[A NOVEL]

The **Book** *of* Portraiture

by Steve Tomasula

FC2
Normal/Tallahassee

Published by FC2 with support provided by Florida State University and
the Publications Unit of the Department of English at Illinois State University.
This project is supported in part by an award from the National Endowment
for the Arts, which believes that a great nation deserves great art.

Address all inquiries to: Fiction Collective Two
                          Florida State University
                          c/o English Department
                          Tallahassee, FL 32306-1580
ISBN-10: Paper, 1-57366-128-7
ISBN-13: Paper, 978-1-57366-128-7

                          Library of Congress Cataloging-in-Publication Data
Tomasula, Steve.
  The book of portraiture / by Steve Tomasula.-- 1st ed.
      p. cm.
ISBN 1-57366-128-7 (pbk.)
1. Experimental fiction. I. Title.
PS3620.O53B66 2006
813'.6--dc22
                          2005033799

NATIONAL
ENDOWMENT
FOR THE ARTS

Cover and Book Design: Robert P. Sedlack, Jr.

For Maria, Alba & Ava

LET'S JUST SAY THAT SOMETIMES A ROSE IS JUST A READ FLOWER

....

LET'S JUST SAY THAT GREEN IS ALWAYS A REFLECTION OF THE IDEA
OF GREEN

....

LET'S JUST SAY THAT WE THINK IT BEFORE WE SEE IT OR BETTER
WE SEE IT AS WE THINK IT

....

LET'S JUST SAY THAT PRETTY UGLY IS AN ASPIRING OXYMORON

....

LET'S JUST SAY THAT MANKIND SUFFERS ITS LANGUAGE

—FROM CHARLES BERNSTEIN, "LET'S JUST SAY" IN *GIRLY MAN*

Chapter 1
In a Beginning

LONG

before the heroes
of martyrdom began to fade

from living memory, before monks (†430) discovered faith

through the malleability of words, long before the heroes of

psychiatry (1900) construed dreams as language, and almost four

millennia before cows began to carry the genes of fish; before

mile-high buildings collapsed into dust, or men and women

everywhere proclaimed their bodies to be, after all, their most

potent weapons, their poems, their canvas, something powerful

had been straining to come into the world. Its silent efforts were

there in the bloodstains aborigines made on boulders—perfect

prints of human hands—first portraits that were repeated and repeated and repeated as if out of the sheer awe that they *could*

be repeated, and wonder at what that might mean. This something

was there in cave paintings—stick figures wielding stick spears as

if to shout *I! I was! I did!* Its silent efforts grew stronger in the

ciphers that ancient Chinese scratched on tortoise shells, in

the tally marks of Minoan merchants, in the runes destroyed by

Assyrian armies, and in the clay tablets listing animals sacrificed

by Sumerian priests. But not until these efforts began to gain a

voice, emerging as it did from the symbols for fish and shields

and owls in Egyptian hieroglyphics could this force—

He was a trader, a teller of amazing stories who would attach himself to whatever caravan would have him. That is, he was a poet or liar, a sometime prophet, a chameleon who years ago had the audacity to merely walk out of his bondage in Egypt and yet still was the first to throw himself prostrate to proclaim the glory of whatever desert chieftain he came in contact with as he wandered the Sinai, more often lost than found....

One day's camel ride from the turquoise mines of Serabit el-Khadim, an ox lowed just as he began to fall asleep, and the image that flashed before his mind's eye was so startling that it made him sit up. Earlier in the day, while the caravan rested in the shade of a *gebel*, he had run his hands over its creamy stone and the wind-worn symbols carved into it: symbols for oxen along with other markings that reminded him of the papyrus marshes he had waded through to escape the halls of Egypt: wavy lines that to Egyptians meant "river," but also symbols of fishes and plants he did not recognize, and so assumed had been carved long ago, back when the desert must have been a lush garden, before Gilgamesh's flood carved this wadi, then receded, leaving only outcroppings and a few parched watering holes. It was the symbol of the ox head that came to him as he drifted into sleep, though, its horns pricking his slumber at the very moment he thought the Semite word for the animal, *aleph*.

Propping an elbow on the camel saddle that served as his pillow, he raised a fist, extending his thumb and small finger to give his fist horns, using moonlight to cast a shadow on the sand—a shadow puppet of an aleph—only elongated, ripples in the sand distorting his aleph no matter how he turned his hand, giving his shadow-ox an ambiguity, an aspect of a skinny, milkless goat. Or a *djinn*. Soothsayers could read a future in the sands' shifting shapes, it was said, and as he gazed into these he couldn't tell if they foretold fortuitous or evil ends—or both?—for he suddenly saw how the marks carved into the outcroppings could be used not only to represent oxen, fish, hides, or reeds—the objects themselves—but also sounds, winds of the mouth that had become his trade. And what were the words he sold if not sounds in a certain order?—a tapestry of verse and half-truths he had woven to exaggerate the plagues of locusts he had seen in Egypt or the sea turning red at the port of Sidon in order to make an omen and thus paint an Egyptian general's drowning, one worth feeding the teller to hear....

Each telling of a history, speech, situation, proclamation, translation, or revelation had to be altered, at least a little, to fit its times or the customs of its hearer. And so convincingly did he have to sell his words, throwing himself into them with the passion of a true believer, that it became increasingly worrisome for him to remember for whom he had invented which chronicle, revealed what secrets, claimed which kinship, or inserted which omissions....

With a finger, he cautiously drew in the sand the symbol for ox

that he'd seen carved in stone, , saying as he did so not the

animal's whole name, aleph, but only its first sound: "Aa."

"Aaaa," he said, reading it back. Then he tried "Hhh," scratching

into the sand ⪅⪅⪅, the symbol for *het*, that is, "fence." The sight

of it caused him to get fully out of his carpet, and while others

snored about him, while the camels shifted against the tongs

that hobbled their forelegs for the night, while the son who'd

been posted to keep watch watched, he picked up a charred

palm frond and wrote, ⬨ Ⅲ Ⅲ ⬨ , then ⬨ Ⅲ ⬨ ,

writing over and over and faster and faster, Ⅱ ⬨ Ⅱ ⬨

⬨ # ⬨ # ⬨, unable to believe the simplicity of

his boon. It was as if the sky opened to reveal a heaven where

he could represent not just things but whatever came into his

mind. Not just numbers and animals as in stone carvings, but

all the knots he had to remember—which camel driver could

be bribed, which gatekeeper couldn't. It was a power, he saw,

a power to record any version of stories, words of men, even

gods unseen, demons—whatever fantasies he had ever imagined

or dreamed—anything he could say.

Then he stopped. Once, in the market of Akkad, he had witnessed a hand being cut from each of two farmers who had tried to forge a clay tablet that bore their debt, and the hairs on the back of his neck tingled. That is, if he could set his speech in stone, could not that stone carry him to the bottom of the sea? Was this what the vision meant?

Resolving to tell no one of his discovery until he had worked it out more fully, he bade the night watch peace, and got back into his carpet. But his shadows of the aleph were even stronger by morning sunlight. As the caravan plodded on, his thoughts raced with the realization that the ancient myths he repeated for others were true: that *Ad-ham*—a name that meant both "first man" and "mud"—that Ad-ham did call plants and beasts and language into existence, bringing them forth from a formless garden by giving them and tigers and gazelles and lilies and scorpions each its name. But this mad creation didn't end with Ad-ham; barred from both the garden and God's grace, Ad-ham's sons—the first murderer and the first victim—and their sons, and yea, the unclean daughters of their sons and sons continued to create and corrupt and destroy with their words, unawares, even unto this day. And he trembled to find himself among their number, for he could see this curse for the power it held, a spell or a power he could multiply over those as blind to it as—

He had to be careful, though, lest it consume him as well.

Over the next journeys, he added to his device as an alchemist adds to his pharmacy, selecting those elements that are strongest, culling from his collection those not as well suited as he had first thought, replacing them with others, noting carefully how other traders recorded their transactions, finding in their symbols signs of the same genie though they did not hear its voice as clearly as he: from Egyptian messengers he learned to make a reminder of foreign names by using symbols such as Υ, that is, *mu*, the mark for an owl, or the wavy line $\wedge\!\!\vee\!\!\vee\!\!\wedge$, their mark for *net* or "river," not as owl or river but as the first sound of the foreign name, an *m* or *n*. Hebrew slaves in the mines of Serabit el-Khadim taught him how the outline of a camel's hump—$\diagup\!\!\frown$—or *gamal*, as they said it, could be used for the guttural *g* that began the name of the Girgashites among them.

His invention became less and less original to him as other slaves showed him how they used symbols for other sounds: a ⌐⌐ or *bayit*—the outline of a house—for the sound of *b*; a *d* sound indicated by the outline of a tent door △ , a *delth*—a set of symbols he also found in use by the Hebrews in the Wadi el Hol, a communion of signs between them. Teaching his *aleph*, *bayit*, *gamals* to a Phoenician sea merchant as a code by which the two of them might conduct business, he found his symbols come back to him by way of the Phoenician's Greek slave as *alpha*, *beta*, *gamma*....

Working out a complete stable of symbols, he also worked out

how if there were an exaggeration, shortage, or abundance to be

discovered, it would be in the merchandise, not the merchant,

and one day, understanding how narrowly he, the messengers,

traders, and slaves had been thinking of this device, he realized

that the time had come for him to test its true strength. On a

papyrus light enough to hide in his robes, he used black dye, a

qualam or reed, and his invention to write out not ciphers, not

recording angels nor hieroglyphs but symbols for the sounds that

would portray—nay, transform—a life, and which when read back

would say for him: *I*—

No sooner had he begun to write then he was given pause. The person he was transmuting himself into deserved a new name, he saw, but what? *Ra-Moses* came to mind, the Egyptian word for "Ra— the son of god is born." Likewise, he thought of *Thut-Mose*, that is, "Thoth—is born" and the more he pondered this Egyptian custom of forging a name out of words for actions, the more it appealed to him and he wrote, *I, -Moses*, that is, born of?—born of what?—writing?—*from the land of*.... Again he paused. He didn't know where he was from. Or even where his parents were born, or who they were, but he knew he didn't want his new person to be a slave to his old, lost kinship, or even the body this kinship had given him, while something from the story that Mesopotamians told about Sargon always appealed to him, especially how Sargon was found as an infant floating in a qualam basket on the Tigris river.... Why not? *I, Moses, born of the Nile, swear by my son's head*, he always wanted progeny, *to the truth of the tale that follows, a tale of terrible plagues, of great migrations, and also God's voice, a tale told by many mouths....*

Chapter 2

The [SKETCH] BOOK OF PORTRAITURE [RESTORED VOLUME]
BY
DIEGO DE VELÁZQUEZ, PAINTER AND COURTIER [HOPEFUL]
AS WRITTEN BY HIMSELF
NEAR THE END OF A LONG AND DISTINGUISHED CAREER

AL CATOLICO
REY
FELIPE IV,
DEFENSOR DE LA FÉ,
GRAN MONARCA DE ESPAÑA Y DEL NUEVO MUNDO,

QUE DIOS GUARDE,

EL SAGRADO BALSÓN DE CATOLICO MONARCA, CONSEGUIDO POR EL REY RECAREDO DE

LOS GODOS, PROCLAMADO EN EL TERCER CONCILIO DE TOLEDO, RESTAURADO POR EL REY

DON ALFONSO DE LEÓN, RESTABLECIDO, Y VINCULADO Á LA CORONA DE ESPAÑA POR

LOS REYES CATOLICOS DON FERNANDO, Y DOÑA ISABEL, CARLOS V, FELIPE II, Y FELIPE

III; SI PARA LA SOBERANA GRANDEZ A DE V. MAGESTAD ES GLORIOSO TYMBRE DE SU

HEREDITARIO ZELO, Y RELIGION, ES TAMBIEN PARA MI HUMILDAD TITULO APOSENTADOR

DE PALACIO, QUE ME ALIENTA A PONERME A LOS PIES DE V. MAGESTAD CON LA PEQUEÑA

OFERTA DESTE LIBRO; PORQUE AUIENDO TODO EL MUNDO EXPERIMENTADO LA PIEDAD

CON QUE ASSISTE A LAS CAUSAS DE LA FÉ, NO PERMITE DUDA DE QUE

NO DISGUSTARÁ V. MAGESTAD DE VER REFERIDO LO QUE SE

DIGNO DE VER EXECUTADO, Y QUE FAVORECERÁ EN LA

ESTAMPA, CON EL REAL PATROCINIO DE SU NOMBRE.

*I*Yo, Diego de Velázquez, painter, invented these physiks to depict human flesh: for a deathly pallor which is intend'd to arouse feelings of compassion, take old walnut oil and add in bone dust. Let them simmer then—

[PAGES LOST]

I never!— *If* Such wit, such audacity! O! to represent this personage in mere oils... Words fail me, my head pounds... But I digress... His Lord Majesty King Felipe IV was receiving Cardinal Derrilieu, a vain princeling of the Church who had come to court to prostitute his Holy Office in the service of French diplomacy. Specifically, King Louis XIII found himself dissatisfied with the Armistice of Pyrenees, a document to end a volatile situation that My Majesty by contrast was exuberant to have settled in his favor. King Louis presently dispatch'd his puppy, the Cardinal, to undermine the agreement—without seeming to do so and under cover of Holy Church. Though the Cardinal had sought to capture the advantage by arriving unannounc'd, his ulterior motive had been discovered by the King's spies; accordingly, orders were given for every diocese in Spain to carry out penitential exercises. Entire villages lay prostrate in supplication to God for a miracle that would prevent the impending erosion of the treaty. War was imminent, all knew, unless a way was found for His Majesty, Defender of the Catholic Faith, to seem as though he was willing to consider all the Cardinal said, and yet somehow work events so that the Cardinal return'd home with only a sack full of wind—and to do so of his own accord. *If* Many devices were found by which to hitch Helios's chariot to a mule: His Majesty's advisors immersed the Cardinal in discussions of Doctrine and of State, especially concerning a mate for the Infanta, María Teresa. More weeks passed while the Cardinal's apartments were refashioned into a sumptuousness befitting his office. All the while, Gaspar de Guzmán, the Count Duke of Olivares, saw to lavish entertainments: Bullfights were held in which no less than sixty horses were disembowel'd by some twenty bulls which were done to death by noblemen on horseback. Concerts, cane tourneys, illuminations and fireworks continu'd without cessation. Without cessation came equestrian parades, masques, balls and combats between wild beasts. Comedies and literary orgies alternated with religious processions and church ceremonies. Heretics were burn'd in autos-da-fe which especially delight'd the crowd. And of course, there were battles royal in which courtly ladies fought one another with perfumed eggs. ℐ In the midst of this, His Majesty bid the Cardinal to sit so that I might paint his portrait—My hand trembles from laughter as I write—and this he did [LATER ALTERED] for though the Cardinal protest'd every delay, he also had his role to play. And play. And play! and play still! All the while a lavish banquet was prepared to honor the Cardinal before his accompanying French courtiers and their papal witnesses: Entertaining a mere cardinal as if he were an Emperor, Felipe knew, would ply the vanity of the churchmen present while the French learn'd the subtler lesson that though Spain's fortunes had in fact declin'd since the glorious reign of Carlos V, she still had riches enough to punish neighboring kings.

ℐThe scene of this event, the Hall of Mirrors, was turn'd into a mass of crimson and gold embedded with paintings of Spanish military victories. Drums herald'd the entry of the Spanish Guard, resplendent on their showy Andalusian horses which clatter'd loudly as they canter'd into the marble hall. Gentlemen of the Count Duke's household knelt as they offer'd perfumes in crystal to the royal guests and their suite of ladies. By rank were distribut'd cloaks trimm'd in ermine; alaunts, that is, war dogs which are sent into battle with cauldrons of flaming pitch strapp'd to their backs; scent'd lace... ℐ The Cardinal himself seem'd overwhelm'd as he was carry'd in by lords dress'd as Mohammedan

slaves in silver'd plush before a hundred other groups, the mention of which would fill pages. ℐ Before this multitude of eyes, Olivares fell to his knees and kiss'd the Cardinal's hands, then hug'd his thighs, and deliver'd how immeasurably glad his Catholic Majesty was at his coming. ℐ An immense curtain was then pull'd back at the far end of the hall to reveal His Majesty, seat'd alone above this lavishness, aloof and dignified—the Sun King, the unmov'd mover. With much pomp, Queen Isabel was escort'd to his side, dress'd like him, like the Infanta who accompani'd her, in simple brown velvet embroider'd with silver thread. Emanating from the Sun King, then, stream'd the ranks of Spanish and French gentlemen, bishops, courtiers, grandees, knights and attendants, the rows of guests aglitter with diamonds that made their wearers shine as light itself. ℐ In accordance with tradition, the Cardinal was also seat'd on the royal platform. But the legs of his throne had been sawn so as to keep his head lower than that of the King and this constant reminder of status caused the Cardinal, a tall man, to sit with his knees near his chest. ℐ When the lower dignitaries were also in position, the King touch'd his hat to indicate that he was ready to dine and the Cardinal, being the most senior prelate, said Grace. Then the feast began. The pheasant-shaped breads that served as centerpieces were cut, releasing live doves that were then brought down by hunting falcons loos'd upon their prey in time with wind musick. An enormous silver platter was carry'd in bearing a whole roast bull which was gilt (a paste of egg yolk, saffron, flour and gold leaf). More gifts follow'd more food though not in the riotous manner of most courts; to His Majesty, a public dinner was more sacrament than meal, a performance of his immutable gravity, and the utmost precision of etiquette was preserved. While the hall clamor'd with the musick, antics of clowns and other proceedings, the King's carver, butler, and cellarman moved with the solemnity of servers at Mass. Each time the King want'd a drink, the cellarman fetch'd a goblet from a nearby dresser, uncover'd it, and present'd it to the physician who was attending the royal feast; the physician then cover'd the glass and, accompani'd by two mace-bearers and a court footman, knelt and present'd it to the Monarch; after the Monarch took his drink, the cup would be carry'd back to the dresser, and the cellarman would bring a napkin with which the King wip'd his lips. ℐ The contrast of opulence of scene and gravity of King creat'd an air of grandeur seen in no other Court on earth. The very dishes were a geography lesson in food: Fish that had been swimming the Mediterranean yesterday, then run by relay to Madrid; ice was deliver'd in the same manner from the very Pyrenees under dispute; paellas flavor'd by chilies, chocolates and other delicacies of the New World—the meaning of which was that the four corners of the King's table were one and the same as the Four Corners of the Earth. ℐ The Cardinal with his compliments, motions and approaches could not draw from His Majesty so much as the least nod, he remaining all the while as implacable as an image of God the Father. Indeed, though His Majesty ate, no muscle in his impassive face seem'd to move and the Cardinal's frustration grew with each course. ℐ Then it came time for the visiting dignitary to speak and the congregation fell to silence. Would there be war or the fervently pray'd-for miracle? Would the Cardinal, with the Pope's witnesses in attendance, let pass this opportunity to force the Monarch's hand? With great dignity, the Cardinal rose from the depth of his cushion. But in so doing, for he was over full of meat and drink, the exertion caused him to let out a fart, awesome and terrible. ℐ The lackeys turn'd away in fear for their lives. The Cardinal's face color'd as scarlet as his robe while Spain and France alike trembled at the horror of this stumble from the pinnacle of etiquette where grandees had been cast into exile for less than the height of their heels. Hard upon this shock, though, Calabazas, the King's idiot, spoke up, addressing himself loudly to the Cardinal: "What saith my lord?" ℐ "I? I saith nothing." ℐ Having thus committ'd the second error of engaging with a fool, the Cardinal was accost'd by the King's dwarf, Sebastián de Morra. Like a matador pirouetting into a poetic kill, the dwarf turn'd so as to project his deep voice as he made this pronouncement: "Pardon the fool, your Eminence, for we all now hear that your voice is indeed different from the one we heard and that the error of our ears was caused by a scent that has the same sweetness as thy breath." ℐ Feigning a stomach indisposition, the Cardinal took his leave.

ℐOn the following day he was conduct'd in state by Felipe to take his leave of the Queen, the Infanta, and Spain herself. All manner of courtesies were exchanged according to the most strict protocol; splendid presents were given on both sides (among which the Cardinal

received an enormous quantity of fine under-garments work'd by the discalced nuns). But even whilst this ostentatious ceremony was being used toward him, other machinations were put in motion: Both Calabazas and Sebastián de Morra were flogg'd within a scantling of their lives, their stripes serving not to punish them but to publish the Cardinal's transgressions; the details of these transgressions were set into a secret paper draft'd by skillful hands in Madrid and destined to precede the Cardinal to Paris. Minstrels in Morris bells were sent abroad to stage a "fiction" in which the bladder of a cow was used to re-create a certain contemptuous noise at play's climax. By these instruments was set before King Louis XIII, as well as the Pope, as well as the courts and villages of France, a vivid depiction of Cardinal Derrilieu's violations and omissions while in Spain, his rudeness, his violence, his lack of diplomacy, his inexpertness in affairs, his pride and insolence in having stay'd so long. The King's advisors, indeed, had determined to make the Cardinal the scapegoat as an additional security for themselves, and they thus laid the foundation of the spoilt favorite's ruin.

[PAGES LOST]

J...since a single color can signify many things, the passion-blood plant can be used for the crimson in a cardinal's robe (or face), or the stripes of a flogg'd back. Violently pluck its delicate flowers when they are in full bloom, for it is in this manner that the petals and stems will stay all red together. Crush them well and wring the red juice into powder'd alum....

J...with these preparations we arrive at the character of the portrait. And yet what can technique add when the impromptu utterance of a dwarf is enough to vanquish tomes of erudite learning? Verily, I did not always recognize the importance of a portraitist's "manner of seeing." As a youth apprenticed to my master don Francisco Pacheco, and indeed afterwards as a young man marry'd to his daughter, I thought brilliant execution was all. But my *Old Woman Cooking* should have been titled *Two Eggs*, for the process by which egg whites metamorphose while cooking is where I lavish'd attention as may be noted by comparing this center with her wooden, lifeless aspect. Instead of Divine Light, my only guide through *Three Men*

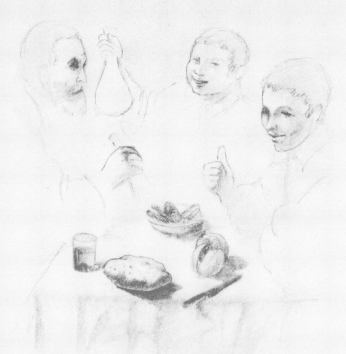

at Table was a hunger for the trials of imitation I had set thereupon: reflecting metal, shadows, a cloth that is seen through air, glass, and also glass and water; a young man, an old one, one of medium age; one laughing, one sober, one of medium expression. ℐ By treating these objects—yes I mean to include the men when I say objects—by treating these objects as if each was isolated from all others and fix'd in amber, I was not making art though many canvases were bought by patrons who marvel'd at my ability to create "portraits"—paintings that I, now more humble, clearly see as mere bodegas: "still lifes," as the English call them, in the sense of the original Latin phrase: *natura mort*
[DEAD NATURE].

Gratefully, God's beneficence is more bountiful than our skill; these techniques, though too feckless to render the character of a dwarf, proved most appropriate in the depiction of a Monarch and account'd for my call to Court at the age of 23.

[UNINTELLIGIBLE ERASURES]

*T*ierra Morena [BROWN EARTH] is how the mesa between Sevilla and Madrid is oft described. The hot solano that blows across it stunts the esparto-grass that grows there, the pastures it once contain'd destroy'd as much by generations of sheep as by the battles of Reconquista [AGAINST THE MOHAMMEDANS] that once raged back and forth across Spain's bosom. *§* The pigments that can be obtain'd from the roots of thorn bushes, the ochers and brick reds available from Her clays provide the painter of this region with a muted palette. Yet if this painter resists the temptation to import brilliant colors from more exotic places, his paintings of Spain, having come from Spain, will be of Spain, no matter what the subject. Who can look at a Ribera and not see the iron pits of the North in its domineering browns?... Or the chalk of the South in the whites of a painting by Roelas, his assistants dislodging chunks of the mineral for his use by shooting arrows into the cliffs where it is found? And, while these painting fade, as paintings must, who cannot be remind'd of this Nation's somber mutability? *§* Riding over Her brown terrain, I couldn't but dwell on this. Cristóbal Colón especially came to mind: Because of the changes to Spain that he wrought and from which She was fading, but also because he had received word that Queen Isabella had changed her mind and approved of his voyage to the Indies while he was riding home after his fifth fail'd audience. I had been home from a fail'd bid to paint the King for only two weeks when word arrived to return. There was now an opening. Rodrigo de Villandrando, one of six painters then employ'd at court, had died. *§* Never was hope given such wing by the death of a man. Back in Sevilla, I had enter'd the narrow confines of my life as Jonah into the belly of his whale, so wasted by cares that I had not bother'd to untie the latchets of my kit. Then don Pacheco, my father-in-law and master, burst in with the news of de Villandrando's death, and it was as if trumpets announced my own resurrection. *§* By mid-afternoon, I was back among human society, on that dry road to Madrid. ℐ Rock'd in the cradle of my horse's saddle, the sun beating down, I drifted in and out of a vision of the arteries that radiate from Madrid peopled with other painters. At each stop, I heard of some local wonder who had pack'd his brushes and was already far ahead. Most would be more experienced, I knew; all would be as hopeful as newly-made Christians, though all but one would find the journey to Madrid as vain as a pilgrimage to Mecca. ℐ But never could I imagine the scene that greet'd me. ℐ Hundreds of painters were there, jostling to gain admittance to the hall where the competition for the one position would be held. Those known by the court, or with letters of introduction such as I had from the many connections of my father-in-law, or those with ready coin to bribe gatekeepers, were all given a space to paint in an immense hall (such as I later decorated as part of my duties). The greatest number of painters were rough, indistinguishable by their speech or country dress from a smith. A few wealthy painters stood out as members of the small gentry whose success in the rental of fields inflated their opinion of themselves as artists or poets. Their pretension to the royal household show'd itself in their equipage: a great train of servants, nicely dress'd, who call'd them "Your Honor" and serv'd them their victuals all in silver. ℐ Most of the mob was kept out even though they and their families continued to beat on the doors for hours. From inside we could hear soldiers driving them back. A stench of burning wood sent a panic through the painters inside for a time as word spread that those without had set fire to the building. Even so, not one artist left for fear he would lose his place. ℐ Then the competition began. El Conde-Duque de Olivares, posed in place of the King. We were told to paint his body in whatsoever pose we desir'd but to leave the face blank. Perhaps a dozen of us would then be select'd to fill in the face of the King himself, who would grant us an audience of one hour during which we would be allow'd to sketch. ℐ It was hard to paint for the commotion that ensued. The slaves and apprentices jump'd to action, assembling elaborate still lifes in which their artist-master would place the body of the King. Crates of fruits and vegetables were brought in. One apprentice was dress'd like Apollo and posed in the posture of the model so that the folds of the costume might be imitated exactly. Another who wish'd to pose the King as a hunter sent his slaves out to shoot deer and, hearing this, others dispatched their servants. When they return'd there was much arguing over who own'd the idea and where the dead animals would be hung. Since there was no scaffolding for this purpose, it all had to be built—as well as entire sets. The hammering went on through the night. By the time Aurora began to tint the balconies of the East, even a horse had been kill'd so that it might be posed. The results were not unimpressive. ℐ Canvases of all sizes gradually fill'd the hall. The King was depict'd as Apollo, as both Romulus and Remus; he was shown with his foot on a stag; fighting a dragon; even ascending into Heaven; and all of them faceless. The eeriness of that variety of faceless Monarchs was emphasiz'd by the complete silence, save the shuffling of feet, as we were usher'd out to await the decision of the judges. ℐ At the time, I thought my chances were fair. A number of canvases could have been done by Orbaneja, a painter from Ubeda whose talent was so meager that it forced him, when he finished painting a cock, to write on the frame in Gilt letters, *This is a Cock*. Other figures were so lifelike, tho', that e'en examining them narrowly, a viewer would expect them to move. The plainly dress'd figure I had paint'd seem'd to disappear among the lavishness of pigments and exaggerat'd styles. So I sat with the others of my station in a tavern, doing my best not to murder Hope. Periodically, reports of the judging came to us. The affair was to have been conduct'd in secrecy, but money loosen'd the lips of servants and other servants in turn had been bribed and so on until every word of Vicencio Carducho and Eugenio Cajés, the two eldest court painters who where judging the work, was publish'd throughout Madrid. ℐ "Quinones del Paso is a painter of rare quality and from an old Christian family," came the first report. Six other names were immediately add'd and my chances seem'd to sink in proportion. ℐ But my fellows said that early prizes always go by bribes and not to worry. Still, over the next two days a taste among the judges had emerg'd: All of the canvases select'd were allegorical. All were beautifully render'd—in the manner in which Homer render'd Heroes as they should be, not as they are. And the list was complete. Then one name was added. "Surely NOT him," my judges were report'd to have said. "He does show a courtly stile, Your Majesty, but his skill is more fitting for rural composition." Yet they could not prevail, and I learnt that I was elect'd to the final round, and ultimately to the post by the King himself— against the counsel of his judges. ℐ Why? ℐ I had been as bewilder'd as others, but I now understand that paintings of royalty are not intend'd to reveal the character of the sitters but rather their status as rulers. That is, the court painter is not a portraitist, but a maker of secular icons. Nowhere was this more true than in the court of Felipe IV, a monarch who by following the customs of his ancestors, sought grandeur not in magnificent display but in regal reticence and court etiquette. To this spirit my stile was especially adept; my icons of the King shew'd him as he act'd in public: composed, aloof, expressionless. What was once a lifeless stiffness in my oils of tavern women became in the King a regal quality of power and prestige. When seat'd on a horse, inanimate as a chess piece, the King became, through my brush, a glyph of capacity to rule. ℐ My rise in the Court was rapid. ℐ Naturally, the older Court painters, Carducho and Cajés, were jealous. Though careful not to mention my paintings of Court, they criticized me for depicting commoners in my other work: Trivial and base subjects, they said, in comparison to the allegorically noble, the sublime exemplify'd by Titian's *The Rape of*

Europa. Carducho left my name entirely out of his treatise on worthy Spanish painters for the reason that I paint'd natural appearances instead of universal truths. "Cartoons," he call'd them, "aim'd to bring visual delight to the ignorant rather than intellectual satisfaction to the wise." Through the paying patrons we competed for, I learnt that these my elders refer'd to me as "the evil genius," an "anti-Michelangelo," even "anti-Christ," who "work'd without learning, without doctrine or study, with nothing but nature before him, which he simply copy'd in his amazing way." ℐ Yet what was all learning, I might have answered, if not a copying? We learn the medicinal benefits of vomiting by apprehending it in the dog. We learn of the dissonance of Mars by seeing its influence in the humors of the body and the humors of the body through tropes in the Kingdom of Plants. Thus it was only by noting a sympathy between the form of the human brain and the meat of the walnut that natural Philosophers learn't that this meat, when mix'd with wine, can ease the pain we sometimes suffer in our minds whilst its shell can be ground up for ailments of the skull. Bearing this in mind, then, is it so difficult to see why art could take its place within the quadrivium of learning?—producing works that were more than illustration, without lapsing into sorcery? ℐ How this was to be accomplish'd I knew not, though in imitation of the scholars, poets, and artists who debated round my master's table I fashion'd this answer to my critics: "It is only by paying stricktest attention to the techniques of representation that we can discover a subject grander than representation." ℐ As the nut of painting after painting refused to crack and give up the meat of this subject, tho', I began to worry that one of the charges against me was true: that I was merely creating sensual, though empty, experience. I especially fear'd that petty jealousies in this form would reach the ears of the Inquisition. Diverse times I watch'd the autos-da-fe pass by my window. Condemn'd

adulteresses dress'd as priests would swing censers made of old shoes that emit'd an incense of stinking smoke; the sight of hereticks forced to ride backwards on asses or otherwise act out the travesties they had made of Biblical lessons was a constant reminder that any words, even Scripture, could be made to mean their opposite. What defense could anyone make against servants and other illiterate witnesses call'd before grim judges to repeat out of context phrases that were bandied about often and eloquently at don Pacheco's table: "poet as a second god" and "painting as a golden world, better than the first"? The sobs of those pleading their innocence?... Or the gagging of those who had "reconciled" themselves to Mother Church and had therefore been grant'd the grace of strangulation before the pyre was lit?... ℐ In more reason'd moments (which later proved to be the most illusionistic), I assured myself that the King's favor was adequate shelter. Indeed, as a reward that particularly irk'd my superiors (in tenure though not in talent), His Majesty grant'd me leave to visit Rome in order to procure art for his collection and to study my craft.

ℐ...from Michelangelo's Sistine Ceiling I learn'd how human figures could be transform'd into emotions....

ℐ...or the great age he gave the dying Christ in contrast with the youth of his grieving mother and how this contrast made the sculpture itself the very embodiment of its title: *The Pity* [VANDALIZED IN 1985].

[PAGES DESTROYED]

ℐ I was to ship back to Spain bronze copies of the best sculptures Rome had to offer, but doing so took the utmost diplomacy. The danger that a cast poses to the original made owners pretend they were out of town or otherwise resist. Thus, arranging for the various favors and pressures necessary to loosen an owner's permission was a wearing task.... As a respite from the particulars of this embassy, a number of us went falconing on the grounds of Monsignor Camillo Massimi. The Monsignor was there, dress'd in a hunting wardrobe of the same peacock blue as his office. With us were the painters Pozzo, Andrea Sacchi and Christsaves Alhambra, a converso and sculptor of little note from Carthage whose real talent was the hawks. *§* With the tenderness of a Madonna, he remov'd the plumed hood from the head of one of his birds and immediately it shot into the sky. "Hark—your bird is taking exercise," Pozzo chided, for to our eyes the sky appear'd empty. Presently though, we understood that the hawk was attacking a bird so far off that none of us had been able to descry it. *§* It soon return'd with a dove in its talons and as a reward, Alhambra allow'd it to feed. The delicate rib cage of the dove snap'd audibly as the talons of the hawk clench'd about it. Its beak and face were soon bloodied with the dinner it tore from the breast of its prey while Pozzo paid off a friendly wager he had lost. "Your bird's eyesight renews our respect for Zeuxis," Monsignor Massimi said, referring to this ancient Greek who had paint'd grapes so realistically that birds came to peck at them. *§* "Ah, but what of Parrhasios?" Sacchi asked. As we moved on, he related the story of Parrhasios, Zeuxis's rival, who announced one day that he had equal'd the realism of Zeuxis's grapes. With a great contingent, Zeuxis went to Parrhasios's studio in order to judge the claim. There he was led to an easel on which was a painting hidden behind a curtain. When Zeuxis try'd to raise the curtain to expose the painting, though, he discover'd that the curtain was not real, but itself painted. He bow'd to Parrhasios, saying in these words, "I acknowledge my master, for though I had deceiv'd animals, you have deceiv'd the second-greatest artist." *§* Naturally, we fell into a discussion of the great artists of the past. The Monsignor told how Rembrandt's pupils paint'd gold coins on the floor of his studio. "They look'd so real that even Rembrandt stoop'd to pick them up." This led to a lively debate upon the progress of painting and the wagering on the hawks became a wager of painters. Which of us, using only our brush, could catch the most doves? ℐ "Excellent," said the Monsignor, "and God's house shall be your proving ground." ℐ The next day, the Church of All Saints (the Pantheon in pagan days) was shut to the public and we were solemnly led in for "restoration" work. For the next hour, I, Pozzo, and Sacchi busily set about painting our traps: Pozzo depict'd gold coins on the floor where the poor box was located; Sacchi render'd beads of water near the baptismal fountain. ℐ For my part, I paint'd a pale disk on the sacristy floor: an ambiguous golden disk not unlike the host in church light. The others cluck'd at my effort, for truly their renderings were amazing. Pozzo even paint'd nicks on the coin's edges that one practically need'd a glass to see, a sliver of shadow such as would be cast by a real coin completed the effect. "We will see," was all the reply I made. ℐ Then we hid to observe the results. ℐ With much difficulty, we stifled laughter at the sight of people glancing about to see if they were observ'd before swooping down like hawks to pick up the "coins" or gingerly walking around the "spilt water." When a contingent of novitiates fell to their knees at the sight of my "host," lying on the floor, Pozzo said, "So it is a draw." ℐ "But the contest is not yet over," I explain'd, for the Treasurer had just enter'd, brought there by the Monsignor's aide as I had request'd. They came to the sacristy where I had paint'd my "host," the portion of the church where the sacred vessels of the Mass were kept, but also the money collected during the Offertory. "Oh look, a scudo," the Treasurer announced, mistaking my "host" for a gold coin. Over the next few hours the same results were repeated: Whenever a man of the cloth approach'd, he would see a host; men of the world mistook my ambiguous disk for a coin. ℐ Monsignor Massimi ran to fetch Cardinal Medici; he was most desirous to see what his superior would see, for Cardinal Medici was then in the process of filling church coffers by offering specially bless'd hosts—hosts that guaranteed eternal salvation—to nobility not rich enough to endow a monastery but who could still pay an unearthly sum. ℐ When Medici's rotund figure appear'd, silhouett'd by the light streaming through the doorway he enter'd, we posed as if discussing water damage to a fresco. The two men approached, and were so near that hands were being extend'd in greeting when Cardinal Medici suddenly stop'd and point'd to the floor. "Look!" he exclaim'd in surprise, "a gold host." ℐ An embarrassed silence followed. But our worry was for naught. When the *trompe l'oeil* was point'd out, the Cardinal roar'd in delight. So immensely pleased was he that he invited us all to sup. ℐ That evening, I praised my colleges for their skill but shared the true lesson of Zeuxis and Parrhasios and Rembrandt: that the most important organ of sight is not the eyes, but the mind. "Verily, the mind will see what it expects, or desires, even if the eyes do not. Thus, the success of Parrhasios's curtain depends on Zeuxis's urgency to see the painting behind it. The success of Sacchi's water lies in the fact that he paint'd it beside a baptismal font. If a painting is made for this organ, the mind, and not the eyes, a few astute strokes can accomplish what no labor can achieve." ℐ The Cardinal invited me back often after that, for he had a large collection and want'd to hear my opinions. Many times during my stay in Italy, I was moved by the fact that I, a painter, was regard'd as a humanist—just the same as scholars and poets. In Spain I was a craftsman, a pair of hands. But here.... Here they took seriously Simonaedis's dictum that a painting was a mute poem while a poem was a speaking picture. Equals, that is—in a land where it was commonly held that Christina of Sweden did not abdicate her throne and move to Rome to convert to Catholicism, as is believed in Spain, but rather she convert'd to Catholicism to be among Italian art. When she, a Queen, kiss'd the hand of Guercino for having produced so many noble works, other nobles remark'd upon the act as if it were a token of her learning, and not a defilement of her position as this act was construed in Spain.

Indeed, I was once summon'd to the Cardinal's palace to find him among ambassadors. A drawing on rice paper was before them: an Oriental work that had been in the Church collection from as far back as Marcus Paulus. Though he had seen it many times, it was only after our talks, the Cardinal said, that he realized that the figure who was listening had no ears, while the other figure, the one who was speaking, had no mouth. "Come, Diego," he bid me, not as a servant, but as a friend. "Enlighten them as you have so often enlightened me." Then he offer'd me his own seat. *J* His own seat! *J* Astonished, I, a lowly stretcher of canvas, a grinder of pigments—or so I was deem'd in Spain—I sat in the plush of a Cardinal's chair to deliver an exegesis to scholars. They listen'd keenly, not politely, not waiting for me to get it over with so that they may rush in with their own opinions, and after some minutes of discourse, finally quitting the chair, it grieved me to think of the status I would return to once home. *J* I wait'd without for the Cardinal's audience to end. For he had been using the Oriental work to illustrate some matter of State. Then afterwards, helping the Cardinal replace the print in its cabinet, I happen'd upon one of the greatest glories of my trip.

As sailors are sometimes caught unawares by serpents at sea, my world and what I believed of art was in an instant turn'd upside down by a few pencil strokes issued from the hand of Leonardo da Vinci. Render'd in red crayon on brown paper, these drawings of horses in action so embody'd the fleeting nature of perception as to render all illustration false; they ascend'd to the point in art where the highest earthbound mountaintop comes nearest the lowest Sphere of Heaven, the peak that the prophet da Vinci had climb'd to show where philosophy and natural philosophy touched: the point where there was as much speculation in one as observation in the other. How static my own conceptions of nature then seem'd to me! Alone in my apartments I laugh'd to think that in this regard, if I had not been an "anti-Michelangelo," I had at least been an "anti-da Vinci." ℐ By my return to Madrid two years later, I had begun my own climb up da Vinci's mountain. ℐ In my absence, Carducho and Cajés had continued to leadenly tread their valley of formulas. Their rut was color'd by Spain's own waning fortunes. During this period, She had lost Portugal and, with it, Brazil. In place of the supremacy over three continents that She had enjoy'd under Carlos V, Felipe's efforts to protect New World holdings were beginning to pinch even in the capital and His Highness sought to combat a creeping melancholy through a war of images. By his order, Carducho and Cajés had begun to decorate the Hall of Realms with painting after painting of historical military victories. In painting after painting they placed the vanquish'd general alone on his knees to the victorious Spaniard who looks down on him from the might of a horse. Through this convention they sang the same song: "Our King Can Crush His Enemies." Yet if Michelangelo taught anything it was that conventional rules produce conventional paintings. ℐ When His Majesty bade me celebrate in paint *The Surrender of Breda* [LOST BACK TO THE DUTCH TWO YEARS LATER], I depict'd General Spínola as he placed a benevolent hand on the Dutch Commander, Justin of Nassau, preventing him from going to his knees. ℐ Spanish virility is still present, represent'd by a thicket of upright pikes which contrast with the bedraggled remains of the Dutch. But Spínola accepts the keys to the city with the words "Justin, I receive them in full awareness of your valor; for the valor of the defeat'd confers fame upon the victor." [FROM CERVANTES] In this way, the painting became a metaphor of Spanish moral superiority, reflect'd by the glory of the King that both his general and his painter serve, and the Faith all are sworn to defend. ℐ The victory in the painting was match'd by the victory of the painting. By it, I had achieved during an ebb of might what no general could accomplish: to recast the signs of military victory into a laurel of morality and dignity of such leverage that Spain would seem victorious even, if need be, in retreat. That is, just as Adam had call'd "tigers" into being by giving them their name, so I had call'd Spanish grace into the light, and soon the Court, and through it all of Spain, had ceased looking for its reflection in Spanish might

and had begun instead to think of themselves as the most intelligent and generous people on earth. ℊ Yet what had I myself gained?—I, mere craftsman, grinder of pigments, stretcher of canvas who was still accord'd the social status of the "artisan" that blackens the officer's boots. ℊ Worms of envy, nay, worms of injustice began their work. At diverse moments I found my mind attending to that portion of Breda that was the world as I had come to understand it: the faces of the anonymous soldiers who gaze out of the crowd, their expressions suggesting a sum of experiences that are otherwise invisible though potent as the gravity that holds the keystone in its arch or the histories that compel the Spanish to say "rio," the French "fleuve" and the English "river." How common must be the example of Nacito Pele, introducing at court in 1490 the first globe? Placing the weight and shape of the globe into the hands of Isabella and Ferdinand, it was this craftsman who had made what follow'd imaginable and therefore possible, though all credit is given the Monarchs, Columbus, and their Generals.

[TEXT CUT OFF]

While the King was away, a feast was held in honor of the widow Marcela de Ulloa, who, having lost one husband to plague and another to conquest, was now being marry'd for a third time. Like the buffoon who is made Pope at Christmas, a woman's third eternal marriage was consider'd an occasion for gaiety—a dance in the face of death—and satire. Accordingly, diners attend'd in costume. Centaurs, satyrs and water nymphs all bow'd heads while over supper was pray'd this in Latin: "When at table think of the poor." ⸗ Also in Latin, an Amen: "A sentiment best appreciated on a full stomach," and the meats were engaged. In the hall, riotous behavior continued. Dancing. Mock ceremonies wed bachelors and maidens for a night. Many fights. The uproarious laughter that always accompanies burlesque was muted by the sumptuous furnishings of the chamber that I and others later retired to for more common entertainments: a game of chess, the harpsichord of Maribárbola, the dwarf, press'd into service so often to re-create weary minds.... Watching her stubby fingers ply the keyboard, never playing what she wish'd but only skillfully executing the desires of the well-born, I could not but see her as a pet of the court. Her movements were alert as a monkey, the diminutive silk gown she wore, all ruffles and fine embroidery, made for the sake of gentle eyes, not her regard. ⸗ I was drawn from this mind by a Gentlelady's voice: "Diego, Diego, come please." It was doña Maria Lopez, one of those great white-hair'd ladies of the Palace who took it as their duty to calm social ripples. In this case, don Juan de Fonseca y Figueroa, Sumiller de Cortina, had enter'd with his entourage, upsetting the hierarchy of seating and I and Carducho were told—by flattery and politeness, but nonetheless told—to rearrange chairs. Taking us to the side as if we were her great confidants, she said, "Only the eye of an artist can put them into a pleasing pattern." (By which it was understood that we could be conveniently blamed for any *faux pas*.) She smiled, then left us to the chairs. ⸗ As I was thus engaged, the memory of Cardinal Medici offering me his own chair rose within me. I saw that I was a Maribárbola to them—my presence among them a token of the generosity I depict'd in *The Surrender of Breda*. Yes, in their eyes, suffering my company made them the most generous people on earth—just as the English believe themselves to be the most tolerant people on earth because they *tolerate* Indians, though they would never, like a Spaniard, take one as bride. ℐ When we had finished, the ladies sat on satin pillows in the estrado [THE ELEVATED PORTION OF THE ROOM AWAY FROM THE FIRE]. As there were now not enough chairs, I and Carducho, of course, graciously offer'd to stand (for what choice did we have?). In this posture, not within the circle the others formed though not entirely without it, we looked on as Señora Lopez held everyone spellbound with a tale of a Spanish beekeeper who had placed a communion host near his hives. It attract'd pious bees who built a Cathedral of wax, she reported, complete with flying buttresses, spires, and altar upon which they placed the Host. ℐ Then Señor Lopez de Rueda told of a pump devised by Germans that could extract the air from a flask, and much sport was had at his expense over the absurdity of this invention. Indeed, ladies were compelled to hide behind fans for fear that their laughter would crack their faces, paint'd as heavily as they were with a medium of wax to smooth the skin. Instead of relenting before this storm of jeers, Sr. Rueda insisted that the German invention was a sign of the spirit of adventure that once guided Spain's search for hidden rivers to Paradise. "Isabella,"—at this name everyone cross'd themselves—"would rise from Her tomb to see Her galleys now occupy'd by the slave trade instead of Christianizing New Worlds—"

ℐ A loud, rhetorical yawn interrupt'd him. It had come from Juan Alaban, the younger, one of those idle *señoritos* court life produced. Venerable white heads turn'd toward his downy ease as he said, "I was just thinking that as we age, we often resemble those on a ship, who as they sail out of port keep their eyes fix'd on the shore and believe their homeland is shrinking as the ship stands still." Then he lay back on a couch beneath a gilt painting of martyr'd fruits. ℐ Don Pedro (who had spent his youth on a Man O'War) took hot exception. As he put himself into a passion over the fade of Spain's rose, the room began to fall into division. I myself did not know which side to take: those who saw the world continually degenerating as in Ovid's ages, or the side exemplify'd by the great progress in painting.... Truly, I felt as Cervantes must have, noting that some who sprung from mighty titles and estates by little and little have become Nothing while those who were Nothing are now Something: a change that is denied most vehemently by those on their way from Something to Nothing but still decide who is pet and who is of rank. ℐ Doña Pedro interposed herself in the dispute, as is the Nature of Gentleladies. "Come now, please!..." She motion'd for Maribárbola to play and the dwarf struck up airy musick. "All these questions without answers when I was so hoping we could play Enigmas. Who will start?" ℐ Menina Palomino at once came to her aid, starting a game by offering this:

> *"My first displays the grace of kings*
> *Another view my second brings*
> *But, Ah! united, what reverse we have*
> *Thy ready wit will my third supply*
> *A Being that is born by eye."*

The game work'd its charm, of course, for avoiding disagreements is the first rule of gentility's survival. And this point of etiquette is so stricktly observed that no mere discussion of worth could hope to transcend it—Especially when the congeniality of an evening was at stake. ℐ As if rushing to harmonize the discordant note that had momentarily sound'd among them, all agreed, of course, that her first must be a nobleman—he who displays that of Kings without being a

King. A guess at "peasant" for her second could not be made to fit, so "craftsman" was tried. Then Carducho, of all people, proposed "painter." "Every man is a son of his works," he explained, "which makes the artist 'born by eye.' And—and makes of her third a 'Nobleman artist.'" ℐ Several of the nobles present laugh'd outright: "One whose medium is paint should not attempt jests." ℐ "Save Spain from the day that Her craftsmen are allow'd to claim privilege—" ℐ "Then become as useful as airless flasks." Even the ladies, paint'd faces and all, laugh'd at this. ℐ Poor Carducho. One would have hoped for the sumptuous feast that this discourse begged. But he only offer'd acorns, growing red in the face with his very heart blood as he enumerated the uses to which drawing could be put: "...especially in warfare, in drawing towns, sites, rivers, bridges...." Painters like him are bound by the belief that paint is only a means to illustrate that which is already known: stigma no different than the rings in a tree or other traces of God's thought and not symbols, like letters, that could be combined and recombined to make what man imagines into what is. As such, their representations remain as idealized as the perfect circles planets were once thought to trace and which perfectly depress the esteem of all artists to that of deserving craftsmen—servants with brushes instead of brooms. Re-arrangers of chairs. ℐ "...citadels, fortresses...." ℐ "My dear Señor Carducho," interrupt'd Enrique Valderon, the dandy. Brandishing a handkerchief, he delicately perfumed his nose as if his smelling had suddenly been debauch'd by some odious thing in the street. "A useful nature is precisely what bars an artist, or swineherd, from nobility. A nobleman is born, not made, and most at his ease when entertaining tired minds at court with graceful witticisms, which he does for no reward." ℐ It is difficult to stand idle as a thing better express'd prevails over one more true. And Carducho was like myself a painter. Or at least he was to those present. Maribárbola only continued to play. So I ask'd if a noble bloodline was the reason El Negro made servants bow to his dogs—or else bark like one as he beat them. "Or perhaps we should look to *Gran hidalgo conde Justin de Avores de las provincias Oeste, Barón de la mar y partes diversos del Mundo Nuevo*," I said. The singing of this name conjured a history that all champions of strickt etiquette would rather leave at the bottom of the inkhorn: a horrific slaughter of the King's footmen that happen'd when de Avores refused to acknowledge a letter of Retreat because its salutation did not contain his full title.... ❧ "Where are those jibes?" doña Pedro interjected, attempting again to steer the conversation to calm waters. "Odd that no one has seen them as they both bear a great love for pranks and masks." ❧ But her husband still chafed. "Do you deny thy natural Lord and Masters?" ❧ Here was a treasonous as well as blasphemous trap that escalated our discourse in the manner of those gentlemanly disagreements that end in a duel. Gentleladies retreat'd behind their fans, feigning to protect their faces from the warmth of the fire, not the words. Gentlemen stood erect. No enigma was offered, nor even a dismissal with the wave of a scent'd handkerchief. Even Carducho, whose aid I had come to, remain'd mute as a fish. When I elect'd not to participate, don Pedro claim'd his victory by turning to Menina Palomino. "Well?" ❧ Fanning herself, she acknowledged that her third was not a Nobleman artist. ❧ Don Pedro beamed. Carducho—whose aid I had come to!—busy'd himself with a tassel. But the sympathy I received from the Lady's eyes convinced me that the answer to her enigma was in fact an enigma of my own that I had seen her admiring several days earlier, standing before it, perhaps even composing her enigma in words, that is, her speaking picture of my mute poem: my painting of her first, Prince Baltasar Carlos, in which I placed a dwarf, her second. Thinner pigments had allow'd my brush to move freely—like the legs of da Vinci's bucking horses—thus enabling me to catch the fleeting effects of light, the fleeting structures of man. The dwarf's shadow'd face

clashes with the porcelain complexion of the Heir speaking at once of the newness of a just social order in contrast to the older, malproportion'd one. The dwarf, a double of the Heir, holds their playthings, an apple (orb) and a rattle (scepter) as he retires from the stage with these the props of Monarchy while leaving the Heir erect, the perfect image of upright Justice, though yet a child, the painting as a whole— *9* While I debated whether or not to break my mind to them and reveal her third, a great tramping and howling sound'd at the door. Beasts burst in. They chase'd Ladies and upset chess boards— Six men had disguised themselves as "wood savages," donning costumes of linen sewn tight around their bodies, then coat'd with paraffin and hemp hairs so that they appear'd shaggy from head to toe. ℐ "By the Holy Mass you'll pay!" the Guardadama swore. Three of the savages had surround'd Menina Palomino and were bandying her one to another when suddenly Barón Palomino, her father and governor of the palace, enter'd as he normally did with torchbearers illuminating his way. ℐ An ember fell, words cannot keep pace, a flame licking up a wood savage's leg. Then the man was a roaring fire that pop'd and crackled, sending sparks that caught onto one of his confederates. This second wood savage ignited like a Chinese illumination, showering sparks onto a third and a fourth and the whole room was suddenly as brilliant as day. The menina whom the savages had accost'd threw her skirt over one, protecting him from the sparks and thus saving his life. Out-cries of horror add'd to the tortured screams of the burning. Enrique Valderon, who try'd to tear away the flaming costume of one savage, was badly burnt as were those who try'd to smother the flames of the others with tapestries torn from the walls. ℐ Of the six wood savages, only two escaped: the bastard son of Bishop Murrio who was saved by the skirt, and Alfredo, the exiled Prince da Gama of Portugal, who flung himself into a vat of water used to cool wine. Don Pedro's son was burn'd to a cinder. Justin and Juan Nieto, brothers, and sons of José Nieto, Aposentador, died after two days of painful suffering. El Negro lived for three days in agony,

cursing his attendants, cursing his Confessor, cursing his dead fellows right up to the moment he join'd them. When his coffin was carry'd through the streets, his servants shout'd at it "Bark!" and "Play dead!" and other such commands. ❧ Here was the future Kingdom: a future guardian of the meninas, a future General, a future Curate, even, possibly, a future King, all born to position instead of the upright justice I had depicted. The reckless disregard they show'd for themselves and others by going about in such flammable garb.... The utter waste.... ❧ An icon of the Virgin stood unscath'd on an Oratory, witness to the char'd stick that had been a sumptuously furnish'd room; gilt chairs were soot blackened, velour curtains reduced to ash. Heat had made the waxen and paint'd faces of the women run like syrup, creating garish portraits where just moments earlier there had been refined artifice. Indeed, the face of the wide world around appear'd differently after the accident: The Catafalque of Felipe II adorn'd with the silver of an entire mine, and just to hold the body of the Monarch for two days; the lavishness of processions and festivals and opulent shows which break the Nation's treasury for displays that end in the narrow space of a week; the habits of mind that bring them into existence—trains of thought that are invisible because of their familiarity—these unseen causes were dramatically bared by the fire and the effect was like being shaken awake from a dream. ❧ As the pathetic sentiments of this tragedy wore away, I felt the discomfiture of having transformed such inner qualities into "noble" likenesses while my own person remain'd *sub rosa*—roots, not flower—and I long'd all the more for Knighthood, the one path up into the ranks of gentlemen that was open to men of my station. Or, if my destiny was to remain in the service and shadow of ill-deserving sons, to at least achieve the family of painters judged Noble by viewers not yet born—those who could read the mind of an artist even in his portraits of the most sin-blacken'd Pope—painters, like those before who are remember'd for their depictions of Monarchs, Bishops and powerful merchants whose own deeds have long since been forgotten. Titian's self-portrait in which he holds a tiny image of King Felipe II loom'd large in my thoughts. ℐ My experiments grew more bold. ℐ The inability of the dwarfs and fools at court to protest the manner in which they were paint'd was the untying of my hands. It is due to their weakness that I, who had paint'd Kings, approach'd for the first time a semblance of a "true" portrait. Not so long after Cardinal Derrilieu's visit, I set about rendering the two instruments to his downfall, Calabazas, the fool, and Sebastián de Morra, dwarf—but—and here is the first secret to true portraiture—to render them from the inside.

ℐPreviously, all rules dictated that a sitter be consider'd from his outside, posed so as to present it to best advantage. Thus, the Conde de Olivares is always posed askance in order to disguise his monstrous girth.

ℐAllegories of a Venus or Diana ask their viewers to regard them with the detach'd distance of a courtier before a tableau of beauties, even when the goddess depict'd is actually the nude lover of its patron (who hangs her in full view of an unsuspecting wife and family).

I But Calabazas [GOURD HEAD] I posed so as to make evident his cross'd eyes, to make manifest a mind as vacant as his namesake. The laws of nature which have play'd a cruel trick on this fool dissolve into formlessness....

I ...collar as halo that has slip'd down around his neck, render'd as sketchily as the unintelligible (to him) hierarchy that serves as his yoke...

I ...inchoate brushstrokes, quite unlike the high finish my rivals gave their allegories: a finish that disguises the painting's status of illusion even as its brushstrokes hide the canvas. Better to gouge an X across a painting's surface for just as the lines we make with a pen cannot be read as "geometry" unless they somehow call attention to themselves as geometrical signs, so it is only by making visible the artist's artifice that the art of painting can express its own essence: the directions by which the viewer is to note the breach between the marks he sees and the things he believes them to represent. That is, it is only when paint represents itself as paint that its craft can become an Art—a form of knowledge that signifies a way of being as well as represents....

[PARAGRAPHS MISSING]

Portraits? No, but almost, and certainly A, B, Cs in a language of portraiture. Yet in painting this dwarf, this fool as I had never paint'd a Monarch or Prince of the church—in coming within a scantling of my first true portraits—had I help'd to unhinge my own claims to ascension? Surely the distance between Sebastián de Morra and myself was not so great as that between myself and the King. Indeed, though de Morra's wit proved the superior of a Cardinal's learning, the stupidity of a fool was even more destructive. Though I laugh'd full from the belly at the time, I now?— ℐ I now marvel at the chaos that would ensue if the rude designs of New World savages were suddenly seen as the equal of the great art of Italy. What would become of me?—or anyone, if by a leveling of the crude and the sublime we reveal'd the crack by which Monarchies could be brought down, and with them all order, including the Order of Santiago to which I hoped to be elevated? ℐ What if my portrait of Juan de Pareja, my slave [LATER FREED IN ROME], was deem'd to be the equal of the portrait of a Count? His bearing is noble. His skill is equally refined for these many years he has been my apprentice in fact if not in name—rendering all but the face in many of the portraits sold under my signature. And yet if he were allow'd to become an apprentice in name as well as in fact, would not succession to artist follow? And if this slave were to one day take my place as I have taken Titian's?— That is, if the quality of the slave's images were confound'd with the quality of the slave.... Must Nature to Chaos fall? ℐ Already he has disrupt'd this History by working his way onto my page, his sudden appearance in this journal a testament to the existence of histories play'd out beyond the frame of our paintings. For like my wife and many other women of this story, he was there from the start, though invisible to you, Gentle Reader, living beyond the frame of this narrative along with— ℐ Oh how fragile is this airy society through which we move unawares! What is Felipe's majesty, I ask'd myself, indeed what is all civilization if not illusion?—a soap bubble born upon the wind—an appearance created through the cut of our clothes, the movements Felipe taught his body till, like paint on canvas, these signs became a second nature. An image, I knew, because it was an image that I help'd nurture. And yet, does not oil naturally rise upon water? ℐ Courtiers exchange gracious bows while in dungeons beneath their slipper'd feet the bones of witches are stretch'd on the strapado—for their good. For their sake, patients are spun at such high speed that blood spurts from the ears. Red hot pincers are apply'd to their nipples, their screams muffled by the wooden apple that is fix'd in the mouth. Their judges pierce birth marks with long pins, so certain that this trial will reveal God's will that even the pious peasant, born with the stigmata that they say mark her as the devil's own, comes to see her guilt and confesses—*Singing in Anguish*, as it is called—finally understanding that her denial of their Truth is proof of her possession. ℐ

> *Judge ye God, what we endure*
> *When Death or Madness are a Cure!*

ℐ The more I try'd to banish these thoughts, the more intensely they press'd in. Looking at my painting of Baltasar Carlos and the dwarf, the rendering of the dwarf seem'd like truth while the rest only paint. I became consumed with the notion that the only difference between myself and a grandee was the ruffled collar that I who had no title was not allow'd to wear. I, who was becoming recognized as a star—if not The Polar Star—of Spanish painters, I must bow to the lowest Hidalgo because some ancestor of his had perform'd a title-granting action in a time so antique that his parchment of commemoration is tatter'd and greasy, held together by bedraggled ribbons that even mice dare not gnaw. Impoverish'd through the pride that keeps these "noble" men from doing honorable work, they come to the city in droves only to compete with each other for the "honor" of chaperoning Gentleladies and thereby being taken into a household of quality and fed. They are exempt from taxation, from the debtors prisons they would fill if not for the collar that marks their station. They parade up and down wearing swords that only their great-grandfathers used while I toil with a brush, producing images that sway the marital union of crowns as well as their martial divisions, a single brushstroke of which has more potency than a thousand of these limp lancers.... ℐ His Majesty, a true connoisseur, was not adverse to my pretensions to Knighthood. Oft he sat in the leather chair reserved for him in my studio so that he might watch me work and at opportune moments, I would venture casual talk of this, my fervent desire. Always I found a sympathetic ear. Like myself, he saw little difference between the service I render'd the Crown and that of the cavalier who in earlier days was elevated to knight for slaying Mohammedans. Once he complain'd to me bitterly because any candidate for a military order, a post in the Inquisition, or a place in university had to first obtain a certificate of Limpieza de Sangre [PURE BLOOD] from a court of people richly adorn'd though intellectually impoverish'd. His Majesty's ire had been raised, not by the law, which as he point'd out was a "just law, good for even the mariscos it banished." Rather, his ire had been raised by the report that a favorite of his who had refused to bribe this lower court was given a genealogy that show'd him to be a grandchild of Luther and condemn'd to death. ℐ He took me at my word that I was of noble, though undocumented lineage, and complain'd that if a law is to be apply'd loosely, figurement should be not for gain but to favor cases such as mine; clearly my presence would help keep Spain Spanish, the ultimate goal of the test of pure blood. Yet he apparently did not see the far-reaching consequences of the humor he paid me, for he advised me in these words: "Diego, when determining whether a work of art is a workshop copy or an authentick wrought by a master's hand, we rely on certain criteria. But by what criteria do we judge the criteria? Not always quality, I assure you. If two statues are seen to be identical except for a broken nose, you will judge the disfigured statue the superior if it is found to predate the unbroken work—if your ultimate criterion is Originality. If the proof of this succession rests on testimony, as it must, then we must judge the authenticity of the testimony and the problem of judgment begins anew, and anew, back to the Mind of God. So it is with a claim to Nobility." ℐ His Majesty only meant that I should build a case for my claim to pure blood in such a way that it must swing on judgment, which could always be sway'd. But I saw deeper into his words. For as Aristotle says, "Not to know that a hind has no horns is a less serious matter than to paint it inartistically." Quixote can be a Knight-errant, Dulcinea his Lady if others are taken up and join in the story, for God, who alone can judge Good and Evil, lets his sun shine upon sinners as well as saints while we, His ignorant, earth-bound creatures, are left to arrange our chairs. ℐ Am I, for lack of authentick proofs, then, to lose what my Valour so justly deserves? Would justice be better served by the want of a punctilio or by some learn'd Historiographer who might beautify my genealogy? Verily, this would prove but a trifle in comparison to the transformations wrought by the Artist who, in giving his wit wing, can bring about heretofore unseen relations. Indeed, I could not but wonder if this had been the greatest work by Titian: setting in motion events that led to his being knight'd to the Order of the Silver Spur by his patron, Carlos V, who was the predecessor of my own, Felipe IV. ℐ While his Majesty did what he could to arrange my case, I began to stretch a new canvas—one bigger and more ambitious than ever before.

[TEXT MISSING]

Ovid's Arachne
(In the Time of Felipe IV)

And the courtier said,
Who does he think he is, this painter?
A common sort, not even dead,
Visions of Grandeur
stuft'd in his head

Indeed, the painter himself didst think,
A golden chain, the likes of them
Who am I to become a link?
—Unless?—unless I am quite amiss
and a life isn't traced like that but this!—

or

that

OR?—

Mercury and Argus Infantas

Fable of Arachne

Villa Medici Sebastian de Mora

Juan de Pareja Venus and Cupid Woman with Fan Mariana of Austria

Francko Lezcano El Primo

Pedro de Barberano

Antonia de Ipenarrieta with Son Infanta Margarita

Philip IV on Horseback Calabazas with Gourds Baltasar Carlos as Hunter Archbishop Fernando de Valdes Philip IV in Black

Pablo de Valladolid Cardinal Infante Ferdinand as Hunter Calabazas with Portrait

Philip IV and his Brothers Hunting Count-Duke Olivares on Horseback Diego de Corral y Arellano

Ochoa the Gatekeeper Landscape with St Anthony Abbot and St Paul the Hermit Philip IV as Hunter

Don Juan de Austria Philip IV in Brown and Silver La Tela Real Baltasar Carlos on Horseback Baltasar Carlos in the Riding School

Barbarroja Baltasar Carlos Philip IV on a Loggia

Baltasar Carlos and a Dwarf Isabella of Bourbon Joseph's Bloodied Coat Present to Jacob Forge of Vulcan Sense of Taste Surrender of Breda

Count Duke of Olivares Count Duke of Olivares Philip IV in Armor

Man with Ruff Collar Mother Jeronima de la Fuent Philip IV Infante Don Carlos Democritus

Cristobal Suarez de Ribera Philip IV Christ after the Flagellation Contemplated by the Christian Soul Portrait of a Man

St Thomas Louis de Gongora Adoration of the Magi

Virgin of St John the Evangelist Virgin of Immaculate Conception Virgin Bestows Book on St Ildefonso Supper at Emmaus Water Seller Christ in the House of Mary and Martha Old Woman Cooking Three Musicians Three Men at Table

Kitchen Scene

Diego de Velazquez (King's Painter)

Pacheco Too Many Books to List Gruenwald

Nacho Silva (Smith) Marco Silva (Painter) DaVinci Alberti

Paco Silva (Armorer) Rubens Bosch FraAngelico Catacomb Paintings

Durer Bellini Donatelli

Michaelangelo Juan Silva de Rodriguez (Merchant) St Peter's Hagia Sophia

Jeronima Velazquez de Garcia Trajen's Column Empress Theodora and Her Attendants Arch of Constantine

Nike

Praxiteler Too Many Paintings to List

Don Ignacio Velazquez de Nobodaddie (Knighted for Valor in 2nd War to Expel the Moors) Apollo

Maria ? Dionysus Pyramids of Ghiza

Raymundo Velazquez ? (Horseman) Ishtar Gate Nefertiti

? ? ? ? Shrine VII, Catol Huyk Wounded Bison Cave Painting Atlania, Spain

? ? ? Cave Painting Lascaux, France Fertility Goddess 15,000–10,000 B.C. ?

? ? ? ? ? ? ?

? ? ? ? ?

Like this!

Not that!

It MUST be so

Even Kings and Popes visit my Studio

To watch in wonder as I give birth,

with brushstrokes powerful tho' light as mirth,

Infused with pathos, grace and strength,

with fire stolen and genius lent

Could such glorious children my brush procreate

If my own lineage be of second rate?

Snigger'd the courtiers:

See our children, Iron Maiden, Tom Screw

And you'll come abound to our golden rule

to confine your ambitions to those painterly

Or discover the powers we've begot

to deem who's noble and what art is not

(your betters will be merciful, but only if you ask it).

Replieth the painter,

Would that I could not see what I see

In your houses, halls and galleries

Windmills, Sunsets, Water Nymphs

By Jove! By Venus! Your gods are kitsch

Pastures, Dancers, Dappled Brooks,

Fowl and Fish on Kitchen Hooks

Marble sentiment, noble faces

Maidens posing jugs in antique places

How can such gilt-framed clowns

Keep art (and me) from making raspberry sounds?

And tell how lineage stays black and white

Once my colors bring to light

That Knights and Noblemen

Dukes and Gentlemen

Even Kings use fields as beds

When on the march

Or on the hunt

For rustic Maidenheads

Yea, there's more royal blood

In Spain's milkmaids' sons

Than in all your hierarchy

Of borrow'd or barter'd

But mostly invent'd

Lineage

pedigree

A contest was set between Arachne and Minerva, the goddess of weaving, who wove a tapestry with the traditional themes: a hymn in wool to the glory of the gods, with ivy running 'round the border. Meanwhile, Arachne, a commoner, a weaver, wove a tapestry that depicted common women who had been abused by the gods: Asteria, Europa, Leda, Danaë, Bisaltis, Isse, Antiope, Aegina, Melantho, Erigone, and many others.... Arachne's depiction of their abuses was so exquisitely wrought that not even Envy could distinguish Arachne's handiwork from that of the goddess Minerva. Furious, Minerva turned Arachne into a spider: less than a craftswoman though yet a spinner. *I* My own painting sought to alter that history by suspending forever the moment of a mere mortal's ascension through art. Arachne's raiment separates her from the rough dress of the craftswomen, the spinners, whose ranks she had risen from. She stands beside Minerva, cloth'd in finery indistinguishable from that of the goddess. In the foreground stands a spinning wheel whose spokes I left out, sure that by so doing viewers would see the motion that is impossible to paint. Arachne gazes out at her accomplices and true judges, the viewers of the painting, while Minerva inspects Arachne's tapestry, which in my painting is—yes, Cajés and Carducho, I have finally paint'd an allegorical scene!—a copy of Titian's *The Rape of Europa* (a fair-use of a painting presently hanging in His Majesty's collection). ℐ If all knowledge is similitude, if all new knowledge is only a change in relations resulting from a change in perspective, then surely it is not so difficult for a new generation to learn that Titian's painting has taken its proper place in mine, just as I have taken Titian's place in the world. Surely it is not difficult to understand how Titian's patron, Carlos V, was reflect'd in my own, Felipe IV, and that so grand and worthy a successor to the emperor, or so I present'd to the King, deserved no less than a court painter who, like Titian, was also a knight. ℐ My Majesty came to understand that I had resolv'd myself to an earnestness of such intensity that I would succeed gloriously or fail so tragically that my failure would become as legendary as success—the inevitable fate of every mortal who challenges the gods.

ℐAt the hearing grant'd me by the Council of Military Orders, 148 witnesses gave testimony that I was descend'd from noble stock, and that I had never accept'd money for my paintings. My depression over the council's rejection of my petition was exceed'd only by the anxiety I suffer'd three days later when summon'd to appear before the Inquisition.

[PAGES LOST]

I

No. 9

Contra la fama

de Diego de Velázquez, pintor

y guardacama de Felipe IV

XXVIII de junio MDCLVI

visto que

La Iglesia Sagrada se reunio para averiguar,

con diligencia, si el fue un Modernisto

Diego de Velázquez: Fathers, I am only a craftsman. I do not invent meaning, I only create decorations in accordance with the instructions given me.

Inquisitor-General: Come Diego, do not place History on an anvil. Did you not say on April 29th to one Gonzalo de Torres that your painting *Sts. Paul and Antony* was "Theology in Paint"? We have it here in our record.

Diego de Velázquez: [I was taken aback to learn that the book before my hood'd interrogators contain'd a representation of myself, obviously drawn by evil angels at court. The thick candles burning on either side of my austere questioners call'd to mind the pyres into which they cast hereticks like so many fleas and I warn'd myself to tread lightly, though honestly, for who knew what grotesquerie my enemies had created, taking an ear from here, an eye from there, a mouth from elsewhere, assembling them in such manner that the whole be lie though the parts true.] I only meant to say that paintings are mute poems as Pope Gregory call'd them [BY WAY OF PLUTARCH BY WAY OF SIMONIDES].

Apostolic Judge: [A painting of mine, *Moses Gives the Law* [SINCE DESTROYED] , was brought out as the Judge read from a heavy, black, Latin Bible] ...*qui videbant faciem egredientis Mosi esse cornutam sed operiebat rursus ille faciem suam si quando loquebatur ad eos.* [Looking directly at me, he translated.] "Exodus 34: 35: And they saw that the face of Moses when he came out was horned, but he covered his face again, if at any time he spoke to them."

Inquisitor-General: Can you explain why [he said, pointing at my painting], among all the artists who have created "mute poems" of Moses giving the Law, Holy Scripture is distorted by only one of them: one Diego de Velázquez, who depicts the Prophet Moses without the horns that Scripture tells us so plainly appeared upon his head?

Apostolic Judge: But with a smile upon his face. A smile that does not appear in Scripture.

Diego de Velázquez: [I was left speechless for clearly, by the light of this court, anything could be seen as an admission of heresy. Searching the storehouse of my memory, I tried the only words—Scripture—that could not be denied.] The spirit quickeneth but the letter killeth.

Inquisitor-General: Explain, Diego.

Diego de Velázquez: I only meant to use these tokens in the manner of my master, Michelangelo, who distorts the age of his dying Christ to increase our sympathy. Who makes David's hands enormous, to emphasize the strength God gave them to slay Goliath; who guided by the Spirit, depicts so movingly the expressions of the damned, utterly lost in his Last Judgment though there is no description of their faces in Scripture.

Apostolic Judge: And since you have been to Italy, you have also seen with your own eyes that your better, Michelangelo, included horns on Moses' head when he carved his statue of the Prophet.

Inquisitor-General: ...Claude Lorrain's *Landscape with an Anchorite*, Pantoja de la Cruz's *Landscape with the Temptation of Saint Antony Abbot*.... [I realized that he was reading a list of the many paintings I select'd to adorn the Buen Retiro, the retreat where Hermits on court payroll live in gardens, performing mortifications for His Majesty's soul.]

Inquisitor-General: ...Nicolas Poussin's *Landscape with St. Jerome*.... Can you explain why church teaching is alter'd in only one of these paintings, *The Meeting of Saint Antony Abbot and St. Paul the Hermit* by one Diego de Velázquez?—an anti-Michelangelo, as you once referred to yourself.

Apostolic Judge: You alone use your window on the world to show the Saint present at one time in various places, here dead, there conversing inside a cave with a satyr, and yet again with the Holy Hermit.

DIEGO DE VELÁZQUEZ: [A morbid chill came over me. My remark was about da Vinci, not Michelangelo, and only meant as a criticism of myself. And obviously my painting was not meant to be a window on the world for I had paint'd it with the light washes of a fresco so that the weave of the canvas would show. After the manner of medievals, I had depicted the various scenes all together. To ignore these obvious directions to interpretation.... Had the Inquisition already decided my fate? It took me not a few moments to order my thoughts.]

Inquisitor-General: Diego, make an answer.

DIEGO DE VELÁZQUEZ: Our Church Fathers teach that the impoverishment of the original present clashes with the fullness of the eternal present; I cannot simultaneously say all that I simultaneously believe so must order what I say. But as every painter understands, the simple act of putting objects in an order is to comment upon them. Thus, carefully, I critique my thoughts by expressing them in this order: First is God's always-ever-present, and it is this fundamental principle that orders the work. Yet our experience of God's composition is in keeping with Aristotle's depiction of time as an arrow in flight and is the source of my blur'd brushstrokes, created in time, my Modern handling of paint which captures exactly what the eye sees—without mediation—yet shows it to be artifice. Without mediation, then, we learn what words cannot express: the gap between word and image that we unveil each time we attempt to depict one by the other.

Inquisitor-General: Do you then claim to have more complete answers than your Church?

Diego de Velázquez: No, Father.

Licenciado for the Defense: Or your Masters?

Diego de Velázquez: No, Father.

Inquisitor-General: Is there any particle of your Church teachings that you do not accept?

Diego de Velázquez: No, Father. [My Interrogators conferred amongst themselves, and with the optimism so common among the hopelessly lost I imagined them to be confirming the acceptability of my answer. Perhaps they would only order me to change the title of the painting, as Veronese had been ordered to change the title of his *Last Supper* to *Christ in the House of Levi*, after the monkeys and women he included in the composition were deemed blasphemous in a painting about the Last Supper but suitable for other scenes in which Christ may have been present. Changing a caption—what is said—always changes what is seen. But when my interrogators broke their congress, their next question showed how naive my hope had been.]

Apostolic Judge: Tell us, Diego, as you understand Scripture, did Moses often smile?

Diego de Velázquez: [The subtlety of this question was only matched by its danger for its respondent.]

Inquisitor-General: Answer, Diego. When Moses gave Israel the Law, did he wear a veil over his face, as we are told in Exodus, to hide a smile?

Apostolic Judge: Or maybe a smirk?—at the jest he was playing on all the tribes? For if Moses were smiling when he gave the Law, how could the Israelites, or any of the ignorant, tell if he was speaking in earnestness or jest?

Diego de Velázquez: Fathers, holy and benevolent Fathers. You must believe me when I say I only depicted Moses smiling because I imagined receiving the Law gave him pleasure.

Apostolic Judge: Pleasure!

Diego de Velázquez: And pleasure made him smile—we lowly painters only have the body as a means to depict our inner thoughts. My painting only shows him as he may have looked—without mediation. I am no theologian.

Apostolic Judge: Then by what theology do you exalt the essence of the visible world?—without mediation.

Diego de Velázquez: Father, my use of the senses only follows Saint Loyola's *Spiritual Exercises*. In this book we learn that the senses, through stimulation by goat-hair shirts or flogging, can bend the mind toward God. When using our senses to take in a painting, we are also taken out of ourselves. We use the senses to eradicate the senses.

Inquisitor-General: Surely you see the potential for heresy in this paradox.

Diego de Velázquez: [No answer]

Apostolic Judge: The Church teaches that Adam and Eve were made of clay, does it not?

Diego de Velázquez: Yes, Father.

Apostolic Judge: So explain, if you can, why in contradiction to this precept you depict Adam with a navel? [PAINTING DESTROYED]

Licenciado for the Defense: Why do you depict Christ's Crucifixion [PAINTING DESTROYED] with four nails instead of three, the number of the Trinity?

Diego de Velázquez: [I resigned myself to plainness of speech.] A navel, like an even number of nails, makes for a more pleasing composition, Fathers.

Inquisitor & Judge: [My interrogators collectively groan'd out in unison.]

Diego de Velázquez: Surely God who is bound only by the compass of His infinite wit might have given His sculpture a navel as an ornament, much like the useless nipples He has placed on us men.

Inquisitor-General: But if man is allow'd to erase nipples, or otherwise change the stigma written on God's creation, how are we to distinguish His hand from the hand of man?

Licenciado for the Defense: I believe Sr. Velázquez has already answer'd this [and here he read]: "...the artist creates a golden world..."

Apostolic Judge: Creates a golden calf.

Licenciado for the Defense: "...The artist is the origin of the work. But the work is also the origin of the artist." He claims, like God, to have given birth to himself. Then like Mohammed, Luther and other schismaticks, he makes a plagiary of his masters in order

to exalt himself. In his words and colors, everywhere a double logic. Everywhere pride—a sin of most erect neck. Everywhere pride and plagiary, plagiary and pride.

DIEGO DE VELÁZQUEZ: [At this misrepresentation, an image of myself as a defiant dwarf loom'd to mind and I made at times answers passionate though less wise.] Fathers, Fathers, you fashion me a Modern yet I more than any subscribe to Augustine's definition of original as not that which is new, but that which has been among us since the Origin. Indeed, is there not only so much "originality" in a work of art as there is ignorance in its viewer? *Cau, Cau,* calls the crow punning its sound with the Latin for *Copy, copy,* and writers use the crow as a symbol of imitation because of its habit of feasting on the food of others. But as a crow brought life-giving bread to Saints imitating Christ in the desert, so I, in making my *The Meeting of Saint Antony Abbot and Saint Paul the Hermit,* fed upon the gift bequeath'd us by Dürer who fed upon the gift of Grünewald who fed upon the gift of the monks who wrote down the *Golden Legend* wherein these Saints are represent'd in words. Truly, the imagination, which may seem to bear much individual fruit, is root'd in a compost of forgotten books. Yet, if it is impossible to create *ex nihlo,* it is equally impossible to copy without change. Thus, in Cervantes's *Quixote* we read, "...truth, whose mother is history, rival of time." But in Pierre Menard we read: "...truth, whose mother is history, rival of time." Do the two passages mean the same? Certainly not, for even if Menard's creation mirror'd the entire book of *Quixote* word for word, it would be different in time and therefore different in meaning and therefore different. If it were otherwise, the most erudite painters would be the least able to paint, burden'd as they would be by an anxiety of influence. The priest who sees most deeply would be the least able to preach, so feeble would his words seem in comparison to the Word. The true artist, then, goes beyond this trepidation and the greater the genius, the greater the theft: Homer steals from all the Greek people, Virgil is a plagiary of Homer. Immature poets imitate as clumsily as apprentices working from plaster casts. The good composer welds his thefts into a whole of feeling which is unique, utterly different from that of the originals. In the manner of a good composer, I only put my raw materials into a composition more fitting to our times, a mosaic of glasses gather'd from diverse places.

Apostolic Judge: A fine speech of many words, Señor Velázquez, but your new relations are serpents bearing apples. Here the thought of a Manichee, there a Christian.

Inquisitor-General: Your images credit Moses with hazy beginnings.

Licenciado for the Defense: And smiling.

Inquisitor-General: Without horns.

Apostolic Judge: Grinning with levity instead of shining with Glory when he veiled his face.

Diego de Velázquez: [No answer]

Apostolic Judge: That is to say, if all is to you a plagiary, then you make of all a useless carnival, an Arab market of discourse....

[PAGES MISSING]

Licenciado for the Defense: If it were possible to create signs, as he suggests, then sorcerers are correct in making the ramblings of our dreams meaningful.

Apostolic Judge: Our artificial signs would grow.... A confusion of origins would replace the Origin.

Licenciado for the Defense: And what of us, Fathers? Would we not appear as Quixotes foolishly trying to instill truth back into empty form?

Apostolic Judge: Remember, Fathers, the Devil is a logician.

Licenciado for the Defense: The Tower of Babel falling—forever.

Apostolic Judge: And gains the point before we discover his cloven foot.

Licenciado for the Defense: And uses fame as a Sorcery—to undermine authority.

Apostolic Judge: And succession.

Licenciado for the Defense: And lineage.

Apostolic Judge: Remember Eve's apple.

Licenciado for the Defense: And Diariu's Temple, one of the Seven Wonders of the World until an obscure fellow burnt it down to immortalize his name.

[As he spoke, two of my secular paintings were brought in and placed before me like additional accusers: *Democritus* and *Sense of Taste*. [LATER PAINTED OVER] Democritus, or the Laughing Philosopher as he is known, consoled himself for the pain of the world by laughing at its follies. A brewer in the city not only thought this to be the height of wisdom, but also the attitude he hoped his brewery would facilitate. He thus bade me to make a copy of my painting, replacing Democritus's globe with a tall glass of beer in the hopes that the beer would be seen as an aide to philosophy and its maker, the brewer, as a kind of philosopher, improving the sense of the world one draught at a time.]

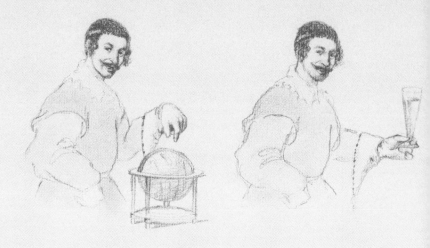

Inquisitor-General: If bastard children were allow'd to corrupt lineage, wars and blood feuds would replace the peaceable transfer of title and land; verily, all society would fall to chaos, would it not, Diego?

Apostolic Judge: Yes, why do you go by the name of your mother's family, Sr. Velázquez, and not Silva, the name given you by the lineage of your father?

Diego de Velázquez: [This shift in subject was a trumpet heralding the real reason I had been singled out to appear before the Inquisition. It was not to settle the petty competition that always exists between living artists. Nor had the Inquisition allow'd itself to be used as an instrument of vengeful courtiers. Rather, the heat of their interest in me, most potent weapon in His Majesty's war of perceptions, was much more serious and potentially fatal: It focus'd on the unknown, to them, beliefs I may or may not hold concerning the source of their authority, a lineage which they traced directly to Christ (Thou art Peter and upon this rock...). It focus'd on ferreting out whether or not my images were a danger to their legitimacy to levy tithes, to interpret matters of Scripture (which is to say all matters), to hold courts such as the one I was in the jaws of and which not even my Monarch could appeal. I should have anticipated from the start their next probe.]

Inquisitor-General: Sr. Velázquez, when you wrote on June 22 that "grandees of all kinds owe more of their elevation to the littleness of the minds of others than to their own greatness," did you mean to include Princes of the Church?

Diego de Velázquez: No, Father.

Licenciado for the Defense: Louder, Sr. Velázquez.

Diego de Velázquez: *Most* assuredly *not*, Father.

Inquisitor-General: [The Credo beads they wore as belts about their robes clack'd as they lean'd toward one another in whisper'd congress.] And this includes Cardinal Derrilieu, even though he is of France? As you know, your Church recognizes neither national boundaries nor other divisions made by men.

Apostolic Judge: Was the rudeness that Cardinal Derrilieu suffer'd in Felipe's court the sort of reception you fancy'd when you wrote [and here he read], "worth and authenticity is less intrinsic than dependent on reception."

Licenciado for the Defense: Was Calabazas the fool knight'd by the applause of the ignorant?—if worth is dependent on reception, as you claim.

Diego de Velázquez: No, Father, I only meant that just as a church is more than its bricks, so a work of art is more than its materials even though the picture hangs on the wall like a hat.

Licenciado for the Defense: Then a chamber pot, if enough people say so, can be a work of art?

Apostolic Judge: Bah, this maker of images has been so dazzled by images that he is no longer able to tell brass from gold, forgery from authenticity, nobility from those more suit'd by birth to the stable.

Diego de Velázquez: Fathers, I beg of you—you see me from the wrong perspective.

Licenciado for the Defense: Then why do you paint more pictures of dwarfs and fools than of Christ?

Diego de Velázquez: My patrons—

Licenciado for the Defense: Why do you make more paintings of pagan myths than of the gospels?

Diego de Velázquez: My patrons—

Apostolic Judge: If your patrons are not more important to you than your God, why do you make art into a thing all together venal and a sort of commodity?

Diego de Velázquez: [The weight of the already said kept my head low as I answered.] Fathers, most holy Fathers, I can only throw myself at your mercy. But in so doing, I beg you to recognize what is reflect'd in my heart: faith that a carpenter became prophet; that the Son, most exalted, was also of profane flesh; that three persons can indeed be one. My whole life, my whole body of work, has been a longing after an imitation of these transformations. If one has contempt for the past, to imitate is easy but foolish; given adulation of it, imitation is mandatory though impossible. The artist who serves the True God, though, the kind of artist I have always aspired to be, instead imitates that transformation in which the Son was both fulfillment and promise: an "originality" in which the artist invokes a descent of which he appears the fruition and invites a progeny of which he appears the seed.

Inquisitor-General: But what misshapen progeny can we expect from your sketchy manner of painting, Diego? A degeneration unto the blank canvas? If answers are not represent'd by the art of painting, but invent'd by it as you claim, what are we to make of your fractured touches of pigment? What do your illusions of light and color say about the nature of the world? Or our ability to know it? What are you telling us with your unresolved spaces when other living artists order the haphazard world of appearance into the harmonious world of Art by a use of linear perspective? Is or is not life nothing but movement or is nature sufficiently well order'd to prove the existence of God?

DIEGO DE VELÁZQUEZ: I don't know.

Inquisitors: *You don't know?*

DIEGO DE VELÁZQUEZ: Can any of us *know*, dear, reverend Fathers, when Faith is the one certain, though partial, way to understand? Though I be placed on the pyre, knowledge will never be as absolute as Faith for knowledge is based on appearance, though the least thought reveals that the most realistic painting is in truth the most illusionistic. My paintings—

Apostolic Judge: Alter the calendar of Saints.

Licenciado for the Defense: And speak as the foolish who say *Por Diez* [BY TEN] for *Por Dios* and think they cheat the devil of his oath.

Inquisitor-General: My assistants mean that we and our world are in fact rushing toward a single and certain earthly end, are we not, Diego? No matter how many words we scatter, Death comes suddenly and shows the intellectual fashions of scholars to be no more than the ruffles of dandies: trifles which they duel over one season only to put aside for flat, Waldroon collars the next. Yet if a transcendent end can only be grasp'd through a figure, as we both agree, is there not Truth in da Vinci's *Last Supper* with its vanishing point directly behind the Son's head? The same Truth that might inhere in a system of the cosmos which depicts all bodies revolving about the Sun? How far from this logic is your portrait of the child Prince with his dwarf—a painting that pretends to be both lofty and vulgar? Or your *Philosopher Democritus* and *Taste in Beer*? Which is mockery, which Sincere? A Philosopher extolling beer? What are we to make of canvases that contain both saints and hornpipes, Cardinals and fools? Laughing Prophets? If the world we know is nothing more than our compositions and our compositions are the world, what are we, finally, to make of any of your portraits?

The Answer I Did Not Make the Inquisition

In the end, the Grand Inquisitor let me take my leave with no more than a token penance of one pound of candle wax (not coincidentally the weight of candles carried by hereticks to the pyre) and a fatherly stricture to be more judicious in the remarks I made to my apprentices or within the hearing of those liable to stir up the chicken coops of criticism. Yet the process of *chiaroscuro*—the creation of form by light and lacunae—fill'd my being. To make a halo bright, a darkness was need'd, such as the black sky that I often placed behind the blonde head of Felipe. And it is I who do this making, it is you, Dear Reader who views it as such, it is we, the absent co-creators in the verse of don Francisco de Quevedo y Villegas:

> *Mighty España ever shrinking shows*
> *things thought solid and of eternal pose*
> *are nothing but appearance and name*

Who giveth Spain this name if not us? Where is Her essence if not in the formations of mind? Yet if this mighty Mother we call'd into being was but an image, why couldn't I, the greatest living maker of images, fashion my own? ❧ For some time, I had scoff'd at the naiveté of Alberti's *Della pittura* in which he so proudly presents the *camera obscura* as a source of truth. But was I being equally naive in believing that by picking our point of perspective we could see whatsoever we wished? If all knowing was a matter of perspective, as I thought, why does a painting by Giotto look more real to us than a Duccio, and why does Michelangelo outstrip them all? What of the single end, quoth by my Inquisitors, to which both Prince and worm rush?—Truly, Death is Death and all are but fish in His net—no matter what name or appearance we give Him. That is, how to reconcile a mute earth, indifferent to our mental formations even as these same formations compose our world? ❧ My Church had Its answer: a powerful dominion, for everyone wants to live in a world that is familiar. This is why a crucifix paint'd from the perspective of one on his knees, then hung at the right height before a pad'd kneeler will act as an invisible hand, bringing its viewer down into alignment. It is only by aligning himself with the assumptions embody'd in the work that it will appear normal. And once the body is in a reverential posture, the mind will follow—and think it is doing so of its own volition. How much greater is the pressure from our Catholic world, its citizens aligning themselves with the millions of appearances, Truths, habits, and Commandments that press in from every side at every moment? ❧ Yet even as Its officers grant'd me leave, their eyes on me, their canvas, they remind'd me of the many painters I have observ'd at work, now moving close to the canvas, now stepping back, now attentive to individual strokes, now to the whole composition, but never attentive to all at once. That is, never can an artist (or Inquisitor) step back far enough to observe himself creating since all acts of seeing are also acts of framing. While the frame limits our view, it is the picture we are born into that determines how we see: a scene that can only be as flat as I make myself writing myself into existence on this page, my quill an instrument of death that transforms the fullness I am to my Author into ink arranged as erudite flourishes. ℐ When ask'd, then, "What are we to make of your portraits, Diego?" I had no answer. My early efforts present'd worlds that pre-exist'd their recording: dead nature, a *lo* [IT], address'd to a world of trees falling in forests and making thunderous crashes whether or not anyone was present to hear. A false world, I later intuited, including faces that gazed out of my canvases: paintings like that of Sebastián de Morra, address'd to an *usted*—a thou—his eyes like those of a Christ that seem to follow a viewer upon whom the painting depends if it is to be more than a dead lo falling in the woods with no one to return its gaze. ℐ But a cold and undeniable endpoint, the inability of any individual to bring a world into existence by his own power, also became self evident; and my interrogator's question suspend'd me in the position of a brush above the stroke it is about to create. Indeed I could not even attempt to fashion an answer until I was back in my studio. ℐ There, before a blank canvas large enough to cover an entire wall of His Majesty's study, I sketch'd in lines of perspective as ceiling timbers that sweep out over a viewer's head. The lines of the floor in this canvas with no frame were drawn to project under a viewer's feet, his entire body absorb'd by the enormity of whether or not it was possible to see through a situation while being part of it—as I thought I had done. Earth/World, Artist/craftsman, God/man, Quixote/Panza, viewer/ subject. The second half of Cervantes's great work looks back on itself, taking as its subject the characters bound'd within its own first half. But could anyone do the same with the portion of their life they were still living? Could I be both a painter and a gentleman? Or was Arachne's fate, like that of Oedipus as father of himself, the most authentic expression of "unnatural paradox"? ℐ A dog is, as everyone knows, a symbol for loyalty. So what do you, as you stand before/within this scene, Dear Reader, Fellow Creator, what do you

make of a sleeping mastiff? The sacred silence of mental labor as symboliz'd by St. Jerome and his sleeping lion? This is how the Saint is always depicted, translating original Hebrew into the Latin Bible that is the foundation of our Mother Church. But if the meaning of paint depends upon a tradition of relations, what are we to think of a sleeping mastiff under the foot of a child? If we see this dog in a foreground that has been reserved by tradition for the central subject, what diminution does that make of the King and Queen who are in the depth of the painting?—a framed depth, fading in a darkness that makes it impossible to tell if their images be reflect'd in a glass, posed in paint or seen through a window. A communion of ways of being—mental image, mirror image, image on canvas, image on eye (an image of images)—a communion that asks if any is more root'd in the earth than clouds or chimeras. That asks if we could even discern a difference, if there was one, when from birth every inflection, every habit of thought, every movement of theirs (and ours) had been mold'd into the second nature they (we) have become: hieroglyphs of their (our) society, fram'd icons of power (or weakness) and capacity to rule (or be ruled). In monastic hoods. (Or with gourd heads.) ✧ Within another frame, the frame of the doorway at one vanishing point, stands the aposentador, José Nieto. Surround'd by scenes from the *Metamorphoses*, his body is form'd by chiaroscuro. He gazes out of the canvas as does the Infanta, the King, Queen, her guardadama, Menina Isabel de Velasco, their dwarf Maribárbola, and myself, the Artist in a painting whose own unframed canvas intrudes from the margin, overwhelming any one of us. To make the scene appear without distortion, you will find yourself, Fellow Viewer, unconsciously move to the one position and distance necessary to do so: the same point I was forced to adopt in order to draw it. It is this point, the point of your (mine) eyes that the gaze of the eyes within the painting are directed: a point outside the painting and center'd before the mirror that appears in its darkest part. Your own gaze will hold you in this spot (for its intimacy, the returning gaze is address'd to *Tu*) as surely as Sebastián de Morra's gaze imply'd no escape for Cardinal Derrilieu. ℐ But if you see the King and Queen as subjects and not your own face reflect'd in the mirror before you, the mirror that I stood before as I painted, what does this say, even if through a figure, but that you are in the place of the King and Queen? That I, don Diego de Velázquez, now posed before the canvas whose back is to you was (am) painting every viewer who is myself painting myself painting this painting?—a scene that cannot be thought to exist without a viewer?—You, I?—the pivot point of all the representations within the work? ℐ In tension with this scene, though, is another: the absorption of Menina María Agustina Sarmiento with Infanta Margarita, the distract'd gaze of the widow'd (for the fourth time) Marcela Ulloa, the tightly shut eyes of their pet, Fide, and the preoccupation with this dog by the young Pertusato: a scene that the viewer has simply stumbled upon and that would exist even without a viewer. A *memento mori* of arrest'd poses and impassive looks, root'd in the world as solidly as still lifes of jugs and wooden spoons address'd to *ellos*, the unengag'd who are uninterest'd in looking at the painting offered: a central character who is being offer'd a glass of perfum'd water at which she is not looking, a mastiff uninterest'd in the play of the child and a guardadama being told by a widow something to which he is not listening. ℐ It is a *memento mori* of people surround'd by real things, not representations. A scene of shadows and melancholy for the inevitable: the passing of our children—despite our efforts—the passing of our art, our theories, our world.... Yes, the five-year-old Infanta died shortly after the paint dried, no matter how eternal I made her youth. It is a *memento mori* of a world whose ceiling is illuminat'd by the dying glow of lamps already extinguished, the fading reflections, King and Queen and the others living in a world where the gap between what the eye sees and that the brush makes is so great as to be independent of you or I or the process by which we see. Through these two means, then, earth (that which is there) and world (that which our minds bring into existence) tie themselves into a Gordian Knot. A fusion of you King and Queen viewer-subject and me viewer-subject looking at you looking at me— they, we—everyone making each other in a world already made—for it is only the I that can give expression to this world that precedes us while the only expression possible is the I itself. The naive (I) eye sees nothing (a dog with its eyes shut). I cannot paint what I cannot see and I cannot see what I am not, for what I see is determin'd by the I's (we) in response to that which creates me, which is to say—and here is the deepest secret of portraiture, the answer I did not make the Inquisition—every portrait tells more of its creator than its subject; every portrait is and can only be a self-portrait; a portrait of its viewer, its author, a portrait of the I (*nosotros*).

Chapter 3

P. Displays R If and Only If S

(a modern romance)

"J'ai horreur des systèmes et surtout des systèmes a priori."

--Paul Topinard, <u>Anthropology of the Criminal</u>

10 February 1917

It is only by removing the 'I' from observation that a psycho-analyst's portrait of his subject can become not an idiosyncratic work of art but a medical diagram. For though it has become popular (in academic circles at least) to think of the mind as an entity separate from the body, experience demonstrates how inextricably mind is bound up with body through the system of nerves that serves them both. Thus, it is only by making psycho-analysis a science of the mind as biology is to the brain that we can avoid transforming advances in technological understanding (e.g. Benjamin Franklin's discovery that lightning is, in fact, electricity) into wasted effort, dead ends, even human suffering (e.g. Benjamin Franklin's disastrous attempts to cure by lightning the invalids who flocked to him after his discovery). In other words, it is only through a meticulous attention to technique that we discover a subject grander than technique.

What follows is a memory recreated on the eve of an advance in the treatment of sexual nervousness that I believe will have as much benefit for society as Freud's popularization of the wonder drug cocaine.[1]

Standing close to our work, we are at a loss as to its significance, or a clear view of how we arrive at point Z from point A. For we create but the latest layer of a palimpsest that has been in the making long before we were born and upon which many others will write in the dust of our graves. I set down this record, therefore, so that those who follow may understand the reasoning by which I arrived at a treatment for Miss Paula's malady, a blight which may very well seem bizarre, or even incomprehensible, to future generations though everyone living at the time I write will recognize the symptoms of a disease which has reached epidemic proportions: a bewilderment and paralysis of capacity, sexual frustration, sexual ambivalence and an undefined sense of melancholy, the symptoms, that is, of nervous exhaustion.

Much has been written about soldiers sent home from the front not due to a physical wound but a psychic breakdown. So frayed are the systems of nerves in these individuals that at times they commit suicide rather than submit to the electroshock cures that would allow their release from the asylum and speedy return to the front. Theirs is but a modern manifestation of a relation between the organic body and the psychic mind that is as old as humanity, though earlier generations could do no better than represent it through the romantic lens of literature. See, for example, the debilitating delusions that both end the life of Don Quixote and begin his tale:

> In fine, he gave himself up so wholly to the reading of Romances,
> that a-Nights he would pore on 'till 'twas Day, and a-Days he

---

1 The list of enthusiastic testimonials from eminent users grows daily (the Czar and Czarina of Russia, President McKinley, General Grant, Thomas Edison, the Prince and Princess of Wales, the Kings of Norway and Sweden, Pope Leo XIII....). The list of ailments cocaine has been shown to cure seems to grow even faster (melancholy, hay fever, sciatica, tuberculosis, the common cold; doctors have also found it to be good for the restoration of memory in the old and the alleviation of teething pain in infants).

> would read on 'till 'twas Night; and thus by sleeping little, and
> reading much, the Moisture of his Brain was exhausted to such
> Degree that at last he lost the Use of his Reason.

But the nervous exhaustion of which I write does not refer to the obvious cases of delusion, or even of the psychic damage we witness in those returning from the front, and whose melancholy duty it was once mine to treat. Nor do I refer to the moral entropy suffered by refugees who experienced the war directly: civilians, for example, attacked by gas and then sent to hospital for internal chemical burns only to be seared alive in the deliberate fire bombing of hospitals.

Rather, I speak of the ordinary citizen: noncombatants living far from the carnage and rubble of Europe, indeed, living in the relative comfort of America. Never coming under fire, the war for this person may only consist of a cousin, or a neighbor, going overseas with his military unit. More commonly, it may only consist of newspaper reports of troop movements, or headlines about battles. Perhaps the war, for this person, was an annoyance at the inability to procure a certain German wine that was in abundance before the war. Perhaps the person of whom I speak simply went about his daily life, too preoccupied by his own affairs to let the war enter his conscious thoughts even as he slowly began to suffer an increasing sense of melancholy, or moral uncertainty, or even twitchy nervousness.

While these may seem like strange phenomena when first encountered, a little reflection will reveal their raison d'être, even inevitability. For the type of person I am referring to lived like all of us in an age when war was thought to be taking its place among other relics: trials by fire, religious inquisitions, and other societal "tools" from an unenlightened past. He believed that as civilization progressed, conflicts would be increasingly settled by force of law, or treaty. Or, and only in the most extreme cases, by chivalrous combats fought according to martial understandings that had evolved over the 2,000 years since Greek City States agreed to bar their armies from destroying each other's temples; to leave standing the olive groves of a defeated enemy; not to place the value of victory above the extraordinary suffering of women and

The Camera Does Not Lie
or
Link to Our Emotional (Animal) Past Revealed by Photography

No one has done more to show how the nervous system knits our mind to our body than Sir Charles Darwin. His breakthrough began with a simple observation: Someone who thinks pleasant thoughts will smile. Sadness involuntarily creates a frown. That is, mental activity is embodied in the nervous system as it controls the muscles used in making facial expressions.

By identifying the muscles of the face used in an expression of terror, for example, and then electrically stimulating the nerves of those muscles long enough to photograph that face, the subjectivity of any sketch artist can be eliminated and a portrait of terror could be said to have been objectively captured. What's more, the ability of the mind, through the electricity of its nerves, to move the body contains profound implications for the ability of using electricity on the body to induce a state of mind.

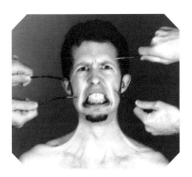

Demonstration of Rage--as seen for instance in Irishmen quarreling and brawling together--produced by electrically stimulating the nerves of the platysma and homologous occipitofrontales muscles by which the instinct of fear causes the eyes to widen and the neck to contract.

Demonstration of Surprise--as seen for instance in intoxicated Irishmen-- produced by electrically contracting the great Zygomatic muscles by which the instinct of Joy draws the corners of the mouth backwards approximately 1 cm as a release of tension (and evidenced by the fact that a person cannot tickle himself).

--Darwin, Charles, The Expressions of the Emotions in Man and Animals, 1897.

children that would be caused by blocking the springs that supply water to a city's population. This person could not imagine, among the white races, anything worse than a pistol duel between nations, nobly contested according to rules of engagement bearing presidential seals and ribbons while noncombatants waited unharmed in the wings.

Then a war such as we could only associate with savages erupted between the most advanced nations on earth and showed the tissue of our civility for what it was.

Not only did the highest achievements of civilization--our science, our social organization--allow us to rain death down upon one another on a scale never before witnessed in the history of earth, but we did so with more venomous hatred than even the most primitive of barbarians could imagine. Young virgins were raped with bayonets as government-sanctioned reprisals; water supplies poisoned; olive groves were burnt then salted so that generations not yet born would feel our hate. From these barbarisms flowered new ruse de guerre. U-Boats sink ocean liners, indiscriminately sending to a watery grave artists, mechanics, rich bankers, destitute farmers, babes in arms, soldiers, pacifists, thieves, priests--the whole spectrum of life--as if an entire village had been destroyed, if it can be imagined, by the push of a button.

And then the perpetrators of every imaginable atrocity return from overseas to live in our neighborhoods, our homes, in our very beds, for they are our neighbors, brothers, sons, and husbands. They are, in fact, us. And recognizing that we are no better than they, a very real and justifiable anxiety begins to poison our atmosphere, causing us to sleep with "one eye open," to be continually on guard against the animal beside us, even within our own selves, driven by blood lust, self interest and sexual desire--no matter how many layers of polite society we gild over the animal nature that man's actions have shown to reside so close to the surface. As a result, we starch our collars stiffer, tighten our religious strictures in an effort to say, Not I. I, Homosapien, Civilized Man, will not admit to the impulses, desires and hungers that are the province of the animal kingdom!

Only the strongest of nerves can bear this unrelenting tension without strain.

My question, therefore, is obvious: Rather than exhausting nervous energy in the struggle to deny our animal nature, would it not be easier on our nervous systems--on us--to give it its due? To admit to our desires, when possible, rather than guarding our thoughts night and day to ensure they remain within the narrow bounds of a lie, refusing to admit, even to ourselves, to biological wirings we suppress in the name of gentility?

Compare our anxiety-ridden civilization with any jungle tribe, for instance. There, the young Negro courts his beloved with his phallic horns and intentions in plain sight: just one example of the ease with which childlike innocence and naked eroticism come together so harmoniously in the black native. Is it an accident that nervous exhaustion is unknown in the wild? If we acknowledge that our animal nature can at times excuse the most impulsive and heinous of crimes--crimes of passion as they are called--can it not also be said, as Freud has written, that free sexual intercourse between our young gentlemen and respectable girls would do much to improve the mental health of our population? From the perspective of "civilization" this is a step back toward the jungle--a regression; but gentility becomes a handicap if it makes our path in life more steep, and to live at peace with one another, and ourselves, has become the Mount Everest of our Modern age.

Such is the frame placed by the world around the case of Miss P. Before I take up her account, let the record show that I have altered certain details in order to conceal her identity. I have also combined some details and omitted others for literary effect--that is, to make those of scientific import stand out while other less essential facts appropriately recede--much as a naturalist might make a drawing of a beaver dam in order to accentuate certain features that would be lost in the haze of unprioritized detail shown by any photo. I stress, though, that I have altered nothing else. This is an objective representation--Excelsior the Objective Eye!

The differences between native and civilized courtship rituals are striking.

I began treating Miss Paula today, a maiden past youth (she was then 26). Miss P. (not her real name) is the eldest of two daughters, her younger sibling having already married. She is an avid reader and connoisseur of the arts in general, having studied at Vassar College, the first to offer art courses to the weaker sex. Her family has a disposition toward philanthropic works and is active in a variety of such organizations. I became acquainted with Miss P.'s family because her father and I belong to the same gentlemen's club. This secular father serves as a balance to a religious mother, and is, in fact, the main reason P. was sent to me: Her parents were concerned by the fact that instead of working to make herself into a desirable mate, she had taken to spending her time exploring the various libraries that the city has to offer, rebuffing the suitors they sent to her, and growing into an independent temperament.

Indeed, her first words to me were, --Is that the couch?

She had been shown into the study where I receive patients and was indicating the couch where, not long ago, I had strapped veterans of the war for their electroshock treatments. Perhaps P. read something of these dolorous experiments in my face and felt a twinge of empathy for me. Or perhaps, like many independently minded old maids, she had a distaste for ceremony. In any case, she did a most extraordinary thing for a lady. Without further invitation, she lay down upon it. Neither by her manner nor expression did she betray the slightest reticence one would have expected in an unmarried woman alone with an unmarried man whom she knew only through the oblique contacts offered by the polite society to which they both belonged. Not knowing what else to do in the face of such boldness, I took my station in the chair positioned just behind her head and proceeded to record our exchange.

P. talked about herself in a pleasant manner, obviously having been prepared for her visit by a lady friend who, I happened to know, was undergoing similar treatment under another doctor of my acquaintance. One might say that she "knew the routine": She related tales revealing her relationship with her mother (loving) and her father (respectful), skillfully interweaving her earliest memories of childhood (delightfully unremarkable). She spoke of a voracious appetite for literature, spending upwards of four hours a day alone reading in the library.... From my position of superior vantage, I was able to observe her freely, mark my own impressions, and create a gloss upon her words much as a painter might work at his leisure, seated at his easel before a pastoral setting.

The landscape was not unimpressive; the location of my chair and her reclining body offered vistas of femininity that were most distracting despite my efforts to stay on task. The clear skin of her neck, her endearing and easy sighs and closed eyes gave her the aspect of a woman in bed and I could not help but wonder if her case could be of import to me for matrimonial as well as professional reasons. Her legs were visible only in outline, lost as they were in the innumerable flounced petticoats worn by all fashionable young women of the distinctly feminine type. Her teeth, her nose, her ears were classic and offered an inventory of small finenesses. She wore her hair piled high on her head and tied at the back in a Greek knot (or as they are now called, a Psyche knot). Her slender, alabaster neck bespoke of a fragile dignity. Yet a corset of steel fingers compressed her waist to the width of a hand as was a la mode and the presence of those bands in my office, that is to say, seeing this feminine device in a medical setting, I was transported to the sanitarium Salpêtrière[2] where iron bands were positioned to press into the ovaries of hysterics in order to control their fits.[3]

---

[2] Literally, "saltpeter works": a factory for the manufacture of the sulfur used in gunpowder and later put in the food of convicts to make it impossible for them to achieve an erection, thereby reducing incidents of buggery.

[3] Indeed, it was these hysterics that first compelled me to abandon my training as an oil portraitist and take up medicine. Rather I should say I was converted to the study of medicine, for the change wrought by my lightning bolt was as thorough and sudden as that of St. Paul on the road to Damascus. Specifically, while touring Europe as an art student I learnt that Michelangelo had used the insane as models for the damned souls in his Last Judgment. Arriving in Paris, then, it occurred to me that I could do some sketches of these character types by attending the public lectures of Dr. Féré. On my first visit, Dr. Féré was using female subjects to demonstrate his theory that magnets could be used to transfer the symptoms of hysterics from one side of the body to the other. One such specimen, Amy L., was fitted with a vest of steel bands penetrated by a screw attached to a pad over her ovaries, which

So strong were my associations conjured by those bands that I feared some such loathsome scene would emerge here in my home. But to the contrary, I soon began to wonder why P.'s parents had sought professional help for her at all, for she spoke of the most trivial matters, girlish confusions put into her head by suffragettes, for the most part, easily dismissed, though her talk of liberation allowed me to understand the rhetoric of her corset for what it was: an attempt through fashion to code her body as available, i.e., wasp waisted, i.e., an advertisement of an available womb waiting to be filled, the rhetoric of its tight bounds contrasting powerfully to the rotundity of maternity. Of course, she, like the creators of this fashion, like the men for whom it was actually designed, would be unaware of this unconscious message no matter how powerful its influence. So I only made a note to myself to open the moment when appropriate. It was this train of thought that called my

----

could be adjusted to any degree of pressure. Ignoring the protests of the patient, Dr. Féré instructed the attendants to loosen the screws. It was like taking the brakes off of an over-heated engine. A pallor of the face changed to a congested red. Then began a slow upward movement of the globes of the eyes until the pupils disappeared beneath the upper lid, and just that quickly the patient lost consciousness. Her facial muscles contorted into a variety of grimaces; the shoulders were raised and drawn forward, while the arms proceeded to perform a peculiar rotary movement, first rigidly and slowly flexing, then pronating, and again extending to their extreme limit with both arms held out like bars of wood in a crucifixion posture.

All at once she began a series of violent bounding movements, executed by suddenly arching her back until she rested on the vertex and the balls of the feet, and then dropping to the bed and flexing her body in the opposite direction to gain a start for a new opisthotonos. The scene became one of violent bounding until she suddenly remained fixed, bent like a bow, resting now only on her head and toes, her pudenda thrust forward, as in coitus, in the position called l'arc-en-ciel, a posture most doctors interpreted as an unconscious plea for male penetration. Soon the body again fell to the bed, and Amy performed various contortions, uttering cries and struggling to escape snakes--obviously penises--which she believed were biting her. She proceeded to go through a series of other passionate attitudes and hallucinations, repeating the above cycle until it became as monotonous as it was distressing. It was then that Dr. Féré ceased the demonstration by applying pressure to the screw on her ovaries whereupon she regained consciousness, and answered questions put to her by students, visitors, and the curiosity seekers who regularly came in from Paris to witness the show. But then, as always happens, someone asked the doctor to see a particular phase demonstrated again, the pressure was remitted, and again the poor girl was put through her exercise.

Amy and dozens like her were kept in the ward as just such educational aids and I determined to join those who studied there, taking meticulous notes on normally fleeting phenomena and able to compose portraits of man's invisible nature with the fidelity of da Vinci's drawings of birds in flight.

attention to the fact that she had not broached the matter of sex.

I probed this area by asking, --Is there an admirer in your life?

She hesitated, though previously her bearing had been disposed to conversation.

--As verb or noun? she finally asked. Around her waist she wore a scarf that had pinned to it a jeweled sachet. As I elaborated, her index finger began to work itself in and out of her sachet, which given her unmarried state, I of course took to be a symbol of masturbation. While she thus masturbated by proxy, we continued to discuss concerns common to young girls. She did in fact desire a husband, she said, yet the prospects offered up by her parents had left her wanting: a dull banker and another genial fellow whose father was in the white-brick business, as was her own, but who failed for reasons she could not explain to interest her. Eventually, she came around to the incident that had sent her to me:

> --The Lyceum had obtained a number of lithographs of paintings I had once been acquainted with. Born of the same experiments followed by Seurat, they were to accompany a lecture entitled, "What Painter Today Would Dare Compete with Light Sensitive Plates?" The lithographs were reputed to be indistinguishable from the paintings, having been printed on canvas, heavily varnished and framed in the style of old masters. Work by the painter Diego Velazquez was represented and since I had learnt in school that certain of the Modern Impressionists adopted their techniques for capturing a fleeting moment by studying him, I was most keen on revisiting the "originals" with the intent to mark the similarities and differences to the modern works they inspired.
>
> --My mother accompanied me. We were seated in a private room and instructed to keep our gloves on while we handled the specimens. Suddenly, a servant opened a door to an inner office and my eyes met those of a gentleman, the curator, seated at a desk within. He smiled politely, then returned to his own occupations, as did I. When the servant retired, though, the

door was left ajar, affording me a view of the curator's shadow, cast by an electric light while he conversed with someone on the telephone about the very image I held.

--When I looked back down to the "painting" I held, the saintly hermits in it seemed to be staring out from the emulsion--"faithful" to the original in the way that mourners often say that a corpse looks natural. And, in truth, it did exert a strange influence over me that I can only compare to the power that photographs of the dead have over us.

--As I overheard the curator discussing the photo's excellence, I couldn't help but think how approaching the aura of the original in the natural light of the Prado, the subtlety of its mystery would only reveal itself slowly, St. Anthony here receiving directions from a centaur, then there a satyr. Then we notice St. Paul hiding in his cave all the while. But in this photograph, the mystery was given the aspect of a photo for the evening post. Imagining a modern photo of a crow bringing manna to two saintly hermits made it, well--not sacred. A parody, not a mystery.

--Nor could I understand the curator's compliments to the photographer since all trace of a human hand seemed to have been eliminated from this reproduction. That is, Velazquez was present but only as a ghost haunting the photograph. Indeed, when I tried to imagine who had made the photo itself, the only answer that came to mind was, was--the camera. It was as if I were expected to believe that a whole work of art could be created with the click of a button.

--The curator seemed to think this a quality to be highly prized. Up until photography, he said, all landscapes, all historical scenes, even those of one's own infancy had been captive to the eye of an artist, a tyranny that had finally been thrown off.

--But I couldn't help wonder if the world had been freed of the artist's imagination only to be entrapped by that of the chemist, the lens grinder, the machinist, and all the industries and habits of mind that make them possible.[4] An interpretation created by an unconscious selection but an interpretation nonetheless, and perhaps more insidious because of its ease and invisibility.

--Never having seen the originals, my mother continued to admire these dead simulacrums while I found myself inexplicably drawn toward the curator who suddenly seemed to me to be the embodiment of a change in the world that had been occurring as slowly as the day-to-day change of a season, and therefore as unnoticed, though ultimately as profound. His shadow was cast by the light of an electric lamp, and as he moved, his shadow elongated, making him seem immense, though diffuse, powerful, though....

--Sensual? I asked.

--Yes. Some minutes later, I realized I was being addressed. It was mother. She was anxiously trying to attract my attention. The attendant was quite agitated because I was handling the new "old masters" with my bare hands. I must have given a start, for the gloves I had unwittingly removed fell from my lap. As the attendant retrieved them, my mother gave me an admonishing look.

--The rest of the day went as usual until alone in bed, I found myself thinking about the curator. The next day I was again distracted by his memory. And the day after that as well. I continued to visit the Wainright Memorial Library and, as was my habit, to find a seat at the Whitehall Memorial Window that had such a nice leaded design and view of the grounds. But it was nearly impossible for me to concentrate enough to read. I found myself thinking about the curator, whose memory

----

4 Darwin's photos of emotions immediately sprang to mind. For whereas earlier artists drew what they were told to look for, e.g., the slack jaw of an idiot, the proud neck of the megalomaniac, the mild smile of the religiously feeble-minded, and etc., the photograph, by contrast, stands to its subject as a mirror does to its viewer. That is, apart. An independent existence. Technology has thus achieved the "mirror on the road of life" that the novelist or painter could only crudely approximate.

became a shadow to me. At odd moments I would catch myself wondering what he was doing, or what our lives would be like together, or what our children would look like, or--

She suddenly gave a musical laugh.

--But I never even met him!...

To the lay eye, this evidence of fantasy may seem perfectly healthy and my first instinct was to bid her good day, and report as much to her parents. Any maid who spent her time sequestered in a library would naturally identify with hermits in a painting. And it would be natural for her to seek direction, as did the hermit in the painting, from a satyr (that horned image of man's lustful nature). Yet the fact that this task was accompanied by a compulsive act of symbolic masturbation indicated deeper waters. The gloves falling away was obviously a token of her shedding her dress; her mother's stricture at her losing her "dress" to a man not intended, a servant no less, was a token of her virginity as well (and it might be added, every mother's nightmare).... "Handling the specimen with gloves," as she put it, is also a very revealing choice of words: a signal of more than the normal anxieties associated with a spinster in the making. That is, her desires were not the problem so much as the fact that she conceived of them as such. This isn't to say that neither she nor I could name the barrier between desire and relief. As numerous cases of derangement demonstrate, a patient with a mental disorder can easily go an entire life without thinking there is anything wrong; in a case of anxiety such as P.'s, the norm is, in fact, for the problem to be completely invisible, only revealing itself slowly to the psycho-analyst who knows what to look for and concentrates until he sees it.

Here was an onion whose layers I must unpeel and examine, one by one, until its black center was revealed. While P. has the misfortune of living in a society that cultivates sexual nervousness, she is lucky that her society is also modern enough to have developed scientific cures.

I asked P. today what associations she makes with shadows and she immediately related the following dream:

--I dreamt that I was walking down an endless loggia lined by statues: the Discus Thrower, Laocoön in the grips of his serpents, winged Mercury... They were all white marble, like grave markers.

--No, wait! That wasn't how it went. Rather, the dream shifted, as dreams do, and I found myself upon a vestibule. Or perhaps the vestibule was beneath me. I can't remember. The door was open, in any case, and I could hear moaning coming from the room it led to. Peeking inside, I was horrified to find my own shadow, quite independent of me, strapped into a chair like dentists use. Men were conducting some sort of experiment, using lights to alter its shape. Or so it seemed. As they worked, I felt a wrenching sensation as if my own shape was metamorphosing to match the shape that the men were making the shadow take on, and I awoke--out of breath and perspiring....

--As I tried to calm the pounding of my heart, I had the peculiar sensation of understanding, intimately, why natives believe that a shadow is a token of the self and guard it with their lives.

27 SEPTEMBER 1917

During the time I studied in Vienna, almost every American student attended Prof. Karl Braun's obstetrics clinic, whether interested in obstetrics or not, as it was a capital place to improve one's knowledge of German. The Professor, being corpulent, sat through his lectures and spoke very slowly with a distinct tone of voice. When, after a long pause, during which many of the German students were audibly snoring, he would ask in the most deliberate manner, "Nun meine Herren--wie viel wiegt--das kind?" A German student once remarked to me that he didn't care a rap about medicine, but to hear Professor Braun's lecture was as good as going to a comedy at the Theatre an der Wien. Nevertheless, Braun was a remarkable man in his keenness of observation. (It is said that the literary character Sherlock Holmes is based upon him.) Taking a patient's hand and looking straight at the class he would say, "This man is a tailor." Later we would find out that he divined this fact by feeling the needle pricks on the roughened forefinger. A hatter he would recognize by the peculiar calluses caused by the tools of that trade.[5] I never forgot his ability to stare at a patient until the traces of a case spoke its own diagnosis.

My sessions with P. had been going on for some weeks at this point, and I felt confident that I had held her in the developing solution of psycho-analysis long enough for a picture to emerge. From our initial meeting on, she repeatedly mentioned the same motifs: the shadow, the photo, the double or simulacrum, and the variety of ways these motifs expressed themselves: waking up from a dream within a dream, or the déjà vu that she experienced whenever she read, or the time she looked upon another woman seated in a neighboring coach, judging her to be overly prim before realizing that she was looking at her own reflection in the glass--manifestations all of her pathological, almost primitive fear

---

5 The student who said he didn't care a rap about medicine later became an officer in the Austro-German army. There he used the techniques learnt in Prof. Braun's class to conduct the Massacre of Maribor, whereby hundreds of Romanian soldiers hiding in that province after their retreat were summarily executed after being identified from calluses on the right thumb and palm peculiar to the infantry man who handles a rifle for an extended period of time.

The Example of Haiti

Never can we see ourselves as clearly as we see an other. Thus, we study the bizarre rituals of strange tribes not to learn about them, per se, but in order to gain insight into our own society, which familiarity has made invisible to us. Therefore, let us look.

Faustin "God" Wirkus and Some of His Faithful.

Though 97% of Haiti's natives are practicing Catholics, 100% are practicing Voodooists, attending blood sacrifices where the metaphoric sacrifice of the Catholic mass that they attended on Sunday morning is by night made literal in the black heart of the jungle. Catholic saints are worshipped as black-magic gods; he-goats are hypnotized to couple with human females before their throats are cut in imitation of Christ's sacrifice, the blood of which is drunk during frenzies of licentious "communion" by the black "parishioners."

Indeed, in Haiti it is common knowledge that corpses are often brought back to life as zombies, many of which are reported to work in the fields of the Haitian-American Sugar Company (HASCO). Consequently, families bury their dead under heavy stones and keep watch until decomposition has made the body useless to the likes of Papa Nebo, a hermaphrodite necromancer and necrophiliac, much feared and respected. They are assisted in this effort by their voodoo priest, or

"Papa Nebo," Hermaphrodite Sorceress Who Digs Up Corpses for Magical Purposes, Garbed as Half Man, Half Woman.

hungman, who gets under the sheet which covers the corpse during the funeral, then shouts out the dead man's name. The corpse shudders and raises as though trying to sit up, then falls back--an inert mass again--the effect of the loa, its spiritual double, leaving.

Virtually all Haitians have seen with their own eyes a dead relative rise in this manner and their reports are sincere, though to an outsider, the priest seems to be merely lifting the corpse and dropping it. Thus it does not take a great effort to imagine these same natives mistaking a pilot, who has parachuted from his abandoned biplane, for a white god, fallen from the sky. That is, Haitian witnesses to the rising of the dead, or the god-pilot descending from heaven, exemplify those observers who are so carried away by faith that all the world is seen in terms of marvel. And herein lies the lesson for us: that even the most outlandish claims can be mistaken for bedrock truth by those submerged in a community that gives them credence and support. Our own communities--religious, artistic, scientific, or medical--all bear witness to this fact by the outrageous claims each has put forth at various times in the past.

-- See William Seabrook, The Magic Island, 1917.

of others using tokens of her "self" to do her harm. Indeed, I couldn't help but be struck by the primitive, i.e., primal nature of her fear, for I had recently read of Lieutenant Faustin E. Wirkus, the U.S. marine who dropped by parachute into Haiti some years back and who was worshipped as a god by natives who believed him to be divinely sent.

Perhaps it were these primitive instinctual fears that were rising up within her when she said whilst describing her dream, "My shadow was as substantial as these marble figures."

In this choice of words we find an equation, in her mind, of her body and the dead. Yet, death has an equally long tradition as a metaphor for coitus. Orgasm is the metaphoric moment of death, la petite mort, as the French have it, which we express when we say, "We died in each other's arms," and other such things. But to P., this is a stony death, an act of coitus as cold as marble. The fact that she is a virgin, who therefore has no standard of comparison for acts of coitus, made me believe that her dread was a form of superstition. Unlike Haitians, our highly regulated culture allows no release for the expression of the "ungenteel" side of our nature.[6] Rather than serving a societal function, our Papa Nebos must bottle up their instinctual nature until it explodes or is vented slowly through neurotic behavior: e.g., the vocification, singing, cursing, aimless wandering or nymphomaniacal excitement that is regrettably so common in clinical descriptions.

In P.'s case, several months of testimony always pointed to her particular form of release: masturbation. The cold substitute for coitus itself. Like dawn breaking in a valley, once I made this realization, the entire geography of onanism came into focus! The reading of literature as well as the other arts were for her sensual pleasures, best indulged in solitude. The cave that continually appears in her dreams is, of

----

6 Indeed, in London, Paris, and Berlin thousands of former soldiers have been forced to walk the earth as the West's living dead: soldiers who survived for years among corpses in grave-like trenches only to have their faces shot away. These unfortunates were saved by a medical science that could do nothing for their horrid disfigurements. Back in polite society, pressures exerted upon them by the norms of decorum led them to revert to the trench mentality that had become a second nature to them, venturing out only under cover of night, wearing wooden masks carved to resemble their old faces.

course, her vagina, the corridor, like tunnels in many dreams, the rite of passage to sexual awareness. But in her dream she merely passes by the figures of nude men and arrives at the vestibule--an anatomical term for a particular region of the female genitals. Anyone who used technical names such as "vestibulum" must have obtained their vocabulary from reading, and not by reading popular magazines either, but from anatomical textbooks-- the common refuge of youth devoured by sexual curiosity. All the time she spent in the library was almost matter-of-factly explained, as was the source of her anxiety.

For far from being glorified as an aide to fertility as it was when a Botticelli or a Titian might have included it in a painting as a symbol of fecundity, masturbation is now widely believed to be the scourge of the young. Even our most prestigious medical journals cite the cause of dementia among the young to:

> sexual excitement, often brought on by the reading of French fiction with voluptuous engravings, which drive the young to masturbate (ergo the name Dementia, i.e., sense-less, and Praecox, i.e., premature, as in pubescence, the onslaught of sexuality when the young are most vulnerable). Excessive masturbation produces toxic sepsis that pollutes the brain, thus weakening moral will, thus leading to further Onanism until the victim, trapped in this cycle of vice, degenerates to a bestial state.[7]

Believing in this wholly organic explanation for Dementia Praecox, the physician makes his wholly organic prescription: to prevent the patient's own self-humbuggery by binding him in a Restraining Chair. In less advanced cases, young men are instructed to fit their organs with engines that will prevent night emissions, day emissions, even erections, out of the fear that to allow sexual energy to run riot will result in nervous exhaustion, irregular bowels, spinal trouble, increasing insanity, paralysis or even death.[8]

Unfortunately, this purely organic explanation ignores the fact that

----

7 Dr. Allen W. Hagenbach. "Masturbation as a Cause of Insanity" in Journal of Nervous and Mental Diseases. 1879, Vol. 6, P. 609.
8 Emil Kraepelin, Psychiatrie, 1909-1913; 2,500 pages.

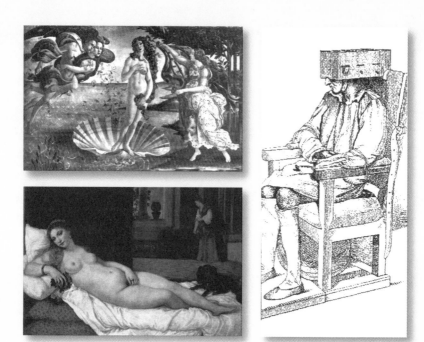

Is masturbation a gift of the gods? An aid to fertility? Or a degenerative vice that must be prevented at all costs to preserve the sanity of its sufferer?

the toxins revealed by dissection of Dementia Praecox sufferers' brains might arise from their anxiety, as a wound exudes pus, causing the sufferer to masturbate, rather than the converse, a toxin produced by masturbation, which drives the victim insane. Many physicians have, in fact, noted that masturbation, in moderation, can actually serve a healthy transitional function. If medical science could only convince America of this, her emancipated youth would send skyrockets shooting upward (pun intended!) in celebration. But since masturbation is condemned by contemporary society, our young men instead find themselves forging psychological, Jacob-Marley chains; with each link they grow weaker, become more timid, guilt-ridden and anxious.

For females, this burden is compounded, and the consequences far more extreme. While females are more prone than males to strong emotions of all kinds, the nervous system that nature has given them

THE TIMELY WARNING
Stop the Vampire of Youth!

A vampire is sucking the vital energy from thousands of men of all ages! The secret vice practiced so extensively by the youth of our land is responsible for lack of ambition, failure, lassitude, sterility, divorce, paralysis, consumption and a thousand and one ills that beset mankind. These delicate parts of young men, like the wet potter's clay, are so easily impressed at this early age by the "vampire of youth" that unless proper measures are taken, what should be a laughing, careless young man becomes instead a timid, shrinking, ambitionless thing, a slimy snake that drags its repellent lengths through a whole lifetime of misery and despair, looking upon life's duties and life's pleasures with a listless eye, hopeless, and despondent.

closed

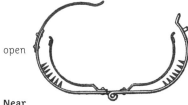
open

Help Is Near

* The Timely Warning device prevents emissions, even at night, by alerting the wearer before a loss is suffered.
* This new device has been allowed a patent by the U.S. Government.
* It is easily applied and can be quickly removed.
* It neither presses on the urethra nor upon the veins on the upper surface of the organ, which have so much to do with causing erections.
* It is adjustable to any size of organ--the spring that holds it in place, as well as the outer band, are supplied with prongs to alert the wearer when the organ enlarges.
* It causes no discomfort to the relaxed organ, nor does it excite erections as do similar devices.

Good For

Stricture, Spermatorrhea, Skin Eruptions, Sexual Insanity, Nervous Disorders, Sexual Neurasthenia, Varicocele of the Veins of the Bag (Scrotum).

Testimonials

Ingalls, Kan., October 17, 1904
Dear Sir:--I received my Timely Warning Ring. It is a great improvement over my old one, which I had purchased from another company. Your appliance has saved me lots of suffering and weakness within the last fifteen months by awakening me in time to prevent a loss. It was the best investment I ever made.

Nashville, Ark., August 18, 1905
Dear Sir:--I am very pleased to tell you that my emissions have stopped, and my anxiety has all gone now. Wish I had known of The Timely Warning years ago.

Culbertson, Mont., March 8, 1905
Dear Sir:--I have had my ring five or six months. I have had just one emission in that time, when my ring was not adjusted tight enough. It has proved of great use to me from the first.

Price by mail, sealed, $2.00
Dr. Foote's Sanitary Bureau, 129 East 28th Street, New York

to carry their elevated emotional loads is paradoxically more delicate. Not only does this emotional burden exhaust the nervous system of their animal frame (and nothing frays the nervous system more than strong passions, guilt and anxiety) but their inherently delicate bodies can also be taxed by a useless increase in heart rate, fainting (and falling), wind in the uterus, ringing in the ears, swelling of the labia, bouts of laughter, bouts of crying, silliness, voluptuous leanings, vacuation sexuelle, erotic imaginings and paroxysms or spasms and other manifestations of a hysterical episode. While committed masturbators are usually male, hysteria, often called the vapors, is the most prevalent chronic illness among women, striking especially those widows or unmarried women aged puberty to thirty-five.

The reason for this range of ages is simple: the sexual drive in women is in actuality the drive to procreate. As any married man can attest, once the need to bear children has been satisfied, it is common for the woman not only to exhibit a diminishment in her willingness to take a man to her bed, but to completely lose any interest whatsoever in sexual relations. Those doctors who insist, despite the massive amount of both folk wisdom and medical research to the contrary, that women derive sexual pleasure--not womb relief--are usually men who project the male drive upon the female out of an inability to see the world through a female's eyes, or feel what a woman feels with a body obviously designed by nature for a single end: childbearing.

This is how oxymorons, such as "female orgasm," come into widespread use, when even a little introspection will show that it makes no more sense to speak of "female orgasm" than it does to discuss "male pregnancy." We speak of female sexual satisfaction and frustration in general, forgetting that what appears to be a craving for a penis can only be, in fact, a craving for pregnancy.9

Masturbation may have served for a time as a healthy substitute for

---

9 Thus grows a whole vocabulary of sexual desire and satisfaction that is no more suited to the normal female physiognomy than the ill-fitting business suits worn by some masculinized variants. It distorts our thinking about women and the problems peculiar to them. Nor are women themselves immune to these fallacies

a man who would vigorously encounter her in bed. But no matter how deeply she buried her real craving it would remain there in her psyche like faulty electrical wiring that has been walled up and lies smoldering until it bursts into flames, consuming everyone asleep in the house. That is, as she sunk deeper into the secret life of lies and deception, as every masturbator must, the store of anxiety she would build up would erode her nervous system and with it her moral judgment. Like an overburdened switchboard, her spinal cord (neuralgia spinalis) would find itself increasingly taxed as it strained to carry the emotional-nervous demands placed upon it (a process already underway as indicated by the hyperirritability she turned on her parents whenever they, quite reasonably, lamented her unmarried state). Wholly engrossed by her libidinal desires, her hysteria might manifest itself in lesbian hysteria brought on by masturbation, or, refusing to stimulate herself, it might erupt into hysteria libidinosian, i.e., nymphomania.

This is the situation that I, her fireman, found when I came rushing in, hose in hand, and I pointed its nozzle at her onastic compulsion by presenting her with the horns of her dilemma. For we had reached the point where it was time to begin drawing her hermit from the cave and see him for what he was!

I began by suggesting that perhaps it was a pity that she had never known man. She looked confused and began to rehearse all of the filial relationships she had already described during the course of our investigations. I could not tell if she was genuinely innocent of my remark

---

of language. It is as if both sexes used the word "twilight" when women mean by it the light before dawn, while men mean the light after sunset--two very different phenomena, similar only in their most surface appearance. The problem is further complicated by the fact that men know nothing of "sunrises" while women know not of "sunsets," with neither sex aware of the other's ignorance. Thus we persist in our common vocabulary, thinking the opposite sex (how aptly named!) feels the same things, and understands the words we use to mean what they think they mean. Given that a need for the two sexes to speak to one another will arise from time to time, we see that miscommunication is inevitable. But always, always, the psychoanalyst must be aware of the distortion inherent in the language he himself uses to communicate with his female patients. Always he must keep in mind that when it comes to sexual matters, the woman cannot possibly mean what he understands her to say when she uses such words as "orgasm," or "desire."

or just found it uncomfortable to discuss what must surely seem to her to be an inadequacy, given the fact that she had witnessed friends and even a younger sister marry. As if to refute me, she detailed her most recent outing with a young man from her father's office, an outing that had gone so well that after he saw her home, she retreated to her bedroom to replay the day's events in her mind.

--And did you touch yourself? I asked.

--I'm sorry, I do not take your meaning.

Again, the veil of gentility was descending between us. In a medical manner, I explained that being a self-toucher was nothing to be ashamed of. No more so than would be scratching to relieve an itch. Or covering one's nose at the onset of a sneeze. Even healthy, heterosexual intercourse is accompanied by fantasies and since nature has endowed women with three centers of sexual sensitivity as opposed to the single one of man, women are naturally predisposed to eroticism.[10]

In situations such as her own, I explained to her astonished expression, a woman with a reputation and future to protect, it is assuredly better and more economical to masturbate--up to a point. Our body knows what is best for us even if society warns us to deny its advice. This was the reason she spent so much time alone: The imagination can work more freely when one is alone. Her love of books was thus revealed as a defense mechanism to mask, even from herself, her true motives. Her face grew as scarlet as passionflowers, her guilt informing me that I had struck a chord. Tuning the instrument, I assured her that she need not be shy with me. The patient on an analyst's couch is an open book that he reads for her betterment. Indeed, her very reason for being here was for me to reveal her secrets to herself so that she might avoid the pitfalls suffered by others.

In order to demonstrate that the danger she was in was not peculiar to her alone, I pulled down from the bookshelf one volume by Havelock Ellis, and read from it a passage in which Ellis reports on the sexual

---

10 One woman studied by Moraglia knew how to masturbate in fourteen different ways. See Lombroso and Ferro. 1915: 43-48.

deviance of seamstresses cooped up in hot quarters all day. Due to the heat of the day, these girls commonly wore no underwear. Theirs was a society where its citizens worked with their legs naked while their neighbor inspected them. The talk of sex that floated over their sewing machines would drive some to quietly masturbate while at their work. Hoping she would see the inherent danger in allowing this temporary method of relief to become first habit, then a way of life, I explained how it was not uncommon for the smell of sex and flesh in the close quarters of a garment factory to lead some girls to pair off.[11]

P. only stared corpse-like at the ceiling, and in order to reassure her that all was not lost, at least in her case, at least not yet, I explained how these woman returned to normalcy once the neural current that caused their fuses to blow was reduced.

Her jaw remained set as I continued to explain that never having found it within herself to give herself to a man, she felt incomplete, especially in light of her advancing age. She longed for the psychological trust shared between a woman and her lover, but her practice of masturbation was, as it were, a hymen preventing this union. This was the meaning of her dream where she was running past the statues of dead men: all nude men were dead to her, she believed. It was also the reason, I said, she lived with her mother and father: her first protectors.

P. endured this lecture stoically, apparently overwhelmed by my acumen.

Of course, I emphasized, since the cloistered life that she found herself trapped in was the result of her own choices, different choices would result in a different life. Nothing she described, I explained, was uncommon for unmarried females of her age, and on the day she finally let a man into her cell, she would, like other women before her, feel the bars of guilt that imprisoned her melt away.

In an effort to lighten the mood, I drew up on my pad the Freudian prescription we used to pass about as students:

----

11 Havelock Ellis, Sexual Inversion, 6 vol. Vol. 2 Studies in the Psychology of Sex. Philadelphia: F.A. Davis Company, 1901, 1915, 1926.

$$R_X = \text{Penis Normalis}$$
dosim repetatur!

P.'s milk-white brow had completely curdled by now, her mouth a tight frown. After more benevolent prodding, she finally confessed-- not that I was correct, but that she had fabricated the entire story my analysis was based upon!

I was stupefied. Then furious! Not only had I wasted months but I had been duped into playing the gullible fool. How could she have lied? Why would anyone lie to their doctor about their symptoms?

She claimed that though she had fabricated the story, she had not lied, at least not in essence. There really had been a man that she could not forget, but it was not the lyceum curator. Rather, this shadow had reminded her of another, a love affair that had ended badly. And while she had fabricated the details, it was the inability to put this affair behind her that had caused her parents to send her to me.

My own level of anger shocked me and seemed inexplicable until I recognized that it was fueled by not a little jealousy. Yet her voice was so remorseful for her fall that.... Passion had raised the colour in her cheeks and as she spoke, I found myself, by degrees, returning to the compassionate role of a physician who knew that a woman could not, should not, be held to the same standards as a man for they are but men arrested in intellectual and physical development. Trapped as they are in an earlier stage of evolution, it is indeed natural for them to have an undeveloped moral sense. As Lombroso and Ferro have shown, the female of our species, being nearer to the savage, has an actual physi-ological incapacity for telling the truth--a characteristic rooted in her primitive biology and reinforced by the need she feels (reinforced by society) to hide menstruation from men and sex from children.[12] We should not be surprised, then, to learn that a woman's natural inclination is to lie--an impulse that we actually condone by construing her libidinal core as a lie that society insists she live within.

----

12 Lombroso, Cesare and Guglielmo Ferro. La dama delinuente, la prostitute e la donna morrale, 1915.

Instead of demanding my fee and showing her the door, then, I composed myself and allowed her to continue her pitiful story, which as it turned out, involved a Spanish painter with whom she had been romantically involved one summer in Europe. He created portraits by first projecting the shadow of his sitters onto the canvas. Whenever she saw her shadow in profile, she thought of him. The liaison was completely unknown to her parents and this no doubt added to her inability to relate the truth to me, a father figure.

The painter had wanted to paint her portrait but she refused, as this would necessitate, he claimed, her going to his bachelor rooms. Over several days he pressed his case, a case that she secretly agreed with: that there was nothing wrong with being alone with him in his rooms, that it was only overbearing social conventions that barred them from the intimacy they had a right to enjoy. In the end, as he promised to be discreet, she consented to visit him in his bachelor rooms in the daytime for the purpose of a fully-clothed posing session. Once there, however, they embraced, then kissed--full on the mouth--first standing, then sitting on the bed, then lying upon it. As he began to admire the delights that were now partly exposed, she heard a click. Looking up, she espied a camera on a bookshelf, pointed at the bed where they lay. Despite his protestations, she became convinced that he had used some kind of remote control to capture her image in this compromising position. She indignantly stormed out and went home. Days later, when the artist came to plead with her to be reasonable, she only insisted that he give her the film. He claimed that the camera didn't even work. That she must have heard the clock click, or possibly a neighbor's door lock. But she remained resolute, saying that just because he was able to fabricate a story that neatly fit the facts, didn't mean it was true.

Could I believe her now, I asked myself? "Dirty knees are a sign of a respectable girl," says a working-class maxim. But how could one tell among women of quality? The answer, I knew, was to be found deeper within the dirt and tangle that are always, always, below the surface.

P. related this dream:

>--I dreamt I was a raven descending to one of the gardens that were so in vogue at the time of Victoria: Vines overgrew artificial Roman ruins of the type that were to inspire meditation on the mutability of life. Hidden within was an "ornamental hermit," that is, one of those poor wretches that the wealthy hire to dress and live as recluses within the confines of their garden.

>--When I delivered the pastry I'd been carrying in my beak, the cave that served as the mock hermit's cell was transformed to the scene of a lavish banquet. Where previously there had been nothing but austere rock there now flowed milk and honey. Succulent melons and peaches glistened with their own juice....

>--I noticed a man pulling apart the wings of the bird on his plate and I....

--You felt a shiver? I suggested.

Tellingly, she crossed her legs at the ankles. However, she answered, demurely.

>--Yes. I hadn't realized it until you asked, but I think I did. And the sensation came at the moment I was changed from a raven back into the form of a woman.

Then her voice took on the tone of women of character who in their reserve forbear from revealing more than they should but also understand the necessity of candor with their doctors.

>--When he noticed me watching him, he had sent to my table two ripe plums. As a thank-you note, I had sent to his table a platter of peeled shrimp. To my consternation, though, he began to share my gift with those beside him. Around us the banquet grew merry. He sent to my table a thick sausage--as if he understood the ravenous hunger that suddenly welled within me. We began sending each other more and more foods, platters of grapes, succulent ears of corn, triangles of phyllo

wrapped around thick meats, chocolate mousse, bratwurst, peaches with pistachio cream, scones oozing cream.... I remember now, there was more: Greek sausages, chocolate raspberry cloud roll, skinned rabbit with duck-blood sauce, puddings, persimmons, pomegranates, figs, cherries jubilee, cheesecake, cheesecakes everywhere-- so much cheesecake neither of us could begin to finish it so we passed it around, our bounty spreading throughout the hall, delighting the other diners as they happily joined in and soon all was a confusion of food, no one knowing or caring who had ordered what for whom: an enormous banana, a blueberry tart....

As she spoke, I realized I had been mistaken to interpret the rhetoric of her corset as an advertisement of an available womb. It now clearly stood out as a promise of sex without fear of pregnancy, the bands that held in her waist a public declaration of this contraceptive covenant.

...wiggly mounds of pink gelatin, each topped by a single cherry, whole salmon glazed with cream sauce, fantastically long bread sticks and soft muffins, and oysters! Oh, the oysters! The oysters!...

These descriptions went on for some time. I filled pages.... When she finally relented, I asked myself, "Where do I begin?"

Often, when we progress through a novel, scenes from earlier sections that we lightly passed over or did not understand begin to become more meaningful as certain themes emerge. So it was in my reading of P. The dropping of her gloves still held up as a shedding of clothes. But what I failed to see before was the purposeful nature of this act. The raven (a bird whose black plumage mirrors pubic hair) descending with a gift was, as P. recognized, a symbol of herself. But what she did not see was that the gift was her virginity, as illustrated more dramatically by the bird on the plate, the man spreading her wings, i.e., her sexual wings, her thighs. An act that contained her destruction: the virginal girl dying to the sexually-aware woman as is evidenced in countless paintings where a bird is used to represent the vagina, shot through by the phallic arrow. It is also interesting to note that the "hermit" that inhabits her "cave" has become an artificial hermit. Perhaps a penis substitute as I originally thought. But this false hermit could be a flesh-and-blood man who would willingly ravish her as opposed to an actual saint who would rather, according to Christian lore, trump desire when it threatened by biting off the tip of his tongue or throwing himself into a thorn bush.

Relating this dream to her actual life, the artist with whom she was romantically involved (and who by training experienced women as aesthetic form), cannot be faulted for his role in the creation of her anxiety. No doubt he unthinkingly planted suggestions in her mind that he wished to "capture" her image as she later formulated it. Her phobia of doubles combined with her denial of sexual desires made her resist and possibly even hallucinate. Indeed, I believed that the camera never clicked. Perhaps there never even was a camera (as P. testified, the artist worked from shadows). The camera was just a perfect symbol of our age. That is, when she confronted the artist, she claims he made the explanation of an inoperable camera and I venture to explain that her imaginings may have arisen out of sexual frustration; she had given him an opportunity to forcibly deflower her, the only way she would allow herself (before marriage) to relieve a maternal itch that was driving her mad.

Conversely, it was possible that P. was not entirely truthful with me in that she didn't visit the artist once, but many times, and not for the innocent kissing and petting she admits but for the full sexual relations indicated by the many phallic symbols of her dream. If this were the case, she assuredly indulged in coitus interruptus or coitus reservatus, practices that only contributed to her neurosis if one remembers that normal women only desire that sex which can result in a child.[13]

Whether or not there was contact of the genitals, the acute sense of unease she felt being in the man's room probably produced a knock, or beat, in her clitoris. Predisposed to perceive what she most dreaded, her mind then projected the sound onto the camera, which she imagined captured her image as she lay nude with her lover.

After some minutes, she said, softly, --I had not realized that a clitoris could "knock" or that a hermit could stand for a penis.

--The audible knocking of the clitoris is a medical fact known by all doctors old enough to have beards, I assured her. And as for the hermit, it is just one of many symbolic figures for the penis.

Her jaw tensed.

At times, we doctors forget that the facts that make up the everyday parlance of our trade are radical revelations to the uninitiated. So I showed her my notes for a table I was compiling to categorize phallic symbols according to their origin in the animal kingdom, the domain of vegetables, those that are mineral and those that are man-made:

> Bananas, bolts, screws, nails, broom handles, mop handles, handles of all sorts, various knifes, swords, pistols, lances, pencils, quills, pens, fingers (middle finger for megalomaniacs,

---

13 Over the years, various means have been tried to relieve infertile women of the frustration, then the hysteria, that they bring on themselves by engaging in useless sexual relations. Dr. J. Marion "The Architect of the Vagina" Sims, the father of gynecology, developed the first contribution to this branch of medicine: the Uterine Guillotine, a guillotine-like device used to remove the clitoris of women. Likewise, Dr. Nikolaus Friedreich has had much success cauterizing the clitorises of patients whose sexual instincts are deemed inappropriate to their inability to be mothers, freeing these lucky patients from the cruel trick that nature has played upon them.

pinky for infertility complexes), nose, ear lobes, monkey tails, rat tails, dog tails, whales, dolphins, barracudas and other fish, pistons and other industrial machinery, candles, tapers, Haley's comet, a thumb, spears, cucumbers, many members of the squash family, sticks, logs, mailing tubes, pipe, locomotives, skyscrapers, stink horn, boat oars, violin bows, flutes, oboes, plows, hoes, spikes, ears of corn, corn cobs, goat horns, sheep horns, bull horns, bull whips, ladders, hoses of all sorts, rifles, cannon, mandrake, snakes of all kinds, worms, lizards, missiles, mortar shells, mortars, hammers, axes, daggers, arrows, asparagus officinalis, augers and other drill bits, wine bottles, screwdrivers, awls, castle towers, Sugar Loaf Mountain, church steeples, the stone megaliths of Brittany, lower-case "l" and upper-case "I", the Washington monument, other famous (and not so famous) obelisks, Belemnitella americana, gearshift levers, Old Faithful, bicycle pumps, billy clubs, chess kings, chess pawns, the Hindenburg, other blimps, blowguns, blunderbusses, trucks, campanile, canes, oil derricks, clarinets, claymores, railway tracks, columns, pillars, Buckingham fountain, stalagmites, stalactites, croquette stakes, masts of ships, the prow of a ship, culverin, cutlasses, daggers, dachshunds, sturgeon, dildos and other rubber novelties (obviously), baseball bats, divining rods, cucumbers, downspouts, eels, elephant tusks, elephant trunks, sentry boxes, gramophone end pins, flag poles, Maypoles, gimlets, smokestacks, hockey sticks, skis, icicles, javelins, lighthouses, minarets, fence posts, barbershop poles, insect stingers, newels, telescopes, hot-dogs, pennywhistles, salt shakers, chemist's pestles, prickets, exclamation marks (!), the arrangement of stars at the center of the Orion constellation, pumps, ramrods, battering rams, reeds, batons, curtain rods, scepters, shaggymane (coprinus cormatus), shillelagh, totem poles, the numeral 1....

One day I hope to do the same for vaginas, coitus, and various perversions, and arrange the categories on a wheel much like those used by students of foreign languages to conjugate verbs. In this manner, the student of psycho-analysis would have a ready and mechanical aid to dream interpretation.

Turning to her case, then--

I explained that no neurasthenia, or analogous neurosis, can exist without a disturbance of the sexual function.

This elicited the same shocked expression Eve must have worn upon discovering that the Tree of Knowledge had roots as well as sexual fruit. And if P. were Eve?--

I suddenly realized that if P. were Eve, then my role was that of the serpent, the instrument of knowledge/the penis; the object of desire. In an effort to reassure her, I told her that she need not be embarrassed by this revelation. Given the high regard that she had for me and my profession, I should have predicted that she would try to make of me the saint who inhabits her cave. Indeed this represented progress! Since I am a secular saint, I explained, her desire for me was not a flight into fancy, but an invitation, set in a poetic manner, like Excalibur in the rock, and intended only for the suitor with the analytic strength to extract it.

--Here is the unconscious reason you lied to me about the extent of your relations with the artist, I said: fear that I would not want to be involved with a fallen woman. Furthermore, I explained, I as a father figure became to you a stand-in for sex with your own father, which of course was socially condemned. By having sexual relations with your analyst, though, my penis could serve as the proxy for your father's penis in the way that your compulsive masturbation was a substitute for marital coitus--

Our interview was ended by Miss P.'s flight from the room.

6 DECEMBER 1917

P.'s flight was no less than an admission of her desire for me: a repeat performance of her flight from her last lover, the Spanish painter. Indeed, I began to wonder if her entire "malady" may have been a ruse to court me after a fashion, which she now believes thwarted by my penetrating analysis that revealed her non-virginity and that, of course, neither of us had any way of anticipating.

But why should this revelation embarrass her? Having witnessed the wholesale overthrow of previous notions of decency between nations, individual decorum, even morality, comes to seem quaint.

What soldier, for example, who has witnessed the summary execution of prisoners under his care, for the simple reason that it was easier to have no prisoners to care for than it was to care for them, what soldier who has witnessed this on a basis as routine as the coming and going of a tram, what soldier would be surprised to learn that a neighborhood grocer has been short-changing the candlestick maker? Or that the minister has been unfaithful to his wife? When the Hottentot discovers a fly about his head, he swats it. When the flies number in the hundreds he learns to accept them. Otherwise the occupation of swatting flies would crowd out all other activity. Likewise, when the community gradually becomes aware of first one, then two, then dozens, then hundreds and thousands of little moral transgressions, it gradually begins to stop raising objections. When the community no longer has its old moral landmarks.... Well, many citizens of the Modern wander lost in a society that has become foreign to them.

Imagine the disorientation--something like what P. must be feeling-- in terms of the relations between men and women.

Yet a return to old habits is not justified. Just as the astronomer must abandon long-held beliefs about the parallel nature of light rays once Einstein's Theory of Relativity shows how and where they bend, so we must not complain when some portion of reality forces us to admit that notions of right and wrong, which once seemed as natural as the rising and setting of the sun, are nothing but the social anxiety by which we are compelled to conform.

Several weeks passed during which Miss P. failed to appear for her regularly scheduled appointment. I began to fear that she had abandoned her cure at its most critical phase and that she would therefore be worse off now than had she never taken to my couch. It was as if my patient had bolted from the operating table in the midst of an appendectomy (a display of the primitive nature of women which causes them to respond to fear by flight, as can also be observed in children, savages, and primates).

Out of fraternal responsibility to her father, as well as professional obligation, I called on him at their home.

Their maid took my hat and ushered me into the library while she went in search of her master. Alone in the library, I waited under the gaze of dead eyes--the glassy stare of gazelles and the heads of other exotic animals, mounted on the walls. The bookcases were taken up by a collection of fossils, rock-minerals and beetles. Pickled frogs were arranged from those the size of a pebble to those the size of a fist, while a collection of mollusks had been divided according to the direction of their spiral with the vast majority winding up clockwise. The minority group, those with a counterclockwise spiral, was labeled Perverse. Just as I was about to examine them more closely, the library doors slid back and P.'s father emerged. A rotund man, his girth made his gray jacket taut and smooth as a seal's skin. He wore no vest, having obviously exchanged a smoking jacket for a formal coat to receive his visitor. Which he did, extending his hand in a firm, manly handshake. We exchanged some pleasantries about the gentlemen's club to which we both belonged, & etc. In order to relax my host, I made some favorable comparisons between the apparent size of his brain case and E.A. Spizka's grand study of the brain size of men of eminence.[14]

---

14 Spitzka, E.A. "A Study of the Brain of the Late Major J.W. Powell" in American Anthropology, 5, 1903.

Also see Spitzka's "A Study of the Brains of Six Eminent Scientists and Scholars Belonging to the American Anthropometric Society" in Transactions of the American Philosophical Society, 21, 1907.

--The jump from a Thackeray to a Zulu or a Bushman is not greater than from the latter to the gorilla or the orang, I assured him.

He chuckled heartily, waving away my compliment though I could tell he was flattered.

Then I answered a few of his questions about "brain mythologists," as psycho-analysts are sometimes labeled by the uninitiated, explaining how the balance between mind and body so central to our practice is partly due to the fact that psycho-analysis has its roots in the ghetto of dermatology and syphilology. This foundation was the very reason we were better able to treat diseases of the nerves than medical doctors who cannot recognize the psychic component of conditions they try to treat through wholly organic means.

This of course brought us around to the business at hand. He listened seriously, stroking the wings of his mustache, as I confirmed for him the symptoms he and his missus had previously observed in their daughter: an indolent, novel-reading life, a tiredness, a melancholy over her lack of marital prospects combined with a hyperirritability over reminders to her that she was long overdue in becoming a wife and mother. By degrees I began to sound the darker waters these symptoms indicated, doing so in layman's language. While he was a man with whom I could speak man-to-man, I realized the necessity in giving him the vocabulary and logic he would need to convey my warning to its true audience, his wife, and through her his daughter. That is, I knew that he would convey to his wife the substance of our conversation, and his wife in turn would be the one to speak to their daughter about this delicate and feminine matter.

Under the cloak of classical allusion--the myth of Psyche, Caeneus, Diana and the like--I gently led him through a vast garden of symptoms and their associated families of hysterias, nervous exhaustions, and hypochondrias that Francois Boissier de Sauvaces had classified, doing for these diseases what Linnaeus had done for the classification of plants.

--Yes, yes, he amplified, whenever he marked an agreement with his own observations of P.: bouts of anxiety, sleeplessness, a certain tinselry, mawkish sentimentality.... His enthusiasm was sobered, however, when

I added further symptoms revealed by our sessions: erotic fantasies accompanied by lower pelvic edema or vaginal lubrication (I surmise), and false imaginings. In sum, symptoms of a nervous condition brought on by the lack of a man. And also confirmation for the reason she had been sent to me. I also alluded to the practice she most assuredly indulged in. In silence, the gravity of this truth hung between us.

Rising from his chair, he rehearsed his frustrated efforts to help his daughter. When he introduced her to an associate from his white-brick factory, and his wife introduced her to another potential suitor, a young minister, she only became all the more irritable at them for trying to help.

In this his daughter was not unique, I assured him. It is oft said, the man who would know women and does not know the hysteric does not know women. Indeed, hysteric episodes are to be expected of aging virgins. Because of retention of the sexual fluid, the heart and surrounding areas are enveloped in a morbid and moist exudation. Thus it was important to usher her through this dangerous period.

--How, exactly, do you mean dangerous? he asked.

Without trying to mitigate the danger, nor be an alarmist, I told him: --Sapphism.

The poor man thrust his face into his hands as though he had just learnt that his only child had died.

--Or spinsterhood, I added to comfort him, wondering all the while how on earth I could tell him the third, and more likely prognosis: nymphomania. He slumped against the mantel, and remained still as a stone sarcophagus while I explained the hard place his daughter had worked herself into. I did so by using the same example I had given her of normal, heterosexual sewing-machine operators who had been turned into raging lesbians from the strong vibrations of the machines they sat at all day. Sparing him my suspicion that his daughter had been deflowered by a foreign painter, I explained how the longer she indulged in her self-inflicted, pseudo cure, the more she would come to rely, and then depend, on it. She would become like the invalid who depends on a crutch for so long that the afflicted limb stops strengthening and begins to wither, necessitating further use of the crutch, causing further atrophy of the limb, until all hope of recovery fades and the use of the crutch becomes a permanent fixture in the patient's life.

Miss P.'s father made such a pitiful sigh I was moved to silence, but being a doctor it was my duty to give him the facts, no matter how unpleasant. It was difficult to predict the manner in which hysteria of a sexual nature would manifest itself, I continued. Once the nerves were frazzled to the point where normal heterosexual energy could no longer stay its course--there was no use in denying it--she could begin to confuse her drive to procreate with sexual pleasure: the first step toward nymphomania. Or perhaps her unconscious mind would transfer her "womb hunger" from the search for a mate to her own genitals, the addiction of the lonely. Or, as in advanced cases, the genitals of any woman. When combined with a nervous condition, even the most healthy of our young women can be converted into a lonely "Spinning Jenny," or a raging nymphomaniac, or the most depraved of all lesbians, or--

--Whatever is to be done, Doctor! he interrupted, taking my arm like a man grasping for a lifeline.

It was possible that intercourse with a caring male would allow her to maintain enough sexual equilibrium to steer between the Calpe and Abyla of nymphomania and sapphism until she was safely docked in a marriage with potential for procreation. But given the religious nature of the mother, this was obviously not an option. I therefore ventured to put forth a treatment I had learned was being used with increasing frequency and stunning success: a course of percussive treatments whereby the hysteric is electromechanically stimulated to spasm.

Just as a safety valve on a boiler can be triggered to release pressure that has grown to a dangerously high level, I explained, so a small hysterical episode can be induced in the woman on the verge of a hysteric collapse in order to put off the more grave event. I first encountered this course of treatment at the Salpêtrière, where hysterics with exactly these symptoms (erotic fantasies and the rest) would be gynecologically

Curing a Hysteric, 1889

massaged to artificially induce their hysteric convulsions. Instead of pouring water on the head to cure madness as was sometimes done in days gone by (such logic!), an attendant would pour the water on the pelvic area. Though patients in general protested their initial treatment, the vast majority came to accept, and even demand further sessions once they saw how much better they felt afterwards. Indeed, it was not uncommon for these patients to report such buoyancy afterwards that they felt as though they had been drinking champagne. In young widows especially, the treatment would produce the most extraordinary effects: weeping, laughing, trembling & etc.

Afterwards it was easy to see that they had indeed received a measure of temporary relief--and this cannot be stressed enough, for it is the key to the treatment--a measure of relief without touching themselves, and thus placing themselves into the role of lesbians-in-training, or masturbators who exhaust their nervous system through the store of guilt they accumulate by plying this vice. Nor do they engage in imperfect intercourse, transferring the act of sexual gratification from the need to have a baby to the desire for a male organ and thus progressing step by step into nymphomania.[15]

I could tell he was hesitant, and surmising that his reservations stemmed from the protective wall every father instinctively erects around the vagina of his wife and daughters, I assured him that since only penetration with the possibility of impregnation can be truly satisfying to a woman, artificially inducing hysterical spasms can not be said to be sexual. Nothing sexual is taking place. Yet clinical production of hysterical paroxysm provided a palliative for female complaints and made patients feel better, allowing them to pass through this dangerous and difficult period of a young woman's life until such time as she found true peace in marriage and children.

--And you say it is modern?

Just as I was about to explain the advances in the electromechanical technology for percussing patients, a burst of feminine laughter sounded in the hallway. The doors slid open and there was Miss P., in all her beauty, and with another woman, equally beautiful though improperly filled out. She looked familiar-- then it dawned on me. She was a patient of the colleague who belonged to the same club both I and P.'s father frequented. The very friend who had, I surmised, coached Miss P. in what to say that first time she took to my couch. The doctor that P.'s friend was seeing had pointed her out to me during a club dinner at which all present were also in attendance. Over dessert, he had bragged to me, albeit in strictest and most professional confidence, about the progress he was making in percussing her and others in his care. The etiology he outlined was very similar to what I had uncovered in P.: a wan complexion, and nervous temperament, resulting from penned up frustration of a sexual nature. Yet seeing her now, I could scarcely believe it was the same girl, so completely had she thrown

---

15 M.L.H. Arnold Snow, M.D., Professor of Mechanical Vibration Therapy in the New York School of Physical Therapeutics; Associate Editor of the Journal of Advanced Therapeutics; Late Assistant in Electro-Therapeutics; Late Assistant in Electro-Therapeutics and Diseases of the Nervous System in the New York Post Graduate Medical School, Etc. Mechanical Vibration and Its Therapeutic Application. New York: Scientific Authors' Publishing Co., 1904, pp. 236-237.

herself into the affectations of the Modern. Along with bobbing her hair, rouging her cheeks, and wearing low-cut shoes, she had obviously taken up that fad called "dieting" that some young women adopt in order to achieve the figure of a young boy.

--Father? P. said, stopping abruptly when she caught sight of me.

Her friend whispered something into P.'s ear, whereupon Miss P. blushed a brilliant red. Then unable to control herself, she collapsed against her companion in a heap of laughter, her scarlet cheek pressed against the artificially-blushed cheek of her companion who held her in a firm embrace, gazing back at us men with her over-weaning egotism: the perfect portrait of an older and more experienced woman who had already begun to instruct her young initiate in the ways of the world. Or was it a portrait of nascent sapphism?--the inevitable outcome of a frustrated sexuality that finds its outlet in the only socially accepted channel available to it?--the tender sympathy of a female companion?

When I turned to see if P.'s father had also seen what I saw, I found his eyes piercing me with pitiful supplication. I nodded, understanding that Miss P. would soon be resuming her sessions.

Miss P. arrived at her appointed hour affecting an attitude as if nothing unusual had interrupted our discourse. And yet, as if to announce that she was picking up where her erotic dream had left off, she arrived wearing an extraordinary feathered hat. Its plumage was scarlet and penetrated by a number of alarmingly large pins. Her toilet was telling me that I had been mistaken in my assessment of her hysteria. That rather than imagining multiple relations with a single man, she spent her time imaging every member of an assembly--passengers in an elevator, perhaps, or even members of a church choir--every member naked, and salaciously intertwined. And of course she projected herself among them: psychologically, there is no difference between her desire to display herself naked or in beautiful clothes. Likewise, her earlier report that she would position herself in a favorite window at the library snapped into focus as an unconscious desire to call down to men in the street, as do prostitutes.

She began, in a mocking sort of tone, by telling me that she had not come back for so long because she had been undergoing treatment from another brain mythologist.

--Another? I replied, trying to repress the catch in my throat.

--My mother, she said flatly.

I laughed, partly from relief, and partly because the notion was amusing.

But Miss P. continued sarcastically, --Don't be so quick to congratu-late yourself. As a way to lecture me on how other explanations could be made to fit my "facts," she described how her mother had decided that the best cure would be for her to get out and do some good for others. Accordingly, she had enlisted Miss P. in the Social Service Agency, that amateurish and self-consciously gracious organization intended to be the embodiment of Sweet Lady Bountiful who ranges through the hovels of the underclass.

--Thanks to your visit to Father! she exclaimed.

--Is it working? I asked dryly.

She pouted, her red lips arching into the shape of cupid's bow. Then, as though sharing a confidence, she admitted that given the choice between me and her father, or her mother, the former did not seem so bad. Indeed, in the beginning when her father first proposed a visit, she said, she had been titillated by the idea. She had been awed by the casual, even sophisticated manner in which her lady friend would report discussions with her own analyst: discussions on topics that, until then, she would not have broached with another woman. Miss P. looked down, then that delicate mouth admitted that I had been correct in seeing a sensual nature in her preoccupations--a yearning of such intensity that some days she could think of nothing else. In an imploring voice, she asserted that despite what I or her parents thought, though, she wanted nothing more than to feel the arms of a loving husband encircle her, to enjoy the freedom from stigma that a married woman enjoys while indulging in what most normal women--and men--desire. Married or not!

She paused, as though to collect herself, then continued speaking in what seemed a rehearsed manner. At home, where she was able to reflect, she had seemed to herself as Desdemona beguiled by Othello. The stories of electroshock that I had told her in the course of our knowing each other, in the small times before and after our sessions, the suffering in asylums I had witnessed, the attendants using wet towels as truncheons to choke patients, these and other trials had moved her deeply, she said.... In the library, she had gone through the Medical Journal and read its volumes as an epic of human suffering: a modern-day Odyssey through pain and longing with me as Odysseus.

In a sentimental, womanly way, she then claimed the most extraordinary ground: that seeing the "id," the "ego," the "wish penis," the "clitoral knock," and other theories I had imparted to her for the stories that they were, a great swell of empathy had gone up for me, for the deep desire to help people that she believed I had, and which had made me, according to her, throw my faith into such unbelievable myths as a way to explain the unexplainable rather than admit to helplessness in the face of the unexplainable, if very real, suffering of others. Indeed, so impressed had she been by my unquestioning faith in my view of the world, she claimed, that I even had her believing it all, at least a little, at least for a while.

Poor child. Living a delusion, that is, living an illusion that is invisible to her as opposed to a magician's trick, dream or other illusion that can be seen for what it is. Nevertheless, it was clear to me what was happening: It was her ego, the almighty ego, trying to protect itself by absorbing me as yet another prop in its view of the world.[16] Like ancient, desert chieftains, the ego knows no punishment for assault other than death. And this has a certain logic, for every injury to our autocratic ego is at bottom a crime of regicide. This is why rather than admit to the sexual gratification that would undermine their authority, papists characterize as "saintliness" sexual perversions such as the masochistic practices common among the anchorites, or St. Theresa, burning the word "Jesus" into her breast.

Can P. be blamed, then, when so many Modern women around her take it upon themselves to remake the world to fit their illusions and thus give each other credence, support and even inspiration? Recently we read of society's jailing of Margaret Sanger for disseminating pamphlets about what some call "birth control." Last year, London's National Gallery witnessed the hysterical attack of a suffragette with a small hatchet that she had concealed in her muff and used to hack at Velazquez's Venus at Her Toilet. The attacker had been inspired by the protest of an even madder suffragette who was trampled to death after stepping out of a crowd of Derby Day spectators and into the path of the king's horse to prevent it from winning. At her funeral, 2,000 of her sister suffragettes turned out to parade her mangled corpse as a monument to what they claimed were the King's repressive policies on women.

----

16 The Neuro-Psychoses of Defense, 1894.

When allowed to flower on a mass scale, the summation of these small acts of hysteria manifests itself as a French Revolution or the war we are currently suffering.[17]

Truly, scenes worthy of a French Revolution are being re-enacted daily in the quietude of our own parlors and boudoirs. Why else does an entire culture embrace a Kafka with his pathological guilt and anxiety? Indeed, why honor his neurosis-ridden fantasies with the title once reserved for that which was uplifting and morally instructive: literature? I concluded our session by contrasting this and other evidence for the Ego to her wishful thinking about paintings, her "Santa-Claus-like fictions" and the "altruism" of her mother's self-serving Sweet Lady Bountiful Society, asking her to consider them by the light of the words of John Stuart Mill: "to believe that whatever received a name must be an entity or being, having an independent existence of its own."

--Be honest, I told her, if you do not believe in my cure. Or my diagnosis upon which it is based. At least a little, to use your words. Then why did you return?

----

17 Many wars are in fact a clash of egos: After the American assault on Manila ended the Spanish-American War, it wasn't the loss of life that the Spanish Monarch mourned but the injury to his nation's ego. "This demand strips us of the very last memory of a glorious past," he said, bitterly protesting the concession of the Philippines that his nation was forced to make, "expelling us from the Western hemisphere which became peopled and civilized through the proud deeds of our ancestors."

P. returned today with a story of her own. It was a story by the sapphist American author, Gertrude Stein: a story about a boy who wanted to make a collection of butterflies and beetles:

--It was all exciting to him and it was all arranged then and then the father said to the son you are certain this is not a cruel thing that you are wanting to be doing, killing things to make collections of them, and the son was very disturbed then and they talked about it together the two of them and more and more they talked about it then and then at last the boy was convinced it was a cruel thing and he said he would not do it and his father said the little boy was a noble boy to give up pleasure when it was a cruel one. The boy went to bed then and then the father when he got up in the early morning saw a wonderfully beautiful moth in the room and he caught him and he killed him and he pinned him and he woke up his son then and showed it to him and he said to him "see what a good father I am to have caught and killed this one," the boy was all mixed up inside him and then he said he would go on with his collecting and that was all there was then of discussing....

--That is your answer? I asked.

--That is my answer, she replied.

--Then we have much work to do, I said.

--Yes, she agreed, we have much work to do.

Did Miss P. see the same thing as I, I have since wondered. Is this why she agreed to go forward with her electro treatments? Or was her motive revealed in the way she herself described "being out of health":

--Water, water everywhere, but not a drop of rain. Have you ever read of sailors lost at sea, who are driven so mad by thirst that they scratch out their veins in order to quench it? Or of the caribou on the arctic tundra who in the summer are pestered by flies, and, having no where to hide, run for hundreds of miles trying to escape their tormentors until finally they die of exhaustion?

Clearly, she knew more intimately than any doctor the pain of Womb Fury, though she could, of course, only use the language of poetry, not medicine, to paint a picture of a hysterical urge to bear children so intense that it is able to drive mad the woman who has no means of release.

The men who surrounded P. daily must indeed be the "water, water everywhere." Yet since all of these men were placed outside of her reach by the stricture of civilized morality, not a drop (of their semen) was available to her. Her analogy of dying of thirst in a sea of water was thus an insightful one. As was her example of caribou. Her friend surely described for her the experience of being percussed. Maybe her testimony convinced Miss P. of the treatment's efficacy. Or maybe Miss P.'s torment was such that she was willing to try any cure offered. Even a "quack" suggestion.

Or maybe a life of depravity placed on the scale against a doctor's sober judgment tipped the balance toward the latter just as some regular churchgoers only put up with their dull regime on the off chance that their superstitious preachers might be, after all, right about the eternal fires of hell. Perhaps Miss P. was merely curious to see for herself if such a simple device could truly induce sensations that some patients liken to the terrifying exhilaration of another Modern invention: the roller coaster. Maybe it was all these reasons. Who can say?

In any case, she cautiously agreed to a test treatment of a light electric bath. I, of course, took the utmost precautions to ensure that her modesty would be preserved. Using a less invasive method (P. fully clothed, one electrode placed upon her abdomen, the other free to roam) than the electric massage she would have received in an institution, we began. Slowly. Ever so slowly. During the first session, I only applied a light electric current (.3 amperes) to her neck, then down her shoulder blades, effecting in essence an upper-body massage.

I ventured slowly downward, directing the vibrating massage locally to her thighs, but I quickly shut it down when P. began to perspire.

--Are you quite all right, Miss P.?

--Hmmmm? she answered drowsily. I was astonished to see that contrary to my fears that I was causing her pain, she had begun to fall asleep! (Though I have since come to learn that weakness of the limbs followed by drowsiness are normal side effects of percussing.)

I increasingly grew bolder in both the intensity and duration of the applied current (.5 amperes, 6 minutes). P. began to moan softly, and though I repeatedly asked her if she wanted me to stop, she only shook her head in the negative. I turned up the current even higher (3.5 amperes, or the equivalent of 400 vibrations per minute). We progressed to the base of the spine, then the nexus of hip and pubis.

Suddenly, a neuro-myotic storm broke out over the subject's uterine musculature, causing waves of spasm to roll through her entire body, and an apparent loss of consciousness.

It was the hysterical paroxysm episode itself!

Never had I witnessed such an uproar of nerves in the female anatomy. For a moment I had the irrational fear that my apparatus had killed her! Throwing the equipment to the floor, I quickly propped her up into a sitting position, patting her flushed checks to revive her.

She only seemed confused and astonishingly her first words were to weakly ask, --Why did you stop?

Over the next few weeks we began to establish a clinical pattern. After the electrodes were applied, her pulse rate would increase, and she would begin to perspire lightly. Moans would soon begin to issue from the subject, whereupon she would soon experience a hysterical paroxysm episode and its attendant side effects: an apparent loss of consciousness, or at least inhibition, flushing of the cheeks, voluptuous sensations, a very brief loss of control--usually less than a minute.

As time passed I grew more adept at the placement and use of the electrodes, using less current to produce symptoms of increasing intensity that Miss P. would endure with the resolve of a woman in labor, violently shaking her head 'no' when asked if she wanted to stop even though a moment before she may have been biting her lip, or even crying out, e.g., --Oh! Oh! Oh stop you devil. Stop!

After the spell passed, there always followed a few moments of confusion, as one sometimes has upon waking up in a strange place, and then embarrassment. Thus far, I have not witnessed in P. the vulgar language, or even singing, other doctors report in their patients during the paroxysms they electrically induce.

While we hold no illusions as to these séances being a substitute for the one real cure, it seems impossible to deny that these clinically induced hysterical paroxysms provide a palliative for her female complaints. In short, they make the patient feel better, even if only temporarily, and until the anxiety again builds to the breaking point--which it must, until she enjoys the one true cure--she is free from her anxious attacks. In this interlude of health, the nervous system has a chance to recover from the unrelenting burden it otherwise strains under while she suffers her particular form of hysteric exhaustion.

As a number of writers on this subject predict, P. seems to have overcome whatever reservations she might have once held in regard to her treatments. She even seems to look forward to them. (Some doctors report that their patients, especially nuns and widows, come to crave their séances, as those with the cocaine habit crave their narcotic.) Her reactions are all within the range reported by other physicians (twitching, an expression of simultaneous pleasure and pain, turbid emissions, an exhausted yet exhilarating sensation). It is also important to note that she did not become incontinent during her seizures, as do epileptics. Yet the mild electric current I pass through her pelvis does not seem to have the desired effect on the sexual nature of her dreams. In fact, she reports erotic dreams more than ever, which makes me wonder if a stronger, and more direct course of electro-mechanical vibration might be more effective.

I considered trials of a number of the more promising electro-mechanical percussors and vibrators now commercially available (many of which had been exhibited at the Paris Exhibition of 1900). That my psycho-analytic diagnosis was correct, however, I am more sure than ever.

The Chattanooga Vibrator

The Carpenter Percussor

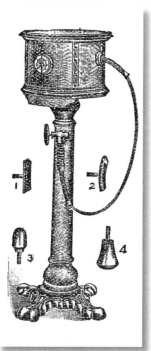

The Percusso Motor

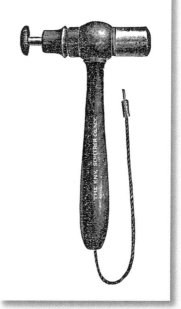

Le vibrotode magic

11 JULY 1918

I suggested to Ms. P. that it may be necessary to remove a few articles of clothing in order to derive the maximum benefit from one of the new devices I had procured. To my surprise, she readily complied. It was only a matter of moments before she stepped out from behind the screen I had placed in my office for this purpose, in only her petticoats, and even more shockingly--completely stockingless.

Given P.'s particular form of mania, I don't believe she is a menace to anyone, save herself. Like Melusina, the traditional figure for nymphomania, she is content to fulfill her social duties by day in such a manner that no one suspects her secret existence as a water nymph by night, the water P. retreats to being the shoreless sea of her own unconscious. And so long as her nymphomania remains latent, her name, and the name of her family, will be safe and no opportunity for marriage and a substantially normal existence will be shut off to her.

This is not to make light of the obstinacy of her condition. In the circus operated by Misters Barnum and Bailey, I once saw Zip the What's-It?, a creature captured by a party of adventurers who were in search of a gorilla when they came upon her, roving about mango trees in a perfectly nude state. Though the carnival barker claimed her to be a freakish ape-man, to the trained eye she was clearly a living primitive like the Hottentot Venus on display at Piccadilly Circus; like that savage, she would sit stoically and completely nude before the laughing stares of her visitors. Indeed, among the pin-heads, Laplanders and elongated giants and human skeletons and skulls of exotic primitives on display at the recent Centennial Exhibition was a live female Botoudo Indian of Brazil, who showed to visitors 104 scars she received as a punishment for 104 adulterous acts--objective evidence of the raging, primitive sexuality simmering just below the surface in civilized men and women: for who can deny that the primitive mind has been bequeathed to us through an unbroken bloodline, and therefore lies within us like a tiger waiting for its cage to be opened?[18]

---

18 Freud himself reports how he once saw a horse shy at the sight of an airplane. This airplane was on a covered lorry which was moving backwards towards the horse, the shape of the plane resembling that of a plesiosaurus or some other prehistoric monster. "The horse had never seen a prehistoric predator before," he writes, "and yet it 'remembered' to be terrified of it."

--Oh! Oh! Ohhhhhh!... (and so on). The ease with which P. underwent what would have been an uncomfortable or even painful experience for most men brought to mind Lombroso's observations on the atavistic tolerance for pain exhibited in criminals and living primitives such as Indians who when punished for straying off their reservations, "sing the praises of their tribe while they are whipped."[19]

----

19 Lombroso, Cesare and Guglielmo Ferro. La femme criminelle et la prostitua. Trans. Louise Meille. Paris: Alcon, 1896. Another useful book when comparing morally depraved females to normal women is: La donna delinquente, la prostituta e la donna normale. 3rd ed. Turen, Fraelli, Bocca, 1915. See also: The Female Offender. Ed. W. Douglas Morrison, London: T. Fisher Urwin, 1895.

24 AUGUST 1918

--Oh God! Oh God you Devil! Oh my God!...

Despite the religious nature of her outcries, P. no longer seemed discouraged by her lack of progress.

Indeed, she rarely misses a séance. That is, does there exist a "rush to health" that is contained within the "instinct for death?" Could they be, in some cases, one and the same? Or does her ambivalence merely reflect the psychological make-up of the weaker sex: a timidity and irregular action in the outer world, submission to the influence of others and an inclination to surrender to elemental forces, such as gravity, as when women throw themselves from heights? Havelock Ellis thinks drowning is becoming an especially popular method of suicide among women and that therein women are becoming more womanly.[20] Perhaps P. sees her sessions with me as a wading deeper and deeper into the waters of the mind. An Oedipal identification with the elemental force of sexual instinct. A modern courtship, per se.[21]

Perhaps P.'s cure would proceed more rapidly if I increase the amperage?.... The length of our séances, the frequency of the applications, the time of the treatment, the placement of the vibratodes. Some patients are better conductors, others less sensitive.... There are so many variables.

---

[20] See also, E.H. Smith "Signs of Masturbation in the Female," Pacific Medical Journal, Feb. 1903, 78-83.

[21] Wilhelm Stekel, "Disguised Onanism (Masked Masturbation)" in American Journal of Urology and Sexology 1 no. 7 (1918): 289-307.

--Yes! Yes! Oh doctor Yesssssss! (And etceteras. Monotonously so, etceteras.)

The hysterical convulsions that the treatment induces in P. seem to grow even more pronounced as she increasingly allows herself to give in to them: rapid breathing, profuse perspiration, hyperkinetic spasm & etc. During her most violent hysterical paroxysms, she clutches the couch she lies upon as if she were clinging to it for dear life. After the paroxysm has spent itself, she falls into the deep sleep of the innocent, and I retreat to my outer rooms to wonder. The desired physical reactions coupled with her lack of psychological improvement is indeed baffling.

In men, the external nature of their sexual apparatus makes the treatment of abnormal desire relatively straightforward. By placing the testicles between the poles of the electrical apparatus, the male who is too easily excited to erection by the sight of a woman (or another man) or mechanical friction, as can happen when wool pants rub the parts, can be made to associate the electric current with morbid desire and be trained to erect no more.[22]

---

22 A Practical Treatise on the Medical and Surgical Uses of Electricity Including Localized and General Electrization, 1913.

The literature on the faridization of woman, however, repeatedly points out the relative difficulty of assaying the effects of treatment, or even of judging whether or not the vibrations have been directed to the necessary spot.[23]

That is, certain hidden and deep-lying muscles peculiar to the internal arrangement of the female organs of generation can only be reached through other muscles and in order to affect any of these internal organs it is necessary that the current should also traverse intervening and surrounding tissues. Luckily, these deeper muscles can sometimes be stimulated by vibrating the more surface tissue, such as the clitoral region, that lies directly above them. By applying direct vibration to clitoral tissue the doctor can induce contractions not only of the muscles but also of the contractile fiber cells, thus stimulating circulation. By virtue of the frequent interruptions of the current as its polarity switches, the action is similar to that of rubbing or massaging movement, and the doctor who cannot tell if his treatment is reaching the necessary spot is encouraged to stimulate the entire region in this manner.

----

23 See:

M.L.H. Snow. Mechanical Vibration and Its Therapeutic Application. New York, 1904.

Abraham Myerson. The Nervous Housewife. Boston: Little Brown & Company, 1908.

John Pechey, A General Treatise on the Treatment of Maids and Widows. London: Henry Bonwick, 1896.

Franklin Benjamin Gottschalk, Practical Electrotherapeutics. Hammond, Ind.: F.S. Betz, 1908.

Joseph Mortimer Granville, Nerve Vibration and Excitation as Agents in the Treatment of Functional Disorders and Organic Disease. London, 1883.

John Taylor. Women's Complaints and Their Treatments by Transmitted Energy and Special Movements. New York: American Book Exchange, 1880.

W.E. Fitch. Bicycle Riding for Women from the Standpoint of a Gynecologist. Hard Books, 1903.

Charles William Malchow. A Scientific Treatise Embracing Normal Sexual Impulse, Sexual Habits, Hysteria and Hygiene. St. Louis: C.V. Mosby, 1923.

W.E. Fitch. "Bicycle Riding: Its Moral Effect upon Young Girls and Its Relation to Diseases of Women" in Georgia Journal of Medicine and Surgery 4 (1899): 156.

I can't put completely out of my mind those first lies Miss P. told me, nor the phenomenon of malingerers: that clan of women known to every doctor with a large practice. Women who, like those soldiers that slip into a debilitating nostalgia or homesickness and thereby prolong their stay in hospital, stave off good health in order to bring to themselves sympathy and attention. These women can become veritable actresses, complete with props. It is not unknown within gynecological circles for some to carry leeches in the mouth to induce the hemorrhaging that would convincingly resemble hemoptysis; deliberate delaying of the act of micturition artificially creates symptoms of urinary suppression. Unmarried women addicted to the speculum make the rounds of gynecologists, seeking relief by feigning a malady which will attract a doctor's attention downward.[24]

Even more disturbing was the change in P.'s disposition. She always approached her treatments in an open, sometimes lighthearted manner. But now, despite the gravity of her situation, it sometimes seems as though it has all become a joke to her. Before our sessions, she sometimes breaks into giggles. Afterwards, after she has awoken and dressed and the inner door clicks open and she shyly emerges to join me in the outer office where I await, she pays me--always with a silver dollar-- saying little other than to confirm the time of our next appointment.

---

24 S.W. Mitchell. "On Malingering, Especially in Regard to Simulation of Diseases of the Nervous System" prepared for The Medical Department of the War and delivered before the Physicians Club of Chicago in February, 1913.

It occurred to me today that P. might never marry. The analyst's task in this eventuality would become one of perpetual maintenance, much like bailing a boat whose hole cannot be stanched. Maybe--as we witness The War to End All War come to a close--all we can console ourselves with is the knowledge that some things will never change. The armistice was signed at 5 a.m. in a boxcar in a wood in France. Yet between that moment and 11 a.m. when it went into effect, the armies of both sides poured death onto one another in a mad rush to expend the last of their ammunition.

Perhaps something similar occurred to Miss P. and this is why she suddenly gave up her treatments. Or maybe she gave them up because secretly she had taken a lover. In lieu of an explanation, or even a notice, I received in the mail an ad torn from the pages of Modern Priscilla, one of those ladies' magazines that are becoming increasingly popular among the young. (Though the envelope contained no letter, nor even a return address, the picture of a nymph running off to life with her seducer spoke volumes.)

From a scientific point of view, of course, the case of Miss P. was not a failure. My record of her affliction is a portrait that contains no brushstrokes, the hand of a portraitist as invisible as the photography that has made the painter irrelevant. The discovery and cataloguing of a new psychosis, erotomania obscura, was in itself justification for the months spent on her case. Those who follow in my footsteps may penetrate deeper than I, the pioneer.

Indeed, I recall that first time I moved her garments to attach the electrodes and her bare thighs lay white and innocent before me; I recalled thinking that the awe I was experiencing must be akin to that of Columbus when he first laid eyes upon his virgin world. The world of the female mind too is a new world upon whose shores we have only just now touched down. Who can say how vast and dark the inner continent may be? This world is so new that even lay observers, no less than trained naturalists, may discover psychic phenomena simply by opening their eyes and cataloging the phobias, predilections, fetishes and other aberrations that surround them. Surely, in the infancy of our explorations, only the most obvious ones, those closest to the shore, are discovered first. Who knows what is to be found at the source of their tributaries? The day may well come when we feel the need for universal psycho-analysis, just as the psychological testing of immigrants and soldiers has led us to recognize the necessity of universal I.Q. testing of children. For truly, as Hamlet told Horatio, "There are more things in heaven and earth, than are dreamt of in your philosophy."

Chapter 4

P__ (a Programmer/Hacker)

I __ (an Investigator for Family Pharmacy)

X__ (a Family Pharmacy Manager)

E

L

S

A _ C D _ F G H _ J K _ M _ O _ _ R _ _ _ _ W _ Y Z

Q__ (an Army Vet/Employee Profiler)

U__ (a Model)

V__ (a Video-graphic Designer)

B__ (a Photo/Digital Retoucher)

T__ (a Pharmacy Technician)

N__ (a Pharmacy Cashier)

08:12:02:18:59

Pecker hopping. Bare chest and thighs shiny with sweat. Nothing they hadn't seen before, thought I__, an Investigator for Family Pharmacy & Foods Inc., trying to make out the face looking at him through the glare of an apartment window across the courtyard, the someone watching him as he jumped rope naked.

He kept up the rhythm while the someone—a woman?—a man with hippie hair?—settled in, watching. As steadily as a camera.

1011 1101 0110 1111 1100 1101 0101 1101 1....—a choreography of bytes....

It was like being in a movie....

Family Pharmacy. Standing before glossy models on the covers of magazines, Q__ felt eyes on her. Instinctively she stashed her meds in her army jacket and looked up—a bowled security mirror collaged her own bowed face with the reflections of a store manager, standing behind the cash register, pretending to work though she could tell he was actually scoping her out; he began diddling with his bow tie—the polka-dot bow tie all Family Pharmacy managers wore—companies as bad as the army about making everyone dress alike so they'd think alike—this stooge looking away as quickly as people always did when she caught them watching her. The Creep.

What kind of movie?

Odd, thought I__, skipping rope in his living room, that he, an Investigator for Family Pharmacy & Foods Inc., a person who knew how surveillance could turn anyone to glass, could be so untroubled....

My Neighbor's Affair?

Name

The View Into Apartment 3-G?

It was like being visited by a shade, U__ thought, naked except for matched black panties and bra (Without-a-Trace™). Ghostly shades, she considered, that were everywhere and therefore nowhere even if night by night they made her a little more like them. She shifted her weight from one spiked heel (Armani) to the other, waiting for the photographer to finish adjusting the flood lights shining into her eyes. They would take her picture—she was sure it was her that they were photographing because her body was there—then one of them would come, make her a little more—a little more obscure—and by the time she saw her other self, the self that appeared in catalogs, on packaging, in brochures and the ads she modeled for, she was different: duskier skin, softer silhouette, *anime* eyes. Different her, yet her.

"Raise the key beam," Photographer told his Assistant. Or at least she assumed it was Photographer. With the lights glaring in her eyes, the people beyond came to her as disembodied voices, fussing about whatever it was that they worried before they took her picture.

She shifted to the other foot. Odd, how something as tiny as a tired muscle or a paper cut could remind a person that the world was solid and too real all around though you yourself could seem so— What?— Not there? And this is how U__'s story began: wondering how the stone walls of the wine cellar she posed in could have such gravity while most of what made up who she was was lighter than the web of stories and negatives and pixels that modeled her career out of thin air. As Stylist put a wrap around U__'s shoulders to keep the cool, wine-cellar air from goose-pimpling her flesh, U__ took inventory: This morning, her bathroom scale said she weighed one hundred and seven pounds; mail addressed to her was delivered to the apartment she inhabited. And of course her driver's license listed a name (Organ Donor?—NO!).

But in an age of interlocking subdivisions and identical restaurants, in a world that each year generated 100,000,000 Miracle Slacks™, each of which had to be filled—HELLO! MY NAME IS:_____—in a country of actuary tables, of ZIP codes, of an endless supply of service manager uniforms (filled out by Service Managers), census forms (filled in by Citizens), personalized mail-order catalogs, identical parking garages and their tiers of look-alike vans (Forest Green or Goldenrod) bearing vanity plates (2HOT4U) stamped out by some 51 prisons (a form of living to be sure), of Neilson ratings, and Frequent Flier Memberships—an age when the Japanese went through thirteen Prime Ministers in nine years without blinking, when every American City greeted tourists with local versions of the same Sports Heroes, News Teams and other types—Bag-lady, Alderman, Shopper, Cop—that is, for the purposes of a story of her time, did the particulars of name matter?

What was important was that the world at this time required Models, just as five hundred Fortune 500 companies required five hundred CEOs, just as airports required Airplanes, just as Hollywood always required about six Action Heroes, four Teenage Heart Throbs, and one, but no more than one, overweight Funny Guy. Just as most divorces still required at least one Jerk, Top 40 lists required forty Top Songs, best-seller lists required Best Sellers to be best sold and talk shows required Hosts to talk, Guests to talk to, and Viewers to call in; Teachers required Students, History required Revolutions, Economies, Wars and Peace to fill it—and Historians to make it mean. If you lit up fluorescent lighting over an expanse of office cubicles, everyone knew, Accountants and Phone Solicitors, Web Designers and Xs and Ys and Zs would soon fill those cubicles, as surely as a crossword puzzle invited Letters or vending machines promised to dispense Product. Thus, if some Photographer set up floodlights, sooner rather than later, a Model would appear to stand in their glare as was U__, dressed in black Lycra, Without-a-Trace™ Panties and Bra (seamless shaping!), shifting limbs heavy with boredom while she waited for him to take his meter readings, adjust his light umbrellas and do whatever it was that photographic apparatus required a Photographer to do.

A movie others were watching

This is stupid, Q__ thought, the store's Manager's eyes weighing on her in that old exhausting way as she brought a magazine up to his register. Even though he probably thought she was shoplifting, she kept the meds she'd

Q ∣∣

X ∣∣

paid for back in pharmacy hidden in her army jacket because— Because she didn't want every Tom, Dick & Harry knowing about her meds. Because she didn't want him to think she was only buying a magazine because—

Because she hated having to ask.

X__ said his Family Pharmacy name tag, the rest of his name hidden by the lapel of his blazer. She placed the magazine—*Look*—on the counter, fished around in her purse—the Manager's ratty, piss-holes-in-the-snow eyes unbuttoning her blouse?—

1011 1101 0110 1111 1100 1101 0101 1100 1101 1....

—to and fro and up into the card reader of the cash register.

On the monitor below the counter, Queenie Qunt, and other info linked to the credit card X__ had just swiped appeared across a live video of her face. Most customers didn't notice the decal on the door giving Family Pharmacy permission to videotape them, he knew, but so what? If they weren't doing anything wrong they had nothing to hide.

APPROVED.

After paying, Q__ stared straight ahead as she asked, "Do you have a public restroom here?"

Store 046616

"**Y**es."

...firm melons....

As Q__ walked to the rear of the store she heard "Nina to register two," come over the store's intercom: the voice of the Manager who'd just told her where to find the head. "Nina to register two, please."

Back in pharmacy, N__ pushed her boyfriend off of her. "Come on, Timo, he's calling me; I got to get back to my register."

Timo Garcia, Apprentice Pharmacy Technician. As T__ adjusted the name tag on his pharmacy smock, he watched his girlfriend's rumba-dancer's ass, even more convex in one of the security mirrors, moving quickly up the Personal Hygiene aisle. Right past the store's rack of condoms, he noted.

$13.13

"**T**hirteen thirteen...." said the electronic voice of the cash register, not the cashier: Nina—according to her name tag, though P__ knew that lots of employees used fictitious names on their name tags.

Webs of laser light continued to parse melons, cough medicine, cupcakes and other merch.

P

Q

X

N

Then she swiped his card.

1011 1101 0110 1111 1100 1101 0101 1100 1101 1....

—a choreography of bytes to and from massive data banks....

Come on, come on, thought P__, the card taking far too long to be approved.

The cashier yawned. "I'll have to key it by hand," she said, and the words made him go clammy.

In the privacy of the Family Pharmacy washroom, Q__ stuck her magazine into her army jacket, raised her skirt, and squatted.

In the janitor's closet adjoining the women's washroom, X__ quietly laid down the ring of keys issued to all Family Pharmacy managers, then stepped up on a chair to reach the rolls of toilet paper on the top shelf. Yeah, baby, if you're a good girl, you've got nothing to hide. Noiselessly, he moved the rolls aside, one by one, until a pinpoint of light shined out from the peep-hole he had drilled through the wall. He pressed his eye to it.

Other data:...   **0110 1111 1100 1101 0101....**

P__ really began to sweat now. Like a lot of the identities he'd borrowed, he'd gotten this one off the fake porn site he'd set up. But this one was tied to local bricks-and-mortar—a vacant house that had been on the market for months and that he had had the charge card mailed to.

He kicked himself for breaking his own rule—to never actually use the identities he borrowed. The TV station where he worked as a programmer would go ballistic if he was caught, he knew, what with their public image and all. They'd never believe that he only used the charge-card and social-security numbers, the mother's maiden names, health care, driver's license, and other info he harvested for a game—a game he and other hackers played to stick it to The Man. Not the Good Man—the good companies that had nothing to hide. Just the evil ones, the ones who did: manufacturers of error-ridden voting machines, or exploding school-bus tires; chain stores that sold designer shoes made by third-world slaves, & etc. But the rightness of bringing dirty corporate secrets into the light would be completely lost on his big-haired Station Manager—a corporate stooge herself. And then, if she began to look into his own records, his letters of recommendation, the grades he corrected—not changed.... Unlike most of the hackers he hung with on-line, he never changed his college transcripts. He only corrected them to reflect the education he actually received, the grades he deserved....

The cashier, *Nina*, a Mexican chick in too much employee-discount makeup, squinted at the name on the card: *Xavier Peterman*. "Huh, what a coincidence," she said, "that's my manager's name too." Her dark eyes were accusing.

"No way!" P__ said, stunned—

"Yeah, he's trying to buy a house but there's some snag with his credit check."

Shit! What he heard was too bizarre to be what she said but P__ wondered if he should beat it anyway. He'd look suspicious. But looking suspicious would be a lot better than having the cashier call in a 44—the Family Pharmacy code for fraud—to a manager whose name he was using....

To distract her, he said, "Nice day today, huh—uh?..." He checked her name tag. "Nina?"

APPROVED.

"Lot'a good it does me," she said, handing him the register's stylus—and mercifully—the card too. "I gotta be here till five."

Limp with relief, he scrawled an illegible **X** on the electronic signature pad, returned the card to the wallet chained to his jeans, then quickly hoisted his bags to leave.

"Psssst!" she hissed sharply. "Aren't these yours?" She nodded toward a small white bag on the counter. A white pharmacy bag, prescription stapled to it, nestled among the candy.

When he looked up to tell her "no", though, he caught the alarm in her eyes: that look the guilty got when they realized they'd been seen. By who? Instinctively, he began to turn—Cameras. She swept the pharmacy bag under the counter with the speed of a pusher seeing cops round into view. Though he didn't know what the scam was, he could smell danger and wanted out.

"Yeah, the Man always gets you in the end," he joked, trying to keep it light, keep it cool, kicking himself because that was the joke that sprung to his lips.

"Let me see your card again," she whispered.

"Huh?" Keep it cool. But keep it moving.

"I overcharged you."

"That's okay," P__ said, heading for the exit.

"Hey, Mister!" she hissed, urgent but keeping her voice low.

An electronic eye opened the door and he rushed out into the light.

Find out the names of everyone on your block: **www.anywho.com**

The realization that he must have left the bag back in the pharmacy hit B__ so hard that he had to sit down. But one of those crazies every public park, library, and museum always seemed to have already occupied the one bench in this museum's Photography Gallery: a woman in an army jacket, jarhead haircut, holding up a copy of *Look Magazine*—as though she was showing one of its glossy ads to the huge, back-lit photo on display. Nuts like her could stay put for days, he knew, so he stepped out of the stream of tourists and art students and gawkers crowding by to see the famous photo: *Las Meninas*—a digital forgery of the painting it was named after; in this version the photographer himself was dressed up as the child princess in the original painting, posed in the photo exactly as the princess had posed for the painter. B__ pushed back his DigiDreams baseball cap, and mentally retraced his steps.

He definitely had the bag when he left the pharmacy counter: he could see it in his mind, a white bag, fake prescription stapled to it. T__, that

Pharmacy Technician, had fixed up ten tabs of Vicodin for him, like always. And like always, N__ had wrung him up at Register Two: $13.13.

It hit him!—to not look suspicious, he'd put down the bag in order to buy a Moonpie and some of the other crap sold at the register, then after he'd gotten out his wallet, and paid, he'd been so focused on getting his card back that he'd forgotten the pharmacy bag on the counter.

How could he have been so stupid!

He dug the receipt out of his pockets: $13.13. Like always, she'd rung up $13.13; then, pretending like his card wouldn't swipe, she'd keyed in by hand $131.13 for the ten pills. Even now he had to admire the beauty of their system: she'd put $13.13 of her own cash in the drawer and at the end of the day the register would come out straight. Perfect. Except for him.

He looked at his watch. **5:10**. N__ got off at five.

Shit. Now he'd have to blow off V__, the woman he'd been dating. Unless he wanted to spend a weekend without his fix, he'd have to blow off V__, go across town and score from his other connection and in the same instant he had his cell phone flipped open. Wait a minute.... As soon as he saw her entry in it—V__—he knew this was a conversation he couldn't win: Ever since she found out his photo was still up at MatchMaker.com, where they'd met, she'd been harder and harder to convince of anything....

He dialed up the number of Alibi.Net, that network of people who would use their own cells to call in sick for you: anonymous people who would lie to your girlfriend, or boss, or wife, or husband, or anyone in exchange for someone else in the network doing the same for them when they needed help. He'd give whatever alibier he got V__'s studio number, he thought. She would have left the station by now, but that way his alibier could leave a message about him being tied up or something, and then he could pretend it was her fault for not getting the message. Yeah, that would work. It did before, but he'd have to make up something good this time. No, he thought, the Alibi.Net switchboard forwarding his call to someone, something bad would be better—something so outlandish that she'd have to believe it. She was going to be pissed. Especially after the last time. But what else could he do?....

As he stood there trying to remember which excuses an Alibi.Net buddy had already used on V__, a tour group glided by. In a loud, projecting voice, the Guide explained how the *Infanta* in the actual, original painting looks out through 400 years of yellowing varnish at viewers looking back at her being looked at by the *Menina* who is seen by viewers, like the Group, looking at the dim mirror in the background of the photo which darkly reflects the King and Queen looking back at viewers standing where they should be, gazed at by Famous Spanish Painter standing before an easel in the painting, looking out at the viewers looking in at him in the act of painting the Menina who in this photo is actually the gay, Japanese Photographer who made this life-sized, digitally remastered duplicate....

"The only one who isn't giving their eyes a workout is the dog," Guide said, "a symbol of loyalty...."

The Next Day....

Today, like every day, V__, a Video-graphic Designer, arrived at the TV Studio to find the work she was to do already scheduled. Taped to the banks of TV monitors and video equipment of her computer workstation was a list of all the graphics she was to create during her shift, the period between the end of the last afternoon soap opera and the beginning of the ten o'clock news. Let's say today's list looked like this:

Mental Health Watch

Storm Tracker

School Yard Shooting

Miracle Diet

Fur Sale

World's Largest Donut

New Computer Virus

Hispanic Population Increase

$hop $ave More $

Diagram of Deadly Flight Path

Our Team Wins!

Peeping Tom Captured

Forged Museum Painting, & Etc....

Her Supervisor would compile the list of late-breaking stories and last-minute ads and the other blurbs and graphics that were to appear over the shoulders of the Anchor Models who worked the news desk, or would be inserted into the edited versions of the satellite feeds that her affiliate downloaded from the parent company, edited, then put on the air for local consumption. Other rooms were blue with the glow of other video monitors and editing equipment, other designers and editors spinning in locally-shot footage and doing the sound mixes, and after creating her images, and clicking on a little mailman that meant **SEND**, the images she made would be fed into the digital stream that fed this flux.

She had to be good because given the pace there was often no time for drafts. Which is to say good meant fast. The moment she sat down at her keyboard and mouse and monitor, she would dive into her list—a list that Supervisor was constantly rushing in to add to or delete from—and let her mind slew into an unspeaking, unthinking dream state where time stopped, or to put it another way, time accelerated so much that the images for heart attacks, and snow storms—**MORE AT TEN!**—flowed like ghosts through her head, through her hand and mouse (for during these times they seemed as one), onto her screen, then out over the airways, through satellites and other nodes and systems and onto everyone's screen as if there were no boundary between the images in her head and the images in their heads, which is probably where the images in her head came from to begin with. It was as if she were a medium, a river running through her, but a river she also swam to keep up with: a bit stream of cartoon hearts and topographical maps and lightening bolts and other graphics she created to communicate corporate desires instantly—or at least in the 2.5 seconds most of her images were on screen.

And she was good. The teasers she had created for news reports on the latest **Global Hot Spot**—silhouettes of foot soldiers with red hearts seen through crosshairs—had even won the Big Award for TV Design and Graphics.

Even so, it was often unreal to her. When she arrived at work the day she found out about the Big Award and the Bean Counters and the big-haired Station Manager and her Supervisor and Co-Workers yelled "Surprise!" and popped open champagne (a form adopted from another kind of celebration), it had seemed like they were toasting someone else. You see, to get through the long, mutable list on time, she had to stay so focused and work so fast, beginning the next image the instant she finished the last, that sometimes she didn't even recognize some of them when they were later shown to her. The time an engineer screwed up and erased an archive of what she'd made, it was like her images, her day, her self, had vanished into the ether. Like she and her images had become ghosts that only existed in the millions of memories of people who had seen them at home. Which is to say they existed no where. And everywhere.

Sometimes, when the whole studio was running late and the TIME-TO-AIR clock was racing toward **00:00** and the Editors and big-haired Manager were shouting so loudly that she could hear them through the sound-proof walls, her images would go out directly into the bit stream. She'd race from one image to the next barely even seeing what she made, just making, and making, and making, and making, and making, and making, and making, and making, a frantic if controlled flow of mouse clicks, and image banks, and **SAVE AS**, and **PAINT**, and **FILLS**, and **CUT** and **PASTE**, and **DRAW**, and **CLIP**, and **PAINT**, until the end of the list hit her with a shock: as if she'd been falling in a dream—Alice down the rabbit's hole—that went on and on with Kings and Queens of Hearts swirling around the Wicked Witch of the West and all of art history—Dali's melting clocks, the raves and dance clubs she went to after her shift, Venus on the half shell—and the earth below so distant that it was just a speck until it suddenly rushed up into her face and she bolted upright in bed, perspiring and out of breath, only to realize it wasn't real.

Still, in a way it was. For even after her shift ended, and the clubs closed, and she was in a cab going home, the images and icons and other cartoons continued to occupy her thoughts. Streaks of rain on the cab window might make her think of the dot screen in video wallpaper. Likewise, the pattern of stage lighting cast in one of the trendy bars she liked, or the tear in the upholstery of a Nautilus machine at her health club. The particular Kelly green that a traffic light takes on when it lights up would remind her of a promo for grass fertilizer she designed months ago, as might the gray-green of a traffic light that was off.

Crosshatching and vinyl, the silhouette of a jet, the glint of chrome.... At night in bed, she'd stare at the shadows on the ceiling, so many images crowding in that it was like having her head full of an upstairs party that wouldn't let her sleep and couldn't be quieted no matter how hard she banged on the ceiling with a broom.

Except today. Today, the world was so much with her that she couldn't shed it the way she had to in order to enter that dream space she needed to do her work. The list was far ahead and gaining so much ground that soon it would be beyond catching. There would be no Awards for the work she did manage to complete. The big-haired Station Manager would soon begin to howl under the crush of her own lists but still V__ couldn't clear her head of the knowledge that B__, her boyfriend, was dead.

Not technically dead.

It was just that as a boyfriend, B__ had ceased to function. With her, that is. For indeed, what made her want to scream was that B__ could be functioning very well as the Boyfriend of **Looking for Love Mailbox 4474**. Or **Come Out And Play Mailbox 0032**. Or any of the hundreds, maybe thousands of women trolling MatchMaker.com, the on-line dating service they'd met on, the digital portraits and bios and come-ons of other women out there 24-7, a horny singles scene that never sleeps: a collage of available bods that was always everywhere even if the real live men and women, unlike their digital doubles, couldn't be in more than one place at a time.

"So like why didn't you call me yourself?" she'd asked, when she got ahold of him the next day. While she'd been waiting to go out with B__, some woman had left a message on her studio voice mail, calling from a phone her caller I.D. didn't recognize to say he was tied up with a client at the Art Museum—an excuse so lame that she wanted to believe it.

"Like my client's secretary told you, I was tied up. I couldn't just walk out on a client that important."

Tied up. She wasn't stupid. The woman who left the message sounded like she was calling from bed, not an office, and anyway, the Art Museum was the classic place for MatchMaker subscribers to meet for their first face-to-face. If the chemistry wasn't there, the museum's crowds provided the perfect cover for escape. If it was, the museum with its galleries and paintings of nudes was handy, an easy conversation starter, excuse to continue the day, a bridge to evening. Or at least it had been for them. And after they'd fallen into serial hookups, she'd thought they'd had an understanding and took her ad off-line—and thought he had too.... "So I forgot!" he'd pleaded when she found out it was still up. "Geeze, it's not like I've been checking my mailbox...."

But what really worried her was his job. Unlike the variety of images she manipulated, the images he manipulated all day were all of a single subject: surreally beautiful women. Models with perfect bodies and skin—or at least as perfect as nature could make them—women who posed for the ads that agencies rushed to him so he could play digital plastic-surgeon. He'd receive the pictures that photographers took of these perfect bodies, then digitally sculpt their waists, or remove their veins and pores to give them a claymation smoothness, or a flatness that no amount of dieting or even real surgery could achieve. He'd add weight here and there to downplay the freak factor of models with lollipop builds, i.e., models so coat-rack thin that their heads appeared space-alien large. He gave women in bikinis tans, made red-heads of blondes or turned brown eyes purple to match the bottle of perfume being hawked by the beauty of the face & etc. Pure fantasy, he'd say, meaning, "Lighten, up, geez!—I never even meet the actual women!"

With so many women passing under the caress of his cursor, though, how could he not begin to think of women the way she thought of the images she created?—infinitely re-arrangeable, highly—as he and the other guys in his biz called models whose bodies lent themselves to digital improvement—"tweakable."

Tweakable. Like the gangstas she once heard on the subway discussing girls as "fuckable."

She liked to think that he was into her because she was special. Not special in that she was better than any of the zillions of women whose thumbnail portraits wallpapered MatchMaker's website. Just special in the way that each person's fingerprints were special. Special in the way someone's yin was special to another's yang. Or at least special enough to not be condemned to a life with her cats and Professional Awards and Coffee-table Art Books. Was that too much to ask of the universe?

Microwavable Soup-for-One. Valentine hearts cracked in half.... She couldn't stand the solo imagery: Cupid's bow unstrung, its string mondo limp, its arrow also limp, the normally lip-lined silhouette of the bow itself not limp but flat—flat as the line of a heart monitor after life has left. To find her head filled with such lame-o clichés was too much. To be one was even worse....

He always was such a sap for glossy.

And if he'd started going parallel again, the least he could do was tell her so she could also re-post her MatchMaker ad instead of just standing around like a dork waiting for him to show. Or worse: enduring his silent lapses like the other night at Club Sade, lights flashing, him acting like he was so engrossed with the video loops of *Metropolis* and *Bride of Frankenstein*, the place crawling with "tweakable" girls, parading their torpedo titties and vinyl minis, his mind obviously on someone not her....

I__ pressed up on a ceiling panel to expose the grid of video cabling suspended above the aisles of Family Pharmacy 028834. Was it the casual way his Neighbor spied on him? Was that why he was so casual about being spied on? Or maybe because of what he always told others?—"If you're not doing anything wrong you've got nothing to hide." He plugged a palm-sized camera into one of the jacks that fed a VCR housed deep in a locker, deep, deep in the manager's office.

Then his company cell phone vibrated—but he could ignore it—it was only someone in the central office activating the phone's global positioning device to check which store he was in....

Name

Sitting on a bench with a view of the park's playground, Q__ tried to ignore the dirty looks she got from the mothers sitting on other benches: dirty suspicious looks shifting from the dog tags tied up in the laces of her boot to the sign on the gate of the playground: WARNING: ADULTS UNACCOMPANIED BY A CHILD NOT ALLOWED. You forget, she wanted to inform them, that everyone is somebody's child. She opened her *Look Magazine* and folded it back so its picture of Mother faced the kids on the swings, imagining what her Shrink would say: that it wasn't really her Mother. And of course he was right. The picture wasn't Mother in the way that other messages meant for Q__ didn't come just to her: Vanity plates—2HOT4U—or the spam that came to her in e-mail at work—**You Like Chinese Food!** in the subject line—at the very moment she was thinking about picking some up on the way home....

Still, sitting on the bench, looking at the picture of Mother looking at the playground, the anxiety that the picture caused Q__ couldn't be explained away. She watched the kids, a redheaded boy with freckles, a girl with a Band-Aid on her knee, and others, wondering which of them would grow up to be the next generation's killers? Every generation made some. Nor could Shrink deny that the picture showed Mother wearing a fur before the very mountains that surrounded the base that Q__ had been airlifted to in Germany, the very snow-capped peaks she had looked onto through the window of her hospital room when she'd had all that time to think and Mother's memory began to fill her to the point of bursting.

No, this was no simple coincidence. For that picture to appear in her hands, trees had been clear-cut in Guatemala, ground into pulp in a Japanese mill while a photographer snapped the picture of Mother in the mountains. Back home, chemical factories created the developing solutions, photo-lab technicians swung into action, layout people, a Big City ad agency, workers in Alabama adjusting a 40-ton printing press, the photo converted to a digital image, turned into dots on printing plates, millions of dots of ink pressed onto countless sheets of paper in an exact pattern over and over and over—thousands of times exactly the same—a river of paper running through the press before being cut up, folded in correct order, bundled into trucks, one of the bundles delivered to the rack of Family Pharmacy where, like a land mine, the magazine lay in wait till her bladder conspired to make her need to use the head, pick up the magazine, and open it to that very page—where Mother posed before the very mountains Q__ used to look out onto while bivouacked so far away, recovering from her wounds, feeling like shit for leaving her.

Q__ believed in meaningful details.

From the map pocket of her army jacket she brought out the only other photo of Mother that she owned: a box-camera black-and-white that someone had taken of her and the Bad Man she lived with before Q__ had been born. They'd been on a picnic, apparently: The Awful Man had his shirt off and was flexing skinny biceps for the camera while Mother sat on a picnic blanket, her long legs stretched out as if, as if—as if she were modeling, Q__ now saw.

As she studied the photo, wondering who had taken it, Q__ absentmindedly stroked the hand grenade sleeping in her jacket's cargo pocket, the grenade's smooth ridges and turtle-like shell, its heft as comfortable as a river rock in her hand. Or a charm. Yeah, a lucky charm proving that not everything could be explained.

Hardly anyone noticed, X__ knew, but a decal on Family Pharmacy's glass front door clearly stated that by entering the store, customers gave their consent to be videotaped. He took a deep breath. Just the thought of the Model passing through those doors, giving her consent while his video camera captured her red apple of an ass from behind one of the store's many one-way mirrors made X__ stiffen as if she were already there. Him and Her: Partners. The two of them: Colleagues. Director and Actress....

Scattered on his desk were the paper collages he'd already made of her: nude bodies he'd scanned from porn mags and then used his digital camera to combine with her head, copying her china-doll face with its large, anime eyes from the boxes of hair dye, condoms and other Family Pharmacy packaging that she appeared on. He'd had them printed out in the Pharmacy's high-res lab, so the skin was smooth, but the angles were off in all of them: Paper Frankensteins. With the software he'd ordered from that porn site, though, he'd be able to take his video of her and seamlessly add her face to the nude body of any one of the women included in the library of women having HOT! HOT! HOT! ASIAN SEX! that came with the software—BE THE DIRECTOR OF YOUR OWN *INTERACTIVE* PORN MOVIE!—and he began to massage himself imagining her coming in the store, posing beside the rack of condoms, his camera set up right where he now stood behind the one-way mirror of his office, zooming in from this bird's-eye-view of the store's aisles to her golden-delicious ass, her pear-shaped tits—jump-cut to her jet-black hair, bobbing away below his belt line, her anime eyes looking up to him, begging for his load, her head—or her ass—a yo-yo he could bobble whenever he liked, once he got the software, just by clicking his mouse....

This was the third dilapidated factory U__ had posed in that week (Full-Length Mink, Red Satin Lining). Before hitting on factories, they had tried to shoot at housing projects and other ghetto scenes. But the locals, mostly Unemployed Young Men, wouldn't let them do their jobs, gathering around to hoot obscene suggestions to her and the other Models. One especially loud man kept repeating, "Boy, I'd like to fuck that Chink," and "Slanty eyes, slanty pussy," and "Spicy Chink chicken!" and so on, referring to the model who was Vietnamese. Finally, one "Chink" too many set her off and she surprised the men by shouting back, "Hey Meester Nauhmber One Dumbass!"—in a phony, Charlie-Chan accent: for she was American, after all, circumstances having made Asian war brides commonplace during the war in Vietnam where her Father met her Mother (unlike the war in the Pacific where U__'s Grandfather had been killed). "Fuck off, 'cause I not even Chink. I a Gook!"

Then someone—one of the ghosts?—got the idea to incorporate the Angry Young Men. So they paid them to strip to the waist and pose with the Models in retro, ghetto-glam shots (lots of sequins/ fros/ big-assed diamond rings) on a chain-link and asphalt playground littered with condoms and those knots of aluminum foil crack was sold in (props other ghosts had planted?). Stylist sprayed their muscular chests to make them glisten, especially where they had branded themselves, using a red-hot coat hanger to make a welt puff up in the shape of their gang's logo: $.

Standing beside one especially sullen fellow (the waist of his polka-dot boxer shorts showing above the belt line of his baggies, his belt, of course, unbuckled), U__ couldn't stop looking at the tattoo on his sinewy forearm: a crude "homemade" prison tat that had obviously been self-inflicted with a sewing needle and ink from a ballpoint pen. *DNR*, it said. This body writing was so different from the petite tattoos that some of the other Models had etched on their buttocks or shoulder blades—butter-flies or rosebuds—that it obviously had a double meaning that theirs did not: that he had been places they would never go, had heard stories they could never tell and therefore saw the Models in ways they couldn't even imagine. So U__ felt an urge to strike up a conversation with him and learn a little about the view from Mars.

But the tattoo was the only thing she could think about. So she asked, "Is that your girlfriend's initials?"

He didn't answer.

They stood together in silence, Mr. No. One Dumbass still hassling the Vietnamese-American Model about her "Moo-goo-pat pie" until

Photographer was ready to begin and the man beside U__ replied without looking at her, "It means, 'Do Not Resuscitate.'"

He and the others scowled beside the Models so "edgily" that the ghosts were thrilled by their own brilliance—until rival Gang Members drove up, trying to muscle in, their threats and hassles ending the other shooting, and the ghosts, furious over the time and money they had already lost, got rid of the Gang Members as if they were so many Mannequins, so much Furniture, which of course they were, and moved the cameras and Models and merch indoors.

After having scary things shouted at them, some of the other Models were furious at the ghosts for having such a flimsy grip on reality. "Put gorgeous us in minks worth beaucoup bucks in front of people with crappy lives—I mean, like *helloooooo!*"

U__ was never sure what to think, though, since so many of those other men themselves were wearing thick gold chains.

"Whatever," she said, getting into the van with the rest of the props. It wasn't her fault, even if a sense of everything being related to everything else gave her the vague feeling that somehow it was. In any case, she was glad that the ghosts had dropped their other idea for moving the shoot indoors—to get rid of all the Models and just shoot pictures of emaciated patients dying of AIDS (100% cotton bed sheets, pin-striped hospital gowns). Thank god another agency had already done that—even if she knew better than anyone that being invisible wasn't the same as not existing.

As they worked, setting up the shoot inside the new location, someone outside would occasionally throw something—a brick or a beer bottle?—at its metal walls. Sirens sounded, and once, there was the faint pop-pop-popping of distant gun shots.

"Please!" shot out from beyond the lights. It was the voice of that toady woman from the fur store who had come along to look after the merch and supervise the Guard who carried a gun and was licensed to kill anyone who tried to heist the skins of the dead minks that U__ and the other two Models were being paid to wear.

As the other Models yakked about the dialog in slasher movies—"I mean, it's so screamy!"—Toady argued with Photographer. Since it was hot, neither U__ nor the other Models would wear anything more than their panties and bras under the fur coats (pale lilac demi bra for her, bikini for the others) and Toady was angry because they were sweating into the linings. But U__ didn't care. After the drive-by hassle, Client, that is, the Owner of the fur store, wouldn't even drive his Expensive Foreign Car out into the Crappy Neighborhoods they used as sets. So let them reclean the coats, U__ thought. Let them reline them for all she cared. Stylist replaced the paper tissue under her armpits to absorb the perspiration.

"Look, you don't need to keep telling me that time is money," Photographer's voice explained again, exasperated beyond the glare, "but her skin is so pale...." U__ knew she was the one being referred to. "If we don't get the lighting right, the flesh tones won't reproduce correctly...."

"...and when he corners her with his ax in that parking garage? I'm like, what was louder?—the grunting or the chopping?..."

Getting the skin right?—what a joke. A bat flew in through one of the broken windows, then after flying around disoriented, flew out through another broken window. Did he think he was fooling anyone? Or was he just that naïve?

Suddenly Toady and Photographer quit arguing.

"We're ready," Assistant said.

U__ threw her head back—Tone of Restful Pride—and took a runway strut toward the camera, one foot crossing the path of the other so her hips would toggle in time with the sweep of her arms though she walked in place so Photographer wouldn't lose focus. Animate the space, she told herself as she performed, looking seductively back through the lens of the camera and into the eye of the man, then laughing, with children, then going pouty, then angry at losing a bet, then surprised to come upon an Old Lover, making the emptiness shimmer all around.... She was Shiva, whirling a world into existence....

Working Girls?

"**C**ity Modeling Agency," a woman answered, her voice so sensual, in that older, smoker sort of way, that X__ found himself speechless. "How may I help you?"

It wasn't that he never spoke to actual women. During one week he'd called the Intimate Apparel Catalog nearly every other day so he could hear the female operators say words like "Nearly Nude Panties," and the names of the other items he bought. During these "dates," as he liked to think of them, he'd imagine that he was talking to the actual models themselves, the models slipping out of the panties and bras they wore in the catalogs to sell them to him, to put them in a box and mail them directly to his hands, his nose, his mouth. But this was different—this was *REAL!*—and it took him a few minutes to compose himself. When he did, he heard his own voice saying, "Hello, This is Xavier Peterman calling from Family Pharmacy & Food Inc. We're planning an in-store promotion, so are beginning to interview models. We were very interested in bringing in one of your girls who has already appeared on several of our products...."

"Are you from advertising?"

"Not exactly. I'm, uh, um, calling about a special in-store promotion. It's sort of a new pilot project. Local. Yes, sort of like having a local football hero in to have his photo taken with a display of Quench-Aide."

"I see." Pause. "Can you hold on while I bring up the girls' schedules?"

While X__ waited, he nervously drummed his fingers on the scanner he used to eavesdrop on cell phones. Through the one-way mirror of his office he could see that Investigator who worked for the Family Pharmacy Chain, disguised as an Electrician, climbing a ladder toward the ceiling. He must be checking on the surveillance cameras above the cash registers....

From up here, he could see everything: luscious melons, a rack of cupcakes....

The cookie-cutter architecture of every Family Pharmacy was as comforting to I__ as the contours of his own living room. To get to Store 049002 he navigated a landscape tagged by ¡Latin Gang! The chrome and glass of Store 023786 mirrored mini-vans and condo landscaping. Like some oddly-shaped congressional district, his territory encompassed customers in factory coveralls and customers in tennis whites. And yet, the Great Equalizer, the identical nets of video cables that hung above all, the identical one-way mirrors and surveillance software comforted him as he climbed a ladder, the way the blind must feel returning from the bustle of streets to the familiarity of their own home.

He hummed as he worked, inserting the needle lens of a camera through a ceiling panel. He trained the camera down upon the spot where the cashier's hands would be, once she opened her register, his thoughts drifting all the while to his hippie Neighbor. Who hadn't been trying to hide his spying. If so, the guy could have easily watched him jump rope naked by peering out from behind his blinds. But no, the guy had stood full faced in the window—as if to make sure I__ saw him seeing him.

Back on the floor, I__ checked his handiwork—the lens was a pinhead, lost in the pebble-grain of ceiling panels molded for just such purposes. Identical in every store. Identical to the ceiling in his living room.

B. Without-a-Trace™ Panty in Buttercup, satin microfiber, guaranteed not to give you away. Bikini sizes XS,S,M,L. W4-232 Orig. $12. Sale $9.

Name

Nice legs and firm buttocks—probably a jogger. Or belonged to a gym.

The Minnesota Modular Approach to Psychosis Prevention

Name

"Thank you for calling Intimate Apparel," the Sales Representative said, "May I have the Preferred Customer Code from the back of your catalog?"

Heavy breathing.

She had only recently completed her training in Neutralizing the Local Accent, that is, in learning to sound American so that Customers who called Intimate Apparel's 1-800 number would feel comfortable ordering from the "girl next door," as "Mr. Oh-So-Proper-Britisher Gupta," their Instructor, put it—even though she was, in fact, the girl on the other side of the world, the girl in a third-world country, in a phone-answering sweatshop that had been contracted to take orders for Intimate Apparel.

"Sir? May I have your code?" she repeated, afraid her Bombay accent had crept in and confused the man. "It's in yellow on the back cover." This customer, Mr. Xavier Peterman, was phoning from a place called 24042 Daphne Lane—how exotic their names sounded! She knew his name because the Caller ID of her computer automatically displayed his name, address, and ordering history—lots of ladies' dainties—the moment it picked up his call. Nevertheless, her company required her to verify all information so they could later sell it.

Xavier retrieved the information, his voice thick as he continued to order, "Without-a-Trace Panties...."

"I'm sorry sir," she said forcing herself out of the habit of saying "very sorry," unable as she was to pronounce that phrase without what Mr. Gupta called the Bombay swing. "Without-a-Trace Panties are finished. I mean, out of stock."

Faster breathing—anxiety?—trying to decide what to get instead? She imagined him in his farmhouse, vast paddies of rice all around, a goodly wife in the kitchen—by Ganesha it could be her!—a new telly in every room, like her cousin Vikram who ran a cold store in Alabama, and Rama and Mrs. Rama who owned their own motel in Omaha, and her other friend Sunita, or Sunny as she now called herself, married to an accountant in California....

She sighed, pulling at her sari to cover the roll of flesh that poked out when she sat at her phone station. Such a rich land. The skimpy bloomers that the man wanted to order cost more than she would earn that day taking hundreds of such orders, speaking American, dreaming Bombay....

> *Module 1: Assessment*
> *The key to early recognition of psychosis in military veterans is*
> *to have it in mind when assaying your patients.*
> *1) Engage the patient through appropriate "greeting" gestures.*
> *2) Establish "rapport."*
> *3) Maintain a high index of suspicion....*

"Have you been taking your medication?" the VA Shrink asked. "Or selling it again?"

"Taking it," Q__ answered—a trick answer for a trick question—"two hundred mg thiorizadine per day." For over a year now she'd been reporting to the VA for her once-a-month visits but this guy was no better than the first. The army doctors she saw were rarely able to fit her in for more than three minutes a visit, and every time she showed up she discovered she'd been assigned to a new doctor. "...Klonopin to moderate anger, Elavil for depression...." Each doctor threw a new pill at her before moving on to their beautiful lives in civie practice. "...Tegretol for mood swings and anxiety...." As he went through the grocery list they'd already given her for her "debilitating conditions," she checked the diploma on the wall. Sure enough, this one graduated last year too. "I'm not crazy, you know," she informed him.

The Shrink put on the standard perception-management mask all of her doctors had been issued in army-doctor school, this one doing so as he double-timed through an explanation of the differences between being crazy and her problem: Peacekeepers' Acute Stress Syndrome, or PASS, as they called it: "a form of hysteria in soldiers who are unable to cope with the trauma of having served in positions where they were fired upon but ordered not to return fire, or had to witness atrocities but had been ordered not to interfere...."

As he wound up the drill, Q__ wondered if he had any clue how many times she'd heard it before. Or how little it applied to her. Her problem wasn't lack of trying. When she closed her eyes she could still see that little girl run in front of her jeep and stop, the driver hitting the brakes to avoid hitting her though he and all the drivers had been trained never to stop, to run over any man, woman, even infant, who stepped into their path. Framed by the windshield, the girl smiled, enigmatic as Mona Lisa, and as though that smile was their cue, others opened fire on the convoy. Q__ had screamed at the driver to step on it, to cream the little bitch. Too late. For him. For all of them. Now she spent her days wondering what that smile meant. Had the girl been happy they were about to die? Was she just friendly? Clueless about the ambush? Relieved that the driver hadn't hit her after she ran into the street without looking? Had she herself been set up?—a dupe to stop the convoy, another victim? Before shrapnel ever peppered Q__'s face, before her fingers had begun to go numb, before she'd even joined the army, she'd seen how the most potent forces in the world were invisible. In fact, desk-jockeys like her, soldiers who operated computers not rifles, probably knew more about invisible forces than any VA doctor could imagine, the data and the tools she'd used to massage it an invisible force as potent as those that guide the path of an arrow, the planets in motion, that call down napalm fire on hostiles. Or not.

As a civilian before all that, she'd operated statistical modeling programs like SR3, translating one form of data into another—an American chain-store's order for shoes from Italy, say, into the slaughter of cattle in Argentina—tracking along the way inventories of hides, boxes, data streams that represented streams of glue, stitching, packaging, payrolls, and all the rest that would come together as "shoe." And it was good. Too good not to use to fix the world, the world being so broken, she increasingly came to see, because of lack of management. Because, that is, its data had been allowed to spill everywhere. So because she was young and wanted to fix the world—maybe like that girl?—she'd joined the army.

She hadn't expected Mother to turn on her for it. Especially given how much the army appreciated her for what she could do, at least at the start, promoting her quickly, moving her from the management of "ma-tier-e-al" as she'd learnt to say it—shipments of k-rations and Kevlar throughout their worldwide network of bases—allowing her by degrees of security clearance into their inner sanctum. A newly minted petty warrant officer, she began to statistically track the tide of hand-guns, rifles, grenade launchers and other small arms that flowed in any army's wake: rockets that were made in Arkansas to Chinese blueprints, then sold to rebel forces who were allies against a common enemy, or American-made, Uzbekistan-bought land mines diverted in mid-flight to peacekeepers without a flag, as well as the great wash of visible and legit pistols, rifles, and mortar shells, weapons that poured in, as water down a funnel, from other countries to those deserts and mountainous places on earth where civil wars made every man, woman and child want to own a gun (a seller's market), and, after the trouble had passed and every man, woman and child who owned a small weapon would trade it for a kilo of bread (a buyer's market), were bought by the metric ton by arms dealers who would import them into the next global hot spot (a seller's market), even if it meant that many of these same weapons that the U.S. first put into the global stockpile eventually resurfaced in the hands of their enemies.

The grenade that wrecked her life surely reached its target via one of these routes: Using the same programs she had once used to track the web of movements and agreements it took to manufacture shoes, she could watch, as in a dream, the just-in-time inventories come together to make a grenade come off its assembly line in Little Rock, go into a crate, then a truck, then the airplane that flew it to Our Desert Friends where it was handed out along with tons of other toe-poppers, rifles, shoulder-launched missiles, RPGs, land mines, and machine guns to rebels fighting Our Desert Enemies. There, the grenade was carried in rucksacks. By donkey. It rode in the toolbox of a Toyota pickup truck for three years till its owner traded it for a few cartons of cigarettes. Its new owner traded it for an WWII vintage Lugar so he could protect his ceramics store. In this manner the grenade traveled from hand to hand, and back and forth across borders till it landed in a open-air market, on a carpet laden with gaudy clocks for sale with more guns, Female Pop Vocalist CDs, ammunition, Soviet watches, imitation Nike shoes, Bulgarian purses, plastic shower sandals from China.... The Syrian who bought the grenade (and an Action Hero DVD) had both stolen from him while re-crossing the border, the bandits keeping the DVD but reselling the grenade to a merchant who was preparing to sell a large number of arms back to associates in Africa, whose son instead gave it to a friend who tied a martyr's scarf around his head, somehow got a little girl to run out into the street and stop an approaching convoy, then threw the grenade onto the hood of the jeep Q__ was riding in, the trajectory of all the lines that made that moment possible converging with a blinding flash as she reported for duty one fine morning.

Funny how she never heard a boom. Then she was in cool white sheets. A hospital bed in Ramstein. That girl's face, her enigmatic smile. Stateside doctors.

"Things okay at work?" this one asked.

Q__ nodded, not wanting to talk about her job as a Profiler, the job she'd gotten after the army kicked her out, or as they called it, gave her an honorable discharge for depression. "Yeah, civilians don't have any problem with me," she said, the spies who watched her at work none of his fucking business.

"And how have you been spending your days off?" he asked, beginning to turn the screws.

"The usual. I go to the public library a lot. And the park," Q__ said, cursing herself for letting her visits to the park slip. "And museums," she quickly added to skip past the moment before her shrink could start in on asking if by "parks" she meant playgrounds. "Last week I even went to an art museum," Q__ added. But she didn't let on that she'd spent most of the day staring at a single, wall-sized photo of a Spanish Master painting. In it, a five-year-old Princess gazed back with the rosy lips and cheeks of a cherub. An enigmatic smile like the girl wore, framed by the windshield of the jeep. The one Q__ screamed at the driver to plow under. The Museum Guide who came by every hour said, every hour, that the Princess had died the year after the painting had been made and the idea had so taken Q__ out of herself that it was only later, after her butt had gone numb, that she realized how long she had sat there, staring at how perfect and alive the little girl was in the painting. "Lots of pictures of kings and martyred saints," she only said now, though.

"And have you seen your mother in any of these places?" he asked, cranking the pressure.

"I already told you where I saw her." Q__ nodded toward the six ads she had laid out on the coffee table—the coffee table, a throw rug, and living-room lamp doing their best to make Shrink's office look like a home instead of a Shrink's office. But Q__ knew better. She was too good at reading the signs to be fooled by disguises so obvious. To let him know so, she stared back till he looked away. Ha! Him and his Sigmund-F. goatee.

Predictable as a rat in a maze, the corners of Shrink's mouth drooped with disapproval at the ads.

The first ad, the one Q__ had found in *Look Magazine* two weeks ago, was still crisp. But she'd gotten some ads by looking through back issues of the newspaper at the library and they were smudged. Another photo was from a box of condoms sold at Family Pharmacy—Mother posed as one half of the perfect couple on a beach before a perfect sunset. Another was on a Family Pharmacy brand of Hair Coloring. Black. Mother's natural color. A fourth picture, a printout on computer paper, Q__ admitted, might not be of Mother. It was the only picture she had found on the Internet though she had spent hours looking. The photo had been taken at a weird, arty angle, making it hard to see the model's features. But still, if it wasn't a picture of Mother, why had her browser turned it up at all? Of all the millions of pictures on the Internet, what were the odds of that?

"And when you see your mother in these pictures, does she ever speak to you?"

Q__ took a breath to keep from going off on him.

"I'm only suggesting," he quickly added, "that maybe your looking for these photos is counterproductive. I mean, maybe by seeking out pictures of this woman—"

"It's Mother! I mean, everywhere I look I see her. I think of her."

"This woman who looks like your mother only encourages you to believe that you see her."

"Don't you get it?" Q__ said, dumbfounded over how stubborn the Shrink could be. "These aren't pictures of just anyone."

"Yes," he said compassionately, "But your mother's been dead for over three years." He paused, looking for a new way under the wires, his grazing fire marking out a new kill box. "It's like this," he began, "sometimes, when we've let someone down, when we feel guilty for not pleasing a parent, our minds can play tricks on us—especially when we are under a lot of stress, when we want a second chance, or a loved one back so badly.... Our minds help us to cope by—" He looked at the newspaper photo again. "She looks like my mother. For that matter, she looks a lot like my sister." Then he looked to his watch. "We only have a little while left so perhaps we should leave that topic for next time. Maybe you can write an account of how you think she could be managing these appearances, and why, and bring it to your next session."

"You don't believe me."

"I believe you believe it's real."

Slippery fucker. "You don't believe in miracles, or my family's story, or ghosts or history, or whatever came before the Big Bang or whatever came after, either."

"No, that's not true. Everyone needs some story they can believe in. Even me. And okay, for the sake of argument, let's say that what I'm telling you is a story. A complete fiction. But it's a necessary fiction—a story you can live within."

"You don't believe me."

"All I'm suggesting is that the woman you're looking for doesn't really exist. We're exposed to so many pictures these days that we're bound to run across photos of people who remind us of others, that make us see connections that aren't really there. Try not to look for any more pictures of her between now and the next session, and we'll see if that makes any difference."

The thing B__ loved most about speeding through his days without sleep was the hyper-precision that pictures seemed to have. Ritalin, especially, gave the Art Museum the clarity of a Surround-Sound, Wrap-Around Photo-Realist painting that he could live within. Even with his eyes shut, he could see the rosy ass-cheeks of Reuben's women, or the geometric women who posed for Picasso, or the flattened queens or birds and oxen in Egyptian art, and he would drift through the galleries trying to work out a way to bring it all into her—the Model he'd been reshaping in Photoshop.

Back in his studio, though, when he began to actually work on her, or even put his finger on the thing all those models had in common, the colors seemed to run:

A Brief History of Women in Art

Did Nefertiti really have such a hydrocephalic head?

Romans, builders of roads as well as men, claimed the ideal woman was divisible by ten.

Two, noted Vitrius, spying on maidens at their bath and judging the pubes to be midway between the soles of bare feet and the top of the head.

If your eye makes you sin, pluck it out, thought Medieval Men, the female body corrupt, a putrid conduit sluicing man's mind from God.

Renaissance Popes weigh in: The Perfect Woman, the Virgin, was 17/18ths the height of man.

While Alberti and Dürer took her measure through their grids.

For what was a heart but a spring; and the nerves but so many stings; and the joynts if not so many wheels? *asked Thomas Hobbes.*

Still, Had Helen's nose been a quarter inch longer, *Pascal replied,* it wouldn't have launched a single ship.

Or would it?

Chinese went nuts for minuscule feet. Bartholomew the Englishman sang the praises of skinny thighs....

The Efik tribe of Nigeria keeps every marriageable girl in a fattening hut until they are pleasingly obese.

Flappers made bodies for a jazz age, thin enough for rumble seats and the Charleston.

In the '30s, Americans competed in Fitter Family Contests at State Fairs, Miss Kansas, Miss Iowa, Miss Indiana, and the rest coming together to crown Miss America, Best of Show.

1950. Photography and calipers; men in white lab coats scientifically find the ideal American woman to be 57% Endomorph, 43% Ectomorph.

The French want a face with personality.

Americans want a face with a cheerleader's balance....

Plastic surgeons in Brazil shape the body to the Carnival Ideal: a breast that can be cupped by one hand, a buttock by two.

Liposuction. Lipoinjection.....

The web of benchmarks, and measurements, and systems that B__ had compiled in his notes went on for gigabytes and was linked to a timeline of aesthetic body shaping: ...sex changes; hair transplants; skin smoothing by laser, by sanding, by chemical peels.... Female bodybuilders and a photo of Famous Performance Artist who used the bone grafts normally used to reconstruct jaws to give her head a pair of horns....

Name

Feet and Ankles
Shoe models must have attractive ankles that do not
dominate their profile, and wear a size 6, the shoe
size worn by most women and therefore shown in most ads.

It wasn't that the woman she was looking at didn't exist, U__ thought, looking at the photos of herself. Rather, it was more like the woman in the photo— the one people saw and advertisers paid to have on their products—had taken her place.

Sitting in her kitchenette (celadon, boxer-style pajamas, notched collar top, silky chameuse lining), U__ took another nibble of the bagel and jam— 295 calories—she allowed herself on Sunday mornings. She continued to examine her tear sheets, that is, the copies of ads she'd been in over the last year. Normally, reviewing her own pictures was one of the simple pleasures she allowed herself, the way others might relax with the Sunday paper and a cappuccino. But today she didn't like what she saw—and it was getting to be time to update her composite: those large postcards that were a collage of her best looks in different lighting, hairstyles, and poses that would be mailed to all the photographers, agencies, clothing manufacturers and department stores—even that pharmacy chain she'd been doing a lot of work for lately. The card was to serve as her visual resume, which meant that it had to project a persona, which is to say what "type" she was, i.e., whether she could be in ads that required a Young Mother or Girl Next Door or an Athletic or Trendy or Exotic type, & Etc. She'd seen Art Directors trying to cast a young-mother catalog go mental when the Young Mother they thought they had hired turned out to be an Exotic type. She'd seen Photographers turn purple because the Model they had hired had been trying to get by on old clips and turned out to be not as hot as she looked in her composite. Which meant her composite had to be accurate. She'd seen Clients turn cruel when the Athletic Type they thought they had hired hadn't been working out, and allowed her body to soften back into The-Girl-Next-Door type. Or a Model who had had her lips fattened when swollen, bee-stung lips were in, disguised them by the way she posed when swollen lips suddenly became the day's cliché.

Just as there were fashions in clothes, there were fashions in bodies. For several years U__ never smiled, the morose, brooding, anemic look of heroine addiction being the fashion in bodies while perky Cheerleader types were so yesterday. Then when the economy got better, and Models were once again required to smile—be Patriotic!—Models by the dozens found themselves unemployable because they looked like heroin addicts (sometimes because they were—you couldn't look the look if you didn't walk the walk), which meant her composite had to be updated constantly.

Art Directors, Photographers, and Clients, like everyone, wanted to know what they were getting before they paid for it, and to be able to tell by flipping through the hundreds or sometimes thousands of women they had on file. So they expected the Model who showed up at the shoot (or interview if the budget allowed for interviewing) to look like the Model in the composite. They also wanted to see what other work she'd done, that is, if the Model was going to be trouble, i.e., if she was a Naïf who would have to be told everything, or a Prima Donna who wouldn't listen to anything, or depending on the real requirements of the job, whether she was going to be Chicken, i.e., young enough to do anything to begin her career.

The problem was that the Model U__ was, i.e., the Model U__ saw when she looked in the mirror, and that Art Directors would see when she showed up in person, looked less and less like the Model she saw when she looked at the finished ads.

There weren't a lot to choose from, at least not of the kind that was supposed to form the centerpiece of any composite: the full-face head shot. Though she worked steadily and always tried to get copies of the catalogs, ads, packaging, labels and brochures she appeared in, once the shoot was over, the promotion offices, stores and clothing manufacturers she had been hired for didn't want to be bothered with remembering who had worked for an agency they had hired six months earlier. Usually they'd only send copies, if at all, after she nagged. Most of the ads she did receive wouldn't work well in a composite: In one, the lighting showed off the features of the chrome VCR she modeled but hid her own features in shadow; in several other ads she had been posed as one among a group of models. A photo that eventually ended up on the boxes of Freedom Condoms sold at Family Pharmacy showed her with a man, forehead to forehead in one of those dreamy "perfect couple" shots. The catalog she'd been in did feature her alone: 32 shots of her by herself. But in each she was only shown midriff to mid-thigh, classically posed in string bikini, thong, classic bikini, and high-cut brief, each in rose, navy, iris, violet, ivory, buff, oatmeal, and indigo. The newspaper ads she'd been in were poor black-and-white reproductions.

After setting these and others aside, what were left were head shots that could have come from a different person. Or a series of people. When she lined them up, her ivory-white skin seemed to get progressively darker. Her nose became less "classic." Her eyes more anime, her expression more exhausted, "languid," Art Directors spun it.

She'd had her images retouched before, of course. Her skin had been made as poreless as Barbie's, her nipples made darker to show through blouses or lighter not to show through blouses. She'd had her breasts enlarged, reduced, muscles painted into her legs, shoulders widened, and all of these alterations made to a body she had starved, exercised and made up to be as perfect as possible.

But this was different. Not a more perfect her, but a different her. Her eyes began to widen and slant, not squint—she had trained her eyes to remain as large as possible, even when the lighting was so bright it hurt, so she was very good at not squinting. It was the shape of the eye itself that was changing, becoming like those saucer-eyed school girls in Japanese comics. When she stacked up the photos and riffled them like a flipbook, it was almost as if she was evolving, turning Japanese. But not quite. Not quite Japanese, but not Korean or Chinese either. In these pictures she could have been Mexican. Or Indian. Or Greek. Or Italian. She could be so many things that the best description that came to her was that she was becoming more "Ethnicky."

Weird.

She thought she had understood the mindset. Cover Models were often composites of several women, or different shots of the same woman: separate photos of hair, face and body, all seamlessly combined, Frankensteins without the stitches. In fact, in addition to her own composite, portfolio, and career, she also had a separate composite, portfolio, and yes, career, for just her hands. It had begun with an ad which read "So Simple You Can Operate It One-Handed" that required her to peer with a surprised expression through the fingers of one hand. Since the Hand Model who had been hired to pose as her hand had been molested by the Photographer on another job earlier in the day, and since punching him while clutching her own torn clothes to her body had swelled her hand and made her miss the shoot, they had asked U__ to hold her own hand in front of her face, and her own hand's career was born. With that ad, and photos she paid to have shot of her hands holding perfume bottles and clothes irons, putting on lotion, & Etc., she made up a composite that her agency mailed out, and jobs began to trickle in.

Gradually her hands became models in their own right, each an actress required to take on roles and project a persona. Why not? In fashion shows, she was only allowed to acknowledge applause by "letting her chin take a bow." Now her hands would delicately hold the champagne glass washed with Client A's soap, while Brand X's beer mug may as well be clutched in a claw. They could hold a pose for hours without the slightest hint of strain.

After this success, she had some intimate portraits of her legs shot and made up a composite for them. Then she made up composites for her feet. Then for her waist. Then her ears and neck. Finally she wondered, if her various parts could be so many models, why not all of their wholes? Though every agency liked to think they owned their Models—would go mental if they caught one of "their" girls working out of another agency—she began experimenting with how many types she could pass for. She created different personas, registered them with different agencies under different names, and sent out different composites; in one she was a Product Model, a Corporate type; in another she was Trendy-but-Sophisticated. She was Fashionable, of course—though at 5'7" she was too short to break into high fashion—so she also had photos shot of herself dressed as a Nurse, a CEO, a Teacher, a Bartender, a Guard in an art museum. She had photos shot of her various types in a casino, in a courtroom, in a doctor's office, in a speedboat with the city skyline glittering behind. In one composite she was the Real Person type though given her bone structure that type was a stretch mainly, she thought, because being Real, i.e., appearing to not be an Actress or a Model was the hardest type of all to pull off. Indeed, sometimes she had to check the scheduler built into her cell phone to remind herself what type she was, especially on those packed days when she had to be Corporate in the morning, Exotic in the afternoon, and Real in the evening. And that didn't even include shoots for her hands and feet and waist and ears, which, of course, also required her attendance.

Even at its most disorienting, though, she had always thought it was a swirl of her own creation—a mosaic of a career whose cracks she could keep from showing by running fast enough—even if she had to work within the constraints of the system (if there had been a market for elbows, she would have made a composite of her elbows, her elbows being, she thought, one of her best parts. But there was no market for elbows). Then this came along—someone changing her—not just her look, but *her*.

Who was doing this to her? And why? When she first realized that the changes weren't just part of the normal mix and flux of air brushing and editing that always went on, she had her bellybutton studded—a small golden dumbbell that she wore like an earring through the pierced flesh of her navel. Some of the other models she worked with thought it was a career move: a jump into the tribal-look that was coming into fashion among Exotic types, not the heavy studdings of real punks, or the belly-button removal that was the fad among Rich Teenagers in L.A., but a punk-lite version: a tasteful, petite golden stud that any Girl-Next-Door Type could hide when posing with her Parent Types. U__ had thought of it more as a joke than anything. A sign to whoever was changing her face that she still owned her body. But then, when the changes continued, when the photos she had posed in showed her other un-self with its wide, anime eyes, classic nose not, tawny skin, and naked, studless bellybutton—even that ad showing her in a police-uniform bikini—it had begun to feel creepy. Sinister. Like some other will had begun to dominate, like someone she didn't know was spying on her and doing whatever they wanted with her body, consistently molding her into something other than her self to the point where her "real" real self, i.e., the fashion persona she had worked hard to project, seemed to evaporate before her very eyes.....

There was a rustling of sheets, then a loud yawn from her bedroom—that Male Model she'd gone to Big Bowl with last night was waking up, and she hurried to get her clips back into their portfolio.

There was the squeak of bed springs unsprung. Then, as if every one of these Guys followed the same script, the tinkle from her bathroom: his morning piss. Bringing him here was dumb, she realized. They were always so hard to get rid of and she had a lot to do today.

The Mummy's Return

Name

When the company screwed her by moving to the suburbs, Q__ was forced to buy a car. Then, because she couldn't stand the messy confusion of street parking, she'd had to move into an apartment that had a space reserved for her car. As she pulled out of it now, a camera recorded her license plate.

55.7 said the radar gun of the first speed trap she drove through, she knew.

53.4 said the second.

102.5FM said the scanner making a survey of the radio stations being listened to in her and every passing car, no doubt.

Just as the traffic began to wind her tight, the green light on her radar detector clicked on, telling her the way was clear. At the same instant, the Family Pharmacy truck that had been rumbling alongside her swerved into her lane, wheeling wide to turn into one of their lots.

"I'll fix your wagon, soldier," she muttered, using her cell phone to dial the number stenciled across one cargo door: *How's My Driving? Call 1-800-2-ADVISE.*

"*Your privacy is very important to us*," said the auto-welcome message of A1 Collection Services, and X__ turned down the volume of the scanner he used to eavesdrop on cell phones, bracing himself for the fight that would begin once a human operator came on. "*...by remaining on the line you acknowledge your consent for your call to be recorded to better serve you or for use in a court of law....*"

"Your case number please," a human finally said by way of "hello."

X__ read the number off the notice the collection agency had sent him and the moment the operator confirmed his name she said, "Our records show you are in default of your payments to MasterCharge. When may we expect to receive payment?"

"That's the problem," X__ said, "I don't have a MasterCharge card."

His scanner crackled to life: *"Yes, I'm calling to report the driving of one of your assholes."*

Q__ arrived at the green, rolling hills of the corporate campus she worked in during the week. Late and agitated, she had to circle the employee lot twice before finding a parking place at the far end. Cameras, like snipers, panned the lot from the roof of her office building. Her efficiency evaluation was coming up, she remembered. For sure her Boss was compiling data on her for his report, tightening the screws, and she made a mental note to look in on the e-mail of her subordinates—just to make sure they weren't goofing off, just to make sure the company couldn't use that reason to screw her over.

On This Date 2001—NY officials propose national warehousing of not just the DNA profiles of criminals, but of everyone, beginning with newborns. "If they aren't doing anything wrong," the Chief of Police said, "they have nothing to hide."

View people at work in an office in England
(or pick from 62 other countries):
www.camvu.com

Grunting?

Modulated by the squishy sound of suck?

Before she had become preoccupied with the nature of the ghost, U__ liked to pass the dead time of photo shoots by making up screenplays about the web of chance and circumstance that had brought her to the moment she filled by imagining movies about the web of chance and circumstance that had brought her to the moment she filled by making up stories about the web of chance and circumstance & Etc....

Today they were shooting in an abandoned electronics factory (a series of Little Black Dresses, sleeveless, retro, & Etc.). The crypt-like gloom of its cavernous space, water-streaked walls and industrial graphics—*NO STEP*—seemed pregnant with ghosts.

Imagining movies was easy here. In fact, so many came crowding in that she had to work to keep them from getting tangled: the Boy Genius who read science fiction and made crystal radios on the kitchen table, dreaming of the day he could teleport himself around the world—*if a person's voice could be turned into radio waves, why not the person?* The other kids only laughed at his dream..... So he lived like a hermit in his parents' basement, she decided, focusing on the Boy building radios, improving them too—*Boy Inventor: A True Story!*—imagining the places he'd go, and growing so tall and gangly that sometimes, lost in a revery of electromagnetic travel, he'd forget where he was, stand up from his sci-fi comic books and his radios and bump his head on the basement ceiling.

Meanwhile, chance and circumstance allowed Scientists, now long dead, to make accidental discoveries that allowed other Engineers, also dead, to stumble upon the principles of vacuum tubes that allowed the Boy, grown into a Young Man, to take a job in a shop that manufactured radios with speakers instead of an earpiece and usher in a world where two or more people could listen together. *That's Show Biz!* The number of Families who wanted to gather around music, news, and stories that could be turned on or off like a faucet kept the shop that the Young Man worked in humming. Then disaster: The War to End All Wars had a sequel. The Young Man rushed off to join the Air Force—*Be a Flyboy!* But they only laughed; someone as tall as him could never fit into a tiny WWII cockpit. And his civilian job was important to the war effort. So he returned to the shop he worked in, which, with the government contracts that came pouring in, grew into a factory, which required an even bigger building, then two buildings, along with Receptionists, and Shippers and all the rest. *Birth of an Empire!*

Young Lovers said passionate good-byes during the melodies of Famous Big Band Leader and other Musicians required by the radio stations to fill airtime created by radios like the ones the Young Man and now lots of other young men and women like him made on assembly lines. *Rosie the Riveter.*

U__'s Grandmother had been among those Young Lovers, becoming pregnant with her Mother to the ethereal melodies tuned in with a dial that was as big as a barometer and that after her Mother was born, and her Mother's Father killed in action, glowed to her like a night-light.

They never found his body.

Across the ocean, the Japanese, who still equated their Emperor with God, were as shocked to hear his voice come over the radio as you would be if God started talking to you through your radio, this God-now-man speaking through radios that glowed like those in America to tell them that their world was ending, and suddenly it seemed like everything was related to everything else. All those bombed-out nations that had to be rebuilt, all those Families that wanted radio and now radar as well, the ghostly blips that would appear on the round, green screens taking their place among other abstractions that people had begun to treat as if they were as solid and real as bricks.

Ground-breaking ceremonies. Industrial railing and graphics—KEEP AISLE CLEAR—a new factory had the streamlined styling that people in the 50s believed was the look of the future. Rock and Roll. Tailfins! Road Trip! Transistors! Plastic! Then there were those ridiculously tiny radios— "Only Nippons have fingers tiny enough to make radios that small—*ha! Ha! Ha!*"—a joke around the water cooler. And NASA! A beep—then staticky transmission of an Astronaut: "*That's one small step for man, one giant leap for mankind*"—*beep*—over a TV that the now Middle-Aged Man may have soldered a part in on the assembly line he worked, and so in his way contributed to the chain of people and machines that brought pictures of a man on the moon into his living room, a fact that filled him with both pride and nostalgia for his own boyhood dreams.

End of an Era.

The downward glide of market share. Markets flooded with cheap product, death of a Founder, lawsuits against export dumping, layoffs, the factory a behemoth nobody wanted, blacks (whose own ancestors had been ripped from Africa—*Roots!*) moving into the surrounding bungalows that had once been lived in by white solderers and white forklift drivers, and white sheet-metal workers, and white drill-press operators who died, or retired to the desert states, their children, like U__'s Mother, now married and fleeing to the suburbs, filling subdivisions around computer companies that did their automated manufacturing in brown third-world countries and had headquarters on corporate campuses in the green, rolling fields, leaving the pension plan of employees, like the Middle-Aged-then-Old Man broke and unable to sell, leaving abandoned buildings like this one for an ad agency to rent for a shoot just about the time that it became chic to pose Fashion Models in scenes of desolation—the Dance of Death being a perennial *fin de siècle* form to be sure—the stark contrast between urban blight and porcelain skin somehow making the clothes they wore more desirable, the clothing manufactures more "aware," even "edgy," at a time when it was fashionable to be scowled at by disdainful runway Models.

Birth of an Era.

The Old Man killed in one of the nearby bungalows had willed his body to science, U__ had read. Men in white lab coats froze the body solid, then shaved it into thousands of microscope-thin slices, taking a body-length scan of each layer as they worked their way through the corpse so that the photos could be reassembled as an anatomy model: the way old biology books used to illustrate a frog's muscles, skeleton, and organs on plastic pages that could be turned one by one to show how the layers went together. Only this man, the Visible Man, as they called him, was digital: a virtual corpse whose organs, muscles, and all the rest could be teleported via phone, radio and satellite transmissions to the screen of any computer in the world. And so he was, at the speed of light, doctors in Japan using his digital body to practice a tricky operation; a plastic surgeon in Brazil using him to demonstrate to a client how much younger she would look after a face-lift; animators in Hollywood using his virtual body to model an army of space aliens; automakers in Germany using him to engineer car seats; fashion designers using him, using the whole library of Virtual People that was being developed as folders of digital information, rearrange-able, collage-able....

U__ paused. Was something like that, she wondered, happening to her? To everyone?

Monitor #5 showed Q__ get out of her car in the employee parking lot. **Monitor #4** showed her walk across the lot. **Monitor #3** showed her enter the lobby where the Receptionist was watching rows of banked monitors.

"**G**ood morning," Receptionist said, "Was traffic heavy?" acting nice, acting friendly, though Q__ knew the little Snitch was just making nice to make sure her lateness was noted on tape.

"Yeah, I was run off the road by a Family Pharmacy truck," she answered in sync with her gray-scale video puppet, hurrying by to an open elevator to get away from the Snitch, a little spy whose back-telling proved how wrong her Shrink was about her being paranoid about nothing.

Run off the road, yeah, right, Receptionist thought, watching Q__ appear on **Monitor #2**, the monitor that showed the stretch of hallway in front of the elevator bank. **Monitor #1** showed their Boss, inside one of the elevators, unbunching his crotch.

In the privacy of the elevator, Q__ adjusted her panties—had to look her best— not give them that excuse to spit her out like the army had. Probably better shadow a few of her subordinates' cases too, she thought, just to make sure that they weren't padding their time sheets. The elevator opened onto the glass facade of her office suite: *Employer Information Services.*

Fluorescent lighting. Office cubicles.

She walked past the "good mornings" of the suckups she worked with, then ducked into her own "executive cubicle." At her desk, she logged in, then hit the "Quilt" function key and her computer screen was transformed into a checkerboard of other computer screens: the screens of the Claims Processors, the 24 men and women she monitored, doing work very similar to her job as a petty warrant officer overseas, her own computer taking snapshots of their screens and displaying them on Q__'s screen so she could watch what they were working on. Along the edge of each, small meters listed their keystrokes per minute, the websites they visited, how many e-mails they'd sent, how many they received, how many of those received they'd read...

The Claims Processors she tracked usually put in more keystrokes than the quotas given them by the company. They knew that if Q__ or someone like her wasn't actually watching them at every moment, she could be—just as she knew she could be watched right at this moment by her Supervisor, who was probably watched by his, who.... She zoomed in on one of the screens.

The Claim Processor, **Alice F. Jernkins**, was doing a credit check on a mortgage applicant, a **Mr. Xavier Peterman**....

Con Artists Steal Your Identity

More at 10!

The glass doors swing open so smartly that at first you believe their lettering: *Welcome To Family Pharmacy & Foods Inc.* But then there you are, framed like a Criminal on a wanted poster that is a 21" monitor.

Fuckers. If they were going to treat him like a Criminal, he was going to act like one. So though gin wasn't his fave, though too much or too fast drinking could make him sick, P__ did what he always did when he transferred buses at this stop: He made his way to the liquor department, grabbed a bottle of the most expensive thing he could consume in the store—Empire Gin—stepped to the blind side of the cameras, and took a deep draw. Then he recapped the bottle and put it back on the shelf. Yeah!—fight the power! The perfect crime. Only it wasn't a crime. Not if he wasn't really a Criminal.

In the parabolic mirror above the pharmacy aisles, T__ could read the lettering on the baseball cap of the customer waiting for his fix: *DigiDreams*....

Just as "day" was meaningless without "night," it was necessary—another word for destiny—that the yin of hardware would require the yang of software. And that software would spontaneously generate Hackers as well as mouses. Money aside, the temptation of an unguarded backdoor would be too great for some to simply pass by. Even more so would be a backdoor with a heart-shaped lock, so it wasn't surprising that P__, that

Programmer from work, would help V__ break in behind B__'s back.

What was surprising to V__ was how easily she decided to do so. After meeting B__ on-line, and then meeting him for coffee at the Art Museum, and sleeping together looked inevitable, she had secretly sent off a strand of his hair for DNA testing. (An age of life-threatening diseases brings into existence, naturally, courtship rituals like this.) After the results came back clean, though, she felt a little cheesy for hiring a lab to check him out. So she promised herself never to sneak around behind his back again and the irony of this was not lost on her as she stood behind P__, watching him use her computer to hack into B__'s e-mail, even getting a little horny as she did so.

Weird—Especially considering who P__ was. When he first took a job as a programmer at the TV station they both worked for, he'd seemed sort of creepy to her. Not in a Biker sort of way, or even because of his nervous, hair-trigger geekiness. "Do you know that plastic pipe can be used to make a gun that won't show up on airport x-ray equipment?" he once asked her, a nervous laugh giggling out though she didn't see what was funny. He seemed to think everything was funny—especially her—breaking into a nervous laugh when they met in the hall as though he knew something that she didn't—that the fly of her leather pants had come unzipped or something just as stupid. Given the grungy way he dressed, always in thread-bare dress pants, she suspected that it was the leather pants (Emporio Armani) themselves that he thought was the joke. As well as her sleeveless black turtleneck (Eileen Fisher) and beaded curtain skirt (Dolce & Gabbana)—pricey, gifts that she'd gotten to spoil herself when she was feeling blue. Or to treat herself, like that time she'd won the Big Award. Oh yeah, the disdain he had for her boutique-ing was written in the jarring contrast her stiletto witch's boots made to his beat-up tennis shoes. The anti-fashion fashion of his Salvation Army clothes a critique of her and her Calvin Kleins, DKNYs, TODs and Hermes—of the fashion mags and catalogs she liked to flip through while killing time during long downloads—his slouch and cigarette an up-yours to the chrome and mirrors of the gyms she worked out in so her shoulders would look buff when she wore those sleeveless turtlenecks.

The way his eyes would dart away every time she caught him checking out her bod made her think, at first, that the dark rings under his eyes were from a social life that only happened on-line. But then she began to wonder if it had more to do with chemicals. Like an addict, he never ate. Even that time her Co-Workers toasted her Award with champagne, she noticed, he only faked it with an empty paper cup. And though the station paid its Programmers well (though nothing like the Anchor Mannequins in front of the cameras, of course), recreational chemicals would explain why the only shirts he seemed to wear were the tees that the station gave away during promotions—as surely as her waxed-python skirt (Salvatore Ferragamo), knee-length merino cardigan (Dolce & Gabbana) and form-fitting trench coat (Borrowed From The Boys) explained her own stratosphere charge-card bills.

Storm Tracker, said the tee he wore the day he came into her office to help. Seeing him in it, in the tornado graphic she had designed for the shirt, his hair as wild as its black swirls—a critique of her own slicked-back haircut—his eyes shooting away the instant they landed on her bare shoulders, she thought he had the look of one of those wired guys who sooner or later comes to work with a rifle.

But now, standing behind him, being a part of whatever it was that was him, she liked the scene. Seated before the code marching across her monitor, he was the calm center of the storm, a stuttering Wallflower who once on stage plays mean and perfect synthesizer. Looking at the veins rising from the backs of his hands as he typed, she recognized the true nature of his addiction—something like her own—his fingers racing clickity-clack over her keyboard.

Was it the software? she wondered. That is, was shared software sexy the way some people said shared food was sexy? Older people, like her Mother who still used an easel to paint pictures of fruit, would say no. They'd point out the stark dif between the succulent flesh of a pomegranate and code. But those people couldn't see how sleek software could be—or how people made themselves sleek, fast and cool by using it—the way a diver becomes a stiletto by pulling on a wet suit. What could be more phallic than a 1?—more vaginal than 0?—mingling with the sexual tension of a single's chat room, the back-and-forth of 1010 101010 10101010 101010 101 0101 01 010 like foreplay at the speed of instant messaging, orgasm with multiple 0s, a force more primal than the sea with its power to move economies, to guide missiles, to deliver to your screen the portraits and e-mails of thousands of Men Seeking Women....

Plus she liked the imagery.

She was also—you know—grateful. Seeing her as a Damsel in digital distress, P__ hadn't hesitated to shed the Dungeons-and-Dragons MUD he inhabited—which he later confided to her was actually—big surprise— a game called Virtual Terrorist in which he, on-line *nom de guerre* Insane Punk, conspired with punks like T-mark and others in Germany and

Wherever to bring down the Information Highway before others like the Greens could grab the glory by doing so first. Or with more collateral damage (a program named Crash Accountant kept score). Players had to use real stock markets and real stolen credit card numbers, and hack into real government agencies, i.e., the only thing that made the real game virtual was that they weren't supposed to actually pull the trigger.

Some teams, according to an anonymous posting, had backing from the CIA, others from the PLO, others from the Aryan Nation, the South Koreans, the FBI & Etc. Unless the posting was a dummy: an attempt at sabotage planted by another team. Maybe backed by Disney, or Famous Footwear, or Diet Cola, or Intimate Apparel, Inc. & Etc.

When he first reached for her mouse and their hands touched, his lingered for a moment too long on top of hers because, they both realized, she had let him.

Not everyone would bust into a stranger's car to rip off its radio as a favor, after all. And what they were doing was at least that illegal. Which also made it at least that exciting. Doing so with the station's equipment—the big-haired Station Manager would flip if she found out—made it even more dangerous—a thrill ride in a stolen car with P__ at the wheel, whipping around curves. Taking that joy ride after work—with another guy behind B__'s back—was like flirting at an office party, the thought of which got her horny in an illicit sort of way. That is, she understood how P__'s game could be addictive. And the temptation B__ might have given into, keeping his MatchMaker ad in play, going parallel behind her back even though he hadn't meant to, even if in her heart of hearts she hoped she was just being paranoid.

When she explained this to P__, though, telling him how she'd checked the MatchMaker site and found that B__ hadn't put his ad back up, he'd only scoffed. "Like. Duhhhhh!—ever hear the word 'Pseudonym?'"

It took a rat—a guy—to think like a rat—a guy— V__ realized, though at the time she'd argued back until it became obvious that all she was really doing was trying to talk herself out of admitting the truth: that not only had B__ begun using a different name, he'd probably moved on to a different matchmaker site.

"Or five or six of them," P__ agreed.

Creating a virtual self was simple: Just set up an e-mail account under a different name and start using it. She'd done it herself. Everyone did— set up one self that was more or less permanent, others that could be ditched—one e-mail name and personality for work, another for friends, another for shopping, another for guys she'd just met. An old roommate had five names and addresses for this last purpose alone: ChiliPepper 1 through 5 that she'd give out according to the hotness of the guys she met and V__ could feel her face turn red for needing P__ to tell her: The only way to find out what B__ was up to was to get back the source—his hard-drive. He could take on another name, another persona—become a Romanian Mail-Order Bride if he wanted to—but as P__ said, code never lies. It can't.

"It might be more fluid than water," he explained, "standing in here for laundered money, there genetically engineered corn, elsewhere a release of toxic gas, or a love letter, but it can't not be what it is and someone who knows how to read it could tell more about its creator's intent by looking at its architecture, than they could by hearing all of the explanations in the world...."

"Okay, we're in," P__ said now, rising to give her the driver's seat—warm. "It's just like his computer is on your LAN...."

Sure enough, when she took back control of the mouse, she could leaf through B__'s hard-drive as easily as if it were her own. She felt a little cheesy opening up the IN BOX of his e-mail. But she got over that feeling of sneaking around much quicker than she had the time she'd had him tested for AIDS. As then, what she was doing was good for them both. And if he didn't have anything to hide he had nothing to be afraid of.

In the main, she found exactly what she was expecting: folders labeled Accounts Receivable, and Billing Correspondence, & Etc. She used a program that P__ wrote and called Mole to scan his thousands of e-mails, using key words like "sex" and "hookup" but she only found e-mails from when they were both parallel, including her own flirting messages. There were a lot from other girls too. She was surprised how many. But she resisted the temptation to spend time reading old business.

Instead she moved on, double-clicking on his V-drive. It didn't open. She double-clicked its icon again: a thumbnail of a woman in white panties, cropped from perfect midriff to perfect mid-thigh the way women modeling underwear were often shown in catalogs. This one had a bellybutton stud. V__ double-clicked on the icon's label, *Venus of Photoshop*—the icon blinked but the hard-drive wouldn't open. "What's going on?" she asked P__.

"I don't know." He leaned across her chest to reach the mouse.

P ....

| ....

V ....
B ....

Had P__ made it not work just so he could lean across her? V__ wondered as he typed commands. The thought was so juvenile it was funny. Endearing, even, and she leaned forward just enough so that as he typed, the tips of her nipples grazed his forearm.

He made a typo, muttering to himself as he corrected it. At length he gave up, flustered. "It must have a chastity belt," he said, his voice now dry. "I mean a physical lock. Some of the old drives used to come with them back in the days when computer theft mostly meant someone physically putting your computer in the trunk of their car. It's the most low-tech security there is, but it's actually pretty good because the drive can't spin without being unlocked. If it can't turn, it can't be hacked."

V__ remembered a key dangling from the front of B__'s computer. He had only bought the NASA-sized hard-drive because he got it for the cost of junk at a liquidation sale. He'd epoxied the key in its lock because he didn't want to lose it. But she didn't think he ever used it either.

08:19:17:23:59

Melons.

Rendered in the grays of black-and-white surveillance, the Family Pharmacy Cashier looked older than the nineteen years recorded in her file, the angle of the ceiling-cam exaggerating her cleavage.

"Rigggggght—now!" I__ pushed the pause button.

Freeze-frame held the Cashier's arm midway between the till and the apron of her Family Pharmacy smock. Using his laptop, I__ ran the history generated by her cash register one more time, and one more time the software alarm that had alerted him to her in the first place went off. Time and date stamps on both video and receipt log confirmed the aberration: she'd rung up $13.13. Family Pharmacy didn't sell anything for $13.13. Even so, even though she'd rung up $13.13 eleven times that day, he still might have passed it over as an honest mistake if she hadn't done that thing a lot of the guilty did in the videos he made: As the tape continued to play, she glanced up at the camera, even though it was impossible for her to know a camera was there.

Guilt. Melons. Guilt. $13.13.

He bit his knuckle; six billion people on earth and everyone but him had some reaction to being watched:

> **Store 023830:** *Embarrassment*
> *The Teenage Girl's giggles dampened into tight-lipped silence as she realized I__ really wasn't going to let her go until she emptied her purse. Her face went scarlet as she did so, a home pregnancy test tumbling out.*

> **Store 030033:** *Anger*
> *"Are you calling me a thief?"*
> *In answer, I__ laid out the employee time sheets that had been short-changed in order to make the store look more profitable and the District Manager he'd been questioning lunged at him from across the table.*

What was his problem?

Say YES! to Caller ID and see who's calling before you pick up the phone!

"**H**ey, the Candy Man's here."

T__ stepped off the bus and into the grip of three Latin Gang members—no, four. From behind, the fourth tore his backpack from his shoulders. "You're late, Candy Man." They shook out homework, textbooks and smock…. When the Ritalin he'd pilfered from work also spilled onto the sidewalk, they dove on it as if a *piñata* had burst. Fighting each other, they stuffed the pills into the folds of the red ski masks they all wore as berets. Then they were off, hooting and bobbing away. "See you next time, Candy Man…."

Slowly, T__ picked up scuffed papers, books, and his own red ski mask. Family Pharmacy Inc., said the bronze name tag pinned to his smock. His theft but not theirs would show up in inventory and seeing his face reflected in the name tag's dull metal—*Timo Garcia, Apprentice Pharmacy Technician*—he wondered how he was ever going to cover it up….

The e-mails and text files V__ read in the following days began innocently enough—mostly clips about body shaping that B__ collected for ideas. There were notes about a Famous Silent-Film Actress who achieved her renowned hourglass figure by having her lower ribs removed, and notes about Famous Performance Artist who had had horns implanted in her head. A PDF from an on-line science magazine explained a genetic basis for ideas of beauty, noting that though Miss America's height has been inversely proportional to her weight, her waist-to-hip ratio has remained a constant 0.7....

Most of the folders on this hard-drive were filled with body parts: dismembered fashion models: images of beautiful ears, lips, breasts, waxed legs, tummies, thighs, tight buns—pictures of parts of the models that he had blown up, sculpted one pixel at a time, and then reassembled, like Frankenstein.

V__ wandered his digital labyrinth, every screen filled with the flesh-colored attention he obviously lavished on them. There were lots of screen-shots of Jenny, the girl who installed web-cams all over her apart-ment so she could put her life on-line: video grabs of her in the shower, or sleeping.... A whole chronology of Jenny-Cam shots documented her gradual slide from perky, co-ed exhibitionist to doughy, computer geek. But that didn't bother V__. Lots of people followed her; many put up their own copycat sites. Rather, the first speed bump V__ hit was a photo he'd shot with his own digital camera at the Art Museum: a photo of a white marble statue of two nude women. The view was from behind, the two women walking away arm in arm, their marble buttocks smooth and prominent, each woman looking back over a shoulder and smiling as though pleased to have caught an admirer spying on them.

The statue illustrated the story of two Roman sisters, his text explained. They'd been bathing in the Pool of Mars when they fell into an argument over which of them had the finest ass. With each accusing the other of being unable to see the truth, they agreed to let a guy decide—the first man who appeared at a certain crossroads. When one did, an Adonis, they resolved to ensure his honesty by telling him that his choice would be his reward. The Hunk immediately chose the more slender and muscular of the two Sisters.

This greatly angered the voluptuous Sister who demanded a second opinion. So they awaited a second man, and when one appeared, equally handsome as the first, they told him as they had told the other that his choice would be his reward. Without hesitation, this man chose the voluptuous Sister.

Rejoicing in the wisdom of the gods, the four of them were married in a double ceremony, and at the crossroads where they met, they erected a shrine to Venus. Their fame soon spread, and pilgrims to love came from all of the ancient world to worship, and to be worshipped, by those who would see in each other their fondest desires.

Below this B__ had typed:

The lesson isn't to design a body everyone would desire. There can be no such body. The lesson is to imagine a body that can be all things to all people, or at least to most shoppers, i.e., the great bulge in the demographic bell curve. I used to think that this body was abstract, pure desire, till I found HER, the source code of desire embodied: her limbs muscular enough to suggest Olympian sex, but not so muscular as to prevent surrender in bed; a face that is at once exotic and mundane; skin that is maybe black, maybe white; eyes maybe Eastern, maybe Western; someone else, mostly me—all of these—terrorist, savior. A body that is both battleground and safe harbor, desired stranger, lover, friend. A body so perfect it intimidates, so intimidating it invites touch, so touchable it is invisible; so invisible it is monumental: a body that is at once classic, of all people in all times and all places, unchanging copies of divine perfection yet simultaneously the face of the New....

The description brought back another night like a kick in the gut: They'd been at Big Bowl, a pan-Asian place with blood-red walls, black leather booths, a touch of theme park—huge rice bowl and chopsticks—a projector crawling Japanese text across chi-chi guys in black linen, chicks in Riviera pants, talking on cell phones while B__ picked at his food—mentally elsewhere—until he recognized one of the Models he worked on, live at another table.

He got so excited seeing her in the flesh—as if she was a Rock Star or something—that he wouldn't shut up about the squareness of her shoulders, her pale skin: the perfect canvas. It was infuriatingly obvious how much time he had spent not only looking at her, but studying her, her and her features that said New Money; E-Trade; The AmericanDream.Com Fulfilled—so sez he—even as the Model still carried a legacy of inheritance in her perfect teeth, her perfect posture and horsy jaw an echo of a fish in water where she was the fish and the water was a lifetime of family privilege and ocean-side homes—the income needed to bring into the world a being with her clean lines and poise greater than the GNP of the nations that supplied their Gardeners and Kitchen Help.... In fact, it was because of those Gardeners and Migrant Workers, and Computer Programmers, and Medical Doctors with diplomas from nations with iffy electricity that the entire nation was becoming darker.

V |||||||||||||||||||||||||||||||||||||||||||||||||||||||||||||||||||||||||||||||||||||||||||||||||||||||||||||||||||||||||||||||||||||||||||||||||||||||||||||||||||||||||||||||||||

B |||||||||||||||||||||||||||||||||||||||||||||||||||||||||||||||||||||||||||||||||||||||||||||||||||||||||||||||||||||||||||||||||||||||||||||||||||||||||||||||||||||||||||||||||

He'd nodded toward the spectrum of skin tones in the restaurant: an older restaurant Owner with the whiteness of a powdered wig, to tanned Gallery Girls on cell phones, to the dark-skinned Busboys—and the continuum was so stark that the truth of what he was saying was clear: So many of the people from those other countries wanted her, or wanted to be her, or at least what she represented, that they were willing to suffer, clean the shit of others, even die for a chance to come here. And so many succeeded in coming here that every year the entire nation was becoming a little more coffee-colored: a skin tone that was easy to tint over the Model's chalky whiteness. Every year, so many of them were here, that is, so many of them had become us, that every year we wanted her to look a little more like us—which he obliged by making her lips a little thicker, her eyes a little *anime*.

And advertisers, squaring desire and demographics, quantifying how the entire country was becoming more like them, and them more like us, like her, had begun to want them/us—that is, her, in their TV spots. Everyone had begun to want her on their package labels and billboards —*¡Comparalo y ahorra!*—their car commercials, everyone wanted her— or at least his version of her.

Catching them looking at her, the Model flashed him a big, beautiful gash of a Model's smile.

"Well, almost everyone," B__ finished, seeing V__ glare back.

"Why don't you just go over and let her shake hands with your boner?" she'd said.

The memory now made V__ feel all crawly, and a sensation of being watched made her turn around.

P__ stood in the doorway of her studio. Instead of looking away nervously as he usually did when their eyes met, he continued to stare at her so intently she said, "Geez, don't forget to blink."

He stepped on one tennis-shoed foot with the other. "Be a carrier," he said.

"Excuse me?"

"Don't be a victim. Be a carrier. Like Typhoid Mary."

"How long have you been standing there?"

"Typhoid Mary wasn't a victim," he continued, "She didn't let people turn her into a dump for the shit of the world. She was a carrier, someone who brought shit to others, tearing up whoever got in her way."

If five years in the FBI and another four as an investigator for Family Pharmacy had taught I__ anything it was that six billion Homo sapiens eat and screw and react to being watched in so few patterns that it had to be the heritage of some deep-seated animal instinct. Yet here was another case, underlining his own apathy at discovering that he himself was being watched.

He switched off the monitor and its screen went black, reflecting the longing in his face for the Cashier's fear. Oh yes, it was fear. Every time she rang up $13.13 she put money in the till. And whenever he caught someone putting money in the till, it was because they were actually putting it back—covering up a previous theft after the wee and small of their data double began to swell in their minds to the prime-time proportions of that poor slob on *Real Cops on TV*, hauled out onto the front lawn in his underwear, over and over, the Cops wrestling down his buttocky girth in the forever of rerun syndication—just because he'd had the bad luck of being drunk enough to fight back on the night cameras were out cruising with Cops, looking for just such a spectacle.

So why was the only bump in his night the fact that he didn't care someone was spying on him?

He closed his eyes to see the Hippie's expressionless face watching him exercise naked. The guy had even begun taking notes, or sketching pictures of him and I__ tried to use that as a motive to hate that face. To summon embarrassment. Or shame or....

Nothing.

Back in the FBI, there were Shrinks for Agents who had burned out. Who had dealt with so many lying Punks that they couldn't see anything but deceit, even in the mirror.... Had something similar happened to him?

> **Store 028830:** *Deceit*
> *The video showed the Employee check the*
> *hallway, then turn back into the lunchroom and*
> *piss in its coffee pot.*

P ιιιιιιιιιιιιιιιιιιιιιιιιιιιιιιιιιιιιιιιιιιιιιιιιιιιιιιιιιιιιιιιιιιιιιιιιιιιιιιι

ιιιιιιιιιιιιιιιιιιιιιιιιιιιιιιιιιιιιιιιιιιιιιιιιιιιιιιιιιιιιιιιιιιιιιιιιιιιιιιιιιιιιιιιιιιιιιιιιιιιιιιιιιιιιιιιιιιιιιιιιιιιιιιιιιιιιιιιιιιιι

It wasn't like he never gave a damn whether he was watching or being watched. After leaving the FBI for Family Pharmacy, I__ had actually felt cheesy using all his high-powered government training to expose Stock Boys, setting up cameras in washrooms and lunchrooms to do so.... Now he knew better than even Portrait Artists that when a person looks in a mirror, the "life sized" reflection they see is only half as big as their actual face. That was why a face in a mirror facing a mirror facing a mirror kept getting smaller and smaller and smaller, until there was nothing there. But anymore, he couldn't even pretend it mattered.

> **Store 034684:** *Denial*
> *"That's not me." In slo-mo, the tape*
> *showed the Pharmacist forging a*
> *prescription for himself. "I swear*
> *to God, that's not me."*

The bus lurched and P__, juggling the didjeridoo he'd just bought, collapsed into the nearest seat to keep the paper grocery bags he also held from bursting. A guy in one of those nerdy Family Pharmacy smocks sniggered. He had a backpack, like a college kid, and also one of those plastic bags from Family Pharmacy that would still be choking the earth a thousand years from now. Go ahead and laugh, jerk, P__ thought. Plastic bags—just so the guy and the millions like him could carry deodorant and whatever other shit he had in there home a little easier.

Was that a gun sticking out?

P |||||||||||||||||||||||||||||||||||||||||||||||||||||||||||||||||||||||||||||||||||||||||||||||||||||||||||||||||||||||

U |||||||||||||||||||||||||||||||||||||||||||||||||||||||||||||||||||||||||||||||||||||||||||||||||||||||||||||||||||||||

The Driver's eyes switched to them for a moment, filling the big mirror above the windshield—the mirror used to watch Passengers, not traffic.

Tuesday nights, U__ attends a class in "World Art" for, as her Counselor put it, "self-fulfillment." This Tuesday her "World Art" prof was showing slides of photos by Famous Feminist Photographer. This photographer, he explained, had become famous for taking photos of herself posed in artificial tableaus that evoked the various genres of old B-movies. Projected on the screen at the head of the darkened classroom was one of them: a black-and-white photo of a woman dressed in cat-eye glasses and pedal pushers (from the '50s), and bent over a bag of groceries (paper) that had burst on the linoleum floor ('50s again) of a kitchenette (mondo '50s, complete with a toaster that had the chrome, teardrop lines of big, post-WWII autos, or sci-fi spaceships). Framed to look like a still from a film with subtitles, the woman, the Famous Feminist Photographer, could have passed for a "Foreign Type."

"...here is a conception of woman as clay with society as the sculptor," Professor Art Historian was saying, and U__ couldn't help but be impressed with how much like her own work these photographs could be—except, of course, for the obvious dif that U__ didn't actually take her own pictures. Or decide what to wear. Or where to pose. And yet, for these exact reasons, wasn't her work a more "direct articulation," as the Professor would put it, of what Famous Feminist Photographer was trying to say?—that she, or any woman, was a "collage of codes" captioned by her society as "Woman"? And if that was true?—

"So what are we to make of a self-portrait that is also a masque?" Professor asked.

The projector *ca-clicked* and the screen filled with a photo of the painting by the famous 17th-century Spanish master, now on display in the Art Museum: *Las Meninas*. Only it wasn't really a photo of that painting. Rather, it was a version of it, the Professor explained, created by a famous homosexual Japanese Photographer: Like the Artist of the original painting, the Photographer had included himself in his work, doing so by digitally altering the picture to put himself in the scene, dressed up in the Princess's clothes and posed where she had stood in the original although it was almost impossible to tell the copy from the original. Both showed a sepia-toned view of a royal chamber with the Princess (Photographer) gazing out at the Viewer while her/his Attendants—Ladies in Waiting, a Widowed Chaperone, Court Functionaries, a Dwarf, her pet dog—all looked to her/him and one another....

"As an entry point," Professor said over the fan of the slide projector, "Think of the common convention for a self-portrait: taller than it is wide and filled by the face, the unique identity of the sitter. Now contrast that mode of visual storytelling to the conventions of the pornography center-fold we discussed earlier: filled by an entire body seen from above so as to present its subject as willing sexual partner."

He went back to an earlier slide, one that wasn't unlike the photos U__ had posed in lots of times: a woman (the Famous Feminist Photographer) lying like a centerfold on a bed seen by a camera looking down on her from above—"the viewpoint of a dominant male, possibly a rapist," Professor said. Her silk bathrobe was open to display her skin, of course, as well as her big ol' nylon bra and girdle—the merch—which Prof. Art Historian called "cultural markers."

"Just as we all 'smile for the camera,'" he said, "that is, just as we mold our bodies to satisfy the expectations of our viewers, women remake themselves according to the expectations of the male gaze...."

As the Professor droned on about how men look at women, but women look at themselves, making themselves over in the image of what they think men want to see when they look at women, U__ squirmed in her seat, feeling her own "culpability in the oppressive erotics of voyeurism," as he put it.

Still, she didn't make the world. Since the first day of school, she couldn't help but notice how the other students in the class—both the men and the women—often stole glances at her long, professional legs. Even the prof did so. And in answer, without even thinking about it, she would let the hem of her skirt ride up her thigh to give them a better look.

As an experiment she arched back in her desk—*lift the torso out of the hips and elongate the body upward*—feigning a yawn, her breasts arching up, the hem of her stretch-tee riding up to reveal a patch of bare midriff between it and the drawstring waist of her linen pants, her belly-button stud an exclamation point in a body she had modeled as an object of desire. Sure enough, the guy next to her, as well as most of the class—men and women—began glancing at her instead of paying attention to whatever the professor was yakking about.

A power. She smiled to herself.

In the same instant, she suddenly saw that that was the big dif about someone digitally changing the color of her skin, the shape of her eyes, the length of her legs. With someone else manipulating her shape, her face, her art, it was as if her ability to use her body was being stripped from her and the realization gave her the sickening feeling of a pianist hearing the crunch of his thumbs as they were broken by goons.

"**W**ell, where are they?" I__ sighed, going behind the camera counter in Store 028834.

"Right here." The Lab Technician pulled out one of the yellow envelopes used to return photos to customers. Usually, when an employee reported that a customer had turned in kiddie porn or other illegal pictures for processing, they turned out to be just naked baby pictures. Or naked Husband and Wife pictures. Or naked Boyfriend or Girlfriend pictures— sometimes screwing—but always a waste of time. Still, he had to check out every report because corporate was worried about lawsuits.

The first ones she showed him were a little different from what he'd expected: photos of naked women with drop-dead beautiful faces. When he looked a little closer, though, he saw that each photo was of the same face though the bodies were obviously of different women. Each photo was actually a collage of photos. Weird. Judging from the stock poses of the bodies in them, it looked like they had been taken from porno mags, and then fitted to head shots of the same model. She looked familiar—eyes like a cartoon character—but I__ couldn't place her. Even so, homemade porn wasn't a crime. He shrugged.

But Lab Technician said, "There's more." She shuffled through the vaca- tion snapshots of another Customer—a man and woman wearing leis in a hot tub—until she found a photo of a Teenager wearing a red ski mask and pointing a gun at passengers on a bus. A Smith & Wesson 9mm semi-automatic, from the looks of it.

"See, I told you."

"Yeah, I'll check with the police to see if there's been any car-jackings lately. Sometimes Punks like to reenact their crimes for their friends. You have the customer's address?"

A Bomb.

A Beauty Bomb.

No, A ~~Beauty~~ Bomb—Rhymes with?

P__ sat diddling in the bay window of his apartment, glancing occasionally at the guy jumping rope naked across the courtyard, trying to translate into words what it was like to be near V__. To be in the editing suite, minding your own business when in she walked and changed the world with the tight fit of her leather pants, or a black sleeveless sweater that you knew, just knew since you couldn't detect an outline no matter how hard you looked, were sheathing barely-there panties and bra—Without-a-Trace™ Panties and Bra that models wore in those catalogs that came to his mailbox, lying back on pillows and beds, looking up at you dreamily, willingly....

Even now the mind-fuck of her femaleness blurred with those catalog models, naked limbs and bellies conflated—images of what she and they must look like naked swirling till he put down his pencil.

He understood why so many suckers kept coming back to the fake porno site he had set up. In one six-hour period alone, he had racked up 78 card numbers from his "secure" site, taking orders for a program that his marks thought would let them paste the face of anyone they knew onto the nude body of women who came with the program. HOT! HOT! HOT!—HOT ASIANS! HOT TWINS! HOT BLACKS! That guy named Xavier Peterman had given him three different charge-card numbers, entering the info from a different card every time the secure site asked him to try again.

It reminded P__ why he had given up poetry to begin with: the utter futility of getting into words the suffering of refugee camps, the utter feeble-ness of rhymes while rain forests were being turned into teak bar tops for people who drove SUVs. Thinking about the political poetry he used to write always made him wince as if he was naked at a podium, reading to other political-poet wannabes when a real Poet walked in, body laden with dynamite, detonator in hand, saying nothing, not needing to say anything, his presence making it impossible for anyone to think about the kind of poetry that was written in words.

What did he know about refugee camps? P__ thought. What could he say that the Famous Central American Poet wasn't saying with his beaten body? Or the Famous South African Poet hadn't said with his hunger strike? Or the Famous Chinese Poet in his gulag? What did he know about gulags? Or alligator clips on testicles? Or truncheons, black hoods and car trunks?...

Looking at the fake porn site he'd set up on the Internet, though, auto-matically gathering what info it could off of the computers of people trying to log in, he remembered how it had dawned on him one day that the ones and zeros of code, too, could be a kind of poetry: a poetry that like the bodies of those imprisoned poets was both message and material. A poetry that he knew a lot about: how it could be a funds transfer, or not; or an order for rifles, or not. It could be part of the system that would eradicate starvation, or not; sell designer purses and teak bar tops, or not; ship those alligator clips, billy clubs and black hoods, or not. He knew a lot more about this system, this kind of poetry, than anyone in a gulag, or car trunk could know: how ones and zeros could be a lyric of love, a political sonnet, Y2K an unfinished epic written by 100 million authors....

> *Module 2: Acute Treatment*
> *Acutely disturbed patients should be treated with*
> *rapid-acting injections.... Lorazepam (Ativan®) is fast-acting*
> *and very sedating and can be used to cover the initial 4*
> *hours.... Afterwards, continue dosages of risperidone, 0.5mg*
> *for the first 24 hrs., increasing to 3mg, twice daily....*

The viewpoint is always that of the shooter, one of the grunts had said back in group, back before Q__ stopped going, and as she sat scoping kids in the park, she wondered why those words had come to her just then.

Kids played "rocket" on the jungle gym—"Beam me up!"—and she tried not to think about them growing up to become a circle of sullen, ex-GIs in group—jerks—in a circle jerk blowing her off because she was a woman, because she'd humped a computer instead of a rifle though she'd probably whacked more rag-heads with the data she crunched than all the rounds they fired combined. She'd stopped going when they started asking her if she heard voices—voices!—like she was crazy!

"Beam me up!"

She tried to calm herself, scratching her armpits to keep the anger from building to the point where it could flip her, keeping her focus on the kids and their small bodies. Running gave their cheeks the angelic ruddiness of the Child Princess in the photo of that old painting she'd seen in the museum—an angel in amber—the Amber Princess—always innocent, never growing up to be played for a tool, to run in front of a convoy so her uncles could open fire—angels too good for this world—unlike the jerks who blocked her view of the kids every now and then, jogging across the grass between her and the playground.

Here came one now. A guy in a designer jogging suit instead of the prison grays that grunts wore in boot camp.

Hey asshole! she wanted to yell, the jogging path's over there! GIs had died so jerks like that could have the freedom to jog on other people's grass, to block other people's view, and she straightened to yell—just to show that the voices she heard weren't only in her head. Not really. Or at least no less real than a voice remembered, or the voice of a conscience, and everyone heard those. She sat back.

The only reason she heard more than most was because she listened better than most. Oh yeah, the shrinks couldn't fool her. She *knew* everybody heard voices. Who hasn't gotten into an argument with her Boss and then replayed the conversation over in her head? But it was never just a replay; the voice in the head would say different things—better things than what the mouth had said during the other argument, the argument with the Boss's mouth. The voices would think of all the things the mouth should have said. Or couldn't or wouldn't say—smarter things—and the mouth, jealous, would sometimes repeat the things when it was too late and it wasn't in the Boss's office but on the bus, or in front of that Manager at Family Pharmacy or with her Shrink or whoever else was at the business end of the next argument, co-workers, or that dick-skinner from Alpha Company, their voices joining the folks already there, psycho-babblists, ex-boyfriends, confusion agents from the army, dictators, TV preachers.... Everything she'd ever seen or heard. *You deserve more meat today!* They were all there yammering away, sometimes taking turns, sometimes jamming each other's bandwidth but sometimes quieting down to just—

Usually Mother.

Queenie, did you clean your room yet?

And why not?—hadn't Mother been there the longest?—sang to her before she was even born, Mother used to say....*A, B, C, D, E, F, G, how I wonder what you are....*

Just before she was born, she used to get the hiccups every evening at six, Mother said, so she'd just rock and sing—*The itsy bitsy spider went up the water spout*—until the pain ended, certain as only someone who knew another as totally as only a Mother could that she wasn't bad. Not in the heart. Not even if the hiccups hurt. Not even if she left her to join the army.

You hurt me, Mother told her over a USO hookup...

Maybe took off years.

Major Minor's First Rule: Keep your hatchet scoured.

Before she could get an emergency leave, it was over.

At ease, sergeant...

Odd, how it took her years to realize that the only one who could really get under her skin was Mother—

At ease, sergeant, I have some bad news for you.

...up the water spout...

The news had hit her dully, a percussion grenade without the bang, the military having done its job well, filling heads with work and words— Higher Ups and other Enemies—so your Mother's dying couldn't get in. Not that they gave a shit about any boot or their Mother, Q__ now saw. They just didn't want to deal with a blip in the routine. Right after the funeral she was shipped out to the latest hot spot. Then flash-bang!—the explosion that put her in the hospital. Then her discharge.

Suckerrrrr!

Use her up, spit her out.

Down came the rain and WASHED Spider out....

But now Mother was back—or at least her memory—no matter how hard Q__ tried to shake her.

But why? as Shrink kept asking. If Mother was appearing to her in these photos, what did she want? Why appear and not speak?—if it were her....

"People simply don't follow others around for no reason," an earlier VA doctor had lectured that other time Q__ thought people were appearing to her, strangers taking turns as her shadow for some reason she never was able to figure out. But every time his arguments began to make sense—that maybe she was becoming a little unhinged—all she had to do was remind herself of the shrapnel in her face. Of months of rehab. Of her hair falling out and fingertips going numb and not one frigging doctor in the whole frigging military able, or willing, to explain why. *Agent Orange. D&D Coverups.* She shivered to think of the grenade in her ruck on a shelf in her closet. Oh yeah, they couldn't fool her—if there was anything she knew for certain it was that sometimes the most powerful things made absolutely no sense—no matter what kind of pressure shrinks put on you to see it their way.

As T__ slept, his Mother crept into his room. His book bag and Family Pharmacy smock hung on the door—such promise—and she swelled with pride for her *Hijo*, her Son, as she considered how much his Family Pharmacy smock resembled the white lab coats worn by scientists in the poster above his bed: serious men writing on clipboards as they conducted an experiment with a cow who stood looking at a life-size painting of another cow. *The Innocent Eye Test*, said its caption.

For his own good—she crossed herself—then tightened her grip on her shears, devoting her last breath, if need be, to turn him into one of those doctors in the poster—she brought the blades near his neck—deter-mined to cut her son from the gangs her Old Flame said he'd begun running with. Last week she'd even found a gun hidden in his underwear drawer—how complicated the world had grown! Her own Mother would have simply taken a few of her Son's hairs to a *Curandera*, but she....

She snipped off the hairs she needed for a DNA test. If her *Hijo* wasn't doing anything wrong he had nothing to hide. If he had a drug problem, she had to find out—before his Father did and beat him for the overtime, for the tons of flock, even, that he had heisted from the paper factory he slaved in to pay the boy's tuition.

As T__ slept, his Father crept into his room, wondering why he couldn't just let sleeping dogs lie. He paused, taking in his *Hijo's* snoring form. The boy was in college—studying medicine, no less. He had a good job, and a hot girlfriend so he wasn't gay even if there was a lot about the boy that he didn't understand—like the goofy poster above his bed: a cow looking at a portrait of a cow. *The Innocent Eye Test.* Could any true son of his?... Then there was the talk of the Neighbors, and his Wife and her Old Flame still whispering together about?— What?

Hijo de mi esposa es su hijo, went the saying, *pero mijo?—quien sabe.*

With a Q-Tip, he swabbed up drool from the boy's mouth for the home DNA test that would confirm whether or not they really were Father and Son. If she hadn't done anything wrong she had nothing to hide.

Name

DNA TESTING
Call 1-800-R-U-MY-KID?

Your Frame
Runway models must be over 5'10" tall and weigh
between 110 and 125 lbs. A narrow body with hip bones
that are narrower than the shoulders (i.e., classic coat-
hanger dimensions) is also required because together
they determine how a garment moves on the body.

The world conspires to make you conform, P__ thought, wishing he still had the hemp bag one of the Mexicans at his old job had given him. Weary from riding the bus, he clutched the plastic bag that held the CDs he'd just bought. The store didn't even offer paper bags and the plastic ones they did have gave off a sickening petroleum smell. The bus lurched—new man at the wheel—the smell of the bags and the smell of the bus beginning to make him nauseous. He closed his eyes against the motion. Tried to sleep, his mind turning as it always did before sleep to his last day at Holiday Paper Products. He'd been working as a programmer for the family-owned business, running the numbers to generate payroll, keeping tabs on the inventory of mis-made tissues and Kotexes that the Company turned into Christmas tree flock when the employees' toilet backed up—again. Making sure his Supervisor was at the far end of the plant, he'd slipped into the lunchroom and called OSHA to report it. As he'd done the week before. And the week before that. As he'd resolved to keep doing until the company stopped making excuses about the toilet. Yeah, that's right; if they weren't doing anything wrong, they had nothing to hide.

The bus lurched. As it groaned along, the stench of the clogged toilet seemed to waft to P__, the one employee john being just off the dirty little closet that served as a lunchroom. It wasn't the stench that had put him on a crusade against the company. It was—dare he use the anachronism?—being treated like a Serf by the Factory Owner with his Armani suits and art collection, and brass and paneled office where he didn't have to breath the dust of ground-up Kotexes. Then Owner himself had fired P__—for taking home a pound of flocking for his own tree—Everyone did that!—convincing P__ that management had somehow found out he was the one who kept reporting them to OSHA. But how? Were the phones tapped? It wouldn't surprise him. The fuckers would jam a telescope up your ass if they thought they could make a dime by examining what you had for lunch. Yet whenever he tried to pin down the moment he was seen, his mind went spinning out of control, the question too big to handle, like thinking about God or Infinity—

The bus lurched.

Is someone barfing?—that fucking Hippie in the back of the bus!

"Hey," yelled the Chick in an army jacket, "don't do that shit in here! Hang your head out a window!"

> YOU ARE ON SURVEILLANCE CAMERA AN AVERAGE OF 10 TIMES A DAY, *said the swimsuit ad, a Model wearing a police-uniform bikini pointing a camera at the viewer.* ARE YOU DRESSED FOR IT?

The Bus Driver's eyes scowled in his mirror.

"Don't worry man, I got a bag," the Dude said, holding up a plastic bag, pendulous with vomit.

"You see the vomit in that bag?" one Black Woman told another, huffing in her own forms: flower-print dress, large, churchin' hat. "He ain't foolin' me. That was gin vomit. There weren't no food in there. Nu-uh, not one single chunk."

The window across the courtyard remained empty as I__ uncoiled his jump rope. He turned on the TV for the noise. Slowly, he unbuttoned his shirt. He dropped his pants. The window across the courtyard remained empty. He stepped out of his BVDs and the breeze hit his pecker. Should he close his blinds? The window across the courtyard remained empty. He pulled on gym socks and laced up gym shoes. Already he'd broken a sweat and if he closed the blinds—

Suddenly—a flash of movement—

His Hippie Neighbor appeared in the window.

Not wanting to tip off that he knew he was being watched, I__ began to jump, telling himself that he was simply willing to pay the price for the fresh air. Yeah, everything had a price and if he wasn't doing anything wrong he had nothing to hide.

After the ten o'clock broadcast, V__ and P__ sat in the handkerchief-sized park that was across from the TV station they worked in during the day. It was a Friday night, so the theme stores that catered to conventioneers and tourists in that part of the city were already closed. But the restaurants were still glowing, and the other benches in the dark, antique park were mostly occupied by people holding hands, waiting to take one of the Romantic Carriage Rides that began near the fountain.

Seeing them, V__ realized how close she was sitting to P__.

Last night they had also sat knee-to-knee so that she could use the wireless connection on her PDA to pass on to his PDA a section of the diary she had downloaded from B__'s computer: the story of the two Roman sisters who were drying off after a bath when they got into a cat fight over which of them had the finest ass. She had wanted P__ to read it because he was a guy—he would give her a guy's take on what to make of it—and they had sat there together like that, knees close, their two PDAs doing the necessary handshaking and recognition as a pair of lovers on another bench slid hands through each other's hair, under shirts, the data passing between the two making V__ feel crummy, as if watching the tiny blinking LED that showed the transfer in progress, she'd been watching herself tongue someone not her boyfriend behind his back.

Now they sat even closer so she could show him her latest discovery in a file labeled **YES!** :

> *Pygmalion made a woman,*
> *Venus, Goddess of Love,*
> *that had greater beauty*
> *than any girl could, and*
> *he fell in love*
> *with his own Workmanship.*
>
> *Often he would run his hands over it*
> *stroke her breast,*
> *praying as he feels the ivory soften*
> *as wax grows soft in sunshine,*
> *And Pygmalion wonders—*
> *O! Words are not enough!*
>
> *The lips he kisses*
> *He can feel them,*
> *kissing back as the girl—she's become real!—*
> *blushes, opening her eyes*
> *on her lover....*

"So. You're a guy," she told P__, nodding toward the screen. "What do you think? Is this chick virtual, or someone he's actually screwing?"

"What's the name of the drive you can't open?"

"V-Drive," she answered. Then seeing what he was getting at, she said softly, "For Venus."

When P__ remained silent she added, "I feel like such a knob."

P__ took her hands. But only to raise her PDA again. Like a scribe using a stylus on an electronic slab, he wrote those odd marks that the character recognition software of PDAs used for letters, $\bigwedge$ for an "A," $\prec$ for a "K," and the others, also giving it commands to send her data. The LED glowed as it had last night. When she looked at what he had sent her, there was an icon in the shape of a black heart: LUVBUG.

"It's a virus," he said, looking into her eyes. He held both of her hands and her PDA together in one grip as he continued, "If you ever want to fix that fucker for doing this to you, e-mail it to him. It sleeps on the harddrive until after it's been backed up. Then it opens up its own box and starts eating data. Destroys not only all the files on his hard-drive, but all his backup copies and the hard-drives of everyone he's been e-mailing, other girlfriends, clients, MatchMakers, everyone. Deadly, deadly shit," he told her. "So deadly it's beautiful."

Tone of Intellectual Musing
Form is the shadow cast by the sundial
of the mind that shows what time it is....

D. Clickable Cleavage Bra lets you create three levels of cleavage. Click once for a little cleavage. Twice for a little more. Three times for the décolletage of Marie Antoinette. Size 32-36A-C. Cat. W132-1313. $65.

Candy Man Special: pink Tranxene t-tabs, capsules of Darvocet, Seconal....

B__ chugged a Vicodin to iron himself out, then put on his *DigiDreams* cap. He had to get it together, especially the giggles. Last time they'd gone out, V__ kept looking at him weird—suspicious-like....

Module 3: On-Going Management
...upon their return from combat, soldiers exhibiting violent or schizophrenic symptoms often benefit from a course of prophylactic anticholinergics....
Build up to 2mg/day haloperidol with a dose increase to 4mg/day after three weeks....patients with a five-year history of problems need 5-10mg; a ten-year history requires 10-15mg; and so on up to 20mg, the maximum safe dosage.

Q__ lay in bed imagining herself as the kid in the stories Mother used to tell— *Twinkle, twinkle little star....*—and how great it would have been if she could just stop time—a childhood held in suspension—great expectations—a moment that she imagined as a big, bright diamond she could turn this way and that—frozen forever like Princess Amber or the girl in the moment before she ran out in front of the convoy....

Instead, she knew, looking at her military ribbons, framed and hanging next to a poster of fairies, she had grown up and made a mess of it. She saw Mother standing at the kitchen sink, washing dishes as she always did when she was beaten down. Disappointed. No furs. No diamonds. No blood chit. Scrubbing, scrubbing, as if she could wash away the mess with a dishrag.

While growing up, Q__ had thought all that washing was just part of Mother's weirdness. A nervous tic. Then lying in her rack in Germany one night, looking out at the white mountains and seeing Mother standing there at the sink, her back to her, the real reason for all of the washing came to Q__: The kitchen sink was the one place in their tiny apartment she could go to to hide her face. To turn away so her daughter wouldn't see how raw her eyes were from fighting with whatever man was living with them, then later, so she couldn't see how disappointed she was in Q__ herself.

Q__ knew because that was the last place she'd seen Mother before shipping out. Running away, Mother called it: "I support you all through college and now finally you have a job and can help and you pay me back by running off to get yourself blown up!"

Q__ had stormed out. Angry. Her Mother just not seeing how bad she had to get out—OUR MISSION: TO *STABILIZE A NATION WRACKED BY CIVIL WAR*. And Mother could have come with her. *PEACE KEEPER*. Even grunts kept family near their home base. She'd practically begged her to come along. But when Q__ walked in after getting her hitch, and found Mother washing dishes at the sink, the way her shoulders sagged at the sound of her entrance told her that she'd gotten her answer.

All right. No hero's farewell. Mother wouldn't even turn around, just stood there with her back to her, her hands outstretched on the sink for support like some kind of crucified saint—NAK that—as Q__ muttered, "I'll be going then."

A year later Mother was dead.

How could she have known that would be the last time she'd see her?—standing at the sink, head hanging, her back turned to her little Princess.

Then, in fulfillment of Mother's prophecy, there'd been the little girl, the explosion. The nightmares. Did the girl smile because they were all about to die? *I know something you don't....* Had Mother put a curse on her? The rehab. How badly she'd wanted to drive over that girl, even though she may have been completely innocent. Smiling because she was sweet. Anxiety and short breath. "If it wasn't a problem," she'd once told that doc in group therapy, "I'd go out and shoot everyone."

Her Shrink had been right about one thing, though: Q__ wished she could go back in time and make it different. If she could, she'd make it different for everyone, go back to the time before it all went bad, and make them stay there—that smiling girl, Mother's little Queenie, her eternal Princess Amber, suspended beneath the varnish of the painting like spring flowers in ice, a serene smile on her face....

The more she thought on the Princess's suspended childhood, the stronger a creeping sensation became, something far off growing closer until it took shape before her: She was too old to go back—instead of Princess Amber's rosy cheeks, Q__ saw her own angry, shrapnel marred features staring out from the ice. But others were still young and pure enough to be like she had once been, like that girl had been before she'd been played, Q__ knew, and she could give it to them. A gift. That only the pure deserved. That is, that only kids deserved.

SEMPER FI, as the Jarheads put it.

The room, even the furniture went very still, very, very still, as if the whole house was thinking.

Is that what Mother had gotten into her head to say?

The next night, the Hippie was already there when I__ got home. He had pulled a recliner up to the window, tied back his long hair, and was sitting there blowing into a didjeridoo. Watching. Waiting for the show to begin.

V__ was just doing her job, googling for an image of Thomas Jefferson to use in the teaser she was composing. A picture of Mt. Rushmore came up along with a caption:

On This Date 1826—President Thomas Jefferson sighed a dying breath, comforted by a life of public service monumental enough to warrant carving a mountain into a likeness of his face.

Then an e-mail popped up on screen:

To: VidChick

MatchMaker.com was the only place she used this name and so the only e-mails that came to it were from guys answering her ad, guys flirting, feeling her out, looking to hook up, and/or answering her flirting feelers to their ads, and like some Pavlovian dog who hadn't forgotten to salivate at the sound of a bell, just the sight of the e-mail threw her into a state of heightened sexual awareness: the tingle she got wearing leotards while stepping into the mirror-paneled gym and having every guy in the room look up to check her out.

Hi,

I joined MatchMaker right about the time you left. In fact, you were the first one I was going to write but before I could figure out what to say, you removed your ad. I never sent my e-mail but I saved your picture on my desktop because you looked pretty cool....

V__ didn't know whether to be flattered or creeped out because some guy she didn't know kept her picture on his desktop. Along with icons for iTunes and other adult toys, no doubt.... Maybe e-mailing it to friends or even pasting into one of those interactive porn programs she'd read about?... Ah, so what? She wasn't doing anything wrong so what did she have to hide?...

...I know you're not in the mix right now, but was wondering, are you thinking of jumping back in?

Your,
WonderBoy

Was she?

Tonight at Ten!—Private Lives and Secrets of the Grave!—DNA testing reveals that President Thomas Jefferson fathered children by his slave Sally Hemings.

The Neck
Concentrate on elongating your neck by reaching upward with the crown of your head while keeping your chin level. Be sure not to tilt it back because this will cause the Adam's apple to protrude....

Back in the FBI, I__ had had teams to help him shadow suspects. One team would follow the Rabbit while two others traveled up parallel streets. That way, if the Rabbit turned a corner, one of the other teams could pick him up without arousing suspicion; in this manner, the teams would leapfrog each other, taking turns being the shadow, or traveling a parallel route, waiting for the Rabbit to turn their way.

Activity Aberration Scores

Store	Cashier	Score
02830	00000501	35% *
02798	00000402	22%
03489	00000470	20%
04902	00000312	20%
03142	00000300	19%
02786	00000201	17%
03065	00000233	16%
03153	00000551	16%
03098	00000781	16%
03241	00000250	15%
02799	00000342	14%
02952	00000215	14%
03065	00000482	14%
03486	00000550	14%
02630	00000208	14%
02931	00000340	13%
03045	00000203	12%
02076	00000339	12%

Pouring over the drug inventory for Family Pharmacy, I__ felt an adrenaline rush similar to the ones he'd get on those hunts. Did you want to know which cashier worked slowest? It was all right there in the volume-against-time summary report. Were you more interested in which pharmacist filled the most Xanax prescriptions? Or who had last touch? Again, the numbers told the tale. No matter which way a Rabbit dodged, their shadow would turn up in another parallel data stream.

Then suddenly the trail went cold. For weeks he'd been tracking Cashier 00000501, Nina Martinez, following the money, seeing a pattern beginning to emerge. Comparing the pattern to the store's surveillance tapes, he'd begun to pick out some of her customers: a woman with a baby, two Chinese or Korean guys who always came in together, what looked like a college student, and some guy who always wore a DigiDreams baseball cap, all of them paying for prescriptions they'd gotten in pharmacy. But the pharmacy inventories showed no aberration. Then just when he asked the Store Manager to rotate the schedule to see if he could get any flags to pop by letting the data play out through a new configuration, it stopped.

Had he been spotted?

Back in the FBI, the only Rabbit they ever lost was that Spy for Airbus. Not shackled to the politics of purchasing committees, the Rabbit's corporate-backed counter surveillance team had used the latest in de-encrypting scanners to trump their counter-counter-surveillance, outfitted with an old administration's govern-ment issue, and the first thing that occurred to I__ now was that he had stumbled onto a bigger, more sophisticated operation than one nineteen-year-old Cashier.

Aberration Reports
Region 0008District 0389
Scoring Type: All Cashiers

Number	Score	Title
Report 1	3	Cash Return/Sales
Report 2	3	Avg. Check Returns
Report 3	4	Returns to Same Acct
Report 4	3	Exchanges
Report 5	3	Post Voids/% Sales
Report 6	3	Cash Post Voids/Sale
Report 7	4	Post Voids/No Sales
Report 8	3	Post Voids/5 Trans.A
Report 9	4	Voids Employee Purch
Report 10	4	Transact. Voids
Report 11	3	Line Item Voids
Report 12	4	Price Modifications
Report 13	4	Sales Not Scanned
Report 14	3	% Sales Keyed
Report 15	4	% Credit Card Scan
Report 16	3	Gift Certificates
Report 17	4	Payouts
Report 18	2	No Sale Transactions
Report 19	2	Sign Off Transaction
Report 20	-	Cashier Profile

Breasts & Bones

Models who have protruding hipbones, ribs or other features that could deflect attention from a swimsuit or article of lingerie will not be selected....

On-Going Management (Cont.)

...if response is poor, consider adding lithium or switching the patient to another drug. Other antidepressants include: Tricyclics: amitriptyline (Elavil®); imipramine (Tofranil®); doxepin (Sinequan®) clomipramine (Anafranil®); haloperidol decanoate (Haldol LA®); benztropine mesylate (Cogentin®); trihexyphenidyl (Artane®); procyclidine (Kemadrin®); amantadine (Symmetrel®); benzodiazepines: flurazepam (Dalmane®); nitrazepam (Mogadan®); lorazepam (Ativan®); chlordiazepoxide (Librium®)....

*Net Detective: The easy way to find out anything
about anybody! www.net-detective.net*

Photographic flood lights shined down on a table set up before the camera. "Hand me those ice cubes," Photographer said, flitting back and forth, arranging the props, adjusting the lights as if he was the busiest fucking guy in the spinning world. If Q__ had brought her grenade, she knew, the fucker would find time to listen.

In her mind she could see it sleeping like a turtle in her ruck on the top shelf of her bedroom closet. *Your ordnance is your best friend, soldier.* Oh yeah, Q__ knew what a great attention-getter a grenade could be, a real clarifier of words, and she wished she had brought hers along so this fucker would stand still a minute and listen.

Instead, the Photographer hopped about with Q__ as his obedient pet, fetching whatever she was told. The ice cubes were made of glass. Phony.

"Real ones would melt under the lights," Photographer explained, taking them from her. He dropped them into a tall glass of cola on the table and then began spraying the glass with an atomizer to fake condensation. As he worked he said, "Yeah, I shot the models for those fur ads. But the one you're after wasn't one of them."

Ad in hand, Q__ looked down to her Mother in it.

"I remember the girls I shot real well," Photographer said, "One Vietnamese, and two whites, not this Italian, or Mexican, or whatever she is. Beautiful. Looks a little like my first ex." He hurried behind the camera. "She must have been added later. Or who knows?" he laughed, firing off in rapid succession a series of shots. "Maybe she dropped from heaven." The film advance whirred. "I'd show you the pictures I took if I had them, but Big Ad Agency makes its outside people turn over everything—all prints, negs—it's all their property." He glanced at the ad again. "I took my photos in a factory," he added, tapping the snowy mountains in the photo. "They must have switched faces when they changed the background. I'd talk to Big Ad Agency, if I were you."

"They're the ones who sent me here!"

Roses 2-for-1 Sale

Yeah, roses, B__ thought, roses would get V__ off his case. A rose by any other name…. He tried to remember how the quote ended.

"…**w**ould smell just as sweet," V__ said.

As would a rat, she thought, taking the roses, her heart sinking. Such a cliché. Such an expensive cliché. Out of the blue—another cliché. What was he hiding?

"Thank you," she added.

Two dozen roses and that's her reaction, B__ thought, like they were an old married couple taking each other for granted. Watching her stick them in a vase with no water, he couldn't help but think how going serial was as bad as being married. Worse. It had all of the bad things, all of the monogamy, and none of the low rent….

Catalogs for preassembled log cabins.

The Urban Farmer.... The slick catalogs that had begun to arrive since P__ started using the charge cards he heisted avalanched into his lap when he sat down before his coffee table. A pop-folk tune played from his laptop instead of the real folk music he used to rip and burn; a Navaho Dream Catcher from Famous Movie Actor's Western Wear catalog hung from the ceiling instead of the *Ojo de Dios* made by the wife of that Mexican at his old job. She'd made it for her husband—to watch over him at work, shredding old Kleenexes and Kotexes, he recalled wistfully. When P__ had been fired, Timo Sr. had given it to him. *Para suerte.* And for fighting management to keep the toilets clean. Now its shabby yarn lay buried beneath glossy models dressed like Cowgirls in a brochure for organically-fed steaks.

P__ cradled his head. What a burlesque of himself he'd become, he thought, the screen of his laptop alive with blondes blowing kisses and wagging their big asses from the fake porn site he'd set up to harvest charge card numbers, using the numbers themselves to buy junk like this CD, or mail-order steaks, instead of fighting the Man, as he had planned. Or even living off the grid: to read. To write a little poetry. To take up the didjeridoo....

He blew a mournful note from the didjeridoo he had also bought with a stolen credit card. To be or not to be.... Hard to believe, what with the way everyone went around parading their thinks, that there once was no such thing as a soliloquy, that Shakespeare had to invent it, and he wondered what he had become, straying as far as he had from the one thing he'd learned in college?—That the only honest man was a naked man.

Naked Man.

Looking out to the window across the courtyard, a sickening thought occurred to him. Had he also misjudged the dude who jumped rope naked? For weeks now, he'd been assuming that the naked rope jumping was an act of philosophy by an honest man, unafraid to exercise nude in the free air—like the ancient Athenians. But maybe the dude was just coming on to him?—or—a horrible thought came over P__: Could the guy just be spying on him? To narc? A Narc sent by the FBI to eavesdrop on his charge-card harvesting! He moved back into a shadow. How could he have been so stupid!—an FBI spy who spied naked, making himself invisible by becoming the most visible, that is, the least suspect, and not to look suspicious, P__ stepped out into full view, into the open window.

B. The Rio Pant has a clean, low waist. Hip-hugging leatherette or chamois in Vanilla (08), Next-to-Nothing Color™ (09) or Black (10). Imported. Sizes 2-16. 32" inseam. BM49-19 $159. Petite sizes 2-14. 29-1/2" inseam. BM49-20 $159.

Before I__ could turn on the lights in his own apartment, he saw that the apartment across the courtyard was lit up unusually bright.

Then the Hippie appeared in his window, his hair pulled back in a ponytail. He raised the laptop he'd been holding like a fig leaf—naked. He was naked.

As I__ got ready, as he began to jump rope naked, the Hippie casually sat before his computer and went about his day, working at his computer, also naked.

V ||||||||||||||||||||||||||||||||||||||||||||||||||||||||||||||||||||||||||||||||||||||||||||||||||||||||||||||||||||||||||||||||||

B ||||||||||||||||||||||||||||||||||||||||||||||||

A God's Eye View: Argus Oversight Specialists simultaneously monitor from a single "command center" hundreds of office cleaning crews, stock rooms, cashiers, customers, ticket booths, clerks, alleys and pedestrians scattered from coast to coast. Argus. We're Automating Surveillance.

The instant V__ got to work, she woke up her computer. Sure enough, there were a dozen e-mails from WonderBoy, sending her links to funny web sites, teasing answers to her e-mails, others telling her how cool she was.

She began clicking furiously on the Venus icon. "Open, damn it! Who are you!" The soft error tone that her computer made every time she clicked on the locked drive continued to beep long after she stopped clicking. She pulled a tissue from the box she kept at her workstation and blew her nose—hating the cliché of the hysterical woman she was becoming—wanting to just e-mail B__ the LUVBUG virus and be done with it. But the swarm of 1s and 0s she could imagine flying from the LUVBUG box as it opened within his hard-drive, spreading its woe and pestilence at the speed of light throughout his world, and hers, eating his software, years of his labor, his business—and them—would be irreversible, and playing Pandora gave her pause. She slid the small, black heart, the LUVBUG virus icon, back into its folder, a creepy thought coming to her: Was WonderBoy B__ himself? Could he be writing her those e-mails, flirting with her just to test her? Is that why he'd been so distant lately? Because she'd been answering those e-mails? Was that why he gave her those cornball roses?—out of guilt? For what? Because everything was fine? Or to make her think everything was fine so she wouldn't suspect he was going parallel behind her back? Or because he'd already cheated on her. Then felt bad about it. Or they meant nothing. Maybe he just liked flowers. Two dozen roses?—in cellophane that screamed drug-store gift aisle? Judas's kiss; Quixote's windmills; Deep Throat; Mona Lisa's smile; the fossil record—why could everything mean more than one thing? Or three or five hundred?.... Why did everything important have to stay just beyond sense?...

Her hand tightened on her mouse.

One last time she sent commands to his Venus of Photoshop drive, using his birthday, his phone numbers, and every other password she thought might be the key.

Nothing. The hard-drive had a real lock, as P__ had said, with a real, silver key. And looking at the icon—a woman without a face—she also knew that the only way to spin it would be for her to go there with her own actual body. And turn the key with her own actual hands.

The Back
Whether sitting, standing, or lying, arch the
back, holding the abdominal muscles firm, to
elongate the body and create a firmer outline....

"I'd like to report that my sex is being harassed."

I__ had gotten so used to seeing Cashier 00000501 as a collection of data that he had to work to get over the disorientation of seeing her in the flesh. Alive. Eyes shining, hair a black no monitor could match, flesh tones without raster. A work of Nature. Each breast a ripe pear, between which a tiny gold man was wrecked, crucified from a neck that had been caressed by?—lightly brushing hair, and hair heavy with a shower's wetness. Shoulders, tummy, knees: bone and flesh bearing the memory of exhaustion, and also goose-bumped suspense, her legs a wonder of utility and sensuousness. In black nylons. And a miniskirt, Ace-bandage tight, that made the Family Pharmacy smock she also wore into the habit of a corporate nunnery.

"Tell me about it," he said, switching on a tape recorder under his desk as she began what was obviously a prepared speech about Xavier Peterman, the Store Manager: how he kept pushing her to pose in her underwear so he could take pictures, how he had started by telling her that she had nice melons, that the cashiers at the last store he managed used to call him Sweet Peter, and Mr. XXX-cicle. In his office, he went weepy because someone was ruining his credit. He began calling her at home, telling her he could take care of her—in every way. In the break room he tempted her with promotions. Then he threatened to fire her, insisting that it was her choice and he kept threatening until finally she did it.

"What? Pose or?—" Something didn't sound right.

She began a dry cry. "Where else would I find a job with benefits?" I__ sat silent, an image of the middle-aged Manager and the Young Girl.... Then from nowhere, she continued, "Timo, my boyfriend is a technician in pharmacy. He's not a thief. He's just.... He's going to college. He wants to be a doctor but a gang in his hood, they make him steal for them. Every week he got to pay their toll to get home. When the manager found out, he said he'd have Timo arrested and kicked out of school if I wasn't a good girl. So I was. But it wasn't enough. I had to keep doing it or he'd tell Timo. Then, he wants a piece of the drug money too. So he sets it up so that Timo fills the 'prescriptions' of customers he sends him; I ring them up and he makes sure the records keep everyone clean."

"You were scrubbing the books right at the register?"

"It's all that motherfucker's fault. He made us do everything."

I__ leaned back, trying to figure out what didn't sound right. When he couldn't, he asked, "Will you wear a wire?"

National Identity Card, she snickered, Thy name is VISA.....

Hips & Hands
Hands can make your hips appear smaller if they are placed on the front of the thighs so that the arms obstruct their outer lines. The effect can be maximized if the elbows are held away from the body so that the indentation of the waist is accentuated.

Every night now, I__ skipped rope naked, lights on, while the Hippie worked at his computer naked, lights also on. He worked at his computer a lot. Was he a writer? A poet? What a difference from the way he used his computer, I__ thought, glancing over at his own computer monitoring the LAN actions of X__, the manager at Store #046616....

The unexamined life is not worth living.
—Socrates, and www.homecams.com, the site that lets you see inside 1,024 private homes....

By hacking through the Naked Rope Jumper's digital cable service, P__ was able to get into his computer and discover that the guy, Ignatius Riter, was always lurking on the Family Pharmacy company LAN. That is, as he had feared, his neighbor was an undercover FBI agent. He knew this because he'd managed to google up a document listing Ignatius's name among others leaving the FBI—a showpiece to let the guy go undercover no doubt—and now here he was, using classic FBI techniques and spy-ware to eavesdrop on X__, Xavier Peterman, the manager of Family Pharmacy and Foods, which meant he was really lying in wait to trap whoever it was that had ripped off Xavier's charge card. That is, him. Shit!

P__ pounded his fist on the table. Shit, shit, why had he ever started stealing charge cards! Keeping one eye on I__, the Pig, jumping rope naked across the courtyard, P__ quickly scanned his hard-drive, doing it sloppily since he could literally see that I__ was jumping rope instead of looking at his screen.

He couldn't find any mention of his own name on I__'s hard-drive, though, nor his address. Or even the numbers he had harvested, but it would only be a matter of time before they traced the charges on X__'s card to him. Or rather to the identity he had set up for himself on-line, and he sank back to think.

What to do, what to do.... He logged off. He closed his eyes to think soliloquy thoughts, blew into his didjeridoo, his bare skin sticking to the vinyl of his chair, naked, the agent jumping rope before him also naked, almost as in a mirror.... Mirrors facing mirrors that came back to him, as he sat there thinking, as a story his mother used to tell about a boy who caught a leprechaun. As per storybook rules, the leprechaun led the boy to the

P |||||||||||||||||||||||||||||||||||||||||||||||||||||||||||||||||||||||||||||||||||||||||||||||||||||||||||||||||||||||||||||||||||||||||||||||||

| |||||||||||||||||||||||||||||||||||||||||||||||||||||||||||||||||||||||||||||||||||||||||||||||||||||||||||||||||||||||||||||||||||||||||||||||||

spot where his pot of gold was buried, beneath the roots of a massive tree. The boy was thrilled, but the roots were tangled and hard as iron and he had no tools. So he tied his yellow kerchief around a branch of the tree to mark it, and made the leprechaun promise not to remove it. The leprechaun promised, solemnly, and on his life, and the boy excitedly ran off to get a shovel. When he returned, he discovered that, sure enough, the leprechaun had kept his promise. He had, however, also tied identical yellow kerchiefs around every tree in the forest, and P__ laughed, clapping his hands above his head for the way out he'd been shown. He did a naked dance in front of the window so the Cop could see. There may be laws against identity theft, but nothing said you couldn't give it away! Nothing said you couldn't put your identity out there on unsecured sites—a big fat golden name—Paxton Lowrance—that may as well have a sign on it, COME AND GET IT, BOYS! Then, after that chick at work sprung his LUVBUG virus.... A fresh start. A new world, clean slate—all he had to do was add a Trojan Horse to the virus and his I.D. would be inserted into every address book of every e-mail program in the e-universe. What better way could there be to disappear than to be everywhere all the time?

But was she going to spring the bug or not? Maybe WonderBoy should send VidChick one more e-mail, he thought firing up his laptop. With a photo of her boyfriend caught in the act to really piss her off....

Wearing a wire was pure theater, I__ knew. The tapes he made would never stand up in court. But he wasn't a cop anymore, this wasn't an arrest, and so he didn't have to worry about stuff like that. Besides, Employees were still somehow more moved by photos and other low-res cloud formations of their crimes than the hard-edged portraits that could be composed from ones and zeros.

He turned back to the fine-grained profiling program running on his laptop, tracing the Manager's movement through the store's data so elegantly that it was a thing of beauty. On the day of the sting, he would sit out in his car, using the wireless card in his laptop—and a remote audio hookup as well—to watch the Manager, to spring out and catch him, goods in hand, data fitting him like a plaster cast. Data was good, but nothing was as convincing as the goods themselves....

...iffy reading habits; iffy credit; complaints to OSHA; fired for stealing, the Case Profiler that Q__ was monitoring wouldn't even have to tie into the data banks of urine analysis to close this case.... The cursor slid Ouija-board smooth to a new field, the Case Profiler that she was monitoring using it in an office two floors down to compile data on a job Applicant, one P__, Paxton Lowrance, for Ever Ready Security. Along the bottom of the screen, a counter tracked keystrokes per minute as the woman applied various demographic sluicers, massaging data on 300,000 names.

The Subject's profile—P__'s profile—was blurry due to a scarcity of data, which seemed to say that the Profiler was slacking off so Q__ called up P__'s college files and saw that though he was applying for a programming job, he had majored in being poor: i.e., philosophy. His college transcripts had been altered to show that he also had a degree in computer program- ming, but he never seemed to have taken any classes in that subject. She skimmed a long list of books that he still owed fines on even though the college had turned his account over to a collection agency. Lots of programming books. And accounting books—enough to have taught himself?... And weird stuff from ex-commie countries—Dostoevsky, Kafka—countries that had recently become less secret but were still iffy. What was it he was applying for? She scrolled up to Position: Night Shift Programmer. Did their warehouses ever store explosives?

Sure enough, the Profiler that Q__ was shadowing typed, **Employer Information Services recommends that Applicant #349099, Paxton Lowrance, NOT be hired for the position of Night Shift Programmer because he distinctly matches the following profile: Malcontent.**

But instead of going on to the next case, she started to milk this one.

All right, Q__ thought, here's my chance, and as she waited to see how long her subordinate gold-bricked, she used the opportunity to open another window to do her own search, using the company's powerful databases and software to find the Digital Guy who had manipulated the photo of Mother. Someone named B__, Robert Barnes.

As she worked at merging databases, confirming first his name, Bob Barnes, then his address, then some accounts, her mind wandered back to a marketing class she'd had as a sophomore. Sales of televisions had been originally stunted, they'd learned, because people were afraid that the TVs could be used to watch them. The class had snickered at that naïveté. But she now smiled at their own, the bit stream that she was able to divert onto her screen from B__'s digital TV allowing her to create a pointillist portrait of him out of what, how and when he watched, the bookmarks in his silicon memory—some poker, lots of fashion shows—a gold mine of demographic information, his activity while surfing detailed enough to reconstruct even the movement of his eyes.

As a Sophomore, spying on someone so naked would have made her feel like a Creep. But B__'s home was her office after all, at least while his TV was on, and if he wasn't doing anything wrong, he had nothing to hide. A double-click and the ATM data she was able to call up for him placed dots on a map to represent each withdrawal. Then she made a map of his charge card use. Then by factoring in the time and date stamps, she was able to figure out his normal routes. Add in his spending, and she had a clear picture of his day-to-day life. Where he ate, shopped, how often he rented movies. Because he always paid his admission with his charge card, she could see that he often went to the same Art Museum she did, and even at the same time as she had once been there, she saw.

Q__ believed in meaningful details.

There were also a lot of charges for $13.13 at Family Pharmacy—the same pharmacy she'd been in when she discovered that first picture of Mother. But oddly, his card also showed charges for $113.13—always just a few seconds later, to an on-line merchant. How was he able to be in two locations at the same time, she wondered?...

The screen of the profiler she was monitoring came alive again: alphanumerics filling her screen with the herky-jerky rhythm of a human typist. Apparently she'd found another Paxton Lowrance who seemed to match the same description as the first. Only this one lived in Nome, Alaska. Then a third appeared—in New Delhi. The screen began to proliferate with Paxton Lowrances, the search program finding so many using the same social security number that they seemed to be replicating themselves—like bacteria in a Petri dish, replicating themselves faster than could be recorded....

U ''

X ''

On This Date 1951— The Miracle of Television: Viewers from coast to coast are amazed at the God's-eye view offered by the first national broadcast—See It Now—bringing together on one screen both the Atlantic and Pacific Oceans. Live!

Static, then the wet suck of sex....

X__ was setting up the video camera he would use to capture U__'s sweet ass on film when his scanner crackled to life. The scanner was under an *Intimate Apparel* catalog, and the catalog was open to Without-a-Trace panties. He'd begun using a scanner because of the thrill of saying "Without-a-Trace panties" to the female operators who took catalog orders, the models themselves manning the phones, he always imagined. Then, during one of these dates, he discovered that he could use his cordless phone to eavesdrop on neighbors. Then he got a scanner so he could zero in on active cell phones.

Now, the antenna he had strung across the ceiling of his office to improve reception was picking up someone: *Moans became squishing, crosstalk, multiple connections...*

Rushing to turn up the volume, he nearly knocked over his camera, the sucking continuing even as a fourth voice moaned his name: "O Xavier, do me!"—

On This Date 1999—Echelon goes on line to monitor all phone, fax and e-mail transmissions worldwide and sort them by keyword and voice print.

L. Essential Silk Skirt. European Fit with classic silhouette. Hidden zip. Bone buttons. Fully lined. Import. 2-14, Petite 0-10 (22-1/4") 84480A $159.99

For quality control and training purposes, your call may be recorded.

01 10101 01001 01 01010 1011110 101101111110 11010 101010 111100101 010 1010.... UPC codes streamed through bundled wires, transforming the slow procession of granola, goat cheese and other groceries on the conveyor belt into multiple packets of information, their prices adding as on an abacus run at the speed of light, generating a personalized coupon for X__, collating the purchases into a profile of X__, reporting X__'s name back to a cat-food manufacturer, adding X__'s name to a mailing list for the health conscious—but then, as cupcakes broke the web of laser beams, taking it off again—and setting a marker that would also drop from inventory the organic apples P__ was buying with X__'s charge card because they were too far off the great bulge in the bell curve of volume.

Why had the store stopped carrying organic apples? he wondered. Then he shrugged. After V__ sprung his virus, he'd be shopping at a different store anyway. He'd just drift away like smoke; with so many people using his identity by then, who would notice if one of its users just vanished?— Maybe he'd be a beach bum in his next life, a hermit crab taking up residence in another ID....

News Leak!

*Political fallout continues over a reported CIA plan to remove rebel
General Savimbi by programming a cruise missile to home in on
and follow the transmission of a conversation as it travels from a
communications satellite to his cell phone. The report detailed
how the missile would destroy him in his palace as he used his cell
phone to order a pizza, a regular Saturday night habit of the general....*

I__ skipped rope, adrenaline kicking in— Tomorrow it would all go down, Manager, Cashier, Pharmacy Technician. He'd even coordinated with the Police so they could grab their most regular Customer—that guy wearing a DigiDreams baseball cap in so many of the surveillance videos, making his buy with N__.

I__ picked up the pace of his jumping.

Where was his Neighbor today, he wondered. Instead of working at his computer naked as had become the Hippie's routine, the widow across the courtyard was empty. The guy's whole apartment looked empty. I__ couldn't remember what he'd been able to see, but there had been something: Indian dream catchers, family photos, something other than the bare wall he could now see through the curtainless window.

> *On This Date 1996—Jenny Ringley, a junior at Dickenson
> College in Pennsylvania, sets up the Jenny-Cam, a camera
> that allows anyone to see into her dorm room 24 hours a
> day, whether she is doing homework, making out, not there,
> talking on the phone, taking a shower....*

www.jennicam.com

Dressed to kill, U__ thought, checking herself out in the reflection of the subway window: tiki-tank with double-skinny straps, waxed midriff glistening between it and her green satin micro with its Chinese dragon pattern, her legs in black slim-tech leotards. Definitely dressed to kill, the way she felt watching her features morph into the face of another, wanting to find the Svengali who had actually made the changes—meeting him face-to-face and asking him Why, and Why her?—

The Family Pharmacy audition she had was only a block from DigiDreams. After it, she had told herself, taking a deep breath, she'd just drop in on the little prick. Pay him a visit, tell him to lay off her face. And the rest of her bod too. The thought of it, the anticipation of the confrontation gave U__ goose flesh, her life suddenly having all the twists of an action movie. Or at least a roller coaster—

The subway car screeched as it rounded a bend in the tracks and she checked the contents of her micro-purse, packed as it was whenever she traveled light expecting action: lipstick; condom, in case; cab fare, in case; and now her designer derringer, just in case. She wasn't stupid. How could she not be suspicious about the man who was obsessing her body, his hand visible in the slant he gave her eyes, his taste embedded in the outline he gave her thighs, her shoulders his opinion, as were all the strokes that made up "her" in the photos seen by everyone not her?

***B**ack in 15 minutes*, said the note taped to the door of DigiDreams, and V__ wondered how long ago her boyfriend had left it. He must be around, but if she worked fast she could be in and out before he even knew she'd

V ||
B ||

been. She slipped the key to his studio into its lock, a rush making her fingers nimble. But V__'s heart sank the moment she opened the door.

She had known it would be a warehouse of beautiful chicks, hundreds of women, a harem vast enough to rubber Ali Baba's imagination: the virtual concubines B__ helped pimp to consumers through products that carried their smiles, their legs, their asses....

She had hoped there would be millions of their photos, billions, his attention so dissipated in their numbers that the presence of any one would be nil. This wasn't the first time she'd been here. Instead, a series of big cibachrome prints dominated the studio, expensive high-definition prints on aluminum, and all of a single woman: the woman he'd cropped for his Venus of Photoshop icon. She could tell it was her from the shape of her waist. After staring at that waist and the stud in its navel during all the hours she'd spent trying to hack his hard-drive, she could pick it out of a police lineup. Except the woman was complete here: her and her collagen-pumped lips, ski-slope tits and flawless face spaced along the walls and luminous as stained glass windows in a church.

V__ walked down a row of them, passing between the metal flatfiles used to store art work. Looking up at the prints of the Model looking down at her, she felt like an unbeliever in another's temple: a temple to a single goddess that her boyfriend had constructed.

Who was she? V__ wondered, comparing the model's wisp of a frame and her own bow-flexed bod. And why? Though the woman in the posters was posed in a variety of the poses fashion Models struck, there weren't any products or logos in the ads. She didn't even seem to be modeling what little clothing she wore. Instead, the photos all seemed to be about her.

Her as a world-weary Vessel, cigarette smoke curling from a nostril; her as twins, walking away arm in arm, both looking back demurely as though having caught an onlooker admiring them from behind; the real subject being her perfect heart-shape rump, the symmetry of her legs stretched out in another poster, her large *anime* eyes, the smoothness of an inner thigh ending in shadow....

B__'s computer was there, and V__ went immediately to its silver key. It hung unprotected from its front so exactly as she had imagined that she began to feel as if she were slipping into one of her own dreams. "Do what you came for," she sighed, knowing what she would find.

When she switched on the computer's powerstrip, the light table behind her also flickered to life. On it were large-format, color slides that some photographer had shot of the same Model: looking sultry into the camera, whirling like a dervish.... But the Model in the slides wasn't exactly like the woman in the posters. Looking closer, V__ could see that the eyes weren't quite as *anime*. Her skin was far lighter. Almost ivory. Her limbs weren't as muscular, and it occurred to her that the woman in the posters was a digital remake of the woman in the slides—or was it the other way around? She placed her palms on the light table and leaned in for a closer look....

> *On-Going Management (Cont.)*
>
> *...chlorpromazine (Largactil®); fluphenazine decanoate (Modecate®); pipotiazine (Piportil L4®).... However, impatient prescribing habits and polypharmacy should be minimized by trying to prescribe only one neuroleptic at a time....*

Q ....

V ....

B ....

DigiDreams. Q__ stood outside the office looking at the lettering airbrushed onto its glass in a way that made the words look like clouds that were evaporating into pixels. The door was open a crack—

Clutching her grenade in the cargo pocket of her army jacket, she used her free hand to silently push open the door.

Dust floated in the light of the studio, then—Huge photos of Mother looked down from every wall and Q__ bit her tongue to keep it in. The photo of Mother wearing fur on a snowy mountain was there. And there were also photos of her that Q__ had never seen—six, maybe ten Mothers....

But Q__'s heart raced when she saw Mother—in the flesh—standing with her back to her at the far end of the room exactly as she'd been the last time Q__ had seen her standing at the kitchen sink, back to her, leaning against her palms, elbows locked for support, her head hanging with the disappointment Q__ had brought on by joining the army. Only this time, instead of steam from the dishes she'd been washing, a bright white light was rising up from the sink, washing over her with its purity to make Q__ understand.

"I won't let you down this time, Mother."

V__ turned from the light table just in time to see a flash of someone dart away from the doorway—who? The bitch B__ was sleeping with?—who else would run away? She hurried around the flatfiles, her clogs clopping like hooves across the old wooden floor of the studio. At the stairwell, she leaned over the banister trying to catch a look at whoever it was that was streaking down the stairs.

Another flash—a glimpse of a hand on the railing, then an army-green sleeve—

"Hey!" she yelled. It was B__'s Bitch!— Why else would she run? "Hey! I'm talkin' to you!" V__ shouted, wishing she had worn her gym shoes.

From the bottom of the stairs there came a sudden burst of light and street noise—the Bitch had flown out the front door.

By the time V__ got out to the street she was gone. A warning horn beeped, a delivery truck backing up to a dock, people going about their day. Miraculously, a cab appeared. V__ jumped into the street to stop it and it was actually vacant. Getting in, she told the driver—a Sikh in a turban—to go around the block in ever-widening circles, as she'd learned to do from that detective movie.

As B__ entered Family Food & Pharmacy, he wondered if he should have written on that note Back in 20 instead of 15 minutes. Maybe he could get T__, the Candy Man, to let him cut ahead of the old geezers and crazies who always seemed to be lined up in the pharmacy for their meds.

"Stop!" V__ yelled at the cabbie. For ten minutes they'd been going up, across, and down the streets, tracing ever larger rectangles with V__'s head on a swivel, looking out this side of the cab, then that, trying to spot the Bitch. Then there she was!—a woman in an army jacket disappearing into a store—Family Pharmacy—and before the cab even jerked to a halt, V__ was throwing some money at the driver, and hurrying out after her.

．

U__ looked up at the sign: Family Pharmacy. It was a little weird that a casting director would have the girls show up at the location itself, but not as weird as the time they wanted her to straddle a surveillance camera while wearing a bikini made out of a police uniform. She looked down the street toward where the Digital Vampire's studio must be, took a deep breath and went in, wanting to get it on, get it over, so afterwards she could go get the vampire. Drive a stake through his heart before she lost her nerve.

She checked her image in the big surveillance monitor at the entrance, then went up to the cashier. "Excuse me," she said, "I'm here for the interviews."

"You want a job *here*?" the cashier said. *NINA* according to her name tag, dark, mascaraed eyes giving her the up-and-down-and-all-around.

"Yeah. I was told to speak to the manager."

"Oh, him," she said as though that explained everything. She motioned with her head. "His office is back by pharmacy."

What's with her? U__ wondered, making her way down an aisle of greeting cards, then shampoo, then feminine hygiene products.... She paused. There, on a rack, were boxes of condoms printed with her picture, her doctored picture, with her posed as the female half of a romantically perfect couple. *Freedom Condoms, Made with American Pride in Thailand to Family Pharmacy Standards.*

Seeing her doctored image, repeated on box after box, was like seeing herself through the eyes of a fly, or in a funhouse mirror.

B__ left the pharmacy counter after T__, the Pharmacy Technician, fixed him up with his usual ten tabs of Vicodin. He had turned up the personal hygiene aisle and was headed for N__'s register when he saw her: the Model whose face he had studied for hundreds of hours, the model who had turned him into Pygmalion, altering her eyes, her skin color—her..... She was standing right there. In the flesh. Heart pounding, he went up to her. "Excuse me," he said, and she jumped, startled, dropping the box she'd been scrutinizing.

"Oh, I'm sorry," he said, stooping with her to pick it up for her. "I didn't mean to startle you, but aren't you a model?"

In the manager's office, peering out through the store's one-way mirror, X__ couldn't believe his luck. Not only had the Model showed up, she paused right there, right in front on him, right at the condom display. When that guy startled her, she'd dropped the box, bending over to get it, and giving him a perfect shot of her tight little ass—the perfect angle he'd need to insert her into the doggie-style mode—the perfect opening to the porno movie she'd be his star in. He had to suck back his saliva. "Oh yeah, baby, that's the money shot...." Operating the video camera he'd set up on his side of the one-way mirror, he zoomed back out as she stood erect, breaking into that big gash of a Model's grin.

"Oh, yeah baby, that's the money shot," came over I__'s earpiece, tuned to the bug he'd planted in the Manager's office. Who was he talking to? I__ wondered, sitting in his van just outside the store. He checked his laptop running a live feed of the activity at N__'s cash register and it showed she was still logged on, still doing business, so it wasn't her....

P ···

Q ···

I ···

U ··

V ···

B ···

X ···

T ···

N ···

Sitting before his computer monitor at work, P__ tapped into the computer of his neighbor, the Cop who jumped rope naked; the guy was logged into the Family Pharmacy network via his wireless connection, lying in ambush at the very cash register P__ had used X__'s card on. But he obviously wasn't on to him yet, and the extra time this gave P__ would be a big help. Relieved, P__ continued to watch I__ track the cashier to make sure he really was tracking her data and not acting like a decoy. **Nina**, was her name according to the screen. **Nina Martinez**, a.k.a. **Cashier #00000501**....

V__ peered through a hole formed by the merchandise on the shelf, unable to believe what she was seeing in the next aisle: her boyfriend B__, red-handed—there with the Bitch, the Model, sharing a joke. And they were buying rubbers!

Q__ emerged from the washroom, trying to get herself together as she headed toward the pharmacy. All she needed was her meds—her meds would iron her out, silence the voices, put the whole day back into perspective. The woman she saw couldn't have been Mother, she knew. As her Shrink had tried to tell her, the world didn't revolve around her or any "I." Closing the distance to the Pharmacy, though, she could see a man in a suit about to speak to a Pharmacy Technician in white lab coat who seemed deaf, standing motionless at his station behind the counter, looking heavenward as though transfixed by a vision, and when she followed his line of sight to see what he was staring at something within her withered. There, in the bowed security mirror of the store, was Mother posed in the center of a group of people exactly as the Amber Princess in that Old Master

painting—a scene that Q__ knew wouldn't exist if she hadn't stumbled
upon it just at that moment, that couldn't exist without someone like
her to put together its pieces: a moment frozen in time like a snapshot
of poses and expressions, a woman at the center of the bowed security mirror who was being offered a box she was not looking at; the man
holding the box with a look of reverence; a Pharmacy Technician about
to be told something by someone to whom he was not listening; another
hidden woman spying through a gap in the merchandise at those in the
next aisle; Q__'s own reflection in the disk of the security mirror—her
face as enigmatic as the girl's and reflected again by the one-way mirror
that ran along the wall—mirrors facing mirrors—like a fun house of the
wider world around diminishing with each reflection till she could fit in
her own mind's eye and as though her life flashed before her eyes she
was chilled by the realization that she had seen her Mother and the girl
and the girl and her Mother were her—within her—and her very body
ached as though it would burst, as though bursting was the only way she
could get them out....

Then the moment broke and everyone began to move along their own
trajectories again. The man in the suit broke the Pharmacy Technician's
gaze by shoving a badge of some kind before him; the Spying Woman
turned, ran away wiping back a tear; the Man who'd been handing Mother
a box was also giving her a pen so she could autograph it; and Mother,
or at least the woman who had been Mother in the moment, broke into
a wide grin as Q__ turned away. Oh yes, it—she—had been Mother,
she saw. More clearly than she had ever seen anything else. Maybe she
wasn't Mother right now, or the girl, but at that moment she had been. Of
that Q__ was certain for even though Q__ had run from that studio, even

though she had run as hard and as long as her breath allowed, Mother had somehow managed to appear right behind, calm in high heels, not even breaking a sweat.

Blood. Q__ saw that there was blood on her palm as she turned away. She'd been gripping her prescription so hard that the staples in its receipt had cut into her palm and she knew this was the final sign. A blood omen. The world snapping into a clarity it had never had before, she double-timed it up the aisle, knowing what she must do, the grenade heavy with significance in her pocket.

On-Going Management (cont.)
If the patient's symptoms become worse, or the patient becomes actively suicidal, Electro-Convulsive Therapy (ECT) should be considered.

> *On This Date 1826—James Fenimore Cooper publishes*
> The Last of the Mohicans *under the name "A Gentleman*
> *from New York" because it would have been vulgar for*
> *his family's name to appear in the news.*

"**We**'re ready to go," an undercover Narc told I__. "You want us to take along these two as well?"

The Cashier, N__, and Pharmacy Technician, T__, cowered on the couch of the Manager's office like the two scared kids that they were. Let them sweat a minute, I__ thought. Let them shit a brick. A squad car outside held X__, the Manager—probably still screaming that he had been set up, that the little Gold Digger had caught him filming Customers and tried to blackmail him, and when he wouldn't give in she said she'd get him. I__ looked at the video camera, set up to peer out the one-way mirror onto the store, equipment and scanners and catalogs that made the story plausible. But I__ knew better. He had them on tape.

"I'll take care of them," he said at last and the Pharmacy Technician, T__, went limp, whispering, "Thank you, thank you...."

"Suit yourself," the Narc said. "If you have a change of heart, you know where to find us," and he waved a good-bye salute.

The kid buried his face in his hands but the girl, N__, sat upright, blinking back, expectant, as if it could have gone no other way.

Finally alone with them, I__ allowed himself the satisfaction of the moment's taut minimalist logic: bare office, metal office desk, single video monitor on the desk. And the Rabbit. Outside, bell-clear skies; inside, clammy palms and the buzz of fluorescent lighting. He took a breath, then began: "There is something that people have that no one can take away. A gang can beat you up, steal your money. But even if they kill you, they can't take away this one thing." He paused for effect. No reaction from the girl. "But you can give it away. You can give it away because that one thing is your self. Sometimes when we're young it's easy to make a mistake. You might want to do something later in your life, though, like go to med school—"

"I do!" T__ interrupted. "How did you?—" Recognition sobering his features, he turned to his girlfriend. She took his hand—patted it the way an older sister might quiet a child.

"Well," said I__, "a conviction for stealing drugs would ruin that forever." Looking at the girl now, he continued. "We do what we think is right at the time, but later we see that it's very wrong. An older guy comes along, he says he'll pay you a lot of money if you just let him take some pictures of you in a hotel room...." Then he dropped a name the Manager had sworn by, "Like The Paradise—"

The boy's head snapped toward his girlfriend. "You never went to The Paradise," he said, some bigger story flashing between them.

"Yeah," the Cashier protested, following another's lead for the first time, that high-strung tone that said, You ain't got nuthin' on me, Copper, creeping into her voice.

For her benefit, I__ arched an eyebrow as if she'd just claimed that the earth was flat. He wanted to tell her of corpses, back in the FBI, with bruises on the backs of their hands that told how they had given their last trying to shield a face from blows; he wanted to tell her how even a field mouse bends the grass; how a person walking down a sidewalk leaves infrared hot spots; how e-mail could be recovered from a hard-drive that had been totally erased....

Instead, he began a slow show of stacking blank videocassettes on the desk as he did whenever he didn't have any evidence. Often, just the sight of cassettes was enough to make the guilty ones confess—the ones, at least, who were basically good. Or at least still had a conscience, even if in a way, those tapes were their conscience.

As he suspected, the Cashier was basically a good kid. When he switched on the monitor, she fell silent and remained mute as a saint, eyes transfixed in its blue glow. "There's nothing you can do that doesn't leave a trace of some kind," I__ continued, "and the memory of data banks is long, unforgiving, and worldwide. Wherever you go, whatever you do, no matter what you say, your digital shadow will always be there and believe me, not even philosophers can jump over their shadows."

Turning away from his girlfriend, the boy mumbled, "I guess that makes us all deep thinkers."

Since sending the LUVBUG virus to her Ex-boyfriend, V__ had moved through her daily routine with the numbness of sleepwalking.

Playground Mayhem—More at Ten!

The words sat leadenly on her computer screen. Of all the days that a story this big had to break, this one had to break on the day she was a zombie. She dragged herself through files of clip art, struggling to come up with a catchy graphic to go with what was bound to be the lead story of every station in the country.

Cracked brain? Voice of God? The Devil?... Nothing seemed right, though by now Designers like her at other stations had spun off galaxies of variations, she knew, stockpiling tag graphics for the follow-ups and teasers that would be used to churn the story in the weeks ahead—What a ratings booster—what with Crisis Managers, and Parents of the Dead, and Parents of the Kids Who Survived, and Teachers, and of course the Dead Kids themselves—yearbook photos—and the Crazy who walked into the middle of a crowded playground and pulled the pin on a hand grenade. How to depict it? How could it happen? How? A chemical imbalance? Dr.

Freud? Wicked Witch of the West? Not everything made sense, and when she gave up trying to concentrate, she decided to recycle a graphic she'd designed for the last war—a heart seen through crosshairs—and set to altering it so it would look new. But the sight of it kept choking her up. Stupid, how much the cliché of a cartoon heart got to her. An empty symbol, like the drunken Cupids on the paper cups used at the last office party. Just a picture on her screen. And what was that?—dots that blur together to form a picture, an arrangement of pixels that was itself the result of a program that was a chain of subroutines—IF<>THEN—macros that were clusters of codes that were bytes of machine language, words of 1s and 0s that could be anything—what could be more abstract that that?—

Click. Cut. Paste. She dragged her cursor in a languid slicing motion. Not all dots were meant to connect.

And yet, when these nothings were put in the right pattern, they could be more real than bricks, porn, or a bank account—love poems that set in motion hormones, or launch sequences more deadly than the digital leprosy she imagined eroding the virtual bodies of his digital women, music files, billing, his labyrinth tumbling down into itself like a house of cards, Kings and Queens and Jokers, that image she had in her head of B__ buying rubbers with that Model, the same woman he was making out with in the photo WonderBoy sent her. Just as P__ had warned her. Wherever he was. Since she'd sent the virus into the world, he hadn't been to work. And when she called his apartment, a recording told her to leave a message after a tone that never followed.

Shadows long in a late summer sun, I__ practically skipped home, happy over how well everything had gone. As a lagniappe, they'd even got one of the buyers, that regular customer in a DigiDreams baseball cap who was in so many of the store's surveillance tapes, nabbing him at N__'s cash register even though the Narc jumped the gun, taking the Pharmacy Technician into custody before I__'s signal. But that's okay. *You don't always catch what you want*, went the words to one song.... But sometimes you do.

A wind shivered the trees that lined his street and he buttoned his collar. A futile gesture. But that was okay too. A time for all seasons, autumn coming so gradually, if relentlessly, that a lot of people wouldn't even notice until some trees were bare.

As he entered the courtyard of his building, a new surveillance camera stared down at him and he couldn't help but smile. One of the reasons his Ex had left him was because he kept bringing the office home. But she would have been proud of the way he gave those two kids a second chance today, letting them resign.

Like the eyes in a painting, the gaze of the camera seemed to follow him as he came up the walk. It was installed because there'd been a rape in the courtyard a few months back, he knew, and it made him wonder why he had been so uptight about not caring he was being watched. Why had his Ex been so uptight about him not being able to shut off his watching others? After all, this place, this courtyard, was his home too, wasn't it? And if people weren't doing anything wrong, what did they have to hide?

The micro lines of the camera looked absolutely millennial against the ponderous Victorian limestone and iron work of the rest of the building. A Hitachi C-U 24X. The same kind of camera that was used outside banks, and over the drive-up lanes of Fast-Food Restaurant, aimed at customers as they ordered their burgers; it had a wider field of vision than the cameras they used in Family Pharmacy, mounted so that a customer's video double was the first thing that greeted him or her as they entered— unlike the dummy cameras that simply gave the appearance of watching. Its optics were coated: When the courtyard was bare in winter, the brightness of snow wouldn't white everything out; with 0.3 lux illumination, its circuitry would be hot enough to see by the sodium-vapor lights that flooded the courtyard at night; its weather-proof housing would allow it to operate in rain or summer's heat as reliably as those indoor cousins that watched people shop in the weatherless weather of malls; or work in factories, or play in parks, in hospitals monitoring newborn infants or those dying under observation....

Anyway, I__ thought, only a schizo could be one person at work and another at home.

Then he was before the doorway that led to his Neighbor's apartment.

While looking up at the camera, he had taken the path that led to the apartments directly across from his own. Realizing that he was before his Neighbor's vestibule, an urge came over him to get his name—the Hippie's name—from his mailbox.... Why hadn't he done it before?

He pulled open the door, heavy with leaded glass, and a motion sensor switched on a light inside the vestibule. Rows of locked mailboxes gleamed, burnished by generations of fingers. A matrix in brick and brass. Third floor, middle apartment.... But the space reserved for a name below the mailbox was blank. Had he moved out? Is that why he hadn't seen him lately? A finger push and the doorbell would ring upstairs. Should he check and see?—surprise him? If a computer virus that was spreading around the globe hadn't crashed the server at work I__ would still be there finishing up reports instead of coming home so early. Surprise or not, maybe he should ring the bell and introduce himself. In a way, I__ realized, he had his Neighbor to thank for making him see that he wasn't nuts. When he remembered how preoccupied he'd been with his own apathy about being watched it was like remembering another person: a nail-biter who had pined to regress to a life behind closed doors even though closed doors had become as quaint as the skirts Victorians once used to hide the legs of chairs.

It wasn't that there was something sneaky about what he did; rather everyone just did what they did in front of his eyes, in front of everyone's eyes. May as well curse the sun for making all grass grow.

I__ stood there a long time. If he spoke to the Hippie face-to-face, he knew, it would be harder to go home to his workout. And yet how could he not be curious about the man who watched him exercise naked? He drummed his fingers on the heavy outer door. Courtyard before, mail-boxes behind. Was it just as well?

The building he stood in with its dark oak moldings, its doors hiding other doors, was built in another century. It was only much later, and gradu-ally, that Tenants had lost their taste for heavy drapery. That the privacy hedges had been cropped to improve visibility from the street. That the night of the courtyard had been turned into halogen day....

He pushed into the open air. From where he stood he could see that the shades were up in not just his apartment, but in lots of apartments. A wall of windows. Through them he thought he heard that mournful, aboriginal *wa-waaa*—someone playing the didjeridoo that he often heard in the evenings. But as the noise grew louder, he realized it was just the wailing of a couple having an argument in one of the apartments. Or maybe it was that poor slob on the *Real Cops on TV*? *"...reports live from the scene of the bombing...."* The flicker of two or three other TVs played more momentous moments, no doubt: ex-commies pouring onto the techno-color side of the Berlin Wall. And smaller moments: secrets of marital affairs blooming across the electronic skies of talk shows, Masturbators, the Overweight, Adulterers, the Lonely, the Angry, the Happy, the Sad and other Plain Folks calling in from home, all of them going about their lives while he.... Cured, a Shrink might say, if being normal only meant acting like your Neighbors, and he took a step toward them. Home. For the first time in months he felt at home.

His shadow rose up to meet him, clinging to each step with a fierce, animal tenacity though it was now being cast by the light that had switched on automatically as he approached.

As U__ shivered, waiting to pose in beach wear, she looked at her shadow cast on the fake beach spread over the studio floor, her shadow and the shadows of the others around her—like ghosts of themselves—moving in and out of each other: the gay Male Models fussing with their hair, the other Girls yakking about *Slasher Movie II*, yet another Stylist, Photographer, yet another Client.... Everything back to normal. So why did she feel so weird? So restless? Was it because this was the anniversary of that weird day at Family Pharmacy, she wondered. The date was easy to remember since that was also the day that that Nut set off a grenade on a playground. But even without the anniversary, she thought of that day a lot: that Guy asking her to autograph a box of condoms that featured her picture; then the Manager she was supposed to see about a modeling job being led away by police. Afterwards, after that weirdness, she'd gone to DigiDreams to kill the vampire as she'd planned. *Back in 15 Minutes*, said a note on the door. But he never showed. Even though she'd waited for over an hour. He was never there any of the other times she tried to ambush him either. Wouldn't answer his phone—as though he'd just vanished. A ghost. Then the janitor of his building told her the guy had been busted; a virus wiped out all his client files—and him without insurance. Then the police showed up with a search warrant and found a small bag of stolen pills, a judge sentencing him to rehab.... "I always thought the place should have been named DruggieDreams," the Janitor had laughed.

It was about that time that she got her body back—that is, since that day the ads she posed for showed photos of her as she was, her face, her eye shape, her skin tone, not those digitally manipulated ones. Still, she couldn't shake the creepy sensation that the ghosts were still watching her, seeing her from somewhere unknown, mainly because of something weird that happened that day in Family Pharmacy. She hadn't thought about it at the time, but afterwards, she realized that the guy who had asked for her autograph said he recognized her from the box. But she didn't look anything like her picture on the box because that picture had been doctored to make her look more ethnicky.

DigiDreams.... Something wasn't right, but she couldn't put her finger on it. And after she got her body back, after she'd stopped caring, she found herself shrugging, like now, when the thought came to her. She could make a thousand stories from the same details, she realized. Like

Scheherazade, why not? Maybe a million. As could any I. or X. or Y. or Z., standing on a beach, or in a field, or an abandoned factory, daydreaming a movie to inhabit while she waits to pose. That is, while she waits to play the role of "a woman who just spoiled her own surprise party" or "a pouty girlfriend" or just the girl she once imagined she had been, flashlight in hand, night all around, trying to see constellations by comparing the connected dots on a chart to a sky full of unconnected stars so that seeing the patterns, mentally drawing lines between the Alphas and Omegas that the chart said to link was more a matter of not seeing than seeing, of ignoring patterns that the makers of charts didn't know were there in order to believe that their Scorpions and Dragons were outside and not just within. Why make yourself crazy? Especially since she'd gotten her bod back.

She looked down to that body and smiled. The stud she had used to pin her bellybutton to herself so long ago was still there, its gold glint piercing her skin, comforting her with the fact that there was always herself, always her body. No matter how it was photographed or digitally manipulated, she knew, her self had kept company with her body. And always will.

Chapter 5

In a Beginning

The neck of a mouse is easier to snap than a pencil, Mary had said. Hundreds of necks later, it was the ease of the words that most bothered Paul. He laid the mouse stomach-down on the lab bench, whiskers twitching, the mouse curious about what its nose was against, though of course, oblivious to the big picture descending from above. Like all of us, Paul thought, wishing he hadn't been so quick to tell Mary he'd help her make an embryo.

He stroked the mouse for a five count, the time one study said was necessary to calm small animals enough to prevent fear's adrenaline rush from skewing the hormone measurements he'd later take. Then he held the rod he used against the base of its skull, close to the C1 vertebrae line as Mary had taught him, twining its tail around a finger. A hard yank and the mouse twitched, dead.

After "Hello," how to euthanize a mouse was the first thing Mary had said to him. It was the reason they'd been introduced, so that first impression partly explained why he remembered her voice so clearly, her tone casual, familiar, the same way she'd later say, "Hey, I borrowed a cigarette from your pack." The same way she'd later ask to use his semen.

Still, waving away the fog of sublimating dry ice he used to make the mice docile, he knew he didn't need Mary to see how anything could become familiar. Even invisible. Once, Dr. Woo had gone off at him for allowing a batch of mice to die. The carpenter who rented space below Paul and Mary's loft had called to complain that water was leaking from his ceiling and Paul had biked over to shut off a faucet, he'd thought. When he got there, though, he found steam billowing from that radiator that never worked right. It streaked windows and six months of art that Mary had been making for an upcoming show—he couldn't just leave—and by the time he got back, Dr. Woo, the Primary Researcher on most of the studies Paul pulled, was angrily incinerating the mice, along with the now-useless data that they carried in their cells.

The board that policed the treatment of lab animals could have made trouble. And as Paul signed a paper stating that he understood the protocol for harvesting livers, or hearts, or bone marrow, or whatever material a study called for, he knew not to say what he was thinking—that there were plenty more where they came from. Even so, working with so many mice it was hard not to know what he knew as he lifted the next by its tail: that there would always be more. Its white body emerged from the cold fog like a Popsicle from one of those carts Mexican vendors pushed around his parents' old neighborhood.

Laying the mouse down, Paul let his mind wander as he often did while he worked, putting the bar behind its skull, yanking its tail, getting into a zone like a basketball player finding his rhythm, he imagined, lifting another mouse, calming it—three, four, five— yank; grab the tail and yank; grab the tail and yank; three, four, five, yank; grab the tail and yank; grab the tail and yank, in one fluid motion yank, hard enough to jerk the spine from the base of the skull, yanking hard enough to kill instantly, but not so hard as to break skin, a touch thing, like shooting a basketball, grab the tail and yank, till an hour later, when he was going good, there'd be a pile of white bodies in the basin of the stainless-steel sink, his trigger finger sore from the yanking.

Everyone was shaped by their world, at least a little, he knew, pinching a flap of skin in one mouse's stomach. Still, though he'd been a premed major and never bothered by the dissecting, the killing always got a reaction from him. Holding the soft underbelly of the dead mouse between thumb and forefinger, he snipped it open with surgical scissors. Not a big reaction; but a little one, like anyone might get when it was their turn to gas the used rats, or do anything unpleasant. Two more snips and the liver was free from the purse he had made of the body. But with her, an artist who only majored in bio because her parents wouldn't pay for an art degree, bodies were something so not to flinch over that it was weird, her words not spoken in a tone that could be called matter-of-fact, or clinical, or even cold. No, she was on a curve so far ahead that he couldn't even see what direction she was going, though he knew that if he could, it would explain a lot.....

It was the delicacy of her bones that most unnerved Saroush. He sat beside the couch his daughter Fatima lay on, worrying her tiny knuckles as if they were prayer beads. "Ye faithful, have you not considered how Allah dealt with the Army of the Elephant," he repeated upon each, praying the surah that told how in the Prophet's time, Allah had defeated the invaders' elephants by sending a swarm of birds to drop stones on them. But the frailty of Fatima's rib cage made a mockery of words, even sacred ones.

Across the room, Saroush's mother prostrated herself below them—

—a tapestry of God's writing, woven like It into an endlessly repeating pattern that Saroush wished he could lose himself in as she did, as he once had. But it was too soon since his vigil in the hospital, endlessly tracing over the words for Wafta, his wife. The relatives of other patients had been there also. They spoke with the confidence that could be had only by those waiting for the end to a hernia repair or other minor operation. It had been during Ramadan so the TV, like every TV in the nation, was on the vast whorl of pilgrims circling the Ka'aba in Mecca. All individuality was lost to the God's-eye view of pilgrims, churning on the TV screen like a sea of tiny white bubbles while Saroush and the others fell into the silence of watching their patterns endlessly form, then dissipate, then reform, knowing that what they were part of had been going on long before they were in the world and would go on long after. Then the recorded devotions of a muezzin sang over the hospital intercom—"*bismillah ir-rahman, ir-rahim*"—calling the faithful to mid-day prayer.

As he bent into the first rakah, the others began to argue. Should they face the television where they could see Mecca, or face the Pepsi machine against the western wall, Mecca's true direction? On TV, the fuzzy image of the faithful began to roll and

Saroush couldn't help but realize that the most modern piece of equipment he'd seen in the hospital was that Pepsi machine. By the time the same recorded muezzin called the faithful to afternoon prayer, Saroush was the only one still waiting, the feeling that something had gone wrong with Wafta's "suspicious ulcer" waxing into even more intense prayer: "Have you not considered how Allah dealt with the Army of the Elephant?"

Finally, a door opened at the far end of the corridor. A surgeon appeared, still wearing scrubs that were the gray-green of a body bag. The bags around his feet made his steps soundless and Saroush had the sensation of seeing the angel of death approach. When the angel bid Saroush to take a seat beside him, he nearly swooned. The doctor explained that they had found a tumor growing along an artery. Slicing it off without nicking the artery had been like walking a tightrope for three and a half hours. It then took them forty-five minutes to reposition her so they could continue cutting. His voice suddenly became weary. "Once her peritoneal surfaces were exposed.... Cancer cells marbled her flesh like grains of sand so fine and uniform that they didn't show on any tests...."

All the prayers. All the words. Against these tiny bodies. "Is there nothing—" Saroush broke off. The surgeon shrugged, helpless. He began to say something about metastases and then chemicals— But the chemicals would be in America and Europe, they both knew. The Emir might be flown out of the country for such treatment, but a woman, whose husband was a bench technician?.... The success rate for these treatments was very low anyway, surgeon offered by way of consolation. "Very, very low. I'm sorry."

And that was before the war. Now, Red Crescent supplies were barred from the harbor. It was on TV daily. The medical supplies that did get in were stockpiled for palace guards and police.... Instead of insulin, the medicine bags beside Fatima's arm carried only sweetwater, her body strong against prayers, her body, like all bodies, determined to have the last word.

Paul often went up to the eleventh floor of the research center so he could eat his sack lunch with Mary. The elevator opened onto a floor that looked identical to his because they all looked identical: porcelain-white corridors, a ring of labs around shared equipment like the million-dollar spectral photometer that his floor shared. The people came from all over—Taiwan, the Philippines—but even they looked the same: the techs like him dressed in jeans, tennis shoes and white lab coats, photo-ID clipped to the pocket; the PIs older, their postdocs already starting to take on the serious, preoccupied look of their mentors. A Korean doctor passed by discussing something with his black intern, and Paul couldn't help but imagine Mary going to one of them if he backed out.

Today he found her and her assistant Pamela, a tech like him, doing rabbits on the opposite side of the window that separated the operating theater from the rest of their lab. Coming upon the two women dressed in their scrubs, blue caps and surgical masks covering all but their eyes—like veiled Arab women—Paul often suffered a moment of disorientation—who are you?—sizing up the shape of their bodies before the boyishness of one gave its answer: Mary Elizabeth Smith. But who was that?

As he entered she greeted him, "How's it hangin' Mengele," glancing up from the incision she was making. It was a joke they shared—him being the Josef Mengele of the Mice—and he answered back, "Yo, Mengele,"—the Mengele of the Rabbits—hopping up on a lab bench with his lunch.

Daughter? Artist? Lover? Friend? She was also the Mengele of the pigs. And of the rats, and the dogs: all of the large animals used in studies that required a lot more surgical skill than he could provide. The bypasses, gene therapies, and other trial procedures she performed were more complicated. They took longer, so when she could she worked in stages, opening the chest of one rabbit while the anesthesia was taking affect on another, while Pamela helped a third come out from under. Today they were juggling six operations, three chests clamped opened at once.

"Hey," she said, tying off an artery to simulate heart disease, "Laura scheduled a late meeting today so I can use the microinjector while they're out," meaning she was going to skip lunch. She used to be able to come and go a lot easier, using the equipment she needed in Microbiology to work on her art projects. Since the attack, though, all the rules had been tightened. Plus, a lot of the equipment was tied up doing DNA identification of victims. The place wasn't set up to be a forensics lab, but the huge number of pulverized corpses made the FBI turn to every lab that could help and theirs was one of them: The automated systems they had in place to handle the large number of genes necessary to create statistically-meaningful profiles also made the lab ideal for matching the thousands of bits of flesh that had been scattered across the disaster site to the saliva of living relatives, or to hairs plucked from the bathroom drains of the dead, or to....

He unwrapped his peanut-butter-and-jelly sandwich on his lap and watched as he ate.

She was good. Seeing her this way, working on her rabbits, it was easy to picture her in a MASH unit, operating on shot-up soldiers, or earthquake victims. The arteries of a human were way larger than those of a rat so he was sure that technically she could pull it off. To do open-heart surgery on rats, she worked by looking through the telescoping lens of the binocular loupe she wore over her head. The arteries themselves were no thicker than red thread while the 10-0 suture she had to use was so fine it was invisible to the naked eye. Yet even working at this microscopic scale her movements were sure. "This is nothing," she'd tell people. "Do you know how hard it is to draw a circle without a compass?" And it was true. Her ability with a scalpel was at least partly the result of her art training. Not long after they'd begun living together, he'd unrolled a bunch of her old canvases, her juvenilia she called it, that he'd found stuffed in a barrel. They were from her undergrad days: still lifes and nudes, self portraits so detailed that she had used a brush with a single hair for some highlights. The paintings were marvels of draftsmanship, but they embarrassed her now for their lack of ideas, and the whole while he looked at them she kept insisting that he roll them back up. She hadn't made a painting in years; no artist she took seriously did. And her ability to draw would never even come up if it didn't live on in her scalpel work, or in the delicate maneuvers she could make with a cell in the microinjector. Still, eye-hand coordination wasn't the main reason she'd make a good surgeon. Once, he had joked that if they were ever on an isolated camping trip and he needed an emergency appendectomy, he'd want her to be the one to do it. He thought she'd make some crack about removing the wrong organ, the anatomy of a man being different from a rabbit, after all. Instead, she'd only said, "Okay." Without hesitation. Without a hint of irony. He wished he had her balls.

"There. That should do, little one," she said, finishing a stitch, and turning the rabbit she was working on over to Pamela. In a few weeks she'd try to cure the rabbit's heart damage by injecting stem cells that earlier studies said could be coaxed into becoming new blood vessels. But of course the rabbit didn't know that part, what with a ventilator making its open chest work up and down.

Finally turning her clear brown eyes fully on Paul, she asked, like always, "So you going to come along?"

...001 010 010 001 001 011...

Mary brought out a tray of petri dishes labeled with the names of PIs and other clinical i.d.s., then opened the one marked ART, an acronym that usually meant Assisted Reproductive Technology. This one held rat blastocysts, her latest project, the pun of its label a secret between them.

While she positioned them on the platform of the microinjector, Paul took a seat on the stool beside her and adjusted its second binocular microscope to his eye height. All a blur.

"Like a virgin...." Mary softly sang to herself.

Paul liked watching her make art more than he liked watching her operate. She had to do a lot of it on the sly, using the expensive equipment for personal use as she did, so only he and a few others at work like Pam and Laura knew she was an artist—it was a link between them. Plus he liked going to Microbiology. Its test tubes and cultures gave the department more of the feel of what he thought of as a real lab, though since Microbiology took on identifying those victims, that part of the lab had taken on the creepy hush of a morgue. Through a pass-through window he could see it: the banks of automated equipment—stainless steel arms, cabling and glass slides—creating the DNA stains that would be used to identify smears of people recovered from the site of the blast. Extra technicians had been hired so the identification could go on night and day, and he didn't recognize a lot of them moving about in their lab coats. He wished the lab would hurry back to the way it had been, but even with the hours that the extra techs put in, even though some dozen other labs around the country were doing the same work, the job was still going to take months. Almost daily a truck would arrive with more samples: stacks of white trays containing a hundred thimble-sized wells, each filled with a clear solution of DNA prepared from the material of a fingernail, a shred of skin, or some body part that hadn't been pulverized beyond hope of even DNA recognition. By the time investigators had finished excavating the site, there were going to be almost a million of these little wells: each a microscopic portrait, each a tiny grave. Each, also, someone's hope for the sense of an ending: concrete proof that their son, or daughter, or wife or husband or lover had been there and had not just vanished one day. Had been taken, that is, and not just left. During the first few weeks of the project, the rock station that the techs in the lab usually had playing was replaced by a lot of silence—except for the whir of machines, the clicking of keyboards as other technicians worked the programs that looked for matches. A few of the regulars had quit. Even the outside phone lines had been disconnected when relatives began to call. Now, two months later, the radio was back on, though turned low. Mary hummed along under her breath as she worked.

Paul looked back to the microinjector, adjusting its focusing ring until the blur in his eyepiece resolved into blastocysts floating like amebas in the medium. Or nebulas. Nebulas that were actually half the size of a period. They swam away from the micro-pipette Mary controlled with a joystick. She had made the blastocysts, fertilized rat eggs, earlier; the male and female protonuclei wouldn't fuse for a while, and before they did she was trying to inject the male protonucellus with the DNA of a third rat. The idea was to make a rat whose DNA fingerprint would show that it was a mosaic of three parents. The technique was common. Most of the mice used as disease models and all of the custom animals were now created this way. She'd gotten the idea to use the method to make a work of art from the lab mice that carried a jellyfish gene; the gene caused their tumors to glow a green that reminded Paul of the brilliant blue or orange stripes on some tropical fish, and allowed the tumors to be studied without killing their host for an autopsy. But a Brazilian artist had beat her to using the technique as a paintbrush, creating a green-glowing rabbit. So she thought she'd leapfrog them both by using the technique on one of her own eggs. It was an outgrowth of an earlier work of bio sculpture she'd made, Self Portrait: an egg she had encapsulated beneath a bubble that functioned as a magnifying glass, placed in the frame that used to house her baby portrait. To make the portrait she had in mind now, though, it was important that she use an embryo that was viable. "My egg, your sperm, and some junk DNA of a third person," she'd told Paul. It wasn't as mechanical as Mary had hoped, though, and this was her fourth attempt to make it work with rats. "It's a touch thing," Laura had said when teaching her how to work the controls, so Paul knew it wouldn't take Mary long to ice it.

She brought the glass pipette, her pedestal, up to the egg and the suction at the pipette's polished tip held it fast. Operating the other joystick, Mary took up her chisel, an even more microscopic hypodermic needle. As she maneuvered the needle into a position that would allow a clean stab into the male protonucleus, he felt himself squirm, thinking of his own protonucleus semi-fused with hers under the light of the microinjector.

"...doing it for the twenty-third time...."

When she'd first brought up the idea, he'd agreed right away. It was only going to be an art work—not a baby. Religious art. She was going to call it Trinity. She had no intention of implanting it in a womb or allowing it to become a fetus, even if it was important for the piece to have that potential, at least for a while. "Integrity of materials, and all that," she'd said, explaining how it wouldn't get anyone's attention if she only faked it....

The idea of his sperm mingling with her egg had been a powerful aphrodisiac, making him hard, horny. A powerful link between them. Or so it had seemed. Then her conception of the piece began to evolve. Mary began to fiddle with its name—Resurrection or Self Portrait(s), she hadn't decided yet—thinking that if she could use the junk DNA from a third party, mitochondria that would serve no function other than to give the potential child's DNA fingerprint the trace of a third parent, why not use junk DNA from someone important? Like the president. Or Christ. Paul's real importance in the project began to show as she became consumed with tracking down the thirteen churches that claimed to have Christ's tissue, his foreskin, removed by circumcision since he was Jewish. Supposedly, the rest of his body ascended into heaven. After failing to find anyone who could get her a piece that wasn't totally iffy, if not an outright scam, though, she decided to settle for any garden-variety saint with good provenance. She didn't even care which, even if she was being picky about the relics that showed up on eBay. Way more picky, it seemed, than she was about the guy who filled his spot.

"Do you know how easy it is to get sperm?" she laughed when, to see how she'd react, he'd joked that getting a sample from him was the only reason she'd let him move into her loft. But he was afraid to ask if she meant get it—$100 per dose—from the fertility clinic she'd contracted to harvest her eggs, or get it herself. Either way, it didn't exactly make him feel vital.

The needle punctured a dark spot on the jellyfish, the male protonucleus. "Damn," she said. "Do you think it went all the way through?" He couldn't tell. But it didn't look like it. So she syringed in a tiny gray stream, a trillionth of a liter of solution containing the junk DNA from the third rat. "Looks like the membrane held," she said. She pressed a button on the first joystick, cutting off the suction and the egg floated away. Then she moved the microscopic glass pipette to capture another one. If this trial worked, she'd have all the pieces: injection technique down; a fertility clinic to harvest her eggs; she'd set up an account with one of the dozens of commercial labs in California that could purify and multiply junk DNA from a tissue sample. They'd FedEx it to her overnight. All she had to do was come up with a saint. And have her roommate jerkoff.

"So that's what you'll do with my little guys," he said, watching her inject the next protonucleus.

Silence. Then, "That's what I'll do," she said, her tone suddenly flat. They'd been down this road before.

She continued to work in silence till he said, "Will it hurt?"

"No one's forcing you," she said, the edge in her voice telling him that this wasn't the time.

"...in an impassioned speech proclaimed that the men, women and children who died fighting terrorism were all American Heroes, and that it would be a shame on the nation if his million-dollar memorial bill wasn't passed...."

"We invite the congregation to join in."

And Job answered,

How else to represent a person?

Oh, would that my words were written down!

How else to tell their story?

knight/damsel

Aliens/Earthlings

Scripture A or Scripture B:

Human Remains Pouch; Case #97-0013; Unique identifier: 0127; Description: Female, partial (torso w/ right lower extremity)....

white hat/black hat

One who died after a long illness:

God of deliverance, you called our brother/sister N. (fill in the name)...

One who died suddenly:

Would that they were inscribed in a record...

Human Material Identifier: D157; VNTR Genetic ID @ 5'-GGCC-3'; Digital Code of Results: 001 001

010 010 001 001 011 001 001 010 010 001 001 011 010 001 001 011 011 001 001 010 010...

Sports Loving Fiancée

...engaged to be married. She said the first thing he did each day at his desk was read the sports page. She arranged a honeymoon to his favorite country club and intended to present him with a new set of golf clubs during...

Lord, as we mourn the sudden death of our brother/sister, N...

Human Remains Pouch; Case #97-0013; Unique identifier: 0045; Description: Male, partial (head w/ blue eyes)....

...010 001 001 011...

One who died accidentally or violently: Our brother/sister N. was suddenly [and violently] taken from us...

That with an iron chisel and with lead...

Seat 27A: Passenger Katherine Novak, 28, Winner of a Fulbright to Pakistan to study the weaving of traffic patterns on highway off-ramps in the third world.

Music in Her Soul

...an accountant with her own country and western band. On her rare days off, she liked to take her nieces and nephews to the zoo....

General (Version A):

Lord, the death of our brother/sister N. recalls the brevity of our lives on earth....

...they were cut in the rock forever!

...001 001 011 001 001 010...

At first Saroush thought that Imam was only trying to comfort him, telling him that if the worst came to pass, Fatima would be a martyr, repeating what Saroush heard often these days: that the embargo was as deadly as bombs dropped on villages, that all martyrs—especially children—who die in jihad went directly to heaven…. "Birds dropping stones on elephants," Imam said. But as Saroush looked toward the room where she lay, wishing with all his might for the worst not to come to pass, the reach of Imam's words began to extend. He told Saroush that Fatima's sacrifice would be meaningless to people whose maps of the world were mostly blank. "For this reason, more words would only be like loading a donkey with books," Imam said, explaining that other ways had to be tried. "As Mohammed did at Badr."

Saroush had been preparing coffee in a brass kanaka, self-conscious that there was no woman in the house to pour it for them. As he lifted it, Imam stayed his hand, saying more emphatically, "I can talk forever to make you remember me. Or I can come to you when you least expect it and fire a gun near your ear. Fear will make you know with your entrails." He paused, then asked, "Do you understand, Saroush?"

Saroush nodded, though he was no longer sure if they were talking about his daughter. He stared at his own face, reflected in the minaret-like spire on the lid of the kanaka as Imam continued, "Now imagine a fear that is able to penetrate so deeply into your flesh and blood that you can never forget, can never board a plane, go into a shop or start your car without hearing my name."

The Glock-17: A plastic pistol that is invisible to metal detectors. When its body is broken down into its pieces, they appear on airport X-ray screens as indistinguishable shadows...

Mary eased her naked body onto his, kissing him. But the condom Paul had on, the non-spermicidal kind used to capture semen samples—a test—made him self conscious, like he was on a microscope slide, and though they went through the same motions, did all the same licking and biting, he was so aware of the difference from what it was like when he first moved in that he knew she must feel it too.

She was six years older than him and had sworn off men for a while after her divorce. He'd just dropped out of pre-med—still a horny college kid, bottled up by books—so when they met, the chemical reaction had been exothermic. The first time he picked her up at her loft, they didn't even make it to the movie that was the pretext for the date. Dressed in a skinny summer dress instead of the scrubs he always saw her in at work, she'd offered him a joint, then ten minutes after that they were fucking, her clogs and panties on the floor, her thin dress hiked up around her waist, him in the condom she'd had at the ready as they went at each other on the mattress she then used as a bed.

She'd switched to the pill after it looked like they were going to become a regular thing. But now, after having gone through the motions on the queen-sized bed they'd bought to replace the mattress, he wondered what she saw when she looked into their future. If she even looked.

Sure enough, a moment later she gave him a pat and was up. A lot had changed since he'd begun to stay here, he knew, watching her pull on the oversized sweatshirt she used as a bathrobe. She carried his sample to the corner of the loft she used as a kitchen. The two of them used to walk around the loft naked without giving it a thought. But no more. Bed sheets hung across its big industrial windows so construction workers rehabbing a neighboring factory into condos couldn't see in—just as a lot of other incremental changes had become second nature. The dirty mop heads she'd been weaving into sculptures when she got her divorce—so important to her then—were now pushed against one wall, the loft big enough to just push things off to one side and forget about them. Even a heap of mop heads four feet high.

"So far so good," she called back, looking through a jeweler's loupe.

In a way, though, it was as if nothing had changed.

"Was there ever a doubt?" He tried to sound enthusiastic. Except for the bed, his bicycle and a few other things, his own stuff seemed to just melt into the junk—materials she called it—that she used to scavenge from dumpsters and demolition sites on her way home from the lab.

"Never a doubt," she said, smiling, coming back to bed. She pulled off her sweatshirt and her brown nipples dangled before him as she bent to put the loupe on top of the bed-side TV. She switched the set on, then lay back in his arms. Now that she wasn't examining him any longer, it was easier for him to see her body and from it he could tell she was more relaxed as well. Glad because what could have been a hard decision for her had been defused? He pushed a hand up her back.

"Mmmmm," she murmured, warmly, her register deepened by age—her body, like his, like everyone's, a portrait of her life. Gray peppered what he guessed had once been jet-black hair, her hair short as a swimmer's so she could easily get it in and out of a surgical cap. The first time he saw her naked, he'd been surprised by how much older her body looked from the other girlfriends he'd had—students like him, mostly younger. There'd been tufts of hair at her armpits because she'd been a girl at a time when some mothers still told their daughters that things like that didn't matter while the smooth girlfriends he'd had, if they knew that story at all, would have thought it a relic of old hippie weirdness, or just plain gross. When he dug his knuckles into her back, she gave a little gasp, the flesh wrinkling before the plow of his palms instead of snapping back even though the muscles below were firm, her calves more muscular than some bike messengers. A mole on one shoulder. Earlobe piercing closed from nonuse. The imperfections and idiosyncrasies struck him as— As particularly her—unlike glossy pictures of fashion models whose symmetry made them unreal—like the plastic casts of Everyman or Everywoman they used to use to teach anatomy— everyone's ideal, and therefore ideals of no one. Especially those old enough not to be mistaken for kids. Time's winged chariot at my back, as an epigram to a chapter on aging said in a biology book he once owned.

"Oh gag," she said, groaning at something in a commercial. "That joke's so old."

Or did coming home to him feel more to her like the routine of laundry day? The last thing she wanted after her divorce, she'd said, was to jump into another relationship. And she never really gave him permission to move in. It's just that he had been coming over, then sleeping over, then sleeping over and coming back later in the day so often that after a while, without either of them pointing it out, he had begun to stay. Now her project and whether or not he was going to go through with it was pointing it out. And the thought of her finding someone else to help her seemed too much like moving out even if he had never really moved in.

"Paul, do you think we're doing the right thing?" she asked, as though she'd been reading his mind. She leaned out of his arms to twist the coat hanger that was the TV's antenna, its picture wiggling back into form. "I'd hate to do anything that could wreck what we have here."

Her question surprised him, and he hugged her for finally coming around to at least consider his reservations. "I don't know, Mary," he said. "I mean at first I didn't think it was any big deal but now that it's starting to seem more real...."

"Maybe we should have just thrown that flier away."

"Flier?" She was talking about getting cable-TV, he realized. Her lease strictly stipulated that the loft could only be used as studio space. She'd needed it for the video cameras and welding equipment she used to use to make art from junk and heaps of mop heads that her then-husband wouldn't let her bring into their apartment. The loft was in an old, Maidenform bra factory with a tar roof that got blistering in the summer and made the place impossible to heat in the winter. It was against code for anyone to live there. But when she fell out with her ex for good, she'd gotten a microwave and moved in. When the surrounding factories and warehouses had begun to be converted into luxury condos, Paul and Mary sort of figured it was only a matter of time before they'd have to get out even if they both said doing so would kill them, the difference between the loft and the sterile research center, the chance the loft gave them to live apart from the grid, an oasis from the lab's controlled atmosphere. Still, when a flier arrived announcing that cable-TV was now available in their area, they debated whether to get it and risk alerting the landlord to their presence.

She sat up in bed and looked at him, the bemused look coming onto her face showing that she realized what he had been talking about. Then she hit him with a pillow. "Would you give it a rest!" she said in mock disbelief.

"What? Why is it so hard for you to put yourself in my shoes? I mean, you're going to do it anyway, right? If not with me, then with some other guy."

She shook her head and laughed one of her exasperated laughs. "We've been through all of this. I'd do it without anyone else if I could, but eggs don't keep. Sperm freezes—that's why it's so cheap—embryos freeze, but not eggs," she said, referring to the way she wanted to display the art embryo: in liquid nitrogen—the way another artist displayed the bust of his head he had sculpted out of a block of his own frozen blood. "If you don't want to help me out, just say so and I'll get a dose from a male donor when they harvest my eggs. I'm not doing 'it' with anyone, if that's what you're worried about." Then she looked at him hard. "Is this a Catholic thing?"

Whenever her logic found no corollary in him, she went back to the fact that he'd been brought up by religious parents. "No!" he said, trying to explain it for her, and himself, without lapsing into sperm competition among apes, or any of those other theories of domination through sex that they learned in animal biology. This to someone who had sold her eggs to make ends meet while getting her master's in art. When he could think of nothing to say other than the fact that he didn't want to think of her eggs in a tube with another man, he said, "Oh, forget it."

Imam hadn't been talking about fear, Saroush thought, standing in his daughter's empty room. They had taken Fatima to the madhab's seminary where Imam said she would be more comfortable, though Saroush wasn't sure how. It was a school, not a hospital. Running the toe of his sandal over the transom she used to always trip over when young, taking in the child-sized chair she used to sit in while doing her homework, feeling she would never be in this room again, he knew Imam had not been talking about fear; rather it was terror. Fear was always fear of something. Terror was what the body did while in that unknown something's fury. He'd learned that the time he had taken Fatima to the beach for Westerners. His wife, her mother, had been dead for almost a year and as the anniversary approached, Saroush resolved to break the choke of memory that had grown over them, to celebrate Wafta's entry into paradise as she had asked. But to do so would require his whole body as well as his mind—a jihad—supreme effort. That's when he remembered Wafta's wish to see the Westerners' beach: to see if Western women were as bold with their bodies as everyone said. They had argued in hushed tones so Fatima wouldn't hear, though the walls of their apartment couldn't keep secrets from even neighbors and he knew Fatima must have grown curious about the beach in the way the young hunger to know of sex but are afraid to ask. Her thick eyebrows arched—so like her mother—when one day, as she copied her Koran for school, he casually asked her if she would like to go.

He had always looked Egyptian, so he borrowed the passport of a foreign engineer he knew at work and used it to get past the armed guards at the entrance to the beach. He could feel all the Europeans staring at him, the only one in trousers, as he hurried his daughter by their briquette fires, their tape players and beach houses built with oil money. Colorful tents flapped in a stiff breeze. Long before desalination plants, Saroush's grandfather used to dive off shore near here; he used a leather bag to capture the sweetwater that flowed from underwater springs, then sell it in the souk and Saroush told Fatima the story, pointing out to the ocean to distract her from women sunning themselves in bathing suits that were little more than strings. Perhaps what she did see would be educational, as Wafta had said.

When they were well past them, he spread out the rug he had brought then stood, back to the water, gazing at one of the mansions that dotted the shore. It was the Emir's palace. Saroush had heard that the Emir kept a palace at the Westerners' beach, but had always thought it to be a rumor spread by zealots for political reasons. But there it was—gold onion domes topped by the green pendants that were his signature, a security fence and guards carrying AK-47s and wearing the maroon berets of the Emir's personal guard— there could be no mistake, the Emir kept a resort home here with this fleshpot as his front yard.

When Saroush turned back, Fatima was gone. Whitecaps broke on shore. The only people visible on the beach were the Westerners some fifty meters away. She simply wasn't there. She must have run off to chase datebirds, something she often did, he thought. But the sky was empty in all directions while the only other place a child could possibly be was—

The water.

The water was as empty as wasteland. If she had fallen in, wouldn't he have heard it? No, he realized, the wind scattering even radio music. How far out could she have gone in a minute?—surely not far enough to drown. Images of Fatima's face bobbing underwater....

Clothes on, he waded into the water to make sure the worst hadn't happened before searching for her on the beach. Stepping from shore he sunk into water up to his waist, Fatima's chest level. A meter more and it was up to his chest. Beach erosion—as if from an underwater spring—had created a drop-off as precipitous as the edge of a diving pool. Only this wasn't a pool. Waves slapped into him, making an undertow and churning the water so that it was impossible to see bottom. He began to breath heavily, fear growing. He worked to move through the water, its resistance like mud. Then he stepped on something—it felt like a toy sand-shovel, the one Fatima had in her hand the last time he saw her? When he bent to pick it up, he was knocked over by a wave. If he couldn't even retrieve a toy... His breath became short, the danger of the ocean magnifying a pale, lifeless face. The weight of his clothes and the suck of the water were already tiring him, a grown man, as he thrashed about trying to see into the water. Should he run for help? Where?—the Emir's palace? By the time anyone came wouldn't it be too late to do anything except drag for a body? Is that what he was already doing? The tiny grave mounds of Al Zingh Cemetery. It was too much to bear. He had brought her to this forbidden beach and now he was being punished. These are the things that devour a mind in terror, Saroush now thought, remembering how in that moment Fatima's face had been most vivid.

Two fat Americans had come strolling along, smirking at the "camel jockey" trying to swim in street clothes. To his astonishment, he turned to them desperately, "Please, sir, have you seen a girl with a plastic shovel?"

"She's over there," one said, pointing down the beach to where the others were and Saroush ran off. As he approached their volleyball net and music, he saw the girl they'd meant—he'd lost his glasses—and was almost on top of her before he could see clearly that she was a stranger. The realization that Fatima might be underwater back there while he had run here to be among Westerners made his blood pound. Then he saw her, crying at the center of a crowd of white strangers. She was lost and so scared that even when she saw him she didn't move. He felt the same and they came together slowly. "Where were you?" he barely managed to choke out.

And her choking reply, "I started making footprints and then you weren't there."

Now, this smooth, tile floor Saroush stood on refused to show Fatima's footprints. Nor those of Wafta, and he felt as though he was trying to strike out at the air. How many other small enactments of terror began with the phrase, a normal day? Festive atmosphere, crowds of happy vacationers, sunshine.... Then the bomb goes off.

All life is but a dream from which we will one day awaken....

...the conventions of story...

"You could use a new set," the cable guy said. He sat on the bed, adjusting the controls of their old portable TV. The channel control worked okay, if you knew how to use it—a touch thing. But the guy didn't know how to use it. No one would ever have to know again, so Paul wedged a toothpick in the control to make the set stay on the channel that the cablebox needed to work. "*Showtime*, *HBO*..." The guy used the new remote to surf the channels in the package Mary had ordered, demonstrating that they were all there. "...and *Court TV*," he said, leaving it on the channel Paul had asked about. Mary liked the reality-TV shows, the channels that just put on footage of murderers confessing, or surgeries being performed, so he wanted to have one of those playing when she got home.

"You been installing a lot of systems around here?" Paul asked as the guy packed up.

"You kidding?" he said, motioning to the rehab going on across the street. "I bet the only reason this building hasn't been sold to developers is because someone's holding out for more cash. I remember when the hospital was in the middle of a ghetto. No more," he said. And it was true. The hospital that Paul and Mary worked in had been an island in a war-zone part of town that ran up to the mostly empty industrial area they lived in. As recently as two years ago when Paul met Mary, riding his bike the couple of miles out here had been creepy. Now he stopped on his way in to pick up a coffee from the Starbucks in one of the condo buildings that a lot of interns lived in; the pockets of new condos and student housing springing up had grown so numerous that they'd begun to connect. "The world's changing, my man," the guy said, hitching up his tool belt. Then he was gone.

Paul found a couple of TV-dinner trays among the junk Mary had accumulated in the loft. He opened the freezer in the corner that was her kitchen, and got the TV dinners he'd bought to surprise her with. Behind them were some of her cultures, and behind those a box with a Korean label. It was the frozen squid they had bought at a Vietnamese market when they'd just begun dating. They had these plans for making an Asian dinner in her loft, but back then it seemed like all they did was screw, and the squid had remained frozen there all this time. He pulled it out, imagining the look on her face when she saw what he had cooked. Was it still good? Behind it, in the deepest part of the freezer were more sealed baggies—had they bought other stuff that day as well? *Joe, Korean 2.5.00.000A* was written in magic marker on one. Inside was a brown bottle that Paul at first thought was the kind Asian markets used to sell rhino horn and other potions. But then, scraping away the frost, he saw that it was one of the bottles used for samples in Microbiology. *Luke, Afro.-Am. 2.15.00.000A* said the next. There were some seven or eight others.

The plodding of someone laboring up the stairs sounded out in the hallway.

When he saw *Paul, Caucasian* written on one of the vials, he knew what he was looking at.

A scratching of keys, the door swung open and Mary was there, carrying her bike on one shoulder.

"Who is Joe, Korean?"

She stopped, her mouth open in mid-hello. Then she put her bike down. "Just some guy I knew before I knew you."

"And Afro.-Amer. 2.15.00.000A?"

"Look, they were all just guys. You don't know any of them."

"I—"

"And even if you did, this was before we met. You didn't think you were the first, did you?"

He could feel his blood quicken while behind his eyes there was a flash, a prom date's mother snapping pictures as he posed grinning in a living room decorated with framed photos of his date in other corsages, arm-in-arm with other guys. "And you were saving their jizz? Like some kind of memento?"

"Not a memento," she said sarcastically. "I thought I was going to make art out of it."

"What?"

"Nothing came of it." She crossed her arms. "I really doubt that old beater of a freezer even keeps them cold enough to be viable."

"That's beside the point!"

"I knew I should have thrown them away," she said more to herself than to him. "I didn't mean to—"

"Great, you harvest their sperm, my sperm, then keep it on ice until you could get around to making art out of it? Without telling anyone?"

"It was just an idea. Nothing came of it. Maybe I should have said something but it's not exactly like you guys were so concerned about what happened to your sperm when you came over here."

"Who the hell do you think you are!"

Several persons:

You gave new life to N. and N. and N....

He hadn't meant to explode like that.

GENETIC BACKGROUND in which the Transgenic Mice Will Be Made? Paul clicked on the radio-button beside *F2(C57B16 X CBA)*. As he continued to fill out the on-line form, placing an order for the genetically altered mice that Dr. Pashvani needed for one of the lab's studies, he wished he hadn't gone there. That is, he wished he hadn't yelled, "Who the hell do you think you are?" and then continue to spray gasoline on the big, blowing oil-rig fire of a fight they had until she was screaming back, "All right, all right, I feel like dirt! Are you happy!"

Alpha 1 (IX) collagen; Alpha 1b-adrenergic... He scrolled down the long list of genes that could be knocked out of a mouse's sequence till he found *Vascular/endothelial-cadherin*, and clicked its radio-button. Mary had issues about who she was, he knew. Serious issues. When she'd been in college, she'd gotten an e-mail from someone claiming to be an unknown sister who said that both of them had been given up for adoption when they were infants. Mary had told the woman she was crazy, but when she searched birth records to prove it, she couldn't find her own. It turned out that she wasn't related to the woman, but her parents denied she was adopted right up until she laid the DNA evidence before them.

Charges for Blastocyst Injections, per targeting (2 clones) $3,000.

After she'd told Paul that story, how she might never have discovered the lie she'd been living if she hadn't seen a billboard—Call 1-800-DNA-TYPE—set up by a company that helped settle paternity cases, he understood a little better how she could sell her eggs. For the longest time she didn't want anything to do with her parents, treated them like kidnappers who had made her major in something practical, something she wasn't. She didn't talk to them through the rest of her senior year, which meant that she had to pay for it herself. When she turned to the ads for waitressing at the local IHOP or Big Boy, she also found the other ads that periodically ran in the school newspaper: ads for healthy co-eds to become egg donors, or to rent their wombs. A friend had already volunteered for the first and had been paid a $12,000 gratuity. On the psychological screening portion of the application that asked prospective donors why they wanted to do it, Mary didn't have to lie: she was glad to help other women have their own kids, she wrote, rather than have to adopt someone else's. But he couldn't stop wondering how many of them were out there—those women with their kids. The thought of her eggs mingling with the sperm of different men—the connection she would have with those men, and women, and kids—gave him a pang of jealousy. If the fertility drugs every donor had to take allowed her to give up twenty to forty eggs, how many other e-mails would Mary be getting in the future? And that's assuming she only sold her eggs once. The egg she used in Self-Portrait came from those days, she claimed. But that would mean she'd kept it for years. While there were "more where those came from," as she put it; and as she'd said, she'd needed money back when she was going through her divorce. No wonder she couldn't get her mind around his reaction. He must seem like a dinosaur sometimes, he thought, clicking on the bookmarks of his browser to reveal all the links he had saved to tomatoes that carried codfish genes so they would be less susceptible to freezing; blue cotton that didn't have to be dyed to make jeans; synthetic skin, ears and noses grown in petri dishes; cow embryos that were part human; goats that gave steroid-laden milk; Dr. Pashvani, Dr. Woo and thousands like them asking if all plants, animals, cells—all nature—could be used as rearrangable packets of information, while he, Mary, and thousands of techs like them, even ordinary people, did the grunt work of stitching together answers....

March 10. New York (AP)

Investigators in the crash of American Airlines flight 384 said today that they may never be able to determine if the 5th jetliner that went down that day crashed as the result of mechanical failure, sabotage, or the scuffle that ensued when passengers....

"...remember also, Father, Your servants Alfred Wiesoki..." The priest was getting to the part Paul came for so he began to pay attention. "...Stanley Stodola, Martin Zwoboda; Dolores Danielewski, Jose Garcia, and James and Jean Krygoski"—Paul's parents—and when the priest finished intoning the names of the dead, Paul and the few others in attendance at this weekday mass murmured, "And let perpetual light shine upon them." It was a mass of remembrance. And though it seemed like so much voodoo to him, his parents had both bought masses for their parents, had attended regularly each and every anniversary of their deaths, or birth into Christ as the church put it. So for each of the six years since their deaths he had paid to have their names said at mass, if for no other reason than to remember.

Scattered around the dark church were a few old people: his parents' generation, too set in their ways to move away when the neighborhood began to go Hispanic. An icon of the Virgin of Guadalupe now hung in an alcove where Paul knew an inscription in Polish remembered those who had died in The War to End War, as people called WWI before world wars had sequels. A woman his age sat in a side pew—stylish business suit, arty glasses—on the periphery like him, and here no doubt for the same reason. It was a connection between them. She also looked a little lost, but tried to go through the motions, following the lead of the others who were not just remembering someone dead but were literally praying to save their souls.

Seeing the old people finger rosaries, Paul was always struck by their belief in words. How they thought words could cure disease. Resurrect the dead. Determine whether a soul burned in eternal hell or basked in perpetual light. Like the woman, he had also tried to pray along at his first mass of remembrance. He could have done it easily when he was a kid and attended the grade school attached to the church. But he hadn't been to mass in years since then, and he felt foolish, like a person trying to sing a Christmas carol he could only half remember. But why not? he thought, glancing at the woman mumbling along. What could it hurt?

Even so, his mind kept wandering to the communion railing and altarpiece, a marvel in carved oak that no one would even try to duplicate today. Had Mary been born 500 years ago, she might have worked at carving communion railings like this one instead of making the art that she did. Had she been born in Europe, that is. Had she been born into the right guild, that is. Had she been born male. He remembered how excited she'd been to see the stained-glass windows the time he'd brought her here. He knew about her interest in tribal art so he wasn't surprised that she also liked religious art – spiritual art, as she called it. She'd stood fixed before one of the church's statues, an imitation of Michelangelo's *Moses*, while he explained why this Moses wore what looked like a gold, two-pronged party hat: Like Michelangelo's statue and its millions of copies and knockoffs, this one had originally had horns protruding from the prophet's head because somewhere in the Bible it said that God gave him a pair of horns along with the Law. It turned out, though, that this was a mistranslation that got passed along for centuries before anyone noticed that "horns" should have said "rays." Since their pastor always thought the horns made Moses look demonic, he had these painted gold in the hopes that paint would transform them into rays of light. But all it did was make him look like a hung-over party animal. "Religious art," Mary had chuckled. Tenderly. Still, he hadn't thought she would actually make any till she returned with a camera to shoot the church's rose window in different light. It was its blue at dawn that she wanted to use she said. And its shape reminded her of a petri dish.

Looking at it, a deep blue circle now protected by bulletproof glass, he remembered the stories he'd heard about it as a kid. It had been made in Lithuania, the master stonecutters, glassblowers, and other craftsmen needed to make a church like this all back in Europe, the connection between the new and old worlds straining from the start. And it did look like a petri dish. He'd never noticed how much body stuff there was in the church till Mary started asking about the cannibalism of their rituals: "This is my body, take and eat?" she had said when he tried to deny it. "What's up with that?"

As in other churches, the body of an emaciated God-man hung crucified at the front of this one. But the thing that struck Paul after all these years, the thing that had most made him think it was all a lot of B.S. and voodoo to begin with was the way they all thought water could turn into wine, bread into flesh. That a man could simultaneously be a dove. Virgin birth. But now, going through his catalog of mice with tobacco genes, his bookmarks to test-tube babies, infants with baboon hearts, and the rest, none of it seemed so farfetched any more.

"This is my blood," the priest said, raising a chalice of wine above his head. A Mexican altar girl in dingy tennis shoes and a surplice as white as a lab coat rang the chimes, just as he had as a kid, to mark the moment of the wine's transformation. It was about words, but also about bodies. Always the body. Even if bodies were becoming as permeable as words: him standing here because twenty-six years ago his forty-year-old parents, good Catholics to the end, bet rhythm against chemistry; his mother's Polish mother before them marrying his Lithuanian grandfather because his first wife had died in childbirth, all three of them coming here after The War to End All War from different parts of a torn-up Europe on the basis of rumors that the Middle West—as if it were a hamlet—was where they'd find people from their village. The rumors themselves had been based on the construction of this church, they later realized—the windows from Lithuania, the communion railing from Poland, and when he thought of the web of words and bodies that had been needed to bring him into existence, he couldn't help but wonder—Who were any of them?—5,000 generations back to African Eve, the last woman genetic reconstruction said all people now walking the earth were descended from, as few as fifty of her descendants walking out of Africa and into Europe to continue a web of chance and circumstance so old and interwoven that it almost seemed as if it was his one true creator; the number of accidents and chance encounters—a world war had to have been fought—and miscarriages, the number of births that it took to get to him was too large to hold in his mind—like thinking about god. Or infinity. No wonder words like "race" were supposedly going the way of words like "miracle." If a person counted back 120,000 generations to Adam, the first ameba, even words like fish and mammal began to blur—forget about monkey/man. Yet in the free fall he understood for an instant how his grandmother could have gotten on a boat to come here. Penniless. Not a word of English. Unknown continent before but an understanding deeper than marrow that she was part of something larger than herself. And as water seeks its own level, she had found his grandfather here in this church.

Trim, aerobicized bod: the lawyer, or ad exec or whoever the woman his age was shot him a frowning glance—as though she'd caught him checking her out. But really he was trying to look past her, to the dark side chapel where votive candles flickered before relics: bone chips or bits of flesh from dead saints. Among the relics, he knew, was the dried blood of St. Paul, the saint his parents had picked to be his namesake and patron, housed in a silver heart.

All people are shaped in Your image...

They were supposed to be celebrating tonight. A piece Mary had made two years ago, *In a Beginning*, had won the Tokyo Prize for techno art and this was its opening. They lay in bed looking at a projection of it, taken from the web, routed through a projector plugged into her computer's video output and cast on the bed sheet that hung across one of the windows of their loft: creases in the sheet rippled the live image, a deep-blue circle speckled with dots that reminded Paul of the night sky seen through a telescope. But instead of the night sky, the circle was a petri dish, and instead of stars, the dots were E.coli bacteria. Mary had contracted a lab to infuse their cells with a synthetic gene whose sequence of amino acids carried a message: LET MAN HAVE DOMINION OVER ALL THE PLANTS AND ANIMALS OF THE EARTH. The actual petri dish was set up in a Tokyo gallery, but anyone could see the same view of it that he and Mary were looking at by going to her website. Once there, they could use their mouse to trigger an ultraviolet flash on the bacteria. When they did, the projected circle flashed whitish, then returned to its deep blue glow, the blue of the rose window in the church Paul's parents had been buried in. The idea was that each flash of the UV light would cause the bacteria to mutate a little, corrupting the message in a way no one would know until she translated the genetic coding back into English.

The loft lit up again, as from lightning, the sheet going momentarily white. Someone somewhere in the world had clicked their mouse. In the flash Paul could see Mary's face, serene, and he took her hand, glad their fight was over. Living in a loft with no walls, it had been hard to avoid each other. Slowly they had begun to talk again. First in clipped answers to clipped questions, then more naturally. What the hell, he thought, beginning to understand what the project meant to her. And wanting the fight to be over before this, her biggest opening, he'd bought a bottle of massage oil—a peace offering—to place on her pillow with an IOU for a back rub as a way to say, if the project meant so much to her, he'd go along with it, even if he didn't know what it all meant. Entering the loft he found a woman-sized pillar of mop heads in the chair where Mary normally sat. She'd made a video of her lips, then connected it to a motion sensor and Watchman buried in the mops so its tiny screen appeared right were her lips would be if she were them. Whenever he came near, the video lips said, "I'm sorry." When Mary showed up, they made up, and backs rubbed, egos massaged, he told her his IOU had another meaning. Instead of being happy, though, she only said that she wanted to think about it. That she wasn't sure what it all meant either.

Right after that she'd found out that *In a Beginning* had won the Tokyo Prize, and she'd be getting 500,000 yen. And right after that they got their eviction notice.

"What will you do with the money?" he asked, refilling her paper cup with champagne.

"I don't know. Maybe buy a dress. Or a new pair of shoes."

After the success of *In a Beginning*, a knockout project like *Self Portrait(s)* would really put her on the map, he knew, at least among the artists who used plants and animals, living tissue, or palettes of bacteria as their medium. And she knew it too. And that the prize money would pay for the harvesting of eggs, if she decided to keep them all instead of donating the ones she wouldn't use to the clinic that was going to do the job. It would also pay for the purification of DNA she'd extract from a tissue sample, as well as its cloning and amplification. Even so, she still hadn't said she'd go through with it. Even though her rats had tested positive for poly-parentage. He knew it had something to do with him, though he wasn't sure what. Though they'd both said they were sorry, though they knew they had to get out of the loft by the end of next month, they still hadn't made any plans for moving elsewhere and he was afraid it was because she was thinking about going without him.

She hadn't said anything to make him think this. They just didn't talk about it. Or her project. And that's what worried him. That out of courtesy to him, knowing how he felt, she wasn't going to involve his body before they split. She didn't want that tie.

The projected petri dish lit up again, illuminating the loft. In the flash he tried to read her face. What was she thinking? Was he in or out? In a way, he couldn't blame her. The thought of giving up the loft for a regular apartment with white walls and a real kitchen was depressing. The kind of depression that made him feel older, like he was turning into his parents shopping for linoleum. How much more so would it be for her—signing a lease with a guy as if she was stepping back into another marriage.

He should have known, just coming and staying as he did, that all along he'd been living on borrowed time. Still....

"You know my parents' church?" he said, pressing the length of his naked body to hers. "I never showed you that time we went to look at the window, but a side altar has the relics of a few saints."

"Oh yeah?" she said, an eyebrow raising.

"Yeah. One of them is St. Paul. The patron saint of public relations, pilgrims, refugees and other travelers to new lands."

"I like it," she said.

"It's in a silver heart just screwed to the wall. And the church is open twenty-four hours a day. In case someone going by gets religion in the middle of the night. It's a Catholic thing."

His words gave her pause. "So what? You're saying we'd just go in and steal it?"

"Not steal. Borrow. After you amplify the DNA, they'll be enough relics for a million churches."

She studied him for the longest time, then said, "You're serious, aren't you."

Saroush held Fatima's child corpse in his arms as he emerged from the mosque and into the eye-stinging brightness of the day. For Wafta there had been no procession. He'd been a technician and processions were expensive. So her death had been private. But Imam had explained that as a martyr, Fatima's death was also a matter of state, and as a gesture of the state's grief mourners poured in from the settlements that dotted a land once inhabited only by a few isolated, desert hermits. They came by the bus load and it was odd to see that the signs some carried were in English, the language of Satan as they called it, written backwards as it was from left to right. Then Saroush saw the camera crews from TV stations in Baghdad and Halab and he understood. The glass eyes of the cameras trained on him as he began to walk; crowds pressed in to touch his daughter. Women wailed—*"Allahu Akbar!"*—their high-pitched warbles cutting into him. As if she had been a great personage, a train of servants fell in behind and Saroush could hear a muffled drum toll that he recognized from Ashurah as the sound of fundamentalists beating their bared chests in unison. They were holding shards of glass, he knew, each blow scratching a wound a little deeper. *"Ya Hussein!"* men shouted in unison. In unison, others would use ceremonial scimitars to rhythmically slash their foreheads, these the Emir's personal replacements in grief, other matters of state unfortunately preventing him from attending personally. Saroush thought of him and his guards in his brilliant white palace on the Westerners' beach. He embraced Fatima's body, shrouded in a flag and as light in his hands as a *qualam*—a reed pen—the first thing created by God. What fool would think he could use it or any body to rewrite a book in which all things were written?—rewriting itself a chimera and lie, even if he did what they wanted....

The crowd of wailing mourners parted, allowing only a single narrow lane through which he could pass.

Even if he somehow managed to break away and hide Fatima's body in the darkest cave, that too would be written. *Insh'Allah*. Up ahead, men on black horses darted back and forth, wailing and lashing their backs, the streaks of blood they drew bright in the sun.

GeneTech. The FedEx package arrived as they were packing to move into their new apartment. Most of the junk—her mops and auto fenders—they decided to just leave behind. But the other stuff, her cultures and sheets and towels, they had boxed up or put in big garbage bags. The boxes and bags and tools and pots formed a pyramid by the door with the FedEx package on top so Mary could hand carry it. Which she did, when the time came, cradling it against her waist as they went out.

The author would like to thank the many people who made this novel possible, first and foremost Maria Tomasula for the drawings that appear throughout this book, but especially for her eye, and advice, during its writing. Also at the head of this list is R. M. Berry, my editor at FC2, for his support and intelligent reading. Robert Sedlack deserves special thanks for his design of the novel. I'd also like to thank Crispin Prebys for his layout and design of early drafts, as well as Larry McCaffery and Lance Olsen for their readings and comments. Brenda Mills, Laura Moran, and Tara Reeser also deserve my thanks for their editing and production advice. Thanks go to models Adam Fung and James Zhang, and photographer Kate Cunningham. Though I have tried to depend on historical documents or actual events and to incorporate the thinking of people from various periods into the narrative that makes up this novel, I have taken many liberties with these materials: the novel is ultimately a work of imagination. Nevertheless, it should be noted that several of the bio-art works described in the last chapter are based on the work of Eduardo Kac; I would like to thank him for a continuing exchange of ideas (as well as cigars and cassis). I would also like to thank Mohammed S. for the hospitality, introductions, and guidance he provided during the time I lived in the Middle East. Thanks also go to Liz Cooper for her hospitality and introduction to modeling; Youmi Shijo for her introduction to broadcasting; and Tim Belka for his tours through corporate surveillance. I'd like to thank Jo-Ann Carbray, Gerald Patejunas, and the rest of the staff at Northwestern Hospital's research center for letting me sit in on surgeries. Several Gulf War veterans (at various Chicago Veterans Administration facilities) were also generous with their time, for which I am grateful. The number of historical sources that influenced this novel is as varied as lived experience so I hesitate to list any out of fear of omitting others, but I would like to acknowledge a few that may not be apparent from the body of the novel: John Man's *Alpha Beta: How 26 Letters Shaped the Western World* on the invention of the alphabet; several visits to the Prado, along with Antonio de Guevara's *Menosprecio de Corte y Alabanza de Aldea* and *Arte de Marear*; Miguel de Cervantes's *Don Quixote* and Jorge Louis Borges's revisitation of this novel; Jaime Vicens Vives's *Historia de España y América*; Luis Díez del Corral's *Velázquez, Felipe IV y la monarquía*; Baldassare Castiglione's *The Book of the Courtier*; Eugène Poitou's *Spain and Its People*; Stephen Haliczer's *Inquisition and Society in the Kingdom of Valencia, 1478-1834*; Jonathan Brown's *Velázquez*; Dale Brown's *The World of Velázquez*. I also drew on a number of documents on the Spanish Inquisition from the Porrua Inquisition Collection at the University of Notre Dame as well as *Records of the Trials of the Spanish Inquisition in Ciudad Real*; Carl Justi's *Diego Velazquez and His Times*; Hayden White's *The Content of Form: Narrative Discourse and Historical Representation and Figural Realism: Studies in the Mimesis Effect*; Barbara W. Tuchman's *A Distant Mirror*; Charles Darwin's *The Expression of the Emotions in Man and Animals*; Earnest Hooton's *Why Men Behave Like Apes, and Vice Versa*; John Shaw's *Essentials of Nervous Diseases and Insanity*; J.M. Charcot's *Lectures on the Diseases of the Nervous System*; George Henry Fox's *Reminiscences*; the Historical Health Fraud Archives of the American Medical Association; numerous books, proceedings and journals at the Library of the Health Sciences at the University of Illinois at Chicago, including George M. Beard and A.D. Rockwell's *A Practical Treatise on the Medical and Surgical Uses of Electricity*; W. J. Morton's "Hystero-Epilepsy, or Hysteria Major" in *Medical Record*; N.A. Cambridge's "Electrical Apparatus Used in Medicine before 1900" in *Proceedings of the Royal Society of Medicine*; John Harvey Kellogg's "Electrotherapeutics in Chronic Maladies" in *Modern Medicine*; W.E. Fitch's "Bicycle Riding: Its Moral Effects upon Young Girls and Its Relation to Diseases of Women" in *The Georgia Journal of Medicine and Surgery*; Joseph Mortimer Granville's *Nerve-Vibration and Excitation as Agents in the Treatment of Functional Disorders and Organic Diseases*; Wilhelm Reich's *Genitalia in the Theory and Therapy of Neurosis*; E.H. Smith's "Signs of Masturbation in the Female" in *The Pacific Medical Journal*; Elmer Ernest Southard's *Shellshock and Other Neuropsychiatric Problems Presented in Five Hundred*

and *Eighty-nine Case Histories from the War Literature, 1914-1918*;
Charles Taylor's *Paralysis and Other Affections of the Nerves: Their
Cures by Transmitted Energy and Special Movements*. I would espe-
cially like to thank Rachel P. Maines for her thoroughly researched
The Technology of Orgasm which led me to some of these, as well as
other sources; Ilza Veith's *Hysteria: The History of a Disease*; William
Seabrook's *The Magic Island*; Richard Loederer's *Voodoo Fire in Haiti*;
Lancelot Law Whyte's *The Unconscious before Freud*; M.L.H. Arnold
Snow's *Mechanical Vibration and Its Therapeutic Application*; Curran
Pope's *Practical Hydrotherapy: A Manual for Students and Practitioners*.
The writings of Michel Foucault, Jacques Derrida, and Sigmund Freud
were very influential in the writing of this book as were Thomas Ste-
phen Szasz's *Schizophrenia: The Sacred Symbol of Psychiatry and The
Manufacture of Madness*; Sander Gilman's *Disease and Representa-
tion*; Wilhelm Erb's *Handbook of Electro-Therapeutics*; and Stephen
Jay Gould's *The Mismeasure of Man*. The passage by Gertrude Stein
comes from her *The Making of Americans* and is used with permission
from Dalkey Archive. Mark Tansey's *The Innocent Eye Test* is used by
permission of The Metropolitan Museum of Art. All rights reserved,
The Metropolitan Museum of Art, promised gift of Charles Cowles,
in honor of William S. Lieberman, 1988 (1988.183). To paraphrase
Wittgenstein, much of a historical book like this must have, if it is to
be meaningful, points of contact with what other people have written—"If my remarks do not bear a stamp which marks them as mine,
—I do not wish to lay any further claim to them as my property."

Last, but not least, I would like to thank the following editors, and
magazines, for publishing earlier versions of portions of this novel as
short stories: Harold Jaffe at *Fiction International*, Elizabeth Mack-
enzie Hebron at *Eratica*, and especially David Hamilton at *The Iowa
Review*.

Colophon

This book was printed on Cougar Opaque Vellum 70 lb. text and 100 lb. cover.

The fonts used are Juvenis, Legato, Metron, and Tyfa.

Design: Robert P. Sedlack, Jr.